Praise for David Mark

'Mark writes bad beautifully' Peter May

'Mark's rich, distinctive prose style and damaged characters compel you to keep reading' *Crime Scene* Magazine

'Aficionados of the grittiest, most trenchant fare love Mark's copper Acctor McAvoy' *Financial Times*

'In McAvoy, David Mark has created a big hero with a huge heart. His skill at weaving threads of light through the darkest fabric has rightly won him a legion of fans who like their crime fiction to be real and compassionate.' Sarah Hilary

'To call Mark's novels police procedurals is like calling the Mona Lisa a pretty painting.' *Kirkus*

'In terms of food analogies, some books are bland or subtly flavoured, while others are like a fiery curry. David Mark's DS McAvoy books are unarguably in the latter category' *Independent*

'David Mark is up there with the best' Mari Hannah

Also by David Mark

The DS McAvoy Series

Dark Winter
Original Skin
Sorrow Bound
Taking Pity
Dead Pretty
Cruel Mercy
A Bad Death: an ebook short story
Fire of Lies: an ebook short story

DAVID MARK

Scorched Earth

MULHOLLAND
BOOKS
HODDER

First published in Great Britain in 2018 by Mulholland Books
An imprint of Hodder & Stoughton
An Hachette UK company

1

First published in paperback in 2018

A CIP catalogue record for this title is available from the British Library

Paperback ISBN 978 1 473 64312 3
eBook ISBN 978 1 473 64311 6

Typeset in Plantin Light by Hewer Text UK Ltd, Edinburgh
Printed and bound in Great Britain by Clays Ltd, Elcograf S.p.A

Hodder & Stoughton policy is to use papers that are natural, renewable
and recyclable products and made from wood grown in sustainable
forests. The logging and manufacturing processes are expected to
conform to the environmental regulations of the country of origin.

Hodder & Stoughton Ltd
Carmelite House
50 Victoria Embankment
London EC4Y 0DZ

www.hodder.co.uk

For Artemisia Violet

'To me, the thing that is worse than death is betrayal. You see, I could conceive death, but I could not conceive betrayal.'

Malcolm X

Prologue

This cold is a living thing. It hungers. It hunts. It *feeds*. When Manu first felt its bitter kiss he feared to look upon his bare arms lest they appear denuded of flesh: chewed to stark white bone.

How strange, he had thought. How strange that fire and ice should have the same desires; the same craven lust for meat.

Manu is wrapped around himself; his arms blanketing a body as flimsy as the shelter in which he squats, trying to keep his backside above the muddy floor. His eyes are pennies; two perfect circles that stare at the flapping wing of canvas that serves as the doorway of his feeble shelter.

Manu shares this patch of scrubland on the outskirts of Calais in northern France with thousands of other men. There is no running water. The ground where he sleeps has the appearance and stench of an open sewer. Most mornings he wakes up semi-submerged. There are times when he has almost drowned himself during one of his midnight hallucinations; plunging nose and mouth into the shallow pool of filthy, fetid water.

He blinks. Stops it all. Cleanses himself in the absolute darkness behind his eyelids. The scene before him is so desolate that to look upon it for too long is to allow cold water into the soul. The image threatens to saps him of the murderous fury that has propelled him this far. And yet he considers himself fortunate. His tent is more luxurious than many. His neighbours protect themselves against the ceaseless rain within a nest of sticks, bin-liners and scavenged pieces of wood.

Manu could not say for certain how long ago he arrived here. Weeks certainly. Perhaps months. He has no recollection of his first few days in camp. He knows that the last leg of his journey almost killed him. He has been a passenger on many vehicles during his gruelling passage from his homeland and has long known the dangers of falling from his hiding place to be crushed beneath the great wheels of the wagons on which he stowed away. He has witnessed such gruesome incidents many times. But he had never expected to arrive in Calais as an effigy, a sculpture built of frost. Icy water had splashed up and coated him as he clung to the axle of the last lorry on its journey north. The water had turned to ice upon him; holding him fast, arms outstretched; Christlike in the freezing dark.

Manu has never known the names of his saviours. He remembers only the sensation of strong hands as they unpeeled him. There was rain upon his face and a burn upon the back of his leg where his skin had touched hot metal. His shivers were feverish, like the malarial convulsions that shook his sister to her miserable death. But kinder, better men gave him warmth. Treasured sweaters and waterproof coats were bundled up to serve as pillow and blanket. He was fed soups that tasted a little like meat. He was given clothes of his own: a sporty jacket of a flimsy, shiny material; American jeans, canvas shoes. A woollen hat that he could pull down to hide the ugly semicircle of risen flesh where his ear used to sit . . .

He did not deserve such kindness. He, who had done such wicked things. But he took it because it was offered and because he had no wish to die.

The chill is a part of him now, in him like memory, like pain. Through his watery eyes, the dark brown skin on the backs of his hands has taken on a purplish hue, like the night sky before a storm.

'Manu. Bread, my friend?'

Manu looks up at the sound of his companion's voice. It is almost lost to the song of the wind as it pummels the side of the small red tent in which they sit and shelter from the swirling rain.

'No, for you, my friend,' says Manu. 'Eat well.'

The Eritrean gives a wide smile, showing neat white teeth. He reaches into the carrier bag and retrieves another plastic-wrapped bread roll. It is stale but still sweet. The supermarkets here throw away food in such quantities that no man, woman or child should go hungry. But there are men here who prey upon the weak. They take all the food for themselves and hand it out only to those who can pay or who are willing to provide some small service in return.

'In England we will have pizza.' The Eritrean smiles as he takes a bite of hard brioche. 'Pizza every night.'

Manu gives his friend the smile he seeks. The Eritrean is called Golgol. He is younger than Manu, perhaps not yet thirty, but his journey to this place has scarred deep lines into his face and his black moustache and beard are tinged with grey. There is little meat on his bones though he is still larger than Manu himself. Manu weighs no more than a child. He is all knotted joints and jagged bones.

'Bad,' says Golgol, as the rain and the wind double their assault on the flimsy tent.

'We are lucky,' says Manu. 'The Sudanese have mud-slides.'

'Mud-slides?' asks Golgol, looking confused.

'The ground,' says Manu, patting the tattered floor of the tent. He makes a bird of his hands and demonstrates the earth moving away.

Golgol points a finger at him in understanding. 'By God's mercy,' says Golgol.

They are silent for a while, listening to the rain. Manu is sitting up, hugging his knees with his forearms. Golgol is lying down, using Manu's shell suit top as a pillow. Neither man

3

speaks the language of the other but Golgol has a smattering of English and has learned more in Manu's company. He has learned about England too. Manu has told him good words to use to make people like him. Told him that 'please' and 'thank you' are good but that 'I'd be delighted' and 'I would love to' serve as currency in the English culture. He has told him not to say 'fucking' or 'cunt' in front of people over fifty. In return, Golgol has taught Manu how to sign his own name in Eritrean and educated him on his people's long battles for independence from Ethiopia. He has told him of his family and his own long journey and the hellish boat ride across black water that he took with so many terrified countrymen as he fought to reach the sacred shores of Europe.

Even so, they are unlikely confidantes. Golgol had not expected to find a friend in the dark-eyed, one-eared man from Mozambique. But God had been merciful, despite his sin. Golgol used to live among his countrymen in the Eritrean section of the camp, but he and another man tried to force themselves upon a young woman whose tent neighboured his own and, when her screams roused the other Eritreans, he was badly beaten and banished from the patch of waste ground where so many of his people had made a home. Friendless, Golgol had redoubled his efforts to get aboard one of the thousands of vehicles heading for the port. His dream was England and he had already suffered endless torments on his long journey to this bleak tip of northern France. Golgol had no luck. The truck drivers saw him and on the occasions they did not, he would be found by the heat scanners or the bastard sniffer dogs trained to seek out him and his kind. His bad luck was contagious. He had thought himself alone in the refrigerated compartment of a meat wagon heading for England. When the doors were opened and the men in uniform pulled him, shivering, onto the road, he learned he had been sharing the vehicle with Manu. They were placed in a police vehicle and driven inland and then dumped on the side of the road. It took them several hours to walk back to the campsite that its starving, freezing residents called the Jungle and which served as home to thousands of desperate souls.

Manu and Golgol have been friends since. They have shared stories. They have told one another their dreams.

Manu looks again at the other man. He looks happy. He has a full belly and the hooded sweatshirt he has wrapped around himself is keeping out the worst of the chill.

The rain rattles against the tent once more and the feeble shelter feels as though it will rise from the ground. Golgol closes his eyes and Manu turns to Aishita, who sits beside him, wordless and brooding.

'It must be done,' says Manu under his breath in his native Portuguese.

Aishita barely turns his head. He has already made up his mind. There is no other way.

Golgol raises his head and sees his friend in conversation.

'Are you weak, little mouse?' asks Aishita, his voice barely audible over the sound of the wind and the rain. 'I can do this. Let me do this. Let me help my little mouse . . .'

Manu shakes his head violently, like a child refusing to eat. It has been this way for a long time. Aishita is fearless. He is cruel. He does what must be done and feels no remorse for the brutality he wields as a tool. Manu does not enjoy the barbarous acts he has both witnessed and performed. They bring him no pleasure, despite the skill with which he executes them.

'He is content. He is happy. It is a kindness.'

As ever, Manu recognises the truth of the other man's words. Golgol is unlucky. He will never make it to England. He will probably die here, of cold, or starvation, or at the hands of some criminal who wishes to relieve him of his clothes or his food or who remembers some terrible act in their nightmares and wakes with a fresh urge to kill.

'Manu?' asks Golgol, propping himself on one elbow. 'Are you okay?'

Manu looks at him with a look of sad resignation upon his face. Truly, it must be done.

The bicycle spoke that Manu has concealed beneath him has been sharpened to a needle-point on a damp stone. The bicycle was abandoned by some tourist who would rather go home without it than repair the buckled wheel. Manu and Aishita snapped the spokes off by the side of the road, neither speaking as they silently agreed upon their course of action.

'Manu?'

Quick as darkness, Manu grasps the silver spoke in a fist that looks like tarred rope. Golgol has only a moment in which to ask his friend why, and then the spoke is entering his chest between the second and third ribs. Above him, Manu releases a slight hiss as he feels the blade punch through between the bones and slide through Golgol's heart. Manu is sprawled on top of the Eritrean, close as lovers, and though he tries to turn his head away he catches the smell of sweet, stale bread as the breath leaves Golgol's body. Manu wants to spit; to vomit out this man's dying exhalation, but he feels the imposing bulk of Aishita at his side and knows that such superstition should only scare children and fragile men. He is a soldier. A man. A warrior.

'Quick now. The flame.'

Manu feels himself trembling but does not pause in his actions. He retrieves the shiny shell suit from beneath Golgol's head. He opens it out as if laying a table and then wraps the garment around Golgol's face.

'This frees us, Manu. Anybody who searches for you – their path ends here. This is where your new existence begins. Become the weapon. Become the man you are.'

Manu nods. He searches Golgol's pockets and takes the damp handful of euros that represent the little he has managed to beg and steal during his time here. Manu does not need to count the notes. He knows there to be a little over 800 euros in his hand. Added to his own savings, it will be enough.

With deft, efficient hands, Manu empties his pockets. He places his own passport in the dead man's jeans, together with the receipt for the cigarettes and cola he had bought last night at one of the few shops willing to serve people from the Jungle, and which was covered inside and out with video surveillance.

'The ear.'

Manu does not let himself display any emotion as he takes the small knife from his sock and cuts a chunk off Golgol's ear. He cannot help but raise his hand to touch the gristled lump of scar tissue that marks the spot where his own ear was severed. He remembers the pain. The helplessness. The sense of becoming less. He puts both blade and ear into his pocket and does not let himself shudder at the touch of dead flesh.

'Good work,' growls Aishita. 'Light him.'

It has been many years since Aishita taught Manu how to kill. Manu had feared that over the years since he last took a life he would have lost his flair for execution. But as he looks at the lighter in his hands, he realises that his hands are no longer shaking and that the chill has left his bones.

'Thank you, my friend,' says Manu, and lights the shiny material. It ignites in moments, the flames spreading around the entirety of the jacket and clinging to the face beneath. Manu slides the spoke from Golgol's chest and bunches up his shirt to conceal the tiny hole in the material. He pulls on Golgol's hooded shirt and slips the skewer up his sleeve. He feels heat at his back and his nostrils fill with the acrid smell of cooking skin and melting fabric.

'Leave him,' says Aishita and both men pull themselves free of the tent.

The storm has driven most of the Jungle's inhabitants to seek shelter in one of the sturdier buildings on the site. Others will be begging for food and clothing from the elderly volunteers who man the charity stalls set up to give help to the helpless. Nobody sees Manu and Aishita as they weave between the ragged tents, splashing through muddy puddles and leaving prints in the churned-up grass.

They do not speak again until they have handed over their rolls of damp, muddy cash to the fat man with the painted arms and thick neck and who leaves the engine running as they climb up to the cab and slither inside. In return, he gives them a phone number and two names, scribbled on a piece of cigarette paper. Manu struggles to say the words. He will practise on the journey – silently repeating the names over and over until they are no longer unfamiliar to his lips.

They lie in the dark, vibrating like the vehicle, soaking and shivering on a carpet of magazines and food wrappers: crammed together in a coffin that stinks of piss and diesel.

This moment should not feel like victory.

But as Manu dares to imagine the prize that awaits him in England he cannot help but let his excitement show in his eyes.

Soon he will be in England.

Soon he will be rich.

And soon he will have revenge on the devil that made him become this terrible, terrible man.

I

Last Wednesday, 3.53 p.m.

The rhythm of heavy, mud-caked hooves. Of iron on stone, iron on soft earth; iron splashing through water. The sound is a pulse. Each step is a tongue tick-tocked: clip-clopped against a wet palate. The pony isn't moving quickly but any song composed to this beat would be a sprightly adagio. It is a cheerful sound.

Walking briskly at the animal's side, Crystal finds herself half remembering a tune she heard on *Strictly Come Dancing*. She can't place it. Wouldn't know its name even if she saw it written down. There were trumpets and the dancers were wearing ruffled sleeves and carrying flowers. She makes a mental note to Google it when she gets a moment. Knows that she will forget.

It rained earlier. Came down hard. The sky is still overcast but the clouds have cried themselves out. Everything looks freshly painted: the grass somehow greener; the tree-trunks a rich chocolate brown. Even the puddles in the rutted track have an attractive rainbow shimmer to their surface, though Crystal presumes that is due to the spilled petrol from the same 4x4 vehicle that carved the great ruts in the bridleway.

The lead-rope in Crystal's hand is soggy against her grubby palm. Muddy water gathers at the sleeve of her blue fleece. Grey hairs from the pony's mane speckle the material. Strands of her own, longer hair cling to the material at her shoulder; delicate loops of golden brown. Mud streaks her boots. Her jodhpurs were black six months ago but have been faded to a storm-cloud grey by sunlight and detergent. They do not embarrass her. She has earned the right to look dishevelled. Her clothes demonstrate her devotion to her profession. She lives outdoors. She spends her time in the muck. She wears her faded work clothes the way rock stars sport their ripped jeans. She likes knowing that nothing about her appearance is an affectation. Her clothes look lived-in because she damn well lives in them.

'Heels down,' she says, surprising herself. The instruction is automatic. 'Thumbs up.'

The girl in the saddle responds to the instruction. She's eleven years old – almost half Crystal's age. Her boots are shiny; her jodhpurs black as ink.

'He keeps dropping his head,' says the girl.

'Show him who's boss,' says Crystal, stepping over a twist of tree root. 'Don't let him try it on. Give him a yank if he needs it.'

'I don't like hurting him,' says the girl.

'It won't hurt him, Primrose. It will reassure him. He'll know that you're confident. He'll thank you for it.'

Primrose gives a tug on the reins. The grey raises his head at once.

'Better,' says Crystal. 'Look at you, eh! Lovely straight back. There're some brambles coming up on the left so be wary of anything snagging him. He can be a silly one sometimes.'

'Remember the carrier bag?' says Primrose.

Crystal grins. Shakes her head. 'Don't know what he thought it was. A ghost maybe. I thought you were going to have a heart attack when he bolted. You did so well. The scream wasn't your finest moment but you didn't come off.'

Primrose sits a little higher in the saddle. Automatically, Crystal reaches up to pat the pony's neck. He is a seven-year-old. Welsh, section A. Primrose's father had wanted to spend a few thousand on his daughter's new hobby but Crystal had told him to save his money. Primrose was just starting out. It would be like buying a Stradivarius for a rookie violinist. She'd laid it out for them straight. *Money isn't always a blessing in the equestrian world. Hard work and perseverance are worth a lot more.* Joel had smiled at her after she said it. Told her she was a philosopher. Told her he would be paying her a lot more attention from now on.

Crystal's breath catches a little as she remembers that conversation. She hadn't had much to do with Joel Musgrave prior to that. It was his achingly beautiful wife, Viola, who had hired her as groom and riding tutor to their only child. Primrose had shown an interest in riding, she said. Wanted to become 'a horsey person'. Later, Crystal discovered that what Primrose actually wanted was a unicorn.

Joel had been perfectly polite during their brief encounters but Crystal had rarely given him much thought. Her focus was always the horses. Joel was just Primrose's father. He was Viola's husband. He was a good-looking, hippyish sort with nice eyes and a beaded necklace and a huge great house in the country. She had no time for fantasy. She was through with all that. Daft men and their game-playing; headaches and histrionics and jealousy. She didn't need any of it. She was happy with horses.

Falling for him was insidious. There was no single moment when she realised that she was in love with him. It stole over her in inches; a creeping, colonising passion that took her over like tangled ivy. By the time she accepted what she was feeling she had no reserves with which to fight it.

'What are you thinking about?' asks Primrose from the saddle. 'You're smiling.'

Crystal presses her lips into a tight smile. Concentrates on the track. It's a cold, blustery day and the pony is easily spooked. The rustle of a leaf or the sudden emergence of a pheasant from a hedge and the silly sod could take off like a rocket. Crystal's palm still bears the rope burns from his last outburst. Her right thigh is still empurpled with a crescent bruise. The kick had brought tears to her eyes. So did what came next.

Joel had witnessed what occurred; had come running from the big house, barefoot and bare-chested, desperate to know if she was okay. She was leaning on the fence, gasping for breath, cursing at her charge through clenched teeth. The daft nag had kicked her with enough force to take the wind right out of her. Dealt her pride a body-blow too. A good groom should never be kicked. Don't ever let a horse turn its back on you. That's what she had been taught.

Her thigh throbbed. She hurt from her hip to her toes. Joel had let her lean on him as he helped her hobble up to the house. Made her coffee with his big expensive machine. Gave her prescription painkillers and a tub of some sweet-smelling gunk that he said was used by tribespeople in one of the African countries where he used to spend his time. Was it Sudan? No, Madagascar. Or was that where the vanilla came from? She can't remember. Her thoughts are too jumbled. She just remembers Joel's instructions. The way he looked at her. His hands, soft and creamy, on the back of her rough fingers.

Take off your jodhpurs. Rub it on slowly. Let it soak in. I can help you if you want . . .

Gooseflesh pimples Crystal's body. She's a slim girl; jointy and knotted and sharp at the shoulder blades. She has sunken cheeks and staining on her teeth and her hair smells of hay and leather and the cheap washing powder in which she washes her Primark bedsheets. But Joel had pressed his nose to her crown and inhaled her as if she were a bouquet of roses.

'It's there again,' says Primrose. 'Same one.'

Crystal looks up, concentrating on the here and now. She squints. The track is winding back down towards the little road that curves round to the village. It is not a place where people regularly park. This is a public bridleway but Primrose and her mother are the only people who ride here. It's a nice spot. The trees form a canopy that shields them from the worst excesses of sunshine or rain and at this time of year there are snowdrops poking through the rich greenery. Sloes and elderberries ripen among the hedgerows each autumn. The air carries the taste of wild garlic; of standing water and crushed rosehips. Sometimes Crystal brings one of the other horses down here and treats herself to a canter. Before Joel laid his hands upon her she did not believe there was a better feeling.

'Same van?' asks Crystal, bemused. 'What do you think they're up to?'

'An affair,' says Primrose solemnly. 'A secret assignation. Is that the right word? Assignation?'

Crystal smirks. When she was Primrose's age she would not have known what an assignation was. But she would have been very aware that sometimes grown-ups meet down country lanes and fuck each other. Without such inclinations, she doubts she would be here at all. Crystal was not born to the privilege that Primrose enjoys. She had made mistakes. Got herself into bother without really meaning to be bad. Helped people who didn't deserve it and ignored those who did. It took an effort of will to get her life in order.

Stop being a silly cow, she'd told herself. *You're better than this. Make a life you want to live.*

She knows she has a tendency to obsess. She becomes addicted too easily. Her unceasing graft with the horses could easily be seen as an exercise in masochism. She is hooked on the feeling of exhaustion that suffuses her limbs. Is that what she is doing with Joel? she wonders. Is he her new addiction? Her new high? She is onto a good thing here. They treat her as one of the family. Primrose could almost be a little sister. She has to stop thinking about what could be and focus instead on what she has . . .

The pony senses the disturbance before either his rider or her tutor. It is a primal thing; a sensory disturbance. The animal pulls. Whinnies. His ears flatten. Primrose reaches down to pat his neck as Crystal looks up from her contemplations and raises a hand to his flanks . . .

The man emerges behind them. His approaching footsteps have been disguised by the regularity of the pony's hoofbeats. Crystal sees him only an instant before he reaches them. She has a blurred impression of dark skin. Bright eyes. A dark coat blackened with rain. A peculiarity to his features; a sensation of some indescribable wrongness; a missing piece . . .

There is a black-handled object in his right hand.

Crystal's thoughts seem to crush together; to bottleneck as they jostle for attention. So she stands, half-twisted, unmoving, mouth open, as the man jabs the device into the pony's rump and pumps the electric current through his flesh.

The pony rears back – a cardboard cut-out, paralysed by the current that surges through his meat and up into the delicate skin of his rider.

The air becomes a dreadful commotion of screeches and desperate shouts and then Crystal is falling onto her back and pain is shooting through her twisted knee and Primrose and her pony are collapsing down towards her like a toppling wall.

'Crystal! Help me!'

The log-jam in Crystal's consciousness suddenly rights itself. She is suddenly absolutely, damnably present. Absolutely *here*.

Somebody is trying to take Primrose.

She raises herself up and glimpses the girl's lifeless body being dragged, ragdoll-like, from beneath the motionless body of the animal. She hears herself shout; a desperate, furious 'No!' as she lashes out and grabs handfuls of earth, baring her teeth and snarling, bellowing – dire threats and vengeful warnings as everything within her becomes one single impulse. She must save Primrose. She must.

And now there is a shape. It becomes a face, swimming just inches above her own. Upside down. Cracked lips and grimy dark skin. Shadow and gnarled flesh where his ear should be. Eyes that burn with an intensity that makes her feel a spear has been thrust into her.

'Tell him.'

She sees the lips move. Soft words, almost song-like. And then a hand, stinking of grass and plastic, closing over her mouth and nose; her world diminishing into one single ugly spot.

His lips, so close that his threat becomes a delicate kiss.

'Tell him I have come to repay his betrayal.'

Her head is yanked upwards from the ground, fist gripping her chin.

A sudden downward thrust and a sickening impact with the rocky ground . . .

Colours turning monochrome; his words black ink on the dirty white that veils her vision.

'Tell him he is going to pay.'

2

Saturday night, 7.20 p.m.

A busy junction, not far from the centre of Hull.

It's all headlights and misty rain; gaudy shop fronts and purplish skies. The scents from half a dozen different takeaways are battling for dominance of the chilly, damp air. Most of the pedestrians hurrying along the pavements look baffled as to why they are suddenly craving a Kentucky Fried pizza with onion bhaji and hoi sin sauce. Up near the traffic lights, a sodden cyclist leans with an elbow on the wet, black railings, unable to manoeuvre his expensive toy through the tiny gap left by a van driver who has no inclination to be benevolent to any grown man who wears Lycra.

A boxy people-carrier, stationary in the gap between a white bus and a pizza-delivery scooter.

It's cosy inside the car. The smell of baby-wipes, Ribena and laundered clothes. The radio is turned down low but something folkish – all bodhrans and fiddles and a stomping right boot – is drifting out of the speakers. The driver and rear passengers are nodding along to the rhythm. Turned up high, the music would have a stirring effect upon their mood. The tune is fast and ferocious. Unfettered, it can make those with Celtic blood come over all wide-eyed and pagan. It is all the driver can do not to draw his claymore and declare war on anybody who has ever mocked the bagpipes or turned up their nose at a piece of shortbread.

An Irish voice, cheery and playful, emanating from the passenger in the front seat. She is petite and dark-haired and is busy writing the words 'help me' in the steam upon the glass.

'Shall we just say we live here? Make this spot our new address?'

Detective Sergeant Aector McAvoy chuckles softly. Places his hand upon his wife's thigh. She smiles, still delighted with his touch.

Fin McAvoy raises his head. Catches his father's eye in the mirror. 'Daddy . . .' he begins, then corrects himself, forcing his voice an octave lower. 'Dad, I mean. If you were a cake, what kind of cake would you be?'

The seven-year-old boy has the same bright brown eyes as his father. The same pale skin and red hair. At this moment Fin rivals his dad for width of shoulders and hugeness of chest, but that is due to the fact that he is wearing his ice hockey kit complete with helmet and shoulder pads.

'Go on, Aector.' Roisin smiles impishly from the passenger seat. 'Answer your son.'

McAvoy gives it some thought as he stares out of the window and stretches some life back into his static right foot. He used to be a good driver, as far as he can recall. Then he moved to Hull. He can't seem to remember having to change gear more than half a dozen times since. The streets are filled with motorists desperate to make it home in time to neutralise the effects of a day's shopping with a six-pack of lager and some undemanding TV. McAvoy has been staring at the advert on the back of the bus in front for the past twenty minutes. He now knows, with absolute certainty, that if he wants a solicitor to take his case on a *no-win-no-fee* basis, there is a first-class chap waiting to take his call.

'Speak, Daddy,' says Lilah.

McAvoy shifts so he can see his daughter. She's sitting in her child-seat doing an excellent impression of a Roman emperor.

He fears that if he does not come up with a good answer she may be disinclined to show mercy.

'I'd probably be a Battenberg,' says McAvoy.

'Why?' asks Fin. 'Is that the pink and yellow one?'

'I'm an acquired taste,' says McAvoy, nosing the people-carrier forward and switching the windscreen wipers on to smear a million tiny droplets into one big streak. 'And I do go pink when I exercise.'

Fin and Lilah have a hurried discussion in the rear of the car. There is a thud as Lilah strikes her brother on his ice hockey helmet in response to some unhelpful suggestion. McAvoy watches them in the mirror and smiles when his wife takes his hand.

'What about you?' he asks Roisin. 'What kind of cake would you be?'

'A profiterole,' she says, without preamble. 'I'd love to be a profiterole. In reality I'd probably be a vanilla slice but I'd never give up on my profiterole ambitions.'

McAvoy looks at his wife. She's wearing a fleecy top beneath her denim jacket and her lower half is clad in jodhpurs and riding boots. Even after eight years of marriage she is so beautiful as to make him catch his breath.

'You're thinking about me as a profiterole, aren't you?' asks Roisin, grinning at him in the way that suggests he will be expected to give her at least half an hour of his time before she lets him fall asleep tonight.

'We've decided you're not a Battenberg,' says Fin solemnly. 'You're a rhubarb crumble.'

'That's not a cake, strictly speaking,' points out McAvoy, drumming his fingers on the wheel and wishing there was a setting for his windscreen wipers that dealt specifically with the feeble and indecisive rain that swirls around Yorkshire at this time of year.

'Listen,' commands Lilah.

'And Mammy is a Smartie Bun,' says Fin.

'I'll take that,' says Roisin, leaning into the back seat to high-five both children.

'What are we?' asks Fin, and his voice is muffled by the helmet.

'You're a gingerbread man,' says Roisin to her son. 'Lilah, I reckon you're something squishy. Or maybe a rocky road, because you're a bit nuts and you melt in the sun.'

The children are still giggling as the lights finally change and McAvoy is able to tailgate the bus across the busy intersection. This part of the city has changed a lot. The Aldi on his left was a nice pub with a stained-glass ceiling when he arrived more than a decade ago. There were definitely fewer takeaways and letting agencies. They are only half a mile from the university but the cut-price accommodation in this area is no longer intended just for students. It is a multicultural hub; a melting pot of ethnicities and cultures. It was in an upstairs flat not far from here that McAvoy discovered how Urdu sounds when spoken with a Hull accent. His ears have never been quite the same since.

'What about Auntie Trish?' asks Fin mischievously.

'Some sort of tart,' says Roisin without pause.

McAvoy concentrates on the road ahead. Another old building is being converted into low-cost flats and, according to the graffiti on the bus stop across the road, Kelly has been shagged by Saleem. The notice fills McAvoy with a feeling of nostalgia. He recently had to deal with an attempted murder case sparked off by something one teenage girl had written about another one's personal hygiene on Facebook. It had made him yearn for simpler times, when writing 'Daz is a Twat' on somebody's pencil case was as close as a person could come to bullying a schoolmate in perpetuity.

'Are you going to take your helmet off, son?' asks McAvoy, looking at his son in the mirror.

'You said I could keep it on,' he protests.

'It's just if you go into the back of Mummy there's a good chance her head will pop,' says McAvoy soothingly.

'Are you willing to risk it, Mammy?' he asks Roisin.

'Aye, I've had a good life,' she says, staring out of the window at two students, huddling under an umbrella and nodding along to some tune. They both have similar hair and clothes and could be conjoined twins who were born attached at the headphones.

'I won't be long,' says McAvoy, as they cruise up Beverley Road and pass the tree where a dozen limp floral bouquets and a selection of soggy teddy bears have been left in memory of the latest group of girls to die in a car crash. 'He probably wants to tell me about one of the local newsagents selling knock-off cigarettes.'

Roisin blesses herself as they pass the spot of remembrance and adds her own extra gesture to the genuflection by slapping her husband on the arm. 'Be as long as you need. We'll be grand. I want to know what kind of sandwich the kids think I would be. We've got ways to keep ourselves entertained.'

McAvoy turns right and into the quiet estate of newer houses. It's a nice area, where three-bed semis and comfortable bunga-lows are shielded from view by the large Victorian properties on Beverley High Road. It's the sort of community where people will check on their neighbours if they haven't brought the milk in off the doorstep within twenty-four hours and where the elderly are invited to other people's family parties because it's less hassle than keeping the noise down.

'You can come in,' says McAvoy, as the car bumps over the speed hump at the entrance to the Autumn Days Care Home. He parks between a Daewoo and a Ford Ka and enjoys the fleeting sensation of owning the most luxurious vehicle in the row. 'He'd like to see you.'

'No, you go. Honestly. He doesn't let himself be himself when

I'm around. He can talk to you better if I'm not there. Anyway, I want to know if I'm cheese and pickle or corned beef.'

'You're strawberry jam,' says McAvoy, undoing his seat belt and climbing out of the car. He closes the door on the final syllable of Lilah's instruction not to be so ridiculous.

McAvoy smooths himself down and tries to make himself presentable. He kept his coat on during the drive from the Ice Arena and, despite the chill and the ugliness of the weather, he is perspiring a little at the temples. He trimmed his greying beard just this morning but already it is growing back, as if on some perverse mission to ensure he always looks a little like a biblical lumberjack. Beneath his expensive coat he wears a checked shirt and black V-neck jumper and somehow Roisin has managed to acquire jeans long enough to be worn with turn-ups at the bottom. At an easy six feet five, he is not accustomed to such a treat. He checks his reflection in the glass of the Daewoo. He doesn't find himself anywhere near as attractive as women seem to, but he feels suitably attired to go and speak to Perry.

The trees that surround the car park are shaking. It's been dark for a couple of hours and the light on the front porch of the red-brick building catches the miserable drizzle in its yellow circle of gaudy illumination. McAvoy wishes he were carrying a gift of some kind. He usually brings a couple of paperback books and a tin filled with home-made biscuits, but on his last visit Perry informed him that he was showing signs of diabetes and McAvoy had decided not to contribute to anything else going wrong with the poor old sod.

'You didn't have to drop everything,' says Perry from the doorway, in an accent that is pure Hull. 'I know you've got a life of your own.'

McAvoy waves a hand in greeting and then gives the old man a look of admonishment as he spots the cigarette in his hand.

'I thought you quit,' says McAvoy.

'I did. Then I started again. I'll quit again in the morning and start at lunchtime. Who are you, my mother?'

McAvoy shakes his head and joins the old man in the shelter of the reception area. From here he can catch the faintest whiff of slow-cooked meat and furniture polish. It almost masks the scent of detergent and urine that lingers despite the best intentions of both staff and guests.

'Beef stroganoff tonight,' says Perry, staring straight ahead at the car park.

'You like beef stroganoff?'

'Couldn't give a shit either way,' he says, rubbing out his cigarette against the wall. He turns his head and looks up. 'Were you up to anything fun?'

McAvoy gives a shrug. 'My boy had an ice hockey game.'

'Ice hockey? Christ.'

'They did okay. Fin scored twice and managed to avoid getting sent off for hooking an opposition player around the neck. I wish I could say the same about his mum. She spent the last ten minutes in the car park cooling off.'

Perry grins. He has met all the members of McAvoy's family. He has little or nothing to say to the two young children but had been happy to tell McAvoy that his wife was a stunner with whom he would happily flatten some grass.

'They in the car?' asks Perry.

'Discussing deeply philosophical matters.'

'I'll bet.'

McAvoy looks at the old man. He's wearing smart grey trousers and a shirt and tie beneath a grey cardigan and a padded coat. The only concession to his age is the burgundy slippers he wears on feet clad in two pairs of socks. He was forced to concede defeat on the shoe front recently and add the tying of his shoelaces to the growing list of activities too hazardous to attempt without supervision.

Perry Royle is somewhere in his early eighties. There's little fat on his bones and his clothes look on him the same way they do on the hanger. It has been thirty-three years since he was last able to flash his warrant card and call himself a policeman but he has never truly attuned his instincts to civilian life. He spent eight years as a security guard in Princes Quay and another few as a guide at the Ferens Art Gallery. At seventy-one he accepted retirement and gave himself over to a life of leisure with the wife who had waited decades for his full attention. She died a year later when an aneurysm exploded in her brain midway through the conundrum on an episode of *Countdown*. Perry had not been able to look at the word 'indelible' since. The couple never had children and Perry had little interest in the nieces and nephews who forgot his birthday with increasing regularity. He lived alone in a house in Gipsyville and looked forward to his two pints each Thursday afternoon with a couple of equally decrepit old colleagues. Then Jim suffered a heart attack and Gordon went doolally, and at the age of eighty-one Perry discovered that he was alone in the world.

He met McAvoy by chance. A teenager broke into the home of one of Perry's neighbours while Perry was mowing his front lawn. He saw the little bleeder making a break for it on a flashy bicycle and instinct took over. Perry grabbed the little sod by the hood of his jumper and slapped the taste out of his mouth for the next twenty minutes. He retrieved the stolen goods and let the kid go on the condition that if he did it again, Perry would be within his rights to cut him off at the knees. The teenager's parents reported the old boy to the police. McAvoy, in his role as emblem of geniality for Humberside Police, was asked by the top brass to go and smooth things over. Nobody wanted the old bugger prosecuted but likewise they couldn't be seen to let him get away with it. McAvoy persuaded Perry to write a letter of apology and then managed to get the teen's parents to leave the matter alone. McAvoy had taken a shine to the cantankerous old sod and dropped him off a bottle of single malt on behalf of his various colleagues at CID who would have otherwise nominated him for a medal. They got to talking. That turned to a sharing of opinions and a heated discussion about the future of the Labour Party. Without meaning to, they became friends and it was McAvoy who helped Perry move here, to the Autumn Days Care Home, when his last mini-stroke left him unable to put sugar in his tea without spilling half of it back into the bowl. McAvoy tries to see him once a fortnight. They sometimes play chess. On occasion, McAvoy has been known to read to him, though neither man is sufficiently at home with their feelings to be able to say how much they look forward to such events. Perry's bedroom wall is decorated with drawings done by Fin and Lilah, even if McAvoy has never handed over a new artwork without blushing and trying to explain what the picture is meant to be.

'I'm not talking shit,' says Perry, who appears to be defending himself despite the absence of attack.

'I've never heard you talk shit. I've heard you talk a bit of bollocks, but not out-and-out shit.'

'Watch it, gingernut,' says Perry, biting down on a smile. 'I've still got enough moves to put you on your arse.'

McAvoy leans back against the wall, waiting for Perry to explain why he had left him a voicemail demanding his immediate presence at the care home. Perry is too proud ever to ask for help.

'House, down yonder,' says Perry, pointing with his foot in the traditional Hull way.

'Bronte Hall, isn't it?'

'Aye. Nobody's lived there for years. Lovely old place but falling to bits. Seems like every new set of builders buggers off before the job gets done. Saw in the *Mail* it's being done up properly.'

McAvoy nods. 'Yes?'

'There've been comings and goings, Aector. Builders, aye, but it's more than that. Something's not right.'

McAvoy straightens himself up. He looks through the windows of the care home and catches a glimpse of the pensioners sitting in a semicircle, watching a young crooner in a purple suit belt out Sinatra numbers from an improvised stage.

'I've taken down the number plates,' says Perry. 'One of them was a VW Transporter. It stopped for a moment while I was having a fag and I swear, even with my old eyes, I could see that the number plate had been tampered with. The "F" was an "L" and the "2" was a "7". It was masking tape and a felt-tip pen. I wouldn't have been looking if it wasn't for the fact that there were more cars than usual heading down to the house.'

McAvoy listens, waiting for more.

'This evening I heard shouts,' says Perry. 'Proper shouts, coming from the house. So I went to investigate.'

McAvoy gives the old man a warning look.

'What? I'm not allowed to take a walk? I live here!'

'What did you see?'

'Security lights came on as soon as I was inside the grounds. Then this foreign prick came out and demanded to know what I was doing. Said some shit in foreign and told me to get off his land because it was private property.'

'And did you?'

'Sure,' says Perry. His lip twitches. His eyes seem to lose focus as he considers his recent memory. He sees it again. 'Had a look in the cars as I went though. Blood, Aector. I'm sure I saw it – the way it looks in the light – the stickiness . . . you know it when you see it, even if it's a flash. I was going to call 999 but I had a feeling they'd think I was some daft old bastard. I called you instead because you already know I'm not.'

McAvoy looks back at the old people who are clapping along to the Sinatra impersonator. Most of them are younger than Perry and if any of them called the police to report suspicious activity at an abandoned house he would likely shrug it off as the result of old age and too much blue cheese before bedtime. Even so, he would check out their suspicions.

'I'm doing my duty as a concerned citizen,' says Perry. 'What you do with it is up to you.'

McAvoy snorts. 'You know what I'll do with it.'

'Aye, that's why I called. And that's why we're friends.'

Ten minutes later, McAvoy is making his way down the dark, pitted driveway that leads to Bronte Hall. To the sound of tuts from Perry he used his phone to skim-read the details on the dilapidated property at the end of the road. He now knows as much about the place as the Hull City Council planning officers who wrote the report. The Hall was built in the eighteenth century by a toff who was destined to become MP for Hull and who would die impoverished in Canada within four decades of its construction. For the past thirty years it has been derelict and though it is owned by a private landlord who once expressed an interest in turning it into a set of luxury apartments, it has fallen into disrepair. Various local pressure groups have been in touch with the local authorities demanding it be brought under the control of the public sector and turned into some form of museum or community resource. The landlord has done little more than put sticking plasters over the cracks, though McAvoy recalls reading about plans for a larger scale redevelopment. It's a twelve-bed, white-painted affair that backs onto the River Hull and is encircled on all sides by a wooden fence topped with barbed wire. As McAvoy makes his way down the path he spots three different placards warning him that this is private property and that trespassers will be prosecuted.

A white light winks into life as he leaves the rocky driveway and makes his way across the short neat grass towards the main doors. The light illuminates a three-storey construction. Up close, the white is more a chalky shade of grey, with rectangular windows divided into squares, which put McAvoy in mind of an old-fashioned chocolate bar. The balconies beneath the windows look a little like bowling pins and the twin chimneys as if they have been drawn in by a child.

Sighing a little, McAvoy climbs the stone stairs to the front door and bangs on the brown wood.

'Humberside Police,' he shouts, and his voice sounds loud against the silence of the early evening air.

McAvoy's shout is met with silence. Out of habit he tries the door handle and is surprised to find it turn. The door hinges give a squeak as he pushes the door open.

'Hello. Hull CID.' And then, for completeness: 'Police.'

McAvoy enters the hallway. It's dark and cold. His feet disturb a pile of glossy papers and as he fumbles with his phone and tries to find a light, he makes his way down a hallway carpeted in chessboard tiles.

'Police,' he shouts again, and his voice is swallowed by the empty air.

Eventually, McAvoy locates the torch on his phone and finds himself standing in the centre of a small circle of yellow light. He looks down at the black and white floor and up to the distant ceiling, with its ruined rose and its trailing wires. He looks down again, for clarification.

To his right is a doorway, hinges and nails sticking out of the frame. The door has been wrenched off and is laid out flat, like a stretcher. McAvoy holds the light ahead of him as he enters a long room with wooden floors and a ceiling so high he cannot see it.

McAvoy sees the thing on the wall almost immediately. Feels the world slow down. His heart punches at his ribcage as fear runs clawed fingers through his hair.

Pursing his lips, letting out a long, slow exhalation, McAvoy stares up at the figure suspended two feet off the floor, pressed into the wall. He thinks of mummies. Fossils. His mind becomes a kaleidoscope of horrifying images. Some are

27

memories, others projections. He realises his hands have become fists. He angles the torch, looking into the face of a man who died in pain. Tries to process the details. Nice suit. Good watch. Probably a similar age to himself. No bruises. Clean-shaven. A smell of decent aftershave under the buzzing stench of festering blood . . .

McAvoy angles his head and peers at the cracked plaster and dark shadows that spread out from the corpse. Looks at the hands. The nail-heads sticking out of the wrists and the clotted pools of black blood upon pale skin. He stands transfixed. There is a pressure on his chest and he feels chill fingers tickling his shoulders and neck. He smells it again. The reek of it. The taste of a life ended amid the sound of screams.

A mannequin, he thinks, and it is more plea than hope. Please, let it just be a mannequin . . .

A flash of movement, the sound of fleeing footsteps. McAvoy spinning as he hears the front door bang; the engine revving on a big car, tyres squealing, a shower of gravel and dirt.

Instinct takes over. McAvoy runs. Barges through the open doorway and down the corridor, slipping on the glossy leaflets and stumbling through the front door and into the dark and the rain. The car is tearing away across the grass. He squints to make out the forms in the back seat. Tries to count the number of heads. Curses as the vehicle disappears onto the driveway.

McAvoy's phone is still in his hand, clutched tight as a grenade as he sprints towards the care home. He slides his finger on the damp screen, punching 999, hearing himself shouting at nothing.

McAvoy emerges from shadow and into the low light of the care home reception area. Blinks sweat from his eyes. Sees, as if in slow-motion, the unfolding scene at the entrance to the car park. Perry stands in the road and holds out his forearm as if it were a shield. The old man is only halfway through saying 'police' when the car bonnet hits him at 50 mph and propels him ten feet down the road. He hits the ground like a bag of sticks and rags.

As the car roars away, the only other sound is the gentle pitter-patter of the downpour, and McAvoy's whisper, over and again, the simple plea: 'No'.

3

'Well, that's not something you see every day.'

Detective Superintendent Trish Pharaoh is peering at the well-dressed man who has been pressed into the wall of Bronte Hall. She glares at his expensive gold watch.

'Why did they leave you this, eh? Wallet too.'

She looks at his brown suede loafers with their Lacoste logo, and the Prada glasses that lie beneath.

'I think we can call you a fashion victim,' she mumbles.

Pharaoh turns to look at McAvoy: huge in the glare of the lurid spotlights being erected by the forensics team. There's a fine spray of blood on his forehead but she doesn't quite know how to tell him. His shoulders are slumped and his hands hang limp by his sides. It is all she can do not to give him a hug and a bar of chocolate. He looks the way her children do when they fall and scrape their knees and can't quite understand how the world has suddenly turned on them.

'What's the film I'm thinking about?' she asks, raising her voice over the mutterings of the men and women in white suits and face masks as they mill around the room.

'*Empire Strikes Back*,' says McAvoy quietly. 'Han Solo gets frozen in the carbonite.'

Pharaoh nods her head. 'Yeah, that's it. Did that have the little bears in it?'

'Next one did. Ewoks.' McAvoy sighs, rubbing his head and looking with dismay at the redness that now stains his fingertips. 'Is that a line of enquiry?'

'Watch your lip,' says Pharaoh, smiling. McAvoy doesn't make many jokes and she appreciates it when he makes an effort.

Pharaoh has only just arrived at the scene. The lipstick she wears today is the same shade as the red wine in the cracks of her lips. She smells of cigarettes and chewing gum and her eyeliner is straighter on her left eye than her right. The flaws do not make her any less desirable and the uniformed constables who have been guarding the crime scene visibly straightened their backs and stroked down their hair when news came through that Pharaoh was on her way. She's forty-seven, a mother of four, and is at once the most adored and hated woman on Humberside Police. To many, she's a role model. Her conviction rate is exceptional. She's fearless and has a personality roughly twice the size of her body. She's all waving arms and flamboyant gestures. She spills half of every cup of coffee and spends large portions of her day trying to disentangle her necklaces from her long black hair. With her curves, biker boots and sunglasses, there are few officers who have not imagined what it would be like to press themselves against her ample chest and let her make all their problems go away. Those who do not like her tend to be the people she has torn to bits with her one of her legendary dressing-downs, or who have tried it on at a Christmas party and ended up with a different kind of groin-based contact than they had hoped for. Pharaoh grew up on a rough estate in a small South Yorkshire town and knows that no matter how hard they try, nobody can put muscles on their bollocks.

Pharaoh looks around and tries to work out which of the figures in white is the forensic pathologist. 'What you think, Prof? We got a Jedi-based serial killer on our hands? Should I be looking for a nine-foot Wookie or a little green fella in a robe? Shouldn't be hard to get enough people for an ID parade. This is Hull, after all.'

Professor Manfred Laurel stops in the act of doing something complicated with the straps of the video camera mounted upon the head of his assistant. He gives Pharaoh his full attention.

'My predecessor warned me to prepare myself for your idiosyncrasies,' he says brightly.

Pharaoh gives a snort. 'Predecessor would suggest the word "deceased", wouldn't it? Which isn't really right, given that Dr Jackson-Savannah remains disappointingly alive.'

Professor Laurel grins and pulls down his mask. He looks like a child's drawing of a grown-up. His head is a misshapen circle and his hair is a squiggle of black curls that stop well short of his forehead. With his sticky-out ears and beaming, closed-mouth smile, he looks as though he should have a gold star and 'good work' written across his legs.

'Come and have a listen, Hector,' says Pharaoh. 'The professor's going to educate us.'

McAvoy steps gingerly onto the metal floor-plates put down by the scene of crime team to protect evidence. They groan and clank under the pressure. He joins Pharaoh and Laurel by the dead man. McAvoy's protective suit is too small for him. Pharaoh's is too large.

'Two days, judging by the lividity and the way the blood has settled,' says Laurel, lifting the dead man's shirt to show the purplish swellings above the line of his jeans. 'No less, possibly more.'

'ID?' asks Pharaoh.

McAvoy shifts his weight. This is his cue. He has acquainted himself with the basic facts in the three hours since the car ploughed through Perry and the old man breathed a series of desperate rasping breaths into McAvoy's face. 'This is Mahesh Kahrivardan,' he says. He has downloaded an app to his phone that tutored him in the correct pronunciation. In his Highlands accent, it sounds like '*my hash caravan*'.

'Local boy, eh?' asks Pharaoh.

'Yes and no,' says McAvoy. 'Lives on Galfrid Road in Bilton.'

'Bilton?'

'Heading east. You pass it on your way to Burton Constable Hall.'

'Is that the big house? Nice scones. Whalebone in the courtyard.'

'That's it.'

'Am with you. Proceed.'

'He's forty-two. Has dual citizenship – here and Sri Lanka, though Yorkshire has been home for more than twenty years.'

'Record?' asks Pharaoh.

McAvoy digs in his pockets for his pad. This time he does need his notes.

'Two years ago he was sentenced to six months' imprisonment, suspended for two years, after admitting offences under the Gangmaster Licensing Act. He was charged after an investigation by the UK Border Agency Immigration Crime Team. Seems he was a small cog in a big operation but there was evidence he illegally supplied workers to several different firms in Portsmouth. Under the Proceeds of Crime Act he was ordered to repay the £340,000 he was said to have made through his illegal activities. He defaulted last summer and was told by magistrates to sell off his assets in order to comply. The assets he shared with the court included four local businesses, two houses in India, the property in Bilton and a caravan in Hornsea, not to mention his BMW X5.' McAvoy stops talking and closes his eyes. He nods towards the road, still damp with an old man's blood. 'That X5.'

'Keep going,' says Pharaoh, looking at the man on the wall with fresh interest.

'He made payment in full within a week of the hearing.'

'Lottery win?' asks Pharaoh.

'Stranger things have happened, but not many.'

33

'Dependants? Next of kin?' asks Pharaoh.

'There's a photo of a blonde girl with her top off in his wallet. She looks about nineteen. Inspector Stade and two uniforms have gone to the Bilton house. Detective Inspector Harte is on standby to take a statement.'

From beneath Pharaoh's face mask comes the noise of a lower lip being sucked in thought. Pharaoh hand-picked her new detective inspector when the Serious and Organised Unit was downsized and remoulded in the wake of budget cuts. She was forced to bring in a new DI and a new detective sergeant to complement her team of six constables and half a dozen civilian staff. Alec Harte is a solid, dependable officer who impressed Pharaoh during the interview process by never once looking down her top. He's a big, bluff Lancastrian with a completely bald head and a nose flattened by a life spent playing rugby. Pharaoh thinks he looks like a cross between a cage-fighter and a puffin.

'Aye, let him take it,' says Pharaoh, shrugging. 'He can fill us in in the morning.'

McAvoy gives a tight smile, relieved. It's clear he wants to go home. Pharaoh can all but read his thoughts as he stands beside her. He wants to hold his family. Wants to wrap his arms around Roisin and decompress in her embrace. Needs to think about the injuries to his friend in the only space where he feels comfortable to let himself go.

'Professor,' says Pharaoh, turning to the pathologist. 'Any idea how laddo here got stuck in the wall?'

Professor Laurel seems delighted to be asked. Unbidden, one of his assistants hands him an electronic tablet and he engages the application that serves as light, recording device and magnifying glass. He runs it over Kahrivardan's torso and stops at a shining point of silver.

'This is the object that's holding him up,' says Laurel. 'He has been skewered to the wall using what looks at first glance to be a knitting needle but could be a drill-bit or particularly thin screwdriver body. As you can see, the plaster was still damp at the time. He's rather a peculiar thing to look at, is he not? I may get a seminar or two out of this.'

'No blood,' says Pharaoh.

'Not much, no. But look at his stomach. There are pints of blood inside the cavity. It's pooled and coagulated there. When we open him up there will be a near flood.'

'Grim,' says Pharaoh.

'Indeed.'

'Any other signs of a struggle?'

'No bruising to the face. No bruising on the hands. No visible head wounds. But you'll see here that nails have been driven through his wrists. Nail-gun, if you want my guess.'

McAvoy and Pharaoh exchange a look. They've got more experience of nail-guns than they would like.

'Could be religious,' says Pharaoh, with an air of hopefulness. 'Nails through the wrists has a rather biblical feel.'

'Nothing in the ankles,' says Professor Laurel. 'If you're thinking down that path, there are some useful textbooks I could furnish you with.'

Pharaoh gives a nod of thanks but from the shape of her shoulders it's clear she is feeling dispirited. The nail-gun is the weapon of choice for a vicious criminal gang that has nearly cost her everything she holds dear. She would rather deal with a crucifixion than the Headhunters. The criminal syndicate has spilled a lake of blood since Pharaoh first saw their brutal calling card. Merciless and professional, the outfit offers expertise and manpower to existing criminal organisations, in exchange for a share of any profits. Those who resist are destroyed – one way or another. Pharaoh looks at the body again. Kahrivardan was wearing jeans, checked shirt and a suede jacket when the metal skewer entered his heart and pinned him to the wall. He's not a big man but it would take strength to ram the implement through him and into the damp plaster behind.

'He hadn't been reported missing?' she asks McAvoy, who shakes his head. She sucks her lip again. Then she turns to Laurel. 'Okay, we're here now and you've already ruined my appetite. Show me the other thing.'

Laurel leads Pharaoh and McAvoy down the corridor. The metal plates creak afresh beneath McAvoy's feet. Bronte Hall has fallen far from its days as Hull's premier residence. It has stood empty for years and none of its owners have treated it kindly. Damp patches now flourish on the peach-coloured walls and wires hang loose from the high ceilings. The wooden floor is littered with food containers and loose papers, leaflets and receipts. Cobwebs have piled up in the corners. One appears to have trapped a mouse. It is a cold, gloomy space and Pharaoh feels she should be barefoot and wearing a long nightdress, holding a silver candlestick and watching the flame stretch out on the breeze.

'I feel like I'm in fucking *Scooby Doo*,' she mutters, in the hope McAvoy will smile. He doesn't.

'In there,' says Laurel, and he indicates an open wooden door, painted white.

Pharaoh pauses before entering. There are three shiny bolts on the outside of the door.

'New,' she says. 'Newest thing in here.'

'Not quite,' says McAvoy, who has already been inside.

Pharaoh enters the room. It is bathed in the same yellow light as the area where Kahrivardan died. The bulbs cast an incongruous sparkle into the drab, half-empty space. The room is perhaps four metres by five. Long ago it had floral wallpaper but the pattern has been turned to a blackened mess by the damp that blooms on every surface. The carpet has been ripped up and the floor is a soggy mess of rotting underlay. A square of hard transparent Perspex has been nailed in front of the solitary window and some kind of sealant squirted around the edges. There is a brown blanket on the floor, its tasselled edges a tangle of knots. There is a black plastic bucket by the near wall, together with a roll of toilet paper and some anti-bacterial hand sanitiser. The food wrappers that litter the floor are all from cheap chocolate bars and there is a bottle of cheap supermarket fizzy drink lying empty on its side.

Pharaoh turns around, taking it all in. She stops when she sees the metal D-ring, screwed deep into the wall.

'Not very comfortable,' she says, and takes her face mask off. She breathes deep and wrinkles her nose. 'What's that smell?'

'A lot of things,' says McAvoy. 'Sweat. Urine. Bleach. Rotting fabric. Damp.'

Pharaoh indicates that McAvoy should pull down his own mask. He does so, exposing more of the blood that patterns his face and blends in perversely with his freckles.

'You've got something to tell me,' she says. 'I can hear your brain whirring.'

McAvoy seems uncertain for a moment. Then his face hardens and he points to the rug. He squats down beside it and urges her to do the same.

'Immediate thought is that Kahrivardan was held captive here and whoever did it went on to kill him, yes?'

'We don't assume, Hector, but that would seem like a fair guess.'

'Alternatively, we think that Kahrivardan had a captive here. Somehow, they've escaped and killed their captor. They got scared when I arrived and they fled, knocking Perry down in the process. Tyre marks show the car was parked by the out-house, tucked up against the wall. I couldn't see it when I came in. Tyres match. The same car hit Perry.'

Pharaoh softens her eyes. McAvoy's voice almost broke at mention of the old cop's name.

'That would seem just as likely.'

McAvoy points at the tangled tassels that hem the blanket.

'These are a special type of knot,' he says, keeping his voice low. 'There's a way of braiding a horse's hair . . . button braids, they're called. A lot of the equestrian crowd think it looks brilliant – others think it's crass. Either way, it's not easy to do.'

Pharaoh considers the twists. 'They're not just a tangle?'

'No, this has been done properly. And here,' says McAvoy, standing up and putting out his arm to help Pharaoh rise. He takes her to the black bucket and motions for Professor Laurel to come closer. He produces a blue light and shines it around the bucket as he had done for McAvoy shortly after arriving.

'No drips,' says McAvoy, and he sounds a little embarrassed. 'I don't want to be crass but a man can't hit the toilet bowl every time if it's the size of a swimming pool. And there are no urine drips.'

Pharaoh peers into the bucket. Smells urine, damp paper, faeces and bleach.

'So you're suggesting . . .'

McAvoy opens his hands. 'I'm not suggesting anything,' he says. 'But this doesn't seem like it has been home to a middle-aged male hostage for however many days it takes to produce this much mess and that much urine.'

'A girl?' asks Pharaoh.

McAvoy looks at her and the light catches in the scars that groove his big, broad face.

'I couldn't get a good look at them,' he says, and it sounds like a confession. 'They were already driving away. And then all I could see was Perry. But I'm playing it back in my head and I can't be certain what I saw. It's all a jumble.'

Pharaoh waits for more. She puts her hand on his arm.

'Hector, don't ever worry about saying things to me. Tell me what you're thinking.'

'I think there was a girl with them,' he says coldly. 'I think they've been keeping her here and I scared them away. And if that's the case, I don't know if I just cost her her life.'

4

The tiny hamlet of Thoresway sits in a green valley on the outer reaches of the Lincolnshire Wolds. While the majority of the county is flat, the landscape here creases like the wrinkles in a badly ironed tablecloth and for several miles in each direction this is a place of steep hills and sudden drops.

There are no more than a score of houses in this tiny community, which proudly claims that it can trace its history back to the Domesday Book. It is mostly farmland and the homes have names like the Old School House, the Old Post House and Chapel Cottage. The properties are solid, sturdy affairs with neat gardens to the front and rear, and sensible rural vehicles in the driveways. The majority of the residents wear riding boots or wellingtons as a matter of course. It is a community where a person's ability to make jam is taken for granted and where keen gardeners actively seek out the equestrian crowd in order to procure the finest manure for their roses. Here, Hunter wellington boots and Barbour jackets will never go out of style.

The Old Hall is set back a little from the road, screened by a procession of tall trees that were planted in the eighteenth century by the same Nottingham lace merchant who built the property and who died within a year of moving in. It is a huge, white-painted building surrounded by so much grassland that it almost appears as an island in a green sea. There is a pleasing symmetry to the main house, with its central double doors and neat rectangular windows. At the rear, the outbuildings are a more ramshackle affair, having been adapted and extended several times over the decades. The stables are a haphazard construction of wood and red brick, overlooking a paddock in which a circular training manege has been scored out by eager hooves. The barn that used to house agricultural equipment is now an office and games room.

The most recent owners have been here nine years. It took them a great deal of charm and strategy to gain planning permission to build the conservatory that squats at the east of the main building and blends in with the general aesthetic in much the same way as moustache and glasses would on the *Mona Lisa.*

Trainee Detective Constable Angela Verity sits in the large, airy space and sips the expensive Ethiopian coffee that her interviewee was only too happy to make. The coffee is strong and smells wonderful and were it not for the fact that the machine used to make it looks as though it cost more than her car, she would be preparing to turn her back on the brown sludge she normally drinks and which the coppers at her station refer to as 'Soylent Brown'. She has had worse Saturday nights, she thinks.

Verity is about to make her third complimentary statement on the quality when she is interrupted by the sudden sound of claws scuttling on the glass above her head. Against the darkness and the soft rain she sees the outline of a fat pigeon, ice-skating across the glass.

'My heart nearly stopped there,' says Verity, with the little nervous laugh that she had promised herself she would stop emitting when she hit twenty-five. Her dad had always thought her giggle was cute but her last boyfriend has changed her mind on this. Apparently it's annoying and makes her sound like a six-year-old.

'Wait until you hear the foxes scream,' says Musgrave, sipping his green tea. 'Don't ever think the country is all tranquillity. Sometimes it sounds like a horror movie out there. I didn't know that ravens could talk until we moved. It came as quite a surprise. Turns out that in times of great fear, I lose all sense of decorum and my vocabulary disappears. If I die scared, my last words are going to be "Jesus Fucking Fuck".'

Verity and Musgrave are seated opposite one another, separated by a low coffee table on which an ornate chessboard has been abandoned mid-game. Verity is not much of a chess player but she can tell that the blacks are winning. There are some officers she has worked with who would probably take that as politically symbolic. Being a police officer has certainly opened her eyes. There are times she wishes she could close them again.

Verity is sitting on a comfortable velveteen sofa set into a base of bamboo poles. Musgrave is sitting in an antique wooden rocking chair, his feet resting on the thick cream carpet. The room is decorated in a dozen different styles. Maps, watercolours, fabric batiks and wooden African sculptures cover the only wall that is not made of glass, while the side tables are a mismatched selection of ancient beer crates and self-assembly units from Ikea. Verity noticed the same peculiar hodgepodge of tastes in the main house, with its twisting double staircases and its movie posters hanging on floral-print walls. It has the look of a house into which several people have moved the artefacts of previous lives.

'This coffee really is amazing,' says Verity, putting the mug down on top of a glossy magazine on the table to her right. It sits on top of a stack of booklets, envelopes and large hardbacks. As she does so she finds herself hoping that if she is ever lucky enough to live in such a home, she will be equally blasé about how to live her life within it. She hopes that she would still be her usual self: messy and slightly hopeless and forever wishing she was just a bit better at pretty much everything. She fears that living in such a property would indeed change her. After all, she was willing to change her laugh just to please a short man with a spotty back who took her to a Nando's for their first date and used 'Shoveltits' as her pet name.

'Ethiopian,' says Musgrave and then shakes his head in self-reproach. 'I told you that, didn't I? I'm sorry, it must sound like I'm showing off.'

'Not at all,' says Verity, and she cringes a little inside. She feels like this is a date instead of official police business. She hears herself gabbling. 'I don't know if coffee from Ethiopia is better or worse. I don't know if it's something to brag about, is what I mean. It's not like telling me that the pork pie in the fridge is from Melton Mowbray. Now, that would be bragging.'

Musgrave laughs. He has a nice smile. Verity knows from her research into his background that he is nearly fifty years old, but he is clearly in good condition. He's wearing a simple T-shirt beneath a pale blue shirt, soft brown cords and battered Adidas trainers. He has a long, nicely proportioned face and a smudge of beard around his mouth and chin. He wears the sort of round glasses that make some middle-aged men look like a sex pest but on Musgrave they seem to work. He has the look of a hippy done well – the sort who can conduct business deals on a solar-powered telephone while doing something devilish with mung beans and quinoa. Verity finds herself wondering whether his wife is still as pretty as she looks in the huge wedding photograph that hangs in the hall. The wedding was an unshod affair on a beach. Musgrave wore a cream linen suit and open-necked shirt. Viola wore a bikini top and floaty white skirt, showing off the magnificent henna tattoo on her mocha skin. The only person in the picture who looked as though they wanted to do things the traditional way was the flower-girl in the foreground, sweating and red-faced in a gold and ivory dress.

'It's not decaffeinated,' says Musgrave apologetically. 'You won't sleep.'

Verity shakes her head. 'I always get eight hours. Nothing

keeps me awake.' She leaves a gap, wondering if Musgrave will fill it with an innuendo-laden remark. He doesn't. He's been nothing but nice. He's been friendly but not flirtatious and Verity wishes she had the experience to know what to make of somebody who appears to be a genuinely nice guy.

'I would never have called this late but your light was on and it just seemed like it would be silly to leave it until the morning,' says Verity.

'I said it was fine. I mean it.'

Verity realises she is far too comfortable. She wants to pull her legs up underneath her and rest her head on the arm of the sofa. She would like to light some candles and maybe have a doze in front of a period drama. She gets cross with herself for such silliness. She wants to be taken seriously. Wants to take herself seriously. But she is a dreamer. Her mind wanders. She loses her train of thought during interviews and sometimes can't remember attending briefings at which she was most definitely present. She has considered seeing her GP to see if there is something wrong with her but both her parents and most recent boyfriends have told her there is no known cure for being 'away with the fairies'.

Determined to compensate, Verity sits up and tries to look businesslike. She reaches into her bag and pulls out the pale blue file into which she has stuffed the few sheets of paper that pertain to Crystal Heathers. She tries to sound professional and is aware just how far she falls short. She stops and starts twice before she can find her voice.

'Mr Musgrove, yes . . . erm . . . just a moment . . . as I said on the phone, it's entirely possible that there is nothing to worry about. Probably, even. But her mother is very insistent.'

Musgrave gives her an understanding look that Verity appreciates. She reads back over her notes. 'Now, you said that you've known Crystal for almost a year, is that right?'

Musgrave takes another sip of his tea. 'The mobile phone

signal is dire, I get used to repeating myself,' he says. 'Crystal is more my wife's friend than mine but yes, about a year ago Crystal was doing some shifts at the Blacksmith's, that's the pub up the road in Rothwell, and she got talking to Viola about horses. Viola is horse mad, as is my daughter, Primrose. Anyway, Viola said Crystal was welcome to come and play ponies at our place any time and she took her up on the offer. We have three horses and my wife is very good with them but given how often she has to be away with work, we felt we needed somebody to lend a hand. We offered Crystal a job on a casual basis. She comes every weekday morning to muck out and do the feed and every evening to give Primrose her riding lesson. That's the plan, anyway. Turn your back and she and Primrose are out on a hack. Primrose is eleven, I'm not sure if I told you that. And my wife is a fashion designer, as you might already know.'

'And remind me of your job, please,' says Verity, writing down every word.

'On one hand I'm pleasantly retired,' he says, smiling. 'I ran a bioscience company for a long time, which was floated on the Stock Exchange and did rather well. On paper I have a few non-executive directorships with different global agro firms. I also serve as a consultant for firms trying to improve their carbon footprint. So think of me as a hippy with short hair and a big house. That just about covers it.'

'And you said that the last time you saw Crystal was on Wednesday morning, yes?'

'That's right. Primrose has become quite proficient at doing the horses on her own but it would be horrid to tell Crystal we don't need her any more. She turned up at 7 a.m. as she always does. Came on her moped, as is the norm. Prim had already started mucking out. I was in the kitchen making breakfast. Viola is in London at the moment. I had a quick chat with Crystal as I always do. Made her a coffee. Asked her if she wanted a breakfast doing and like usual she said she was fine. Then she went home, or to whatever it is she does when she's not here. She was due back in the evening but didn't arrive so Prim didn't go out. I won't let her take the horses out without supervision. I texted Viola in London to tell her and she said she would text Crystal and see if she was coming. Then Viola told me that she'd seen on Facebook that Crystal was going on an impulse holiday and not to worry, she'd be back after some sun and sea and sand. I was a bit put out and so was Primrose but that was the last I thought of it. Then you came to see me.'

Verity stops writing. She looks up and smiles. It's one of her good smiles. She knows she's not great looking and that she falls more into the 'cute' than 'sexy' category but her smile has been called 'disarming' by the male admirers who know what the word means. Her boss at Brigg Police Station has warned her that with her long dark blonde hair and blue eyes, when she becomes a fully-fledged detective constable her supervisors will use her mostly for honey traps and undercover jobs with Vice. She has not yet decided whether to be offended or pleased.

'That's very helpful, thank you,' says Verity. 'As I explained, as far as the police are concerned Crystal is an adult who is perfectly able to go where she pleases and with whom she pleases. The reason we have involved ourselves is because of the Facebook post. Her mother read that and contacted us immediately. You see, Crystal has never had a passport. She's never been abroad.'

'It could have been a holiday in England,' says Musgrave tactfully.

'Yes, but it's February. And it's also worth considering that the last time Crystal went on a short break she had to borrow a bag from her mother as she doesn't have one of her own. Her mum has also been to Crystal's house and it appears there are no clothes missing.'

Musgrave does not look away. He spreads his hands. His

46

whole manner screams of apology – a burning dismay at being unable to assist.

Verity scratches at the back of her hand and looks up, hoping for stars. She can only see her own reflection. Pale face and cheap clothes and hair blown into knots by the wind. 'We've rung Crystal's phone several times without success,' says Verity, looking back at Musgrave. 'My sergeant says that we should leave things alone and that she has probably just gone off with a boyfriend but her mum says that would be completely out of character. She hasn't been in a relationship for some time and has always said that she could never just go off because she feels the horses are her responsibility.'

Again, Musgrave looks as though he would like to be more helpful.

'You mentioned you would ask your wife and daughter if they had any light they could throw on the matter.'

'I did,' says Musgrave. 'Sadly they had nothing to add. Viola is very concerned. Prim too. But we're her employers, not her parents. People can be flaky at times. Am I right in thinking she had a bit of a past?'

Verity doesn't let her smile drop. 'I can't really go into that,' she says.

'She was very candid about it,' continues Musgrave. 'Said she had her problems as a teen and went a little off the rails before she decided to sort her life out. Good on her, I say.'

Verity returns to her notes, trying not to let her irritation show. Her sergeant had pointed to the exact same fact when he told her to leave well alone.

'Could I have your wife's number?' she asks, not looking up.

'Of course,' says Musgrave, after a pause.

'Your daughter too.'

'She doesn't have a mobile,' says Musgrave.

'She must do,' says Verity. 'She's posted on Crystal's timeline several times over the past few months.'

'She does that from her computer in her room. She's too young for a phone.'

Verity nods and hands over her notepad. Musgrave scribbles down his wife's number and passes it back.

'It's nice you're so concerned,' says Musgrave, and it comes out a touch patronising. 'You must be one of the good ones.'

Verity gives a polite nod. They eye one another and Musgrave drums his fingers on the arm of the chair. Verity takes it as a sign she should probably leave. It's getting on for midnight and home is another thirty miles away. She stands up and hears a scrape as a stone lodged in the grips of her steel-capped boots scratches along the bamboo frame of the sofa. She winces and pulls one of the stones from the grips.

'Bloody driveway,' says Musgrave, smiling. 'Cost a fortune to shingle it and I spend half my life picking rocks from my shoes.'

Verity extends her hand. 'I gave you my card, didn't I?'

Musgrave nods. 'Here, come out this way,' he says, and walks to the glass door. He opens it to a night that is cool and freckled with tiny spots of rain. Verity's Ford Ka sits on the gravel of the driveway. It looks faintly ridiculous next to the splendour of the house, like a mouse squaring up to a lion.

'If anything else occurs to you . . .'

Musgrave holds her gaze and gives a nod. 'I'm sure she'll turn up safe and sound. She means a lot to us. If you hear from her first, would you let us know she's okay?'

Verity likes the way he says it. He seems a good guy. He's an environmentalist, for God's sake. She doesn't know what 'agro' is but she doubts it means the same thing as it does when she is accused of being a little that way inclined.

She crunches over the gravel and climbs into her car. As she turns the key in the ignition her music system blasts into life and she feels embarrassed and juvenile, switching off the sound of Jason Derulo before the foxes start screaming.

She drives away in silence, more uncertain than when she arrived.

Musgrave stands in the doorway of the big white house he can't afford and watches the lights of the silly little car disappear beyond the trees.

Only when he is sure she has truly gone does he allow himself to sag. His knees buckle and he is suddenly awash with sweat; upon his brow, beneath his arms, at the small of his back. The effort of control has made him nauseous.

It is several minutes before Musgrave feels strong enough to go to the kitchen. He makes a sandwich with ham and brown bread and cuts off the crusts. Then he divides the remaining bread into bite-sized portions. He adds some grapes to the plate and cuts a chocolate bar into four meagre pieces. He takes a carton of drink from the fridge and pierces the hole with a straw.

He is about to head out to the wine cellar when he remembers the fork. He knows from past experience that if he feeds the girl by hand she will bite. She is a fighter.

He pulls open the back door and walks swiftly to the old stables. The mud sucks and slurps at his boots. He stops at the tumbledown archway and feels around tentatively, rummaging with his boot. Kicks the hard metal ring. The trapdoor is covered with mud, hay and leaves, which fall with a whispered rush as he yanks open the hatch. He is about to descend into the dank blackness when he hears the faintest sound of screeching on the cold, eager breeze.

'Foxes,' he says out loud, in the hope that he can convince himself that other people will think the same. 'It's just foxes.'

He hopes she hasn't got the gag free again.

He hates it when he has to hurt her.

5

Roisin's eyes seem to blur and distort. Her irises are two inches from McAvoy's and he presumes his own brown eyes are similarly distorted thanks to the nearness of Roisin's gaze. He blinks and she gives a hiss of victory. She kisses him. Her mouth tastes of toothpaste and hot chocolate and as he pushes her dark hair behind her ear she nuzzles closer into him.

'Beat you,' she says, and her lower lip brushes his as she speaks. 'Now, are you ready?'

'Do it,' he says.

She places her freezing cold feet on his shins and his eyes widen at the contact.

'It's like having a seven-foot hot-water bottle,' says Roisin with a smile.

'I don't understand it,' says McAvoy, grimacing. 'You literally just took your socks off.'

'I do it for bad. I stand in the toilet bowl for five minutes before coming to bed, just so I can make you squirm. I hold my hands out and pretend I'm a tree.'

McAvoy readjusts himself, rolling onto his back. Roisin, naked, lays her head on his chest and he holds her small, delicate hand in his big palm. They move with the easy grace of a couple who know one another's gestures and night-time choreography. Within moments they are breathing in tandem: comfortable in the half-light and gladdened by the nearness of one another's skin.

The family have only recently returned to the bedrooms of their little cottage on Hessle Foreshore. The front windows look out across a strip of grass and shingly beach before disappearing into the murk of the estuary. When they sleep with the window open, they can hear the sound of the River Humber kissing the stones. To look up is to feel small. Above them is the bridge; a great tangle of concrete and steel that serves as a loose stitch between Lincolnshire and Yorkshire.

For a long time the McAvoys were forced to live in a caravan in the back garden while repair work was conducted on the main house. Roisin, raised as a Traveller, had felt perfectly at home. McAvoy had felt like a Great Dane trying to fit into a shopping trolley. Now they have moved back in and are enjoying having a proper roof over their heads, even if they disagree fundamentally on the bedroom decor. McAvoy gave her carte blanche to create the room of her dreams. He now presumes she was suffering from a high temperature on the night she conjured up her vision. She has papered it entirely with a huge panoramic scene that she ordered off the internet. The whole room is now a garish sunset: a perfect stratum of reds, golds and crimsons, punctuated by skeletal trees and ragged wisps of cloud. While it is beautiful, McAvoy has not yet grown used to the sheer exuberance that greets him each morning. On several occasions he has opened his eyes and panicked that the house is on fire.

'She made it home then?' asks Roisin, running her finger along the puckered tissue of one of McAvoy's scars. 'The wicked witch.'

'I got a text,' says McAvoy. 'No problems.'

He feels Roisin give a tiny nod. She has a difficult relationship with Pharaoh. She admires her and trusts her to keep McAvoy relatively safe but Roisin is a Traveller by birth and she still finds it difficult to put faith in the police.

'How many hours do you think we'll get?' asks Roisin.

McAvoy reaches out for his watch and squints at the dial. It is a little after 1 a.m. The light from the bedside lamp barely reaches the foot of the bed and he enjoys the sensation of being in a private circle of illumination. He likes to imagine that the bed is a raft, sailing on gentle waters to somewhere peaceful and safe; somewhere that men aren't skewered to walls and old men mown down in front of his eyes.

'I'll get up about six,' says McAvoy.

'You have to?'

'Not strictly speaking, no. But they should have logged most of the contents of the two main rooms by then and I want to go through them before they get jumbled up.'

Roisin gives another little nod. She accepts him for who he is and what he feels he must be. Over the past few years he has gone from being the pariah who brought down the old head of CID to the man who has risked his own life time and again in pursuit of what he sees as his duty. He is given a begrudging respect by those who used to detest him.

'You really think they had a girl there?'

McAvoy wishes he could give a glib answer but he truly isn't sure. 'It didn't seem like the sort of room a man had been kept in. It just didn't feel right.'

'Are there any girls missing at the moment?' asks Roisin. She has long been his sounding board and his conscience speaks with her accent.

'There are always girls missing,' he says. 'We'll start working through the list.'

'They're not just dealing with the guy in the wall though, are they? There's Perry too.'

McAvoy kisses the top of her head. He keeps hearing the awful thud as the old man's frail body slapped down on the tarmac. Roisin and the children had still been in the car when it happened so they did not see the collision. But they all heard McAvoy's voice and both Roisin and Fin had run to the scene while Perry was still gasping and gurgling on the floor and coughing thick blood into McAvoy's face. McAvoy had waved a hand, telling them to get back. Neither had obeyed. Roisin and her son joined McAvoy by the dying man. She put her hand upon her husband's shoulder as he pumped at Perry's chest with his huge hands. Blood had bubbled up and out with each push. The paramedics took over as soon as they arrived. It seemed near miraculous when Perry started spluttering and swearing and telling the ambulance staff that if they went near him with a rectal thermometer he would stick it in their eye. The old bugger was simply too cantankerous to die. He'd been taken to Castle Hill Hospital where his condition remains critical and mood murderous.

McAvoy turns his attention back to his wife.

'The assumption is that whoever killed Kahrivardan was involved in running Perry down. The helicopter has been up but there is no sign of the vehicle. Uniform started a house-to-house but by the time they were briefed it was already too late to be knocking on people's doors. It will all start properly in the morning.'

'What if you do find they've got a girl?' asks Roisin. 'Cases like this . . . it hurts you. It affects you . . .'

McAvoy holds her closer. He knows what she is referring to. For months he obsessed over the disappearance of a young woman. 'I have you,' he says, and it seems insufficient to explain his feelings. 'You and the kids, I mean. You keep me sane and safe.'

'You've never been without us. Not really.'

McAvoy kisses the top of her head again and reaches behind himself to switch off the light. Roisin switches off her consciousness with the ease of a child. In moments she is snoring softly.

McAvoy focuses on nothing but her inhalations, her

exhalations; the rhythm of her heart. He doubts he will sleep much himself tonight. He will lie awake in case his children have bad dreams. He will watch the shadows change on the wall. And he will hear the thump of Perry's body against the unforgiving metal of the stolen car.

6

Sunday morning, painfully early.

'Andy, could you put your ukulele away?'

Detective Constable Andy Daniells stops strumming on the toy-like wooden instrument. He has been trying to master it since Christmas. He keeps it beneath his desk and picks it up in his quiet moments. Despite recurring promises not to let the sound of the strumming rise above a whisper, he occasionally finds himself playing with an unacceptable level of gusto and he is now painfully aware that his colleagues, while fans of music, are not above making good on their threats to beat him to death with the offending instrument if they hear one more chorus of 'House of the Rising Sun'.

'Sorry, Sarge,' says Daniells, grinning. He's a round-faced, corpulent chap whose default setting is one of cheerful good humour. He has been with the Serious and Organised Unit for a couple of years and has proven himself a thorough and diligent member of the team. Last summer he giggled his way through his marriage vows at Hull Registry Office as he tied the knot with his partner – a probation officer called Stefan. Andy didn't really concentrate on the ceremony, preferring instead to enjoy the embarrassment of the dozens of his fellow cops who stood shoulder to shoulder with his friends from the city's gay scene and who had taken him seriously when he said he wanted all the guests to wear pink.

McAvoy waits for the ukulele to be returned to its position beneath the table and makes a mental note to put it somewhere safe before DC Ben Neilsen arrives for the morning briefing. Ben has been particularly imaginative in his descriptions of what he intends to do with the ukulele if he sees it in Andy's hands again.

It's coming up to 8 a.m. and McAvoy has been in Major Incident Room One for the best part of an hour. It's a drab, chilly room painted in a shade of white that looks like scum on standing water. There is a large whiteboard set up at the far end of the square space and a score of hard-backed chairs have been laid out in lecture-hall formation. A projector has been plugged in to the laptop that sits on a Formica-topped table and a stack of briefing notes is arranged on a desk by the door. A trio of sturdy old wooden desks have been arranged like a boardroom table and McAvoy feels a little ashamed to be sitting at the head of it like a company director. His colleagues left him little choice by automatically selecting seats that would not put them in any position of authority. He presumes it must be out of respect for his new suit rather than his own innate leadership qualities. Roisin recently remodelled him in the style of a band she saw in a pub in London. He wears a blue suit with red braces over a floral black and purple shirt. His feet, clad in bright striped socks, disappear into brogued, tan and cream boots. She has also insisted that he grow his beard a little thicker and has bought him a gift voucher to have it styled with a cut-throat razor at the hipster barber in Beverley. He intends to attend his one appointment around the same time that hell freezes over.

'You've got Sophie's,' says Gemma, indicating the mug in front of him. His hot chocolate looks like frothy mud.

'Is it Sophie's? How can you tell?' Guiltily, McAvoy examines the plain white mug he had helped himself to in the kitchen area of the unit's main workstation.

'You'll see when you get to the bottom. She's had a picture of herself looking furious printed on the inside.'

McAvoy cannot help himself. He downs his drink in one huge swallow and finds himself staring into the angry eyes and scowling brow of DC Sophie Kirkland. Through the foam, he notes that she has 'Get Off My Mug!' written on the plain red T-shirt she sports in the picture. McAvoy apologises at once. 'Sorry, sorry,' and feels himself beginning to redden as he realises he is talking to a photograph at the bottom of a cup. A couple of years back, such an incident would have been around the station like the winter vomiting bug. These days, he's earned the right to be a buffoon from time to time.

'Mad as a badger, that one,' says Gemma. 'Did I tell you about what she did in New Clarence on New Year's Eve? Well, she was with her sister, and she's no better—'

'Yes, you did,' says McAvoy firmly. He needs to curb the conversation. Gemma is one of the civilian members of staff employed by the unit and, despite her obvious competence, she is an Olympic-standard chatterbox. She has a degree in criminology and is a huge asset to the team but she and Joanne, the other civilian analyst, sometimes seem to be involved in a contest over who can spend the most time babbling on about anything and everything but casework. Pharaoh has warned them repeatedly for their endless chatter but they only really get the message when she stands over them holding a staple-gun and threatening to stick their lips together.

'You want the blinds opening?' asks Andy. 'Grim in here.'

McAvoy shakes his head. He knows the view beyond the glass too well. The station is on the Orchard Park estate, which has a reputation as one of the city's most down-at-heel neighbourhoods. The sight of half-empty tower blocks standing like piano keys against the grey-black sky does not disturb him as much as the vista of so many people waiting at bus stops in the ceaseless drizzle. He knows himself well enough to predict that if he were to gaze too long upon their miserable shivering he would need to run outside and offer to drive them to their destinations.

With the blinds closed, the only light in the room comes from the dusty strip-light that flickers whenever a lorry rumbles past and which serves as a transparent coffin for countless dead wasps and bluebottles. It is a soulless, unappealing room that still smells of stale cigarettes almost a decade after the arrival of the smoking ban. The briefing is scheduled for 9 a.m. and he is glad that he will not have to give it. He knows that his voice drops to a mumble the second he feels more than a couple of pairs of eyes upon him. Pharaoh will be the one to address the team and it is McAvoy's job to make sure she is up to speed.

The Humberside Police computer generates a random name for each major investigation and the death of Kahrivardan is to be probed under the name Operation Florizel. Gemma and Joanne have been typing up the notes since the early hours. They both look a little wide-eyed and number-blind but neither has complained. They both know what the job entails and for large chunks of the year they are able to go home on time. During a major incident, time is no longer their own. Gemma is the older of the pair. She's in her early thirties, with long brown hair and an upturned nose that would look adorable on a six-year-old girl. Joanne has only just left university. She's a redhead, whose blue spectacles sit like pince-nez upon the bridge of her nose. McAvoy finds it unnerving the way she peers at him over their frame. The other officer present is Detective Sergeant Roseanne Mackintosh. She is new to the team but has already impressed the troops. She's a middle-aged Glaswegian with short, bottle-black hair. She walks with a stick following an incident at her previous station that almost forced her into taking a disability pension. She and Pharaoh go way back and Mackintosh was persuaded to transfer to Serious and Organised rather than turn in her warrant card. She serves as Pharaoh's office manager and general sergeant-at-arms and is a no-nonsense kind of person who McAvoy will admit to being slightly frightened of.

'Up to speed, Sarge?'

McAvoy scans the document for the third time. He feels as though with each rereading he is taking great bites of information and swallowing it down.

'Post-mortem at eleven,' says McAvoy, half to himself. 'DNA scrapings from under the fingernails are on a three-day turnaround. Is that right, Gemma? That's pretty good.'

Gemma smiles, pleased with herself. 'I was charming. They've promised three days and said we can hold them to it.'

'And everything else?'

'Lap of the gods,' says Gemma. 'There's so much to process. They've already bagged over a thousand different exhibits of physical evidence. The sheer volume of rubbish in there is extraordinary. But we're implementing the sifting criteria the boss prefers. Anything that's come into contact with the body is first and then we move outwards in circles from the victim.'

McAvoy gives a nod of approval. He returns his attention to the notes and then realises the room has become uncomfortably silent. He decides it would be better to hear some of the information spoken out loud and turns to Joanne.

'Phone. Wallet. Keys . . .'

Joanne sits forward, eager as ever. 'Phone has gone to the Telecoms Unit. There's a pin code but they were through that in a flash. The entire history is being downloaded and sent across before 9 a.m. but the key findings are already in the notes. Last call made on that phone was at 6.14 p.m. on Thursday. He rang a pay-as-you-go mobile that Telecoms have tried to contact but which is no longer in service. Prior to that he phoned his girlfriend and a car wash on the road into Beverley. He wasn't a social media user and his text messages are dull to the extreme.'

'We'll get Ben on tracing that mobile,' says McAvoy. 'Wholesalers, stockists, the lot, yes?'

'Sure. The wallet contained nothing out of the ordinary. Pictures of his girlfriend; three credit cards and a member's card for Napoleon's Casino; £120 in cash; Caffe Nero loyalty card and two driving licences.'

'Two?'

'One with his new address, one with the old one.'

'The vehicle?'

'No sign of it yet. Description has been circulated. We've liaised with HMRC and Border Force. Associated British Ports have been notified. We've followed the right processes.'

'Formal ID?'

'The girlfriend is coming in this morning.'

'And Perry?'

Joanne looks uncomfortable. 'Still critical. We haven't been able to find a next of kin.'

McAvoy swallows and there is a taste in the back of his throat that he does not like. It's a metallic flavour; all rust and ash. He looks down at his notes and scans the list of evidence numbers already photographed and logged by the scene of crime specialists. The majority relate to the room where Kahrivardan was found but the fourth page begins to detail the scraps of paper found in the nearby room where somebody was held against their will.

'Fibres from the blanket,' he muses. 'Bar code for the bottle of pop. There were no abrasions on Kahrivardan's wrists or ankles consistent with having been tied up. We need to check for any form of adhesive on the skin in case he was gagged with gaffer tape. Sophie can take that on, if it's okay with you, Roseanne?'

Mackintosh nods, happy with the way he is dividing up the tasks.

'This one,' says McAvoy, pressing the tip of his pen to an

evidence number and staring at it quizzically. 'Receipt from Thomas Bell of Brigg.'

Joanne and Gemma share a look. It had not struck them as any more interesting than the other, seemingly endless lists of paper scraps and assorted rubbish logged by the forensics officers. Joanne suddenly pulls a face, aghast that she had not spotted the peculiarity when assembling the briefing document. 'The equestrian place?'

'Yes. Brigg. Over the river.'

'Unusual,' says Mackintosh, and in her broad accent it sounds for a moment as if she were saying 'noodle'. 'Or maybe it's not. The murder room is full of rubbish. Could be any number of people who've dropped the litter from their pockets. What's the date?'

'Eleven days ago,' says McAvoy, looking at the paper. 'It's charged to a trade account. Two bags of feed, hoof-shine, hoof-pick, salt-lick . . .'

'Kahrivardan doesn't seem like he spends a lot of time in the saddle, but, of course, I don't want to make any assumptions,' says Daniells.

'Gem, could you go and see if you can get the name of the account holder please? I know it's early but I'd imagine there'll be somebody at the store. Rural communities – they're up with the lark. And horses don't worry about weekends.'

Gemma nods and heads out of the incident room. As the door opens, McAvoy hears the sound of voices coming from the team's regular offices. He hopes they stay where they are until he hears Pharaoh has arrived.

'The girlfriend,' says McAvoy, reading through the notes from Harte's interview with the victim's teenage partner late last night. 'Hadn't seen him in three days and she hadn't reported him missing?'

'She said it wasn't unusual,' says Mackintosh. 'Sometimes he would go away on business and she would get the odd text from

61

him but she didn't want to be the kind of partner who would nag.'

'Her general demeanour?'

'She cried,' says Joanne, spreading her hands to indicate this could mean something or nothing. 'She certainly didn't indicate he had been living in fear of his life or that he'd told her which shoe box to look in for the name of his killer if anything ever happened to him. She seemed upset. Said they were a good couple and that they had talked of getting married.'

'And why was he at Bronte Hall?'

'She didn't know for sure but he owned different properties and she says he might well have owned that one too. Land Registry says it's owned by TK Holdings, which is registered to an address in Surrey. Director is a Timothy Kimmell. We've called and emailed without success. Local PCs will be door-knocking this morning.'

McAvoy takes a breath and wipes his mouth with forefinger and thumb. He makes sure he looks down as he speaks. 'Missing girls?'

'Full list at the back of your document, boss.'

'Locals?'

'A lot of usual suspects. Teens that Social Services are well aware of and who bugger off every couple of days. A seventeen-year-old new mum who's left her three-week-old baby with her parents and gone off with her boyfriend. Long-term missing, there's no shortage but there's nobody on the list that screams out as being anything to do with this.'

McAvoy wonders if he is being chastised. There's nothing in the briefing notes to even suggest they could be dealing with a missing girl. He should put the idea from his mind and concentrate on what happened to Kahrivardan. He should be focusing on Perry.

'And we've contacted other investigative agencies, yes? We could use some input from the team that investigated him for the gangmaster activities. If he's fallen foul of people-smugglers . . .'

'That's certainly an avenue for investigation,' says Daniells. 'The boss has got good contacts at Border Force.'

'And the weapon,' says McAvoy, nodding. He pulls a face as he reads the description of the implement that had been plunged into the dead man's frame. 'Sharpened bicycle spoke. Now, that's not the obvious way to kill somebody. We need a full breakdown on other instances where such a weapon has been used. And the plaster too. If it was wet when he was killed that must surely suggest he has been doing work on the building but given the state of it and the way he was dressed, it's probable he had somebody else doing the manual work. We need to find out who they are.'

McAvoy stops, short of breath and realising how much work lies ahead of them. He wonders, after the different tasks have been divided up, what he should do himself. Sometimes he fears that there are those within Humberside Police who see him as no more than Pharaoh's errand boy but he has been called so many worse things that he does not let it upset him unduly. He just wants to do something helpful and if that means carrying Pharaoh's bag while she asks the questions, he is willing to do it.

The door opens and Gemma returns. Her eyes are bright.

'Trade account at the horse supplies shop is in the name of a Viola Musgrave,' she says animatedly. 'Lives at an address in Thoresway, near Market Rasen in Lincolnshire. I've looked on Google Maps and it's a great big place. Worth a fortune. She's married to a Joel Musgrave. One daughter, Primrose, aged eleven. The manager at Thomas Bell's knows them well.'

McAvoy waits for more. 'Connection to Bronte Hall?'

'None I can see. She's a fashion designer. He's involved in biosciences.'

McAvoy rubs his temples. His brain is starting to throb inside his skull. 'Fashion designers use unusual buildings. Photoshoots, that kind of thing. She could have dropped a receipt and it could well be irrelevant . . .'

Gemma grins, enjoying having a little piece of information all to herself. 'A young woman named Crystal Heathers was reported missing several days ago. She works for the family as a part-time groom. It's being handled by a TDC in Brigg. Angela Verity. I called her earlier. Mentioned the connection and your name. She's very eager to talk to you.'

McAvoy digests the information. He is about to speak when the door opens and Trish Pharaoh barrels in, sipping from a massive Thermos mug and frowning at the smell in the room.

'We'll have those blinds open,' she says. 'And those tables look daft pushed in the corner. Hector, show me how to use this bloody projector, I never know which hole's the right one, which is remarkable after four kids. And just so I know, you did spot that receipt for the horse place in Brigg, yeah? Definitely an odd note. Are we on that?'

McAvoy rises from the chair and shares a smile with the individuals seated around the table.

'I thought I might take that on myself, Guv,' says McAvoy.

'Good,' says Pharaoh. 'It'll keep you out of mischief. Now, remind me what I'm supposed to be doing. Is Ben in yet? Could somebody get me a breakfast on a tray? And Andy, if that's your ukulele under the desk you are a fucking dead man.'

7

There are no windows down here. The square room has thick, damp walls and words have been carved into the plaster with enough force to make great chunks fall away. In the near darkness the cavities become shapes, like the points of new constellations. Manu watches the images shift and eddy: at once a face, aghast and admonishing; now a village of scattered huts, untethered goats; women running; women falling . . .

Manu closes his eyes. Forces the images away. He tries to be the master of his own memories. Tries to think of home; of that moment: the silent bushveld slipping away as the plane glided higher. He remembers feeling like an arrow, drifting lazily towards the sun. He had gripped the armrest of the seat and felt his heart thudding but he had not been able to remove the smile from his face. His friend had grinned and patted his arm. The sun was casting gold and purple light onto the ochre and green of his homeland. The villages were dark patches; the spots upon a leopard's pelt. *Here* a sudden flash of silver as the light caught the river waters. *Here* a scratch of grey and earth; dust rising from the dirt roads. And then they were over an endless sea of deep, deep green – the landscape a collage of verdant hues; so deep and fertile that it had seemed to Manu as if the roots of the rice paddies and crop fields must stretch into the very centre of the earth and that his tutors had been wrong: the world did not form around a core of fire but around a pure blue pearl of mineral-rich water.

He had felt like a man.

Like a Westerner.

Like an American.

Manu was going to do something important. Manu was going to matter.

The joints in Manu's ankles crack as he repositions himself in the battered swivel chair. He has been sitting still for an age. His legs ache and he knows that when he stretches out his limbs, his knee joints will make a sound like snapping twigs.

The girl looks up at the sound, jerking awake as if startled by an animal. Manu curses his disloyal body. He has spent the past hour waiting for the medicine to take effect. He does not want her awake when he takes what he must.

Manu watches as she swishes her head this way and that; a horse fighting flies. The sleeve of a shirt has been wrapped around her face and it not only obscures her eyes but muffles her hearing. Even so she remains alert to the slightest sound. Manu admires her. She has cried, of course, and she tries to plead with him when she senses there is somebody near: whimpering and trying to force the sponge from her mouth with her tongue, swallowing down her own foul medley of spit, snot and tears.

'Sleep,' he wills her. 'Slip into the dark.'

Then gradually she begins to drift. She lowers her face to the dirty cord carpet and her breathing changes. Manu waits. He wants her to be fully asleep before he punctures her. He knows how his actions would seem to one who does not know him. He remembers with anger the questions they asked him in that place; that sanctuary of healing. He remembers the questions and the gentle way their voices drifted like song. He remembers white hands on his brown skin. Kind eyes.

'What did you feel, Manu?'

'Did you take pleasure in the violence?'

'How did you feel about the people you hurt?'

'Tell us again about your commander. Tell us how he taught you to kill.'

66

Manu had tried his best to answer them. They seemed so interested in him. Nobody judged. They saw in him another victim. He was a boy. He was not yet fully grown. He had taken lives before even starting to live his own. They did not look at him and see a monster. They saw a fourteen-year-old who had witnessed unimaginable horror and carried out acts of barbarism in a bid to stay alive.

'Don't think about it,' says Aishita in his ear. He has been so still that Manu had almost forgotten he was there. 'You're remembering, aren't you? The Centre. The questions.'

Manu gives a tiny nod. He bites his lip and hunches into his jacket so that his features seem to be peering out from between the zip of his coat and the bottom of his woollen hat.

'Be strong,' says Aishita, and the words are so quiet that Manu wonders for a moment if he has imagined them. 'This must be done, Manu.'

It seems strange to hear the bigger man speak in whispers. As children and then as soldiers it was always Manu who was known as the quiet one of the pair. Aishita's voice has always been as imposing as his physique. Manu turns, slowly, and considers his comrade. The journey here has not withered him. He remains the big man he has always been. In wartime it was Aishita whom the new soldiers feared. Aishita who could snap a man's neck with his bare hands. Aishita who talked in machine-gun fire and who spoke to his troops of values like family, comradeship and loyalty to the cause, even as he held his Kalashnikov to the temples of wailing husbands and made them witness the degradation of wives, daughters and sons.

'The only memories that matter are the ones in your heart, Manu. The words of the Americans will sow doubt. I was your friend. I am still your friend. Without me you would be another crippled fool begging for scraps with your food bowl. This must be done. This is right. This is just.'

It was Aishita who led the raid that turned an eight-year-old boy into a soldier. He is only a handful of years older than Manu but he was taken by Renamo soldiers at such a young age that he has little or no memory of the person he was before he was trained in the art of war. He grew up knowing himself to be a crusader against the evil of Frelimo, Mozambique's ruling party. He had no family except the rebel unit that led raids on countless villages and carried off children to join their cause. He killed his first man at seven years old, putting a bullet in the skull of a runaway. He had enjoyed the kick of the gun. He had learned to equate cruelty with reward. In battle he was fearless. Merciless. His capacity for brutality was unequalled. He once told Manu he could not sleep unless he had killed at least one person that day. And when he spoke of Renamo's mission his eyes shone like a zealot's.

Memories blur. Manu screws up his face as his mind fills with ripped pictures and fragments of nightmare. Manu remembers screaming. Bullets hitting skin, stone and earth. Remembers the pain in his chest as he ran, feet slapping through blood. He remembers shame. He had not stopped to look for his parents or his sisters. He had run the moment the rebels emerged from the trees.

The memory folds in on itself. Twists. And now he is there; terrified, gasping, being dragged by his broken arm to be thrown at the feet of a huge man who stands naked before him; shadows and flames dancing in the contours of his scarred flesh. He drinks from a bottle of whiskey, like an American, and he clutches his blade in a hand caked in red. 'You are my little brother now,' says Aishita, in Manu's mind. 'You are a soldier. You will rid this land of our enemy and you will become a man. A man like me.'

Manu wraps his arms around himself and forces the memories back. He cannot allow himself to think of such times. He knows what Aishita has helped him become. Without him he would never have made it here, to this cold grey place so many thousands of miles from home. Aishita gives him strength. Aishita enables him to do the things he must.

Manu can wait no longer. He takes the needle and cord from his pocket and silently moves towards the girl. He finds her cold pink arm and takes it in his. Expertly, he wraps the cord around her forearm and waits until the vein in her arm swells up. He slides the needle in without waking her. He leaves it in the vein for a moment and removes the vials from his pocket. Then he begins to drain her. He wishes they had not had to leave the other place. The shock of their sudden exit weakened the girl and now he is unsure how much blood he can safely take. The girl is no use to them dead. He has to concentrate. Has to do things right.

Manu rubs his fingers together and feels the dried blood of the man that he and Aishita skewered to the wall like an animal. He does not wish to clean himself. The man was not an easy kill and Aishita told him he should display some emblem of victory. Manu does not have the will to refuse. He has accepted the truth of himself. Aishita has shown him who he is. Aishita has made a lie of all that he learned when the war came to an end. He thinks of himself on that aeroplane and the lunatic smile upon his face. He scowls at the recollection. Pities the man he tried to become. Scorns his weakness and ignorance.

Manu holds up the vial of blood and stares into the red liquid as if it could predict the future. This is the blood of his enemy. It is the blood of the man who betrayed him. Before he is done, he intends to spill an ocean's worth.

8

Rural Lincolnshire, Sunday, 3.20 p.m.

Ugly grey clouds, pressing down upon the land like fists; black thunder growling in their palms.

A tiny car, travelling too fast on a rutted grey road, passing through a dizzying blur of green fields, brown fields, yellow fields. Gravel sprays up like slush as the tyres burst through a puddle of spilled diesel and muddy rain.

'Are we in a rush? I wouldn't ask, but I rather feel your car is using me as an air-bag.'

McAvoy has pushed the seat back as far as it will go but he still looks as though he were a passenger in a child's pedal car. His knees are touching the dashboard and he keeps apologising, instinctively, every time Trainee Detective Constable Angela Verity touches his hand or thigh while changing gear. He is not a fan of the Ford Ka, which always makes him feel as if he were running at 60 mph wearing a tinfoil suit. He likes it less when he is being driven by his new companion. It feels as though his spleen has just hit him in the lung.

'I know these roads,' says Angela, throwing the vehicle around a hairpin bend. A tractor suddenly appears before them but Angela swings the car through the long grasses at the side of the road and careers past. The sudden diversion throws McAvoy to his left and he has a close-up view of two startled pheasants that take off from behind a thick privet hedge. They cluck and flap their way skyward, eye to eye with McAvoy. He senses a moment of connection with the birds. The leading one looks as though it feels slightly sorry for him.

'We could have taken my car,' says McAvoy, righting himself.

'I told you, it's no trouble.'

'I'd rather hoped to be able to read your notes on the journey.'

'What's stopping you?'

'Well, my eyeballs are now back to front.'

Angela looks across from the driver's seat and gives him a smile. She has a solitary dimple in her left cheek. Playful eyes. Blonde hair. She has girlish mannerisms and talks without employing many commas. Despite her erratic driving he has warmed to her already and when the car eventually comes to a stop and he is able to put his spleen back where it belongs, he doubts he will say anything unkind.

'That's the road to Brookenby,' says Angela, taking a hand off the wheel to wave to her left. 'Crystal lives up there. We can see it afterwards if you like. I've got a key from her mum.'

'Maybe,' says McAvoy. 'But we're walking.'

'Bit of a hike. She'd use her scooter for the journey.'

'And that hasn't been traced?'

'No. It's in the system but nothing so far.'

'So she could be mobile, or could have been picked up.'

'If she's gone anywhere at all,' says Angela.

There is a straight stretch of road ahead so McAvoy is able to consider the view without fear that it will suddenly start swinging left and right as if viewed from a porthole in a storm. He likes this part of Lincolnshire. It is a collage made up of a thousand shades of green; a rag-rug of avocado, emerald, kiwi and lime. McAvoy feels like an intruder in the silly little white car; a speck of imperfection amid this billowing cloth of grass and trees.

'Nice pub down there,' says Angela, nodding at a vertigin-
ously steep road that McAvoy finds himself praying they will
not take. 'Real ale. They have a right good do on Valentine's if
you're looking for somewhere to take a lady-friend. Right
romantic night. I see you're wearing a wedding ring, but you
could pick up some flowers for the missus on the way back, eh?
Don't let her spoil your fun.'

McAvoy shoots a look at her, trying to work out why she is
being so familiar. He considers the lack of grey hairs and the
smoothness of her skin and realises she is simply young and
energetic. Roisin would probably take to her immediately. He
decides not to be offended by the way she expresses herself and
to concentrate instead on not getting wedged in the window
frame in the event of a head-on collision. He imagines it would
be awkward for the paramedics.

'I thought Lincolnshire was meant to be flat,' says McAvoy,
looking down into the vale.

'It is,' says Angela. 'We just got lucky around here. A few hills
and valleys. Good for the leg muscles and it means the kids get
to go sledging when it snows.'

McAvoy closes his eyes as hedgerows pass in a blur. The
landscape of his youth was like this. He grew up on a croft in
the mountains above Loch Ewe and while the landscape was
truly stunning, anybody who wanted to practise football quickly
learned that dropping the ball meant a long run downhill.
McAvoy's father always claimed that it was Highlanders who
invented rugby for that very reason, and complained bitterly
that toffs from England were nothing but liars when they staked
a claim for ownership of the game.

'He's quite charming,' says Angela, and she nods through a
gap in the hedge at a large white house. 'Beautiful wife.'

'Child?'

'One. Primrose. Haven't met her. Lovely looking girl in the
picture though.'

McAvoy closes his eyes again and is grateful to feel the car slow down. He takes a moment to let his equilibrium settle and then looks at the splendid country house. Immediately he finds himself imagining Roisin as lady of the manor. She would adore this place, although McAvoy imagines she would prefer to add a few sequins, sparkles and swatches of leopard print to the portico.

'He's not poor,' says McAvoy appreciatively.

'No. I've emailed you everything I've got on him.'

'I'd imagine you know it all off by heart,' says McAvoy, and turns in his seat. The young TDC is sitting up, eager and wide-eyed. It was the same when she greeted him at Brigg Police Station. She'd heard of him, of course. Heard of Pharaoh too. Told him, with some enthusiasm, how she dreamed of one day being on the Serious and Organised Unit. Told him how she had always wanted to be a detective. She was delighted that Humberside CID were taking an interest and had not been content with McAvoy's bland assurances that the enquiries were purely routine. She had pressed him for more; demanding to know what other investigation Crystal's disappearance was linked to. Through sheer force of will she had persuaded him to let her drive them both out to Musgrave's big pad in the Wolds. When McAvoy texted Pharaoh to alert her to his movements she had responded with a picture of a fur-trapper culling a seal pup and the words 'your future' written underneath. She had spared him too much distress by adding a smiley-face and a kiss.

'We've had no reason to request his financial records,' says Angela ruefully. 'But a little light digging suggests he's not going to start moaning about paying for somebody else's side-salad when it comes to splitting a bill.'

McAvoy considers this. 'Not all Scots are frugal,' he says.

'I never said anything.' Verity smiles.

'I could sense a tone . . .'

'Honestly, I just meant he's got cash.'

McAvoy peers at the property. The sun is already starting to dip below the horizon, seaming the sky with lines of purple, silver and pink, and in this light the mansion house looks like something from a classic romance. McAvoy briefly wonders how many years of work it would take him to pay one year's mortgage on a place like this and then stops himself before he starts doing the depressing arithmetic.

'He's a biosciences and new-agro consultant,' says Verity, getting out of the car and joining McAvoy on his side of the vehicle. He is leaning back against the passenger door but is not putting his whole weight into it for fear it will tip over.

'So I'm told,' says McAvoy.

'You know what that is?'

McAvoy carries on looking at the house, hoping that some-body inside will see them and come to the door. He wants to see how the homeowners look when they are inconvenienced or perturbed. He learned the technique from Pharaoh. In their experience, people who think of themselves as reasonable and sophisticated are very good at appearing kind. They can answer the door, invite a police officer into their home and make them tea and biscuits, without ever once seeming the sort of person capable of brutality. But by allowing the suspect to feel slightly off-kilter, sometimes it is possible to glimpse the murderer that lurks behind the kind smile. Almost all police officers have got it wrong at one time or another, having been taken in by somebody who seems simply too nice to have done something violent. McAvoy likes to see what a person looks like in temper, if only to take a mental snapshot of what their victim may have witnessed in their dying moments.

'Car isn't here,' says Verity. 'He drives a big thing. BMW.'

'Popesco, yes? That's the name of the company.'

Verity pushes her hair back behind her ear as a sudden gust

of wind shakes loose a mist of raindrops from the evergreens that line the curving driveway.

'You know them?'

'By name. Huge firm.'

'He started a company called Greenchutes when he was in his early twenties. Future farming technologies. Environmental advice. Looking at which crops grew best and in which places. They got some big contracts and became a big player. They were bought out by Popesco a few years back and he was made a director, though it seems he's only really with them on paper. Does lecturing and consultancy.'

McAvoy gives a little jerk of his head and they crunch over the pebbled drive towards the house. Despite his hopes, the door does not open to greet them. Both he and Verity try the bell and knocker but after a couple of minutes they realise the property is empty.

'Shall we have a mooch around?' asks McAvoy.

'A mooch?'

'A potter. A stroll. An amble.'

'Are we permitted to mooch?'

'We're permitted to try the back door,' says McAvoy. 'I can tell you the exact wording in the guidelines if you want but if it got back to my boss she'd make me eat it.'

McAvoy puts his hands in his pockets and stoops a little as he walks beside Verity. He knows his size can be daunting, though Verity seems as if she is not easily intimidated. Their footsteps take them around the rear of the property, where an outbuilding has been transformed into an office. A security light comes on as they enter the courtyard but the glare of the bulb shows that the office, too, is empty.

'Horses,' says McAvoy, sniffing the air. 'We may as well.'

McAvoy leads the way through the courtyard and down a muddy, hoof-pitted track towards the stables. The building is a modern, wooden affair with a corrugated roof. It looks like a

Scandinavian holiday lodge. The heads of two splendid-looking ponies poke over the doors and they turn, in unison, as McAvoy and Verity approach.

'I like that one,' says Verity chattily, as if she were having a day at the zoo with a favourite uncle.

'Welsh section A, I think,' says McAvoy, and leans on the wooden fence. The stables are a few metres away and the space between himself and the ponies is muddy and decorated with dung. 'They need Crystal, that's for sure. Poor things need mucking out.'

'Apparently the daughter, Primrose, has been taking on that responsibility.'

'Not very well, she hasn't. Hasn't been done for a couple of days. We should check her attendance record with the school.'

McAvoy stares at the ponies. Their ears are pricked, as if listening to his voice. He wonders how long they have been inside. They do not seem in distress, so he presumes they have enough food, but the air is thick with the stench of wet straw and manure. These are expensive animals that live in quality stables but they are in need of some attention and affection. Roisin would not be impressed.

'Shall we come back?' asks Verity. 'Maybe we should have called.'

McAvoy turns to look at the rear of the house. The sky is growing dark but he can still make out the shape of the glorious property. A quad bike is parked at the rear double doors and a loose pile of logs has been stacked against the wall. He can make out the shape of some grand garden furniture and a swing. He turns back to the ponies at the sound of a faint whinny from the stables.

'Ventriloquist?' says Verity, smiling.

'Pardon me?'

'Must be another one inside. It wasn't those two.'

McAvoy stands still, listening hard. A moment later there is another faint whinny and McAvoy recognises the sound of an animal in pain. He gives a shake of his head, knowing that what is right and what is legal are two very different things. He unfastens the rope holding the gate closed and steps into the quagmire in front of the stables.

'Everything okay, Sergeant?' asks Verity, and she shows no sign that she wants to follow him.

'Just a moment,' says McAvoy quietly. 'I just need to see.'

The two ponies snort as he approaches the doors but he talks to them in the gentle, sing-song voice that Roisin talks to the children in and both animals respond as he gently pushes them back. 'Easy, easy,' he mutters, keeping his mannerisms soft. He unbolts the door to the stables and slips inside. It's dark and the smell of horse urine and rotting straw is strong. The ground is soft underfoot and as he reaches around blindly for the light switch he feels the gentle bumping of one of the ponies as it nuzzles at his shoulder. He strokes its flanks and feels the bones beneath the soft hair. The animal hasn't been fed properly in days.

'Sergeant?'

McAvoy finds the light switch at the moment Verity calls and he throws up a hand to shield his eyes as the overhead bulb blares into life. The two ponies jerk backwards, startled, but McAvoy gives a gentle shush and they retreat to the corner, nuzzling one another. McAvoy peers at the two horses. One is roan-coloured and McAvoy, although no expert, believes it to be a New Forest gelding. The smaller pony is grey. Welsh section A or B. Its coat is matted and its mane is tangled. McAvoy takes a step forward, eager to see if there are button braids in the mane, and as he does so the ponies snort and jostle one another. Through the gaps in their legs he sees what they have been protecting.

The pony that lies in the straw at the back of the stables is in pain. His stomach looks distended and around his nostrils the skin appears swollen and sunburned. There is dried mud up the animal's legs and sores on his back.

'Look at you,' says McAvoy softly, and he kneels down beside the pony's head. He pats his neck and the animal shivers, pitifully trying to reach up towards him. McAvoy feels a great rush of feeling – a desire to pick up the pony in his arms and rock him. 'Shush now, my friend. Shush now.'

Carefully, McAvoy runs his hands over the shivering body. He looks into the pony's eyes and examines the sores around his nostrils. He fumbles underneath his swollen belly and the pony gives a cry of pain as McAvoy dislodges the hard metal object he has been lying on. He smells blood and sweat.

'Sergeant,' shouts Verity. 'Here please.'

McAvoy stands slowly and keeps his gestures gentle as he moves away from the sick pony and emerges back onto the muddy ground.

'Do you mind telling me what you're doing?'

The voice is not confrontational but it contains an edge. It belongs to a man in soft cords, a black T-shirt and a row of surfer beads. He is shining a torch directly at McAvoy. If he is daunted by McAvoy's size he does not show it.

'I'm Detective Sergeant McAvoy. You have an animal in distress.'

The light flicks to Verity, who winces. McAvoy squelches across the muddy ground towards them and steps through the gate, pulling it closed behind him. 'Could you get the light away from my face?' asks McAvoy, raising an arm that is wider than the other man's leg. 'Thanks.'

The light clicks off but there is still enough spilling from the stables for McAvoy to get a good look at Joel Musgrave. Musgrave stands his ground, keeping his eyes on McAvoy. His stance suggests that he is far from happy but that he is willing to pretend he is not.

'You have a sick pony,' says McAvoy. 'Laminitis, would be

my guess. Colic. And buttercup burn around the nostrils. Have any of the conditions been treated?'

Musgrave spreads his hands. 'You're obviously aware that my groom is not currently available for work. That's why you're here, after all.'

'You told my colleague that your daughter tends the horses.'

'When she can.'

'And is there a reason why she currently can't?'

Musgrave looks to Verity for support but her stare is as hard as McAvoy's. 'Look, officers, I'm more harm than good when it comes to horses. My wife's away. Did I not say? My daughter's with her. I can get somebody in from the equestrian centre, if it makes you happy. I don't have much to do with the horses.'

'I can tell,' says McAvoy. 'But you know what an animal in distress sounds like. You have a duty.'

'I'm sorry,' says Musgrave, and seems to mean it. 'I've had a lot on. I'll get to it. Viola will be furious if not.'

McAvoy gives a curt nod. 'We're here about a separate matter, as it happens. Mr Musgrave, do you have an account with Thomas Bell's Equestrian in Brigg?'

Musgrave looks confused. 'Yes, I believe my wife uses that place a lot.'

'Can you think of a good reason why a receipt from that account would be found at the scene of a murder in Hull?'

Musgrave freezes. He jerks his head towards Verity, seeking confirmation. She remains still.

'A murder?' he asks. 'Whose?'

'I can't reveal that,' says McAvoy, wishing he could.

Musgrave seems shaken. His breath flutters slightly. As he speaks he seems to be working things out.

'A murder? Bloody hell. No, no, of course you can't say. But Hull. Did I read about that? The one in the papers? A man, yes? Middle-aged. An old man got run over too. No ID as yet . . .'

'You know a lot about that case,' says McAvoy, and he keeps his tone stern.

'Just what I've read.'

'So could you answer the question please, Mr Musgrave? The receipt?'

Musgrave is staring past McAvoy to the stables. He seems entranced. It is only when Verity shifts her position that he seems to come back to himself. He gives a little smile of apology.

'Truly, I couldn't say,' he manages, running his hands through his hair.

McAvoy gives him an appraising stare. He's thinning at the temples. There is stubble in little tufts at his jawline. He has shaved erratically.

'Give it a stab,' says McAvoy. It has been a long while since he felt intimidated by people with more money than he has. There is something wrong about this place. About this man.

Musgrave spreads his arms. 'I don't think I've been to Hull more than once or twice in the past couple of years and then it was just to give some boring lecture or another.'

'Your wife? Your daughter? This was a recent receipt.'

'Perhaps,' says Musgrave, looking exasperated. 'They see the odd show at the theatre. Go to the Deep. There might have been an event but I don't know if there is much of an equestrian scene in Hull.' He looks at McAvoy and tries charm. 'I'm told the only horses in Hull are in the sausages.'

McAvoy regards him coolly. 'It's where I live. I like it. And my wife loves horses.'

Musgrave clams up, closing his lips so tightly that they all but disappear.

'You're a bioscientist, is that right?' asks McAvoy.

'Something like that,' says Musgrave.

'And can I presume your wife and child are unavailable?'

'Well, they're in London but I believe they're seeing a show . . .'

'During term time?'

'You've got me – we're terrible parents,' says Musgrave, trying to laugh it off.

McAvoy nods. He jerks his head at Verity. 'Mr Musgrave, I'm going to come back at some stage and I am going to ask you some more questions. When I do, I will want to see a marked improvement in that animal's welfare.'

Musgrave scratches his face and gives a nod. McAvoy tries to read him. Musgrave strikes him as a contradiction. He seems the sort of man who would be happiest eating a vegan burger and watching the sun set on a beach in Cornwall. And yet McAvoy wonders if he is being misled by the bead necklace. Put Musgrave in a suit and he could easily be a ruthless operator. It would not be a stretch of the imagination to picture him sitting in a high-backed Chesterfield in a private members club in Mayfair, sipping a fine port and sharing a cheese board with floppy-fringed junior ministers. McAvoy gets the sense that he will not see the real Joel Musgrave until Musgrave wants him to. He finds himself disliking the man. He is surprised at himself. McAvoy tries to keep his personal feelings out of all investigations. He does not usually admit to an aversion to people until they are kneeling on his chest and trying to stab him. He feels a need to be away from here; to put his thoughts in order. He grunts a goodbye and stalks back towards the house, Verity running to keep up. When they have put some distance between themselves and the stables, Verity allows herself to speak.

'Did you not like him, Sergeant? What was all that about? Receipts? You really didn't warm to him at all.'

'I don't like anybody who mistreats their horses.'

'But if Crystal's missing . . .'

'That poor pony has been loose. He's been grazing wild. He's got a stomach ache that could kill him from eating too much green grass. And he had his tack on for a couple of days before it was removed – you can see from the sweat sores.'

'His tack?'

'Saddle and such.'

'So what does that mean?' asks Verity.

McAvoy walks towards the car – the sound of his footprints on the gravel loud in the stillness of the open air He wonders what he is thinking. Sometimes he does not know his opinions on things until they are pointed out to him but right now he is all about instinct and everything tells him that something here is wrong.

'We've got a missing groom. We've got a dead people-trafficker. A sick pony. A man who's lying about something, even if I don't know what it is. There are pieces here, Detective Constable. And pieces can be put together to make a whole.'

Verity pulls her keys from her pocket and watches as McAvoy folds himself angrily into the passenger seat. She stands outside for a moment, looking back up at the house. She climbs into the car and turns to McAvoy, who is holding up an object to the last of the light.

'What's that?'

'It was under the pony.'

'But what is it?'

The weak light catches on a curve of dirty silver.

'It's a spur,' says McAvoy.

'Like cowboys use?'

'No,' says McAvoy. 'Like little girls use when they're learning to ride on a horse that doesn't want them to.'

'Right? So?'

'This was stuck in the pony's flank,' says McAvoy quietly. 'The other end should have been attached to a riding boot.'

Verity waits for more but gets nothing. 'So?'

McAvoy rubs his forehead. Something is twitching in his

mind. He can half remember something that he knows to be important but he cannot seem to grab for it.

'I need to see Crystal's family,' says McAvoy, talking more to himself than his colleague. 'Something's wrong. I don't like what he's saying.'

'And me? What do you need me to do?'

McAvoy stares at the spur and then slowly turns to face her. 'Keep doing what you're doing. But harder.' He looks up at the house. 'Keep him on his toes.'

9

There was no rest when sleep came. In her dreams, Crystal was again on the bridleway. She was watching the bad men take Primrose. She was fighting. Screaming. Squirming out of the big man's grasp and clawing at his eyes and neck with her stubby fingernails. She wakes into a fog of bewildering darkness and pain. Her face feels as though her head has been crushed in a vice. She's nauseous. There is a pain in her belly where he kicked her and she thinks her wrist broke when he slammed the door and told her that she had to listen to him: had to do as she was told. Her arm is one great throbbing blur of agony. Crystal gags as she tries to swallow. Her throat is almost closed and she cannot seem to close her mouth. She tries to raise her hands but the straps around her elbows bind her tight.

Memories slam into her consciousness like fists.

He hadn't panicked when she told him what had happened. He'd sat very still, thinking hard. He'd only reacted when she tried to call the police. He'd taken the phone from her hand. Told her that he needed time. That he knew people. That this needed his whole attention. She should sit still. Keep her mouth shut and leave it to the grown-ups.

Crystal had thought she'd misheard. Or perhaps she hadn't made herself understood. Perhaps he was making some sort of off-colour joke, the way some people do in extreme circumstances. So she'd tried to call the police again. Ducked outside for a better signal. And that was when he came for her. Grabbed her. Hurt her, as proficiently as he had once thrilled her.

You might die here.

The thought occurs to her without ceremony or preamble. It arrives in her head like any other occurrence; like a sudden reminder to herself to pick up milk or call her mum. The banality of it makes it somehow more terrifying, and Crystal feels tears on her cheeks before they fall into her open mouth and pool upon her tongue.

He'd almost seemed to enjoy fitting her with the bit. Had she imagined it? Had he been punishing her for knocking over the piss bucket and soaking his shirt? He'd bound her slowly, harder than he needed to. He'd lingered as he bent over her and yanked at the buckles and straps and the soft leather of the bit pulled at her cheeks and the cold metal pushed down on her tongue. He had told her it was her own fault. It could all have been so different. He was doing what he had to. She had made this so much harder than it needed to be.

Crystal lies in the dark and drools onto the cold, musty floor. She has a recollection of a sudden, flaring hope, as if she had glimpsed an exotic bird through a prison window. She had heard voices in the house. Soft. Low. She'd opened her mouth to scream and the next moment her world had been a cacophony of bells; a jarring carillon that rang out as her body struck the wall and her head snapped backwards.

Crystal thinks of Primrose and finds herself shivering. The little girl has never experienced fear. Never been hurt for somebody else's amusement. Her life has been all about skis and salopettes, Pony Club and pedicures and costumed sleepovers at the homes of children with names like Maisie and Miles. She thinks the whole world is full of nice people; of waiters who bring her dinners that aren't normally available because her dad is rich enough to view the menu as a list of ingredients. She's seen New York and Milan; sat on a tree swing at the rear of a farmhouse in Brittany and held a smile and a balloon while a professional artist captured her likeness. Her favourite snack is pâté on rice cakes and she hopes to help people in Africa when she grows up. She is an innocent, and when Crystal imagines what she is enduring, it fills her with such a strength that she can almost tear apart her bonds.

Stay strong, she says, though whether she is telling herself or the little girl, she could not say.

She begins to chew at the bit the way Storm likes to when she slows him from a canter. It's a movement that speaks of unspent energy. She is young and full of fight and she will not let him treat her this way.

She tugs again at her bonds. Hears the clank of metal touching metal and then she is filled with a fizzing blue pain as she touches the electric fence wrapped tight around the D-ring through which her bonds trail. Her muscles spasm and she bites down on the metal bit. Her head is so full of static and screeching that when her back molar cracks down to the nerve, she merely finds herself grateful for a change in the quality of the pain.

In the main house, Musgrave can smell the girl's piss on his hands. She knocked over the bucket as he held her above it like a child; arms hooked through hers and holding the backs of her thighs as she looked at him and spat his name through blood-speckled teeth. He lost his grip on her sweaty skin and they both fell to the floor in a clatter of arms and legs and urine. A few days ago she would have used such an opportunity to escape. This time she simply curled into a ball and mewled pitifully as he cursed and batted ineffectually at the spreading stain on his shirt. That's when he saw the light come on. Saw the silly girl and the massive man poking around his stables. He hadn't thought them to be coppers. He'd hidden, shaking, in the cool dark of the wine cellar listening to their voices eddy and recede; their footsteps loud above him. His heart had felt like a shard of glass as he furtively raised the trapdoor and watched them disappear into the stables. She had called him 'sergeant'. They were police. He ripped off his shirt and willed himself to appear calm as he scrambled back towards the house, took a breath and then swivelled in a swift U-turn. The young detective constable looked embarrassed at his sudden appearance but he had seen something else entirely in the expression of the Scotsman, who loomed over him like something carved of marble. He had half expected it to end there and then. Had expected the Scotsman to sniff the urine on his fingers and know, without further need for enquiry, about the girl in the basement. But the odour of the horses masked the vile aroma on his hands and clothes and he had escaped with little more than a warning. As he walked back to the house he had known he was on borrowed time. Things needed to happen fast or he would not be around to ensure they happened at all.

Musgrave stands in the kitchen, running the hot tap until little ribbons of steam begin to curl upwards. He stares at the roiling twists of vapour and knows that were his daughter here beside him, he would likely tell her a story about a dragon and make her giggle. Perhaps he would not. He finds himself counting up the number of times in recent months that he has been too tired to tuck her in or else disappointed her with endless reassurances that they will go swimming or to the cinema or for a walk on the Wolds 'sometime soon'. How much time has he wasted? And for what? To sit on the sofa with a nice glass of wine and a documentary playing on Netflix? Or playing some game on one of his expensive toys? He has acted as if time were an infinite resource – as if she would always be his little girl and look at him with those great doe eyes, admiring him without question. What he would give to have his chances again. He will do things differently when this is over.

Musgrave's desperation for a second chance sits like a stone in his gut. He feels jittery; his bowels watery. He feels an absurd need to drink something sugary – to eat the kind of snack that he always mocks Primrose for enjoying. Crisps. Chocolate. A fistful of Haribo. He wants to feel closer to her. He pulls his phone from his pocket and calls up a recent video he shot. His daughter sits at the kitchen table, drawing pad open in front of her; a glass of milk and some slices of apple on a tray by her left hand. She's playing up to the camera. Soft brown hair and a plain black T-shirt, tanned skin and kind brown eyes. She's trying to explain the plot of *Macbeth* to her mum and keeps getting stuck on the names of the characters. She begins to giggle as she refers to the murder of 'Dunquo'. It's a joyful, infectious sound. She throws her head back, happy at the attention she is getting. Musgrave hears his own voice on the recording, telling her to carry on. Primrose explains that Macbeth cut a man's throat so he could become queen. She corrects herself too swiftly and the sound comes out as 'Quing'. She falls into fits of hysterics. Musgrave hears himself laughing. Hears his wife repeating the word, over and over, letting the laughter in the room build. Musgrave finds himself smiling as he watches the recording through eyes that sting with caged tears.

'The Quing of all Scotland!' Primrose laughs again. She turns as another figure enters the room. Her face twists into a huge grin as she sees the skinny girl with the mud-streaked leggings and cold-slapped face who plonks herself down at the kitchen table. She looks up and sees Musgrave recording her. Smiles, coyly, and raises a hand to her face. 'Are you recording? Why? Look at the state of me! Get it off. Video your wife, she's the stunner!'

Musgrave watches the clip with his fists clenched. This was his normality until a few short days ago. The whirr of the extractor fan as he sliced vegetables for a stir-fry. The chatter of his wife and her groom. The delicate touches and the scent of perfume as his picture-perfect wife glides by like a Disney princess. Gone. All gone, because of a situation over which he has never had any control.

In the clip, Crystal starts to relax. Mugs for the camera. Pulls a silly face and performs a puppet show with her muddy hands: two emus, their beaks made of fingers and thumb, kissing passionately, while Primrose falls into fits of laughter. Crystal grins with satisfaction. They could be sisters. He has always known that Crystal would look good if she smartened herself up a little but it was always her dishevelment, her grubbiness, that he liked. His wife is always so damnably perfect. So crimped and pampered and pruned. Not a pimple or an ingrowing hair. Crystal is the opposite. Mud smears on her cheeks and horse-shit under her fingernails. And always that big smile, as if she had found her heaven and still cannot quite believe it. What he would give to see that now! What he would pay . . .

Without preamble, Musgrave pushes his hands under the scalding water and lets out a hiss as his skin turns instantly red beneath the burning jet. He needs this. Needs the agony to clear his head. He's better than this. Self-doubt is weakness. To conceive of failure is to guarantee it. He has been in harder situations than this. He needs to stop thinking like the child he used to be. He needs to access his sense of outrage.

Unbidden, the face of his tormentor swims into his vision. Musgrave tastes blood as he chomps down on his cheek. Tries to force the memories from his mind. His thoughts pay him no heed. His whole self is suddenly awash with hatred and regret. He had thought the man dead. Thought that the betrayal had died with him. Musgrave had felt as though he were staring at a demon when the message appeared on his mobile phone. White eyes; stained teeth; scarred black skin and a missing ear. A look of absolute malevolence scored into every pore. That voice. Soft and persuasive. Almost charming. Musgrave had used that voice for his own advantage. And now it was warning him what would happen if his demands were not met.

Musgrave finds himself prickling at the unfairness of it all. The betrayal had not been his alone. Musgrave was a small part of a big operation. He had not made the decision that cost Manu his sanity. Indeed, Musgrave had allowed Manu to prosper in a way he would never have been able to consider. He had given him a new life. Helped him put his demons to bed. It wasn't his fault that it had all gone wrong. Some things were beyond his control.

He holds his fist under the scorching water. Revels in the agony.

'Bastard. Ungrateful fucking bastard.'

To come here! To pursue him to England and to take what he considers most precious? Joel shakes his head. Too much. Far too fucking much. He needs to turn this situation around. There is a chance to come out ahead. To gamble and win. It could be his greatest victory yet. Keep the girl chained up. Keep her silent until this is all over. Make some money. Wrap everything up at once and come away ahead.

'That won't help anybody,' says the man who stands in the doorway, inhaling an electric cigarette. 'You don't have to atone, Joel. Don't be silly.'

Musgrave withdraws his hands from the steam. The skin is red but not blistered. Wincing, he stuffs his phone into his pocket.

'Cold tap,' says the man in the doorway.

Joel does as he is told and enjoys the blissful sensation of icy water cooling his reddened skin.

'They know,' says Musgrave. 'The Scotsman. He looked right through me.'

'He doesn't know. He doesn't even suspect. He just has his doubts and that means something else entirely.'

'But he'll be back.'

'It will be done by then.'

'And you're confident, yes? You can do what needs to be done.'

The man in the doorway smiles. 'We have the package. He's having a bit of quiet time before he opens it, poor lamb.'

Musgrave turns from the sink, water dripping from his aching hands onto the floor. 'You don't think badly of me?'

The man shrugs. 'Seen it all, Joel. Seems like you're dealing with this in a sensible way. No harm in turning a bad situation to your advantage.'

'I wouldn't have done this if my hand hadn't been forced,' says Musgrave, like a sulky teen.

'We don't need to go into that now. This is what's happening. You've got friends. Powerful friends. Blue Lightz does this shit every day. They've got good at it. The boss doesn't let his friends fall. He's very good at making sure people do what pleases him. Mr Roper has ways and means.'

Musgrave leans back against the sink as the man enters the kitchen. He has a neat grey beard and close-cropped dark hair. He has the straight back and sharp eyes of somebody who has served in the military, though Musgrave doubts that it is the British Army that has been his sole paymaster. His allegiance is for hire.

'What's that?' asks Musgrave, indicating the envelope in the other man's hand.

'It's what we asked for,' he says. 'Proof of life. I understand if you don't wish to look.'

The man places the package on the table and removes a pair of long-nose pliers from the pocket of his black jacket. Then he takes a recording device from his trousers and mutters the time and date. He places the device on the table. From an inside pocket he produces a box the size and shape of a spectacles case and opens it to reveal the empty plastic vials within. Finally he pulls on a pair of blue latex gloves. He will test one blood sample himself and decant the remainder into the other vials, which will be sped off to the lab for independent verification. The policy's smallprint dictates things be done properly.

'Up to you, Joel. Whatever's happened to her, it can't be undone. They wouldn't release the money without proof of life. We need this to proceed.'

'Just do it.'

Carefully, the man takes the gummed flap of the short, fat envelope between the ends of the pliers. Cautiously, he begins to peel it back. He just manages a fleeting moment of triumph. Of relief.

The tiny explosive charge inside the envelope would not be enough to knock over a pint glass on a bar top. But it is enough to puncture the transparent wallet full of Type O-neg blood that was left on Joel Musgrave's doorstep this afternoon.

There is a small, damp *thwump* and then the packet of fresh blood explodes with enough force to drench the man in the latex gloves. He falls backwards off his chair, dripping crimson onto the wooden floor; wiping blood from his face and gagging on the taste.

By the sink, Musgrave throws up his hands to protect himself. It is not enough. A fine mist of blood seeks the gaps in his defences and in a moment he, too, is retching and gasping; turning to vomit into the sink. He tastes acid. Coffee. And something else. Primal and metallic. Copper and fresh meat. Feels himself shudder and his eyes fill with tears as he pukes out his daughter's blood: pink bubbles in his spit and crimson upon his tongue.

'There's a hot tub on the roof of this place.'

'Yeah?'

'Fancy bar. Cocktails. I've always imagined it would be awesome to sit in a Jacuzzi during a thunderstorm.'

Detective Constable Helen Tremberg examines her boss for any sign that he is joking. He doesn't seem to be. If anything he looks a little wistful, as though his mind were full of pictures of a life he would be leading if he had made different decisions somewhere back down the road. Tremberg's been on secondment to his team for the past four months and has learned to admire the short, stocky man who can switch personalities like an actor in a one-man play. His accent is pure north London but his family are from Grenada. He is an estate tearaway who turned his life around and who would probably be a borough commander by now were he not more interested in catching crooks and killers than playing politics. He runs the National Crime Agency task force tackling a very specific area of organised crime. He's a good boss: firm, fair and unwilling to put his officers into any danger that he would not face down himself.

'Sounds a bit dangerous,' says Tremberg, and realises she might be coming across as a kill-joy. 'Fun though. One of those bucket-list things. I have a different name for the list of stuff I want to do before I die. It's called the "oh fuck-it list". Going well, actually.'

DCI Jay Pramana doesn't turn around. He's leaning against the wall by the huge, floor-to-ceiling window, staring out at the night-time crowd as they do battle with taxis and white vans on this boisterous street on the edge of London's Soho. This hotel is a lavish affair: all blue lights and textured walls, black and white prints and scarlet chandeliers. If it were a woman it would be wearing a fur coat, suspenders and six-inch heels. The bedroom where she and Pramana are making awkward small talk is designed around a towering four-poster bed and the drapes and sheets have all been chosen for maximum tactile enjoyment. There is a mirror on one entire wall and soft red lighting bleeds from the bedside lamp. The carpet is thick as snow and it is all Helen can do not to rip her boots off and start making fists in its opulent surface with her toes. She is determined not to let the words 'shag pile' enter the dialogue any time soon.

'Are you all right, boss?' asks Tremberg. There is a tension in Pramana's shoulders. He looks tired.

'Too many late nights,' says Pramana, turning from the window to give her a smile that doesn't reach his eyes. 'I'm not as young as I was.'

'None of us are,' says Tremberg, and she wishes she were better at comforting people.

'I shouldn't complain. You're the one with the young child keeping you up at all hours.'

'She's pretty good really.'

'Perdita, isn't it?'

'Penelope.'

'Sorry. Nice name though.'

Tremberg nods her thanks. She has told him her baby's name a dozen times. She wonders what it is about her that screams the word 'Perdita'. She wonders what Pramana would think if she told him how hard her father had worked trying to persuade her to call his granddaughter 'Steve'.

'He'll be late in ten seconds,' says Pramana, though he is not looking at his watch.

'He'll be here,' says Tremberg, and is surprised at how confident she sounds. Her informant has never let her down and even though he would dearly like to stick both thumbs in Pramana's eyes, she knows he respects their arrangement and the fact that she will not meet him without having a second officer to back her up. Any evidence given to a serving police officer without the presence of a second officer for confirmation is considered largely invalid by the courts system.

Pramana sighs and turns away from the window. His skin lacks lustre. He looks like he needs a shower and a sandwich, or half an hour in a hot tub in a thunderstorm.

'I just saw a bloke cycling on a Boris Bike wearing a full gimp outfit,' he says, shrugging. 'I think that's that, in terms of visual stimulus.'

'Really?' asks Tremberg. She's sitting on the bed, tapping at her laptop, huffing her hair out of her eyes. She wonders where Pramana will sit if he abandons his vigil by the glass.

'No, not really. I did see a bloke in assless chaps.'

'What are they?'

'Trousers without an arse,' he says flatly. 'Or a good name for a private members club.'

'This was my dad's big fear, y'know. That I'd find myself in a brothel in Soho, talking about gay things.'

'That's a fairly mixed bag of neuroses.'

'He's a northern male.'

'How would he feel about you being in a four-poster bed with a black man?' asks Pramana, with a touch more animation to his face.

'He'd probably be delighted,' says Tremberg, grinning. 'He's under the impression you all know each other. In his head, you'd probably increase his chances of meeting Lewis Hamilton.'

Pramana opens the mini-bar and takes a can of Coke. He presses it to his forehead and sighs, then puts the drink back unopened.

'ID's through,' says Tremberg, shifting her position on the bed. She sucks her teeth as she concentrates on reading the report from the specialist science and forensics team maintained on a full-time basis by her specialist unit. Pramana comes to the side of the bed and leans over her. He smells of bodyspray and damp clothes, coffee and tobacco. His shape reflects in the computer screen and Tremberg has to angle herself differently to be able to read. Pramana seems to realise he is being obtrusive and picks one of the sheafs of paper from the bed, pretending that was his intention all along. He starts reading Tremberg's notes on the victims, although he is already well-versed on the IDs of the men found brutalised at a boarded-up pub on the road near Gatwick Airport. Their fingerprints set off alarms on databases in a dozen different law enforcement agencies. The fingerprints suggest the two men were both soldiers in a branch of an organised crime family operating out of Kiev and both corpses are decorated with tattoos that are undoubtedly Cyrillic. Pramana has already called in expert help on translating the baffling map of churches, stars, demons and gargoyles that cover the men's torsos and limbs.

'Well, blow me down,' says Tremberg, under her breath. And then, for emphasis: 'Fucking hell.'

'Sorry, Helen?'

Tremberg finds herself grinning. She reads the report again, just to make sure.

'He gets bloody everywhere,' she says quietly.

'Senior officer here, Helen,' says Pramana, pointing at his chest. 'Head of the unit. Your boss. Whenever you're ready.'

Tremberg raises her head and pulls a face in apology. 'I know this guy. I know his name, anyway. And I know somebody who can give us chapter and verse.'

'Are you being awkward deliberately? Is it some perverse technique of yours? You don't make sense until I jump on you and slap you around?'

Tremberg cocks her head and enjoys the moment that passes between them. Then she spins the computer screen to face her boss.

'Owen Lee Swainson,' she says. 'Until a few months back he was an inmate at Bull Sands Prison on the Lincolnshire coast. He served four years for possession of an illegal firearm.'

'Bit steep.'

'Just be quiet a second please, boss. There's more.'

Pramana settles himself on the end of the bed and opens his hands. 'Proceed.'

'Owen was a journalist in Hull. Press Association and some freelance work on the side. Well-known. Well-respected. Did a lot of investigative work and had a good relationship with CID. Got on well with the boss and was always first in line for exclusives.'

'Went sour?'

'In a big way. Five years back there was a girl went missing in Hull. Ella Butterworth. Twenty years old. Beautiful girl. Picture was in the *Hull Mail* every day for weeks. Family were the sort the press prays for – real, decent types who had done nothing to deserve all the horror. Owen and another journalist called Tony Halthwaite pretty much stayed with the family 24/7 and every spit and cough was reported. Then Ella's body was found. She was in a house not more than a couple of streets away from the family home. Her corpse was in the bed of a fat waster called Shane Cadbury. He was your archetypal nobody. Low IQ, watched a lot of porn, did recreational drugs and spent his benefits money on DVDs and takeaways. He was arrested and in no time at all he was charged with her murder. Forensics showed she had been raped but it was impossible to determine whether that was before or after death. She'd been killed with a khukri – a Gurkha blade. More than fifty hack and stab wounds.'

'Christ.'

'Quite. So, should have been open and shut, right? But it

wasn't. Owen had spent enough time with the family for them to open up about Ella's fears in the days before her death. Somebody had been following her. A handprint had been left on her bedroom window. Some of her clothes had gone missing. She saw a footprint on the cistern of the toilet and some of her bottles of make-up and whatnot had been knocked over.'

'Difficult to reconcile stalking behaviour with the man in the dock.'

'Precisely. So Owen did some digging. Found other examples up and down the country. Called in favours. Found half a dozen cases of girls killed in similar circumstances. He took his findings to his mate, the head of CID.'

'And?'

'And the next thing, a girl came forward to say that Owen had raped her at the Country Park. Uniform arrested him and a search of his house turned up a handgun.'

'Timely,' says Pramana, without need for further comment.

'Without doubt. It happened just as Cadbury's trial was starting. Trouble was, a detective sergeant on the Major Incident Team had found the same pattern. And he had some serious misgivings about Cadbury's guilt. Cadbury's defence was that he had found Ella's body and brought it home to play with. Not nice, but not murder.'

'And if there was somebody else out there killing girls, it would be nice to catch him, don't you think?'

'That was what the detective sergeant thought. So he spoke to his boss. Told them they had the wrong man. After that it gets a bit hazy in the official record.'

'But?'

'There was an incident. The detective sergeant ended up fighting for his life. He was off sick for months. Terrible injuries and lasting scars. The reporter I mentioned – Tony Halthwaite. He was committed to a mental hospital on the same day as the detective sergeant was hurt – though he had to spend a lot of time in hospital first to repair the gunshot wound to his groin.'

'Christ.'

'Indeed. And Owen was re-arrested before he'd put any distance between himself and the custody suite. Rape was dropped but he was charged with the weapons offence. Pleaded guilty on the assumption he would be given a lighter sentence and ended up doing a hefty stretch and suffering like hell on the inside.'

'Cadbury?'

'Trial went ahead. Found guilty of murder. My old boss has been trying to get the top brass to re-examine the case ever since but he's been told to back off.'

'And the head of the MIT?'

'Early retirement not long after.'

Pramana scratches at his jaw with a rasping sound that makes Tremberg think of playful claws on a wooden door.

'You know a lot about this,' says Pramana. 'You've barely looked at the screen.'

'Owen was released last year. The day he walked out of prison there was an incident at the pub where inmates traditionally stop for their first free pint. Somebody attacked the landlord. Knocked him out cold. When he called the police the first officers on the scene could tell there was something very wrong. They could smell cordite. Chemicals. You know that way a room just feels different? They followed their gut. Forensics carried out a limasol test and a hell of a lot of blood had been hastily cleaned.'

'Owen's?'

'No. It belonged to a gun-for-hire named Stan Renfrew. Forty-six. Convictions for wounding and one attempted murder trial, where he was found not guilty.'

'Body?'

'Never found.'

'And Owen?'

'No sign. This is the first I've heard of him since then.'

Pramana considers her. 'Seriously, I know you're thorough but that's a lot of information to carry in your head. What's your connection?'

Tremberg smiles, shaking her head. 'My old sergeant was the officer who didn't believe it was Cadbury. He was the one who nearly died.'

'McAvoy, right?'

'The same.'

'And the boss of the unit. You're going to tell me his name was Doug Roper, aren't you?'

Tremberg nods. 'Doug Roper. After he quit the whole of CID was restructured. Trish Pharaoh got the job. Brought in officers she knew and trusted, and a couple of others she got lumped with.'

'This is your Colin Ray, yes?'

'DCI Colin Ray. He and DCI Sharon Archer. Good officers but hard to work with.'

Pramana rubs his stubble again. 'So, Owen appears to have gone to the dark side. In your mind, he's killing people we know to be connected to the Headhunters.'

'Not on his own he's not.'

Pramana looks at her warily. 'This is the old man you told me about.'

'Raymond Mahon. Enforcer for Mr Nock. Nock was King of the north-east and tougher than a blacksmith's thumb. Stayed in the shadows for decades. Lost his marbles a bit when he got old and the Headhunters finally saw him off. Killed him up on an East Yorkshire clifftop. Mahon won't rest until everybody involved is hanging from a barbed-wire noose.'

'The same Raymond Mahon who died two years ago?'

'His body wasn't found.'

'What's their connection?'

Tremberg considers it, rubbing her hands on the soft velvet of the bedcovers. 'Hatred,' she says at last. 'Mahon is after the people who killed his boss.'

'And Owen? The only person he could be bitter at is Roper.'

Tremberg stays absolutely still. She doesn't want her body language to betray her.

'Is that really your theory?' asks Pramana, and his face is impassive. 'You think Roper is connected to the Headhunters? I know he was shady and cut corners but he was the head of CID. And yeah, I know, I've seen *Line of Duty*. It's possible. It's just not very likely.'

Tremberg squeezes the soft sheets in her hands. She has kept her thoughts to herself for so long that she is afraid to finally speak in case her words rush out like lava.

'He works for a security consultancy in London,' she says, choosing her words carefully. 'A lot of interesting branches. He heads up a division that I suppose you would call "special projects".'

Pramana is about to speak when there is a soft rap at the door. He holds up his hand to tell Tremberg to hold the thought. He crosses to the door and Tremberg sees him give a curt nod of welcome. He is followed back into the room by a tall, middle-aged man with short dark hair and a pronounced limp. He jerks his head at Tremberg in greeting.

'Hello there, Helen.'

'Hi, Teddy. You well?'

'Mustn't grumble.'

'How's the foot?'

'Only hurts when I breathe.'

Tremberg climbs off the bed and gives Teddy her hand. He takes it in a firm grip and she makes the effort to pat his elbow as they shake. She likes her informant. On paper he is a thuggish, merciless killer but Tremberg has spent enough time with him to know that, in his own mind at least, he is not such a bad guy. A year ago Tremberg gave him the choice of twenty years in prison or the opportunity to work as a snout. He made the sensible decision. He is only a low-level operative with one of the crime families paying protection money to the Headhunters but he sees enough to be invaluable. She trusts him both to provide the information her unit is officially tasked with procuring, and also to keep his eyes open for anything that reinforces her private suspicions.

'Bad business,' says Teddy, crossing to the mini-bar and helping himself to a miniature of Glenfiddich. He drains it in one swallow. 'They're not happy.'

'They wouldn't be,' says Pramana. 'We've just found a couple of delightful corpses in a boarded-up pub. Their soldiers just got blown away.'

'It shouldn't have happened. They were under instructions not to show their faces without absolute certainty they weren't being set up.'

'Poor decision-making.'

'They were trying to milk more than was agreed. That's where so many people go wrong. They get greedy. This outfit isn't about that. They come to an agreement and they do it properly. I don't know if this prick was trying to skim but if he was, he'd have died anyways, and in a far nastier way.'

'Who've they got pegged for it?'

Teddy shoots a look at Tremberg, who gives a nod of assent. 'Same again. Ratty bloke. Old bloke. Handsome bloke. Like the Three Musketeers, but shit.'

'Do you know an Owen Swainson?' asks Pramana, and he lifts the laptop to show Teddy the mugshot. Teddy peers at it.

'Can't say as I do. Handsome though. Do you like him for one of our three killers?'

'The other thing,' says Tremberg, ignoring the question. 'Developments?'

Teddy seems unsure about talking in front of the other officer but Tremberg assures him it's okay.

'The boat,' he says. 'Two of the girls from the club on Thursday of last week. Looked sore when they left but they went back to the place on Wandsworth without complaint. Then she arrived. Saturday morning.'

'She?' asks Pramana.

Tremberg pauses for a second and closes her eyes, weighing up her options. She hears the sound of laughter from the street below. A taxi driver shouts abuse at a lost tourist trying to do a three-point turn on a road barely wide enough for a car. She wonders if she will remember this moment. Whether she will come to view this instant, this heartbeat, as the moment it all changed.

Tremberg takes the laptop back from her boss and keys in a quick pitter-patter of letters. She turns the screen and shows Teddy. 'You're sure?'

He nods. 'Saturday until Sunday. Big bloke dropped her back at her car. Range Rover, parked up in a health club in Richmond.'

'Are you going to tell me what you're talking about?' asks Pramana testily.

Tremberg shows him the screen. It is filled with a picture of a dangerously attractive blonde, all glossy lipstick, artfully tangled hair and hard eyes.

'This is Detective Chief Inspector Shaz Archer. She's head of the Drugs Squad with Humberside Police. She's also the lover of Doug Roper. And she was one of the last people to see Colin Ray before he disappeared.'

Pramana stares into Archer's pixilated eyes for a time. Slowly, he raises his gaze to look hard at his detective constable.

'You're going to lose friends with this one,' he says resignedly.

'Fuck it,' says Tremberg. 'I've got a daughter. That wins.'

'You really want to start looking into him?' asks Pramana,

twisting his face. 'We've had no intelligence on this. We've been looking into it for years and he's never cropped up. And suddenly some DC from up north and an unregistered informant tell me that an ex-cop and a serving cop are mixed up. You expect me to put resources into a hunch?'

Tremberg looks at him with the cold glare that she learned from Trish Pharaoh. 'He was corrupt. He let innocent men go to jail. He fitted up Owen and I know he was hooked up in what happened to McAvoy. You should be grateful I just want to investigate him. Every fibre in my body says it would be quicker just to shoot the fucker.'

Pramana gives a begrudging nod. Teddy backs it up.

'I don't know if this matters, but the man you're interested in – he had some lilies sent to the boat,' says Teddy. 'Special breed, came in under the radar and delivered by a little Russian bloke in a flat cap. I wrote down the name of the flowers, if you want it.'

'And that helps how?' asks Pramana.

Teddy glares at him, his eyes once more those of a professional killer. 'I know the bloke. And he did eight years in Belmarsh for bringing in smack.'

Tremberg and Pramana glance at one another. Tremberg stops herself from saying anything for fear of spoiling things. She looks at her phone, for something to do. There's a number. One she doesn't recognise. A message. Two words.

Stop Looking.

Tremberg breathes in deeply. There's a tension across her shoulders. She sucks her lip. Then she crosses to the windowsill and peers through the blinds at the quiet darkness of the street. She sees nothing save a few still cars and a flurry of moths dancing in the sodium-yellow glow of the streetlight. She glimpses her own face, pale and tired but flushed across the cheeks. She gives the slightest of nods. Fiddles with her mobile phone. Calls the sender, expecting to hear that the number is unavailable. It is answered on the eighth ring.

'Hello?' asks Tremberg, as if checking a cold dark room for occupants. 'This is Helen Tremberg. Somebody texted me? I'm a bit in the dark . . .'

The quality of the silence at the other end of the line seems to change. She wonders if she will be expected to do all the talking.

'You can talk to me.'

The silence seems to spill out from the phone. Tremberg shivers. Closes her eyes and presses on.

'I was just thinking about a man I used to know. Caused me problems. Mark, that was his name. Dead now. Went over a clifftop at Flamborough. We've learned a lot since then. He was barely even mid-level. He was just a tool the Headhunters used. With some people it's money. With others it's family. They got to me through shame. They've been doing this for a long time. They do it well. Coming out the other side is something to be proud of.'

Tremberg hears a rasping breathing. Wonders if she should try a name.

'I'm piecing it together. Two years ago one of our officers was duped into beating up a suspect in the cells. He was suspended and he tried to redeem himself by taking down a solicitor being used as a mouthpiece by the Headhunters. He went to his friend, his protégée, with the information he unearthed. Then he disappeared. Most people think he's abroad, living a debauched life in the sun. I don't. I think he's suffered. Suffered more than anybody should have to endure. But I think he's got himself free and he has joined up with the kind of men he spent his life trying to stop. I think he wants revenge.'

This time her words are met with a sniff. She finds herself picturing him, the last time they met. His ratty features and greasy skin, his slicked-back hair and his look of broken-hearted rage at the idea that Shaz Archer may have lied to him for years.

Tremberg stops talking as the man who listens to her words clears his throat. It's a grotesque, rattling noise that sounds as if somebody were stirring his tonsils with a screwdriver.

'It's not what it seems,' comes a slurred whisper. 'I'm not like them but I don't know what I am. I can't feel my brain any more. There's stuff in me. Stuff that isn't who I remember. They want me to tell them what happened but it's all just grey.'

'Colin,' says Tremberg, and realises she has never used her old DCI's Christian name before. 'Colin, we can still put things right. You're not a killer. You're a policeman. Let me help you.'

'I'm beyond help.'

The phone goes dead.

II

'That one,' says Verity, and nods out of the passenger window at the front door of a neat terraced property. 'That's her mum's car. Lesley.'

'Same surname?'

'No. She's a Jameson. Like the whiskey.'

McAvoy digests the information and concentrates on keeping his internal organs where they should be as Verity swings the car off the quiet road that leads through the village of Brookenby. The terraced houses are set back from the thoroughfare and are accessed by a separate slip road. Of the cars parked along its length, none is newer than six years old and several have had their suspension lowered, their exhausts replaced and transfers stuck along their length. Were he feeling judgemental, McAvoy would suggest that some of the residents of Brookenby enjoy racing their souped-up hatchbacks around the county's dangerous roads. He glances at Verity and briefly wonders whether she has family here.

'You know Brookenby?' she asks, bumping the car onto the grass verge between the slip road and the main street and ignoring the scrape of kerb on the underside of the car.

'My first time.'

'Odd place. Nice enough but looks a bit out of place to me. It's like somebody picked up an inner-city estate and dropped it in the middle of the Wolds. It's all a bit *Prisoner*, if you ask me.'

'Prisoner?'

'The Patrick McGoohan thing. Big white balls.'

McAvoy scratches his eyebrow, searching for the correct response. He comes up with nothing. Turns back to look out of the window. Verity's right. The view to the left is all rolling fields and neat woodland. To his right, the houses and the cars and the sloppily drawn curtains make him feel as though he were about to knock on a door in the middle of some sink estate.

'Council moved a lot of tenants out here from bigger towns,' says Verity, opening her door. 'That's what I heard, anyway. Can't swear to it.'

McAvoy disentangles himself from the vehicle and considers the house that Crystal Heathers has called home for the best part of the last year. It has a white door with a floral pattern set into the glass and there are little teapots containing wildflowers on the step. The curtains are drawn but he can see the backs of picture frames on the windowsill and a vase containing dried poppy-stalks. The door opens as he approaches the house. It's a woman in her fifties, wrapped in a blanket and wearing mismatched socks. Her face is pale and her bottle-black hair is grey at the roots. She has the skin of a hardened smoker. She raises her hands to her face as she sees McAvoy and Verity approach.

'Angela? Oh God, don't tell me it's bad news. Please, if it's bad news I can't, I can't . . .'

McAvoy darts forward as the woman in the doorway begins to crumble. She falls like something made of playing cards; collapsing in on herself and slowly slipping lower.

'Please, Mrs Jameson, don't upset yourself, it's just routine. I'm so sorry.' McAvoy reaches down and puts his arm around the woman's waist and uses the other to hold her elbow. Gently, like picking up a child who has twisted their ankle, he raises her back to her feet. She presses her face against him and sobs, just once. It sounds like a dog, barking in its sleep. Then she pushes herself away from him and gives an embarrassed laugh. Her arm, held in McAvoy's hand, is trembling.

'I'm sorry, I thought . . . I just . . .'

'Hush yourself, Lesley,' says Verity, joining McAvoy on the front step and placing a hand on Lesley's shoulder. 'This is Detective Sergeant McAvoy. You can call him Aector, if you can pronounce it. He's from a special team over the river.'

'Hull?' asks Lesley, looking up at him with the suspicious eyes of somebody who grew up thinking of the city as the enemy.

'That's right. I'm with Humberside Police. I came to talk to Mr Musgrave in connection with another incident we're investigating and I met Angela here and she told me about your missing daughter. I think it would be helpful if we had a little chat. Could we perhaps come inside?'

Lesley looks at him, weighing up whether it would be an ill omen to allow a person from Hull into her daughter's home. She relents after a moment.

'Come on in.'

She leads them into a small, square living room with an L-shaped leather sofa angled to face an old-fashioned boxy TV. The pictures on the walls look as though they have been passed on from other family members. They are churches and land-scapes, hay carts and watercolour dogs. They do not seem to be the taste of a young woman but McAvoy notes that there is no dust on the frames or glass and the pink carpet beneath his feet is spotless. He wonders whether Lesley has been tidying in her daughter's absence or whether Crystal is a natural homemaker.

'Lovely home she has,' says McAvoy, and doesn't sit down until Lesley invites him to.

'Thank you,' says Lesley brightly. 'I wasn't sure myself. I'm from Grimsby. One of the terraces near Blundell Park. Football ground, if you know it.'

'I do. Nice part of the world.'

'Do you think so?' asks Lesley, seemingly troubled by the

compliment. 'Stabbings are down, but there was that shooting not long back. House prices are still through the floor. Hull must be knee-deep in bodies if you think Grimsby's nice.'

McAvoy colours and brushes over his embarrassment. 'Your daughter. She's been here nearly a year, yes?'

'Loving it,' says Lesley. 'Rent is a challenge but she's never missed a payment.'

'That's refreshing. Most young people are up to their eyes in debt.'

'Not just young people,' scoffs Lesley, and she dabs her nose with the cuff of her jumper. 'I don't know anybody round our way who isn't robbing Peter to pay Paul.'

'Peter won't like that.' McAvoy smiles.

'No. But that's when you make a call to Patrick and he smashes Peter's knees with a baseball bat.' Lesley raises her hand to her mouth as soon as she has spoken. She cringes. 'Sorry. Old saying round our way.'

McAvoy softens his face. He takes her in. She's wearing a black skirt that reaches to the floor and a pair of flat shoes that look no larger than a size three. Her gestures are quick and manic. She starts playing with an electronic cigarette, moving it from palm to palm. McAvoy feels like closing both of her hands in his and telling her that everything is going to be okay. The impulse is as much a part of him as his height and hair. He has to fight it. Has to force himself not to make any more promises.

'What do you do for a living, Mrs Jameson?' asks McAvoy, his voice neutral.

Lesley reaches down and picks at a non-existent speck of dirt on the carpet. 'Hotel receptionist. Stallingborough Grange. Bit of bar work. Why do you ask?'

'Just routine,' says McAvoy. He smiles and opens his note-book. 'Can I ask you about Crystal's relationship with her employer?'

Lesley shoots a glance at Verity and receives a tiny nod. 'I think she liked him.'

'Liked in what way?'

'Liked, y'know. Look, Crystal's had some bloody awful boyfriends. She's made some silly mistakes and I'm not going to pretend I've been the easiest mother but she's always had a good heart and all she's ever really wanted is a normal life. Nice house, couple of kids, bloke who takes her for a meal now and then and doesn't knock her about. It's not a big dream but it's not a lot to ask.' Lesley stops and her eyes begin to turn glassy. She sniffs, noisily, and swallows.

'Horses too, so I understand.'

Lesley smiles indulgently. 'Always loved animals. She held a funeral for a neighbour's goldfish when she was four years old. Couldn't stand to see an animal in pain. She'd go and walk neighbours' dogs, even though she wasn't allowed beyond the end of our street. She would run them up and down and between the lampposts – puffing herself out just so the dogs got exercise. But it was horses that she adored. There were some old nags on a bit of waste ground not far from our house and I'd forever catch her sneaking out of the house with carrots she'd nicked from the cupboard. She'd spend her pocket money on apples for the buggers. Her dad, God rest him, he would have loved to have bought her a proper pony of her own but the best we could do was ferry her about to all the different stables where she did mucking out in exchange for tuition and a chance to ride. She was a natural. If she'd had the right accent and whiter teeth she'd have been a champion, but y'know how it is, the horse crowd can be a bit snobby. I never felt very welcome but I always saw her compete.'

'Did she get her own horse?'

'Eventually. Twenty-two years old but still had some spirit. Good practice horse and a friend of a friend said she could stable it with them if she helped them around the yard.'

McAvoy waits for more but Lesley spreads her hands.

'People go off the rails at different ages. Crystal had her crazy time at seventeen. Got into boys. Drinking. Motorbikes. Rebelling, I suppose. Never neglected her animal but you could see her priorities were altering.'

'But she sorted herself out, right, Lesley?' asks Verity.

'Aye, in the end. I think she realised she was heading in the wrong direction. Moved herself out of the way of temptation. She got this little place. It was a godsend when the Musgraves offered her work.'

'She must have been thrilled,' says McAvoy warmly.

'She thinks the world of that little girl. Primrose. I had some image of a right snotty little princess but turns out she's a lovely kid. Head full of stories. Great imagination. Lovely manners.'

'You met her?'

'I did. Crystal had taken me to the Blacksmith's for Sunday lunch. Musgraves were in. Joel's wife, I forget her name – what a stunner. Very friendly family and you could see Primrose just idolised Crystal.'

'When was this?'

'Couple of Sundays ago? Primrose came and sat with us so Joel and the missus could have some alone time. That was when I got the impression Crystal was a bit sweet on Joel. I can't blame her but she knows better than to set her sights there. No, we just chatted with Primrose. She did some drawings and we talked horses. It was all very nice.'

McAvoy stops scribbling in his notebook and looks around him, pursing his lips. He looks as though he has abruptly woken up in a strange place and is not sure what he is doing there. He finds himself suddenly very aware that he is way beyond the boundary of what his team are investigating. He found a body last night. Felt an old man's blood splatter into his face. Shone a torch on a corpse. A man was skewered into fresh plaster by somebody with the strength of a bull. Instead of helping the team work the evidence he is out on his own, lifting up rocks and peering beneath in the hope that the answers will be written there in gleaming white paint.

'Last time we spoke you said you were going to see Joel yourself,' says Verity, appearing to sense McAvoy's preoccupation.

'No answer.' Lesley shrugs. 'Don't know what I expect him to say. You know as well as I do, everybody just thinks she's gone off on holiday and like your lot keep telling me, she's a grown woman.' Lesley picks at a frayed thread in her cuff. 'She's not though. She's my little girl.'

McAvoy stands up, as if to give himself more room to breathe. He pulls a face. 'This is a stupid question but you've tried her mobile a million times, yes?'

Lesley nods. 'Soon as I saw the Facebook message saying she'd gone on holiday I started ringing. Went to voicemail and then I got a message saying it was switched off. Like I told Angela, she's not got a passport.'

McAvoy turns to Verity. 'Have you requested the communications data?'

Verity shakes her head. 'No urgent threat to life. That's what the DS said when I made the request. Doesn't meet the guidelines.'

Lesley looks aghast at the very idea that there should be guidelines dictating how best to find her missing daughter. She looks down at the floor, working her jaw in angry circles.

'Call this chap,' says McAvoy, writing a name and number on his notepad and handing it to Verity. 'Dan. He runs a private company dealing with telecoms and databases. Home Office approved. Used to run our in-house service. Not a bad lad. Tell him you know Trish Pharaoh, he'll get on it.'

Verity smiles, looking eager, and makes her excuses. She heads outside to make the call.

'I just want to know she's safe,' says Lesley, looking up at McAvoy with eyes that plead for a gentle resolution to her nightmare. 'I've even walked the route they used to hack out on, in case she was lying there, injured or something. I know it's crazy but I can't just sit . . .'

McAvoy holds up a hand to stop her talking. He realises the insensitivity of the gesture and turns it into a somewhat incongruous royal wave. Irritated with himself, he sits back down next to Lesley – close enough to smell her Avon perfume and cheap cigarettes. Musgrave's mansion is a decent walk from here but it feels more like a world away. McAvoy tries to get a picture of the girl, sitting here on an evening, drinking tea from a mug, playing games on her phone, eating microwave meals and thinking about her horses. It's a pleasant enough mental image but McAvoy cannot help but wonder if she was hungry for more. Crystal would have been an anomaly if she had never allowed herself to fantasise about being lady of the manor.

'Was there a man in her life?' he asks, feeling like a maiden aunt enquiring whether a niece were walking out with any gentlemen callers.

'Preferred her horses,' says Lesley. She pulls a worried face. 'Not that she thought they were her horses, of course. I mean she looked after them . . .'

'I understand,' says McAvoy. 'And you're quite sure she didn't have feelings for anybody? Her social media posts are rather enigmatic.'

'I'd give my arm to see her happy,' says Lesley. 'I wasn't always a brilliant mum. I want her settled. To know love the way people seem to on the telly.'

'Any friends?' asks McAvoy. 'People who might know if she had any secrets? We all have secrets, don't we?'

Lesley scratches at her arms, scoring white marks in her pink skin. She seems to be struggling with something. 'It's just a fantasy, you know that, don't you?' She looks at McAvoy, tears in her eyes. 'She's not a bad girl. She went there just for the horses. Whose head wouldn't be turned?'

'Whatever it is, you can tell me,' he says, voice soft as tears falling on snow. 'All I want to do is help.'

Lesley sniffs. Gives a little nod. Reaches down to her handbag and pulls out a purple journal, patterned with unicorns. 'There aren't many entries. Got her it for Christmas. Told her she should write some of Primrose's stories down. You'll look after it, won't you?'

McAvoy reaches out and takes the notebook as if it were a priceless roll of parchment. He decides not to read it here and now. He doesn't want Lesley's eye on his blush as he digests the missing girl's words.

'I should have given it to you,' says Lesley, to Verity, as she comes back into the room. 'I don't know what I'm thinking half the time . . .'

McAvoy blushes as he sees the look on Verity's face. She looks cross with herself, as if she has missed some great learning experience; a chance to watch him in action. He feels ridiculous to be the subject of any such admiration. He sees himself as a blunderer who stumbles upon insights by accident. He clears his throat. Tries to steer them back to the present. 'You said you've walked the route. You know exactly where they used to hack out?'

Lesley nods. 'Primrose did all sorts of drawings. Drew a palace for horses and a lovely one of a unicorn. And some favourite bits from their usual route. She did a proper map of the circuit.'

'Do you have them?'

Lesley nods and pulls herself off the sofa. She leaves the living room and is back moments later, holding a sheaf of papers. 'They were stuck to the fridge,' she says, by way of explanation. She hands the pictures to McAvoy.

'Good eye,' he says approvingly, as he flicks through the images. They are clearly drawn by a child with a talent for art. The horses do not look like the squashed giraffes or big dogs that children in his experience tend to produce. They are good sketches, showing an enviable understanding of light, dark and shade.

'That one,' says Lesley unnecessarily.

McAvoy looks at the route that Primrose and Crystal have taken most days over the past months. The woods are swirls of dark green pencil and the paths made of deft brown strokes. Primrose has even drawn contours to show where the route is steepest. It is an aerial view and her home is represented as a pleasant assemblage of white boxes. The village and nearby farms are coloured in autumn tones and the cars are little cubes of blue and red. McAvoy takes in the whole picture and then peers at a small black rectangle that stands at the edge of a pale green field containing two sheep that, if the scale is to be believed, are slightly larger than a Ford Ka. The black oblong is concealed by trees on three sides but angled to face the road. Judging from the way Primrose has drawn the other vehicles, it looks to have reversed into the field.

'When you walked the route, was that vehicle parked there?' Lesley seems to be trying to get her bearings. 'No. Few tyre tracks, if I'm thinking of the right place.'

McAvoy rubs his cheek. He is thinking of a sick pony with a spur in its flank. He is thinking of a little girl with a fierce intelligence and an eye for detail. He is thinking of a black car and the way his friend's body thudded into the ground. Without another word, McAvoy pulls out his phone.

'Guv. It's me. Yes, yes, I know. I know. I am. You're right. Look, please, shush a moment. I need Ben to get me everything we have on a Joel Musgrave. And then I need every science officer we can lay our hands on.'

McAvoy stares at the picture in his lap. He just hopes to God that Pharaoh doesn't ask him what he's got to go on.

12

Trish Pharaoh ends the call and stares at the phone as if it were personally responsible for all the troubles in the world. She decides not to break it, though she does give the screen the sort of flick she reserves for wasps who have landed on the lip of her wine glass. Her children have insisted that she start buying cheap disposable mobiles that she can smash to pieces without worrying unduly about the cost. She has been through three smartphones in the past year and each has lost its life in a catastrophically violent manner. She almost bit through the screen of the last one when the man she was speaking to at her broadband supplier told her, for the eighth time, that he could not tell her at which point between 8 a.m. and 8 p.m. the engineer would be arriving at her house. Although she had rued the financial cost of replacing the phone, Pharaoh had felt thoroughly justified in taking out her frustration on an inanimate object. Plan B involved finding out the name and address of the person who was manning the customer helpline and then bludgeoning them to death with a phone book.

It's a little after 8 p.m. Pharaoh has already decided not to try going home tonight. Her eldest daughter, Sophia, is just about capable of looking after her three younger sisters on her own, though there is a good chance their evening meal will now consist of cereal and crisps. Pharaoh accepts this as part of her job. She runs the Major Incident Team and has received enough commendations over the past few years to be guaranteed a job as assistant chief constable with whatever force she chooses to apply to. Pharaoh is occasionally tempted by the idea of regular hours and more time with her children but in her heart she knows what she is good at. She's good at this. She's good at catching killers and rapists and gangsters. Moreover, the idea of wearing uniform again, albeit with pips and stripes on the shoulders, does not appeal. She never felt like she had the calves for flat shoes.

And then there's *him*. Her tame werewolf. She knows that if she were to take a position with another force she would have to take McAvoy with her. She finds the thought of their separation intolerable. She can just about stomach their situation as it stands. She sees him every day. He is the most significant man in her life. Her children view him like a favourite uncle and she is referred to as 'Auntie' by Lilah and Fin. She can live with this. She knows that Roisin owns great bites of his heart and soul. But she likes knowing that whatever crumbs are left over belong entirely to her.

Pharaoh wipes her forehead and her hand comes away damp. She has to keep flapping the V-neck of her black jumper to get some breeze onto her skin, and when she went to the toilet it took a major effort to get herself back into her tights. She's been having these hot flushes more and more often. Sometimes she feels like a baked potato that keeps cooking even after it has been removed from the microwave – that she could easily explode in a shower of jacket and mash.

Huffing her hair from her eyes and wiping her hand on her skirt, Pharaoh leans forward and places her forehead on the cool metal rail that overlooks the staircase on the second floor of Tower Grange Police Station. She is aware that her position is not particularly flattering but at the moment she doesn't much care. After all, a lot of her jealous colleagues believe she only reached her rank by spending a lot of time bent over and sweating.

Pharaoh doesn't know this station terribly well but it made

sense to conduct the interviews here and for the evening briefing to be held in one of the meeting rooms. It's an old-fashioned station and still retains the lingering odour of cigarettes and whiskey and poorly aired clothes. It stands on Holderness Road, the main artery heading from the heart of the city towards the coast. The locals in Hull take the east and west divide seriously. Back in the days of the trawling industry it was a recognised truth that those who lived on Holderness Road were the shore-based filleters and processers. The Hessle Roaders were the trawlermen. The industry has been dead for decades but the divisions still remain, though they are largely confined to which of the city's two rugby teams a person should support based on their geographical heritage. Hessle Road is Hull FC. Holderness Road is Hull Kingston Rovers. Pharaoh has long considered that rugby is a sport practised entirely by people who have not learned to appreciate football.

'Boss? Coming?'

Pharaoh turns. Ben Neilsen has poked his head out of the meeting room door and is looking at her nervously. She can tell that the other officers in the room have been nudging him and trying to persuade him to be the poor sod who goes and hurries her up. She can understand why he was selected for the dubious honour. After McAvoy, she rates no officer higher than Neilsen. His mastery of the databases and his eye for detail are extraordinary and he's a hard worker who never complains about the seemingly mundane tasks that he is so frequently handed. He's also a handsome devil who falls in love with a different woman each weekend and has never found a way to start a new relationship without some degree of overlap from the previous one.

'He makes my brain hurt,' says Pharaoh, turning on him with dark eyes. 'Flying Bloody Scotsman. He's swanning around in bloody Lincolnshire. He's got something but won't say what. And he wants the cavalry. Does he think I just snap my fingers?'

Neilsen gives an awkward smile. 'You will though, won't you? I mean, he wouldn't ask. It's not like he would be wasting your time. I mean, he's the sarge. This is what he's for.'

Pharaoh pulls a face. 'Still wearing your "I Love McAvoy" underpants are you, Ben?'

'With pride,' he says, grinning.

Pharaoh sags. She was only five minutes into the 8 p.m. briefing when her phone had rung to the familiar tune of 'Da Ya Think I'm Sexy' by Rod Stewart and she had hurried from the room amid a chorus of giggles from officers all too familiar with McAvoy's personalised ring tone.

'Mind if I sit in?'

Pharaoh turns at the sound of the unexpected voice. When she sees who has spoken it takes all her self-control not to let her face contort into a mask of intense dislike. When she sees who is trotting along behind him, she loses the battle and her mouth twists into a scowl.

'We won't make a sound, Trish,' says ACC Bruce Mallett. 'Just listening in.'

Behind the round, red-faced senior officer stands DCI Shaz Archer. She looks like she just stepped out of a salon, though Archer never looks anything other than spectacular. Her blonde hair shimmers as it catches the light and her cream silk blouse and tight faun pencil skirt cling to a size eight body that betrays not an ounce of fat. Her shoes cost more than Pharaoh's car. She's the head of the Drugs Squad and, despite her being a tenacious and determined officer, Pharaoh would like nothing better than to get her in a headlock and stick two fingers up her nose.

'Oh please do,' says Pharaoh, plastering on a fake smile. 'Perfect timing, actually. We were just getting started.'

'You have a suspect in the cells, I understand,' says Mallett, showing teeth that look as though they have been purloined from the corpse of a long-dead dog.

'Misinformed there, sir. But we're working on it. Good to see you, Shaz. I've got some sweeties in my desk drawer if you want to go watch *Peppa Pig* while the grown-ups talk.'

Archer smiles sweetly. She pushes past Mallett and her expensive perfume fills his world.

'I hope you don't think I'm intruding,' says Archer, in an accent that an elocution coach would find impossible to improve. 'Nice to be back with the old team. Might bring back memories. Some of them might even be good ones.'

'If they'd known you were coming they'd have shit in a cake,' says Pharaoh, under her breath, as she leads them towards the briefing room. Louder, she says, 'Intrude away. We're not a closed shop, and if you think there's a drugs angle you're not alone. Come on in.'

Pharaoh enters the briefing room. She glares at the unit and seeks out Andy Daniells, trying to impress upon him the importance of shutting up and behaving himself. She's pleased to see that the team understand immediately and sit up a little straighter in their chairs. She feels like a teacher telling an unruly class that they have special visitors today and that they should refrain from carving their names into one another's limbs.

'At the back, there, sir,' says Pharaoh, waving an arm. 'There should be a chair. DCI Archer, you might want to sit down the front there, next to DI Harte. Don't be frightened, he's actually quite good-looking if you ignore the nose. Are you acquainted? No? Well, we'll do the niceties later. I just want a quick catch-up and then we can be on our way, yes?'

Pharaoh stands in front of a whiteboard onto which several photographs have been pinned. Two show Mahesh Kahrivardan. One is a smiling, brown-faced man with nice eyes and short black hair flecked with grey. He lies on a pillow; the purple cover creased and dishevelled. Although the image stops half-way down his bare chest there is an air of nakedness about it and the smile on his face suggests that whoever was sitting astride him when the photo was taken was doing things to him that produced a more genuine grin than simply saying 'cheese'. The other photo shows Kahrivardan in death: head slumped forward, shoulders and torso stuck fast in the dry plaster and a small puddle of red in his shirt where the bicycle spoke went into his chest. There is only one photograph of Perry Royle. At Pharaoh's request, the image distributed to the press and the one used for her officers are markedly different. Today's cover story in the *Hull Daily Mail* showed Royle as an old man: frail and vulnerable. The image that stares out at her team from the board shows Royle in his prime, standing in crisp blue uniform and tall helmet complete with chin-strap. She wants her officers to think of Royle as a fallen comrade.

Pharaoh glances at the clock. 'The time is now 8.15 p.m. and this is the second briefing of the investigation team looking into the deaths of Mahesh Kahrivardan and the attempted murder of Perry Royle, which the computer has opted to call Operation Florizel. I'm not going to spend too long going on with speculation or repeating things you already know, but it's probably a good idea if we take a look at where we're at so we don't end up doing things twice or giving the brass any reason to think badly of us. You know how I lose sleep if I think those hard-working men and women on the top floor are feeling despondent.'

There is a titter of laughter from the officers but Pharaoh does not bother looking at Mallett. She does not like the man. Doesn't trust him either. And were she to truly think about it she would have some very hard questions for his preening little pet. Instead, she looks at DS Roseanne Mackintosh. She receives a nod, a tiny gesture of assent. She's happy for Pharaoh to carry on talking. It is Mackintosh who has put together the briefing notes and who has worked damn hard on making sure the investigation is being run efficiently. She's entitled to the credit in front of Mallett. But Mackintosh is an experienced officer and knows how to play the game.

Pharaoh takes a breath and launches in.

'You have the briefing notes in front of you thanks to Roseanne here, who may be the best thing to come out of Scotland since the deep-fried creme egg – absent company excepted. You can read them at your leisure. But for the benefit of the newcomers here's a swift breakdown. I think the correct word is précis but I've only ever seen that written down and don't know how to say it.

'Last night, Detective Sergeant McAvoy attended Autumn Days Care Home to speak with a gentleman by the name of Perry Royle. This was a social call but during the course of the evening, Royle alerted Hector to peculiar comings and goings at the neighbouring property. McAvoy dutifully went to examine the house. Once there, he discovered the body of Mahesh Kahrivardan. A black BMW then departed at speed from the property and Mr Royle, sadly, tried to stop it departing. The vehicle ploughed through him and he suffered a massive catalogue of injuries. The tyre marks would suggest that the vehicle was travelling at 40 mph when it struck him and there was no attempt to brake. If anything, whoever was driving put their foot down when they saw him. So it would be fair to say we're looking for a nasty bastard. With the best will in the world, Mr Royle was in the wrong place at the wrong time. He reacted like a cop and he may still die for it and I want you to remember that as you proceed.

'Mahesh Kahrivardan does not appear to have been a victim of circumstance. He didn't trip and skewer himself, let's put it that way. Now, what do we know about him? Well, we know quite a lot because he had previously been investigated for his part in human trafficking, which seems to me to suggest that he moved in circles where people were not 100 per cent nice to each other. We know he'd experienced money problems and had failed to pay court fines but that recently he became a lot more financially stable and had plenty of cash to splash around.

123

That cash no doubt helped buy the affections of his loving, live-in partner Abbey Poole, who is currently crying her eyes out in the comforting arms of a family liaison officer. Abbey has given us very little in terms of real intelligence but we have seized the family computer, iPad and Kindle and they have been analysed by our old friend Dan and his team of cyber cowboys. They've also been very helpful in securing access to his accounts. In terms of real information let's say that Kahrivardan had a rather complex income stream. On paper, he receives an £18,000 salary from a telecoms agency run from an address in Leicester, and which has been linked to various money-laundering scams over the past twelve months. The rent on his property is paid up for another year and the owner has reluctantly informed us that it was paid in cash, which has since been banked. So it would be fair to assume that the fancy car and the exotic holidays and the jewels that drip from Abbey's every digit come from somewhere else altogether. Abbey has admitted that Kahrivardan referred to himself as a property developer and, as far as she is aware, he had interests in several old buildings that are due for renovation.'

Pharaoh sucks on her lower lip and glances at Archer, who crosses her legs with a whisper of nylon and gives her a little smile, as if she's doing well.

'Bronte Hall is owned by TK Holdings Ltd. Director is Timothy Kimmell, who has an address in Richmond, Surrey. That address turns out to be sheltered housing. And Timothy Kimmell turns out to be ninety-one years old. Used to run a building firm when he was a younger man. Perfectly nice life but nothing to suggest he wanted to use his twilight years as a property tycoon. And, according to the local plods in Surrey, he hasn't known who he is or where he is for years. TK Holdings Ltd owns an awful lot of very tasty property. Some are owned through subsidiaries, and there is a separate firm, registered under the same name, responsible for security at the empty premises and for renovations on another. They all lead back to this poor old bugger who has no idea that on paper he's a bloody millionaire. We're trying to tie them together into one easy-on-the-brain package but that's going to take time. For now all we know is that there are a dozen places owned by TK within an hour's drive of Hull so it would make sense to start checking them one by one.'

Pharaoh pauses, taking a breath.

'The car,' she says. 'The BMW belonged to Kahrivardan. A little over eight hours ago it was recovered from the car park at the Odeon cinema on Kingston Retail Park. Now, Ben has been working his wonders and has managed to secure the CCTV from that region for the preceding twenty-four hours and has been going through it in a way that makes me wonder if he's actually human. Benjamin, do you want to share with the group?'

Neilsen gives a nod of thanks to Pharaoh. 'The vehicle was deposited at 12.05 p.m. We know it was on Castle Street prior to that and we think we may have a glimpse of it passing Yorkshire Bank on Hessle Road around five minutes earlier. What we have for certain is an image of a solitary figure getting out of the car at 12.05 p.m. in the car park of the Odeon. The figure is unidentifiable facially because they are wearing a hooded top but there is a white flash on their footwear that we have been able to follow through the network of cameras.'

Neilsen pulls a sheaf of papers from beneath his hard-backed chair and hands them back over his shoulder. There are mutterings of thanks as the documents are passed around.

'The suspect left the vehicle and headed through the car park on the retail estate. He then turned left on Castle Street. The next we see of him is as he crosses the roundabout at the bottom of Hessle Road. His face is still covered. Some 220 metres further up the road he calls in at a newsagent's where he purchases two bottles of cheap orange fizzy drink and a scratch card.'

Neilsen smiles, listening as the officers turn over the next page in the bundle. Then the mutterings of approval start.

'He didn't spot the camera mounted behind the till. So we're looking at our prime suspect.'

Pharaoh finally lets herself look at Mallett. He isn't smiling but he looks as enthused as the rest of her team.

'Facial recognition software has already given us a match. This man is Vasiliy Stroitelev, thirty-eight years old. Native of Kutaisi in Georgia. He made a claim for asylum in Belfast in 2007 but then disappeared from the system. His name was given to Operation Trident in 2013 as being a minor player in a people-smuggling operation. We know he has connections with organised crime in Kutaisi because just about everybody in that part of the world can count some uncle or cousin as a victim of the local mafia. But his record in Kutaisi seems largely clean. We have his face in the database as part of the Trident operation, which, as with so many of their brilliant ideas, led to nothing. What we do know is that Kutaisi is linked to the man on the next page.'

Neilsen waits a moment. He was right to anticipate the mutterings of 'fuck' and 'Jesus Christ'.

'Meet Sebag Sotkilava. He's fifty-three, though I'll admit it's hard to tell. He's a very, very nasty piece of work. He's got convictions for blackmail, drug-trafficking, kidnapping, racketeering and witness tampering. Until 2009 he was a soldier with the Kutaisi branch of the Georgian mafia. He was a true soldier. In 2013, at the same time Operation Trident was learning about Stroitelev, they learned that Sotkilava was in the UK. Information received suggested that he had been sent over from Kutaisi to shut down an outfit that was competing against their interests in Britain. Trident's informants were vague about what happened next but none of Sotkilava's men made it home. It was presumed that Sotkilava was at the bottom of a river somewhere but six months ago he was spotted by a surveillance unit meeting with a Hungarian who we simply know by the name Basil. Basil helps people make it to Britain. You pay him, he'll find a way to get you here. Pay him enough, it might not even be too uncomfortable.'

Pharaoh sees her team starting to squint. Their heads are swimming with names and information.

'Thanks, Ben,' she says gently. 'So, we have a murdered people-trafficker. And we have a low-level criminal from Georgia who possesses a tenuous link to a very, very bad man. We have a senile pensioner who owns a multimillion-pound property business. And oh yes, we have the icing on the cake. Sophie?'

Sophie Kirkland turns in her chair to face the other officers. 'The murder weapon,' she says casually. 'A sharpened bicycle spoke. We've run that through Europol for matches and we've got a hit. The immigrant camp outside Calais. A man was found dead inside a makeshift tent, laid out on the floor and with his face burned down to bone. It would be fair to say the authorities there have taken an "I don't give a merde" approach to the investigation but he was identified by other members of the camp as being called Manu and an unusually thorough pathologist found a hole right through him. Said he had seen such injuries before – during work with NATO in West Africa. ID in camp suggests the victim was Mozambican. There's some story about how he arrived in camp frozen to the underside of a lorry. Kept himself to himself. Some talk of a friend called Aishita but again, not much concrete.'

DI Harte pulls a face and gives her his attention. 'Are you saying it's connected?'

'Earlier today I oversaw the search of Perry Royle's bedroom at the Autumn Days Care Home. In the back of the book on his bedside table he had written down the number plates of any vehicles he saw coming and going from Bronte Hall. We've checked. Some belonged to the builders working on the place. The other three? All reported stolen in the past two weeks. If they're professionals they'll know to keep changing vehicles but they didn't reckon on old Perry. What's more, he gave descriptions of the individuals he glimpsed coming and going from the property. In police speak, it would be fair to say one of the individuals was an IC3 male. In Perry's words, it was a skinny black man in a bobble hat.'

'A black male and two white men,' says Harte, sounding unimpressed. 'And we've dreamed up the rest from conjecture and hope, have we?'

'We don't dream in this department, Detective Inspector,' says Pharaoh icily. 'We think. We speculate. We take imaginative leaps. And that's why we have a clean-up rate that every other force wants to emulate.'

Harte seems about to argue but instead raises his hands in surrender. 'Sorry, boss, just seems a bit weak . . .'

'Don't let that trouble you,' says Pharaoh, thawing a little. 'I have a reputation for letting my officers pursue their theories.'

Nobody speaks for a moment. One or two pull embarrassed faces.

'Where exactly is the sarge?' asks Kirkland, as tactfully as she can.

'Following up on some of the material evidence,' says Pharaoh blithely. 'There's a chance that this investigation may be linked to a missing girl enquiry in Lincolnshire but McAvoy is on top of that. We'll feed back to the team as and when.'

In the front row, Archer coughs and slides her legs against one another, like a cricket playing a tune.

'Sotkilava could actually be the same man that we have been hearing whispers about,' she says. 'A couple of informants have been claiming that the status quo has changed. There has been a vacuum in the drugs trade for nearly two years and Sotkilava may be one of the men trying to fill it. We've had reports of an Eastern European operation but we were told it was run by a Kosovan.'

Pharaoh cocks her head and pushes her hair out of her face. 'Kosovan doesn't always mean Kosovo,' she says. 'There are people round here who refers to Kosovans from Kurdistan and Albania. They think it's a term for all immigrants. Have you had a physical description?'

'Big. Bald. Scary.'

'Could be any number of people. But it's worth knowing. Thanks, Detective Chief Inspector.'

Archer nods and sits back, satisfied. Pharaoh cannot help noticing that Ben Neilsen has glanced at her several times and his eyes have lingered on her strong calf muscles and the tiny triangle of flesh visible between the buttons of her blouse. She wishes she could tell him, out loud, not even to think about it. Rumour has it that she's in a relationship with a rich married man who pays for the large house on the road to Beverley where she has been living for the past year. It's far too palatial for a copper and even though there is no doubt that Archer comes from money and gets handsomely rewarded for running the Drugs Squad, Pharaoh finds it extraordinary that she has not yet come to the attention of the professional standards department. Pharaoh is no stranger to their suspicions, although it is many years since she had a house or lifestyle that anybody could consider ostentatious. Her semi-detached house in Grimsby does not scream 'corruption'.

'We're going to work through the list of addresses held by TK Holdings and see what we can come up with. Dan will alert us to any technical data and we have uniforms and Police Community Support Officers making patrols within three miles of the newsagent's where the last footage was taken.' Pharaoh puffs out her cheeks and glances at Mallett. 'So, we're either very close to a breakthrough or we're pissing in the wind. But let's be positive, yes. And for God's sake, order some pizzas.'

Chairs scrape against the cord carpet. Bottles of pop hiss open. Tired men and women stretch and mutter and drop their papers and take the piss.

Pharaoh watches them all. Watches good men and women trying to do something that matters. Feels proud of them, even as she finds herself staring at the empty patch of air where her sergeant should be. Archer catches the look in her eye and gives the tiniest grin. Pharaoh turns away, reddening at being caught in such a daydream.

'I'm turning into him,' she mutters to herself. Then she pulls out her phone and looks at it, wondering whether to text him, call him or send him something funny.

'Good stuff,' says Mallett, and his warm hand lands on her waist; two fingers veering perilously close to her left buttock. 'Not a lot of evidence but I know better than to interfere. You'll keep me posted, yes? Be a help if you didn't upset Lincolnshire Police without going through the right channels though. Chief constable is a golfing buddy of mine.'

Pharaoh nods, promising to play nice and do nothing to cause him problems. Then she watches him leave and mouths the word 'twat' at his retreating form.

She turns and sees Neilsen and Archer, sitting on a desk, knees touching, making one another laugh. There is something between them. Something Pharaoh wishes she had not seen.

She returns to her phone.

'Andy,' she says, grabbing DC Daniells by the elbow and pulling him in close. 'The sarge wants to know everything we can find on a Joel Musgrave. Lives in Lincolnshire. Softly-softly.'

Daniells looks at her, and gives an overtly conspiratorial wink. 'Catchy monkey, eh boss?'

'You're a fucking idiot,' she says, smiling.

'But I'm your fucking idiot, boss.'

Pharaoh looks back to Neilsen and Archer and sees that their hands are touching, locked at the pinky-finger as they sit on the desk and go over a report.

'You silly bastard,' mutters Pharaoh.

'That too,' says Daniells.

13

Dirty fingerprints smear the cream page: a labyrinth of whorls and horseshoes picked out in grime. The prints are smudged but readable. They would serve as evidence, were it required. They blend with the sketch that has been scribbled into the inside flap of the diary. It's a drawing of a rosette, decorated with sparkles and stars. Inside, Crystal's name is written in large, looping letters. Each letter is a different colour. It reminds McAvoy of the graffiti he has glimpsed on the folders of schoolgirls – declarations of love; hearts and balloons; breathtaking in their innocence.

He flicks through the pages. Reads about Primrose's progress. About what the missing woman had for breakfast, dinner and tea. About her money worries and irritation with her broadband supplier. About her growing infatuation with an enigmatic man whom she refers to simply as J. McAvoy is good at crosswords and Sudoku and has read several textbooks on code-cracking and cyphers. The effort seems a bit wasted. He would recognise Joel Musgrave from Crystal's journal even if she had written his alias in Mandarin.

He rubs his forehead as he reads the passage from 4 January.

I touched my waist today. He was playful. Friendly. He was trying to move me out of the way but the way he did it meant something, didn't it? He let his hand linger longer than he needed to. I froze. Why did I do that? I'm such an idiot. What does he think of me now?

He flicks forward to 9 January. Bites his cheek.

This time it wasn't an accident. He didn't make a joke of it. Came right up to me and stuck his nose right against the skin on the back of my neck. I squealed and told him I reeked of horses and he just looked at me in this way that made me feel like I was going into a gallop. What does he want me to do? I haven't done anything to make him think I want him in that way. I haven't, I promise! I don't know how to do that stuff. I'm crap at flirting. I don't know how to face him.

He turns the pages: 11 January.

OMG!!! He kissed me. A genuine, full-on, tongues and tits and touches kiss. What am I going to do???!!!

14 January.

It happened. It was always going to. I think I'm happy. I don't know. He was funny with me afterwards. Not mean, just distant. This wasn't what I wanted. It was over before it started. I don't want to be that girl. I need to talk to him. I don't want it to be a mistake.

19 January.

He won't even look at me. I feel like I'm dying inside. I keep deciding that it's okay, that we both had fun and it's time to move on. But this little voice tells me that we have something special. Things could be so different. So GOOD!! I feel awful for V but we only get one life. I don't know what to do to get him to notice me again . . .

McAvoy breathes out slowly. Places his glass of lemonade on the wooden table and swats at one of the moths that seem to think he is some kind of lantern. They keep landing on his bare wrists and making his skin feel prickly.

'Are you some sort of Disney princess?' asks Verity, nodding at the latest creature to attempt to colonise his limbs. 'Could you train them to do the dishes and hang out washing and stuff?'

'I just met you today, Angela,' says McAvoy, with a mock scowl. 'It takes some people a lot longer than that to think they can start making fun of me.'

They are sitting outside the Blacksmith's Arms, waiting for the science officers to arrive. It's almost 9.30 p.m. and McAvoy is fighting the urge to call home and ask Roisin whether he is allowed to get a second packet of crisps. She regulates his diet with a strictness that is not present in other areas of their lives. While she never nags or tells him off about his long hours or his tendency to bring his work home with him, she thinks of it as her mission in life to ensure he lives to a ripe old age and never suffers type 2 diabetes along the way. As such, he eschews the takeaway food and snack-machine confectionery with which his colleagues sustain themselves. But his stomach is making the sort of noises normally associated with boats that sail too close to shore and he firmly believes that he would take a bite out of the picnic table if somebody put a little jam on it.

McAvoy looks back down at the diary. He doesn't know what to think. Doesn't know if he is being patronising by feeling sorry for the girl who wrote such wistful words. He has allowed his suspicions to become a fear. He knows that there is a very good chance that Crystal has been abducted. Held hostage at a tumbledown stately home across the river. Somebody is squeezing Musgrave for money. A ransom, for the safe return of his lover. And Musgrave is either struggling to pay, or refusing to.

Distracted, McAvoy starts reading up on the kidnap and ransom insurance policies of some of the big multinationals in the agricultural world. It's a billion-dollar industry. Companies like Popesco would have colossal policies with insurance firms in the event of a hostage-taking at one of their overseas plants. McAvoy clicks on a link. Case studies, outlining the benefits of using a K&R specialist. McAvoy wonders whether Popesco's policy covers affiliates or just direct members of staff and their families. His thoughts turn to Primrose. Begins to wonder. He's shaking his head when the buzzing of a mobile phone interrupts his train of thought.

'That's Dan calling back,' says Verity, and pulls her mobile from her handbag, sitting open on the tabletop and exposing a zipper that looks a lot like a shark.

McAvoy pushes his hair back from his face. Although Verity has given a few theatrical shivers it's not intolerably cold outside this old-fashioned pub with its thick walls and sloping roof, where the silence in the little beer garden is absolute. McAvoy plays with his own phone while Verity talks. He sends Roisin a message, apologising for the lateness of the hour and asking her to give the children an extra kiss from their great Battenberg of a father. She responds a moment later, having drawn a face on both of her feet with a felt-tip pen. Her right foot is a representation of herself and the left displays a larger set of features topped and tailed with unruly hair. In the five-second clip the right foot is whacking against the left like players in an end-of-the-pier Punch and Judy show. McAvoy has to fight his giggles.

'Something to share with the class?'

'It was a Snapchat. I can't play it back.'

Verity looks momentarily hurt but she regains her enthusiasm quickly. 'Dan's everything you said he was,' she says, slightly begrudgingly. 'Primrose appears to be where Joel claims. She just isn't answering her phone. Viola's mobile phone hasn't left this area in the past fourteen days. So if she's in London, she hasn't got it with her.'

'And Primrose?'

'She has a phone registered to her mother's account, despite what Musgrave said. Very hit and miss whether she takes it with her when she rides. It hasn't been active in nine days. Last contact with a phone mast was within a mile of home.'

McAvoy drums his fingers on the table and a moth takes off from the back of his hand. He follows its path, watching it flutter upwards to cast a silhouette onto the black line of trees and houses that sit, broodingly silent, across the curving road.

'Crystal?'

'Same. The Facebook message was uploaded in this area and she's been in contact with no other phone masts. Dan's also been back through her Facebook and she's admitted to a little crush on somebody she shouldn't have a crush on. A few of her friends liked it and one of those who said "tell me more" was Viola. Read into that what you will.'

McAvoy rubs at his forehead and looks back at the road, hoping to see the lights of the science unit. Half an hour ago a patrol car from Brigg turned up, followed closely by McAvoy's bulky people-carrier. The surly police constable who had been driving told him his tyres felt a little bald and that the steering pulled to the left. Then he joined his partner in the squad car and took off, leaving McAvoy feeling as though he had just experienced the worst kind of valet parking.

'And Joel?'

'A lot of phone calls over the past few days to a mobile registered to a Gert Van Vuuren. That mobile has been pinging around. Johannesburg, Malawi, then Amsterdam and London two days ago. I've Googled him. Board of directors at Popesco. Same company Musgrave floated a few years back. Seemingly just an old friend.'

'What else?'

'Not much in the way of work calls. Joel's received three video messages over the past few days but they were via a Snapchat forum so once they've been viewed, they're history.'

McAvoy chews on his lip. His stomach is rumbling and he feels like he has flies in his hair and on his skin. He can't work out what he is feeling. He hears his thoughts in Roisin's voice, telling him that she understands; it's normal to distract himself rather than focus on what he really feels. Is that what he is doing? Last night he saw an old man come apart in front of him; an old man he had grown to care about.

As McAvoy mulls over the new dead-ends he hears the sound of an approaching vehicle. 'This them?' asks Verity.

A green Land Rover cruises past, sending up a fine spray of mist from the grass verges. McAvoy glances at the driver. He's a stocky man with short hair and he scowls at the road as if it has done him harm. The other man's face is only visible for a moment, peering over the driver's extended forearm as if sneaking a glance over a wall. Then the vehicle has gone and McAvoy and Verity are staring at one another.

'That was Musgrave, or am I totally going mad?'

McAvoy nods his assent. 'You get the registration?'

'Last three letters. You?'

'First two. Enough for a partial. I'll ask for it to be run.'

McAvoy pulls out his phone while Verity rummages through her bag for a scrap of paper. They jot down the number plate between them. McAvoy is phoning through a vehicle registration search when the bright yellow lights of the forensics van illuminate the pub garden. Behind the wheel is a young, enthusiastic Asian man called Hardeep who greets McAvoy with a flamboyant wave and grins at him as he pulls into the car park. The sound of some hideous dance track emanates from the sound system.

'I'm going to see where he's going,' says Verity, nodding, as if making up her mind. 'You look after your unit. I'll radio if there's anything out of the ordinary.'

McAvoy turns to her. He feels a sudden need to protect her and then feels grotesque for the impulse. She is a police officer. An adult. A professional. Would he have felt the same had she been a man? McAvoy gives the matter a moment's thought and realises that yes, he probably would. He is about to urge her to call for the assistance of another officer. But as he opens his mouth to speak, Hardeep honks the horn and shrugs at him, raising his hands to indicate that he wants to know where he's going and that he hasn't got time to hang around.

McAvoy feels like he is being pulled in too many directions. Too many people need his attention. He barely takes in the information as the civilian officer at the control centre informs him that the Land Rover is registered to a London security company. He ends the call and turns back. Verity is already walking to her car. 'Hang back,' he says loudly. 'Just keep an eye out. Don't spook him. We don't even know what we're looking for.'

Verity waves her hand like a teenager acknowledging a parent's instructions not to talk to any strange men. Then she climbs into the car. An instant later the little white vehicle is roaring up the sloping hill to the sound of a gear stick being badly treated.

'McAvoy. You're on the clock here. I started charging Pharaoh an hour ago. Where do you want me?'

McAvoy stares after Verity's vehicle long after it is out of sight. He can feel a prickle in his fingers. He looks down, wondering if the moths have landed in number upon his skin. He shakes his hand as if scalded but the huge, spindle-limbed spider grips to his flesh as if glued in place. He flicks it away, shuddering at the sensation of its fat, meaty body against the nail of his index finger.

As he shivers, a moth flutters down and the wings touch his face. He tries to tell himself that the feeling is a pleasant one; a kiss from something pure and natural.

But as he walks over to the van he cannot help notice that the place where the moth touched him feels unnaturally cold. It tingles like a kiss from dead lips.

14

The girl has lost some of her fight. Her eyes are dull and her posture has gone slack, as though something important has snapped inside her. Her jaw hangs loose, lolling against her chest, and her hair dangles like pond weed in front of her pale face.

Musgrave stands in the doorway of the wine cellar and uses the torch from his phone to examine her. Her chest still rises and falls, like that of a sleeping cat. But she has only eaten scraps of the food he has brought her and her skeleton seems to be loose inside her skin.

The wine cellar used to be Musgrave's retreat. It smelled of earth and solitude. He used to enjoy breathing in the dust from the old bottles that glinted and winked in their hundreds, rack after rack disappearing towards the brick arches in the distance. He used to come down daily to shake the older of the vintages, rattling them in their nests of straw like a father massaging a child. He fucked the girl here, not so long ago. Didn't take long but it had felt exquisite. She'd been flaunting herself at him for an age. Reminded him of the hippy girls who used to come out to Africa on work placements. Bare feet and bangles. He's never been able to see a Maori tattoo on a bronzed calf without stiffening in his trousers. The girl was all pheromones and earthiness. He thought she'd understood what she was for. It was an animal act, not to be repeated. She couldn't talk about it. Couldn't tell. Not if she wanted them to still have something special.

Musgrave doubts he will come in here again. It stinks of her. Of piss and sweat and spilled food. It's been spoiled. Taken from him like so much else.

Musgrave considers her again. He finds himself wondering whether he wants her to die. The clarity of the thought shocks him. He had never thought himself capable of such a question. He has made his pact; he will atone if all goes well. He will get her medical help and he will do all in his power to help her forgive him. He had no choice. This had to be done. Were she to die, he might get away with everything and suffer no further penance. Could he allow himself such freedom? Did he deserve it? Perhaps, if not incarcerated, he could perform some good deeds to compensate for his actions. Perhaps, if she were to die, he could devote himself to benevolent works. He could give money to the poor, perhaps. He could be the best man imaginable.

He stops himself before his whispered thoughts become too persuasive. He considers the girl again. Reminds himself who she is.

'Lost in a daydream?'

Musgrave turns at the sound of the voice behind him. He hadn't heard the man approach.

'Come on back up. We're nearly ready.'

Musgrave follows the man up the stairs. The cellar opens into the stables. He smells fertiliser and rain on the air as he walks back through the mud to the house. Then he is walking back into the kitchen. On the table a disembodied head stares at him with sympathetic eyes.

'It's going to be okay, Joel,' says the man on the laptop screen. 'You've done everything they've asked. The samples match and it's clear from the plate counts she's in relatively good health. We can get through this. Just be strong.'

Musgrave slides onto a wooden chair and gives a short, nervous nod.

'You give me your word, yes? They won't try anything risky? It's not worth it. We shouldn't have made them wait . . .'

'Linskey has never let us down. He's very experienced. And he knows the priorities here.'

Musgrave turns and looks at the man who has lived in his home for the past four nights without ever leaving a trace of his presence. He's shorter than Musgrave but stocky and his razored hair parts around a horseshoe-shaped scar. He's dressed in his habitual black. His jacket looks bulky and uncomfortable and Musgrave knows, having lifted it from the back of a chair, that it is lined with Kevlar and too heavy to be worn by anybody other than somebody very fit and unconcerned with comfort.

'You understand, yes?' asks Musgrave. He's asked the question countless times before but needs confirmation.

'We have our orders, Joel. This is what we do.'

Musgrave turns back to the screen. The man he talks to looks older than Musgrave. He has neat white hair and a tanned, handsome face. His checked shirt is open at the neck and the chest beneath looks lean and well-muscled. This is a rich man in the prime of his life.

'Gert, I don't know if I can do this. There are things I haven't told you . . .'

'We know, Joel,' says the man on the screen. He says it soothingly and with kind eyes. 'That can all be taken care of. None of this is your fault. Leave it to us. This is what we pay for.'

Musgrave nods and drops his head. Behind him, Linskey gives a loud sniff. He looks around the kitchen, as if for the final time.

'We've had the final instructions,' says Linskey, to the room in general. 'One of my boys is picking up the bag. We've got two hours so by midnight this will all be over. Don't worry, it will all go off like clockwork. They're professionals too. It's an unusual situation but if we don't think of it like that, it's just another job. Relax, Joel.'

'I'm so sorry,' says Musgrave, to nobody in particular. 'I should have taken better care.'

'Don't worry,' says Linskey. 'We all make mistakes.'

'Just do it right,' says the man on the laptop.

Linskey smiles. The light in his eyes suggests he is looking forward to what is to follow.

As he closes the laptop, Musgrave has to fight to keep his true nature from showing in his face. He has taken steps to ensure tonight is turned to his advantage. He is already half a dozen steps ahead. Manu has given him an opportunity to win. The money buying his daughter's freedom is to be split down the middle. Half for him, half for the mercenaries brought in by Popesco to see his daughter's safe return. Before the night is over, he'll have his daughter, he'll have a nice stash of cash and he will be watching Linskey cut Manu and his associates into strips of jerky. He knows it's a gamble, but he also knows that in any competition he represents a good bet. He's too clever to mess this up. He's almost bulletproof. He's had Crystal in the wine cellar for days now and the big Scotsman didn't suspect a thing as he stood over the trapdoor and worried about the state of the horses. Musgrave looks up. He shivers as the man in black produces a handgun from a holster inside his jacket and checks the clip. A red light appears on the wall above the sink, bouncing back off the window to place a glowing beam on the back of Musgrave's hand.

Looking at the weaponry, at the sleek machines and polished boots and camouflaged features, Musgrave almost feels sorry for Manu. The poor bastard has no idea what he is walking into.

He will understand before the morning, thinks Joel. Before daybreak, he will have bled his apologies into a blood-blackened floor. And he will understand that when you come after Joel Musgrave, you come after a man who can always find a way to win.

15

Manu is adrift in a place that is more memory than dream. He has tried to keep himself awake but sleep has stolen over him and under him like oil and now he feels as though only his nose and eyes remain above its surface. In this place, caught between sleep and wakefulness, his recollections are vivid. The sensations he experienced before feel real to him again. His skin experiences the heat and the flies and the searing pain the way a mouth can remember the texture of favoured foods. His body betrays him with its vivid celebration of agonies he worked so hard to lose. Suddenly he remembers the feeling of the weapon in his hand, the taste of the sour beer on his tongue and the strange, jerking energy that seemed to affect his movements. Feels again the raw power of the handgun and the way his short, brown fingers wrapped around the black rubber grip like vines wrapping around a tree . . .

In his mind, Manu is back in Mozambique. He is a youngster again. He is about to take a life.

'He is nothing,' whispered Aishita, and his spittle flecked Manu's cheek. Manu had licked his lips and tasted blood. 'We are your family, little brother. We are your community. This is a cockroach. An insect. A bug. And you, Manu, you are a giant.'

Manu looked at the man. He was not old but his skin was sagging and his beard salted with grey. He tried to look up at Manu, to plead with his eyes, but the two Renamo soldiers held him face down and his cries were muffled by the dried earth.

'Be a man. Be a brother. Be Renamo!'

Manu heard cries. Heard distant gunshots and the sound of a woman crying as her husband's corpse was used as a mattress for her rape. She called for God and Jesus. No answer came.

Here, now, Manu remembers pulling the trigger more by accident than through any conscious decision. His muscles felt as though they were not his own. His limbs spasmed and his head seemed to fizz, as if insects were crawling into his ears and through his nostrils and biting at parts of him he did not know could feel.

The sound of the shot was almost drowned out by the raucous cheering of the other boys who had learned to bellow their support at any mention of their glorious cause. 'Renamo! Renamo!' Manu had deliberately kept his eyes open as he squeezed the trigger and, for an instant, he wondered whether, if he just concentrated hard enough, he could somehow rewind the past moments. He could suck the bullet back into the gun. He could pull it, softly, tenderly, from the smashed and mangled tissue and bone. The wounds in the man's head could come undone. And Manu would not be a murderer. He would still be a good son. He would not have shot his father in the head as the soldiers held him down. He would not be watching as they raped his sisters and burned his village. But the moment of regret was fleeting. His transformation was complete. He had become a man. Had proven himself loyal. Proven himself worthy of his place as Aishita's right hand . . .

'Manu. It is time.'

Manu jerks awake at the sound of Aishita's voice. The soldier squats in the darkness like a bear; white eyes like jewels, staring at him with the same intensity they always did. Aishita does not comprehend peace. He is a creation of war and blood; horror and murder. He has always been the man of whom Manu is afraid. Aishita is the face of his nightmares but also the creature who gives him strength.

The door to the small dark room opens and the two men enter. The older man is in the lead. He answers to 'Sebag' though Vasiliy rarely uses his name. He is a big man. Bigger than Aishita. Older than all of them. He has a straggly beard and his face looks as though it has been assembled from pieces of other men's flesh. A vivid white line runs across his brow and is bisected by another that runs from the line of his short grey hair to the tip of his nose. When he first saw it Manu had wondered if the wound had been self-inflicted; a statement of religious zeal and eternal emblem of Christ's martyrdom. Vasiliy told him the truth. Sebag had been shot in the face and the operation to remove the bullet had required the detachment of his face.

'They agree,' says Sebag, looking hard at Manu. He ignores Aishita. Ignores the girl. 'It was a good suggestion. The explosive charge was a statement. They got what they asked for and now it is our turn for the reward. You have earned your keep, Manu.'

The sound of voices causes the girl to stir. She looks like a sick dog, laid on her side with her arms and legs in front of her.

'She needs to be tidied a little. Can I trust that to you, Manu? I fear my friend Vasiliy would be ill-suited to the task. I presume you like boys more, eh? That's what I'd heard.'

Sebag laughs at his own joke and the sound bounces off the walls. Something occurs to him and he drags his fingernails through his beard in a way that looks painful. He flashes a scowl at the walls.

'They call this a prison? I've had homes that would fit in here twice. They do not know what we endure, Vasiliy.'

Manu disentangles himself from the chair. His bones crack as he moves. He smells his own sweat and the rank foulness of the enclosed space.

'He is not to die,' says Manu. 'The man. Father. I want him to feel the shame of this for ever.'

Beside him, Aishita clambers to his feet. He looks like he is being formed of shadows. When he stands he blocks Vasiliy from view.

'I want him dead,' says Aishita. 'I want to eat his heart and take his strength. But Manu is weak. He believes in the agony of shame. I feel no shame so I cannot understand.'

'Get her ready,' says Sebag, pointing at the pitiful specimen on the floor. 'Be gentle. If she bleeds she will arouse suspicion. She must understand what is needed. Can you make her understand, Manu? Can you make her do what she must?'

Manu looks at the girl. She is a broken, frightened thing. She no longer screeches or fights back. She no longer asks him his name or tries to bite through the gag. He knows how to talk to her. Knows how to make her do what she must. How to make her run to the other vehicle and not look back. Knows, above all, about the power of fear.

'Yes,' he says. 'I can make her see.'

16

Somehow, the surface of the water looks blacker than the sky that presses down upon it. The pond is roughly the size of a decent back garden and it reflects the moonlight in a way that makes him think of demons and nightmares. It is hard work to stop his imagination from expressing itself. He can imagine the splash a body would make upon cracking the still surface. Can all but hear the revolting sucking sound that the mud would make as it took a young girl's body into its dark embrace.

'Pretty spot. Think she's in there?'

McAvoy turns. The man who addresses him looks like an unfinished drawing of something vaguely humanoid. His blue protective suit covers his entirety and the part of his face that is not entombed in the flimsy material is covered with a breathing mask. It feels like being addressed by a loquacious Jelly Baby. Were it not for the bushy eyebrows that seek fresh air like weeds bursting through the gaps between paving slabs, McAvoy would not recognise forensic scientist and Hardeep's boss, Brian Drew.

'We don't even know if she's missing,' admits McAvoy again. 'But we have to be sure.'

'Divers on their way?'

'I've made the request.'

'They won't like it.'

'No. But it's important.'

Drew looks at him, as if considering an interesting new

specimen of barnacle. 'Wish I had your confidence about what constitutes important.'

McAvoy is standing like a statue. A knobbly footpath leads through a landscape stitched together from different shades of green – all stained charcoal and grey by the dark sky. This is where a black, vaguely rectangular vehicle parked up for long enough for Primrose Musgrave to notice it. It could be anything from a 4x4 to a particularly sombre ice cream van. Standing here, trying to make sense of his thoughts, McAvoy cannot help but admit that the location appears nothing like the drawing that the child had sketched in the nearby pub.

'Crystal is a young woman who loves horses and makes a little girl smile,' says McAvoy. 'She might have been harmed. That constitutes important.'

Drew examines him again. He shakes his head gently. 'Hard to put that on a budget sheet.'

'I don't worry about budget sheets. I worry about missing people.'

'I thought you'd be too busy for this palaver,' says Drew, pulling on his latex gloves and waving at the two other officers who are backing their white van down the pitted bridleway. 'Body stuck in a wall off Beverley Road? You were there, am I right?'

McAvoy did not know he was on such good terms with the middle-aged, heavily bearded man who served as the collections officer on the private unit used by Humberside Police whenever a case hinged on forensic evidence. Drew is pushing fifty and his accent is from somewhere in the Borders. McAvoy would have asked the large, ebullient science officer exactly where he comes from but he does not want him thinking that, as a fellow Scotsman, the two should automatically be friends.

'It's Pharaoh's budget, yes?' muses Drew. He shrugs, reaching a conclusion. 'She won't mind. She'd pay for you to fly to the moon if you asked her to.'

McAvoy turns away from the man in the blue suit and focuses instead on the mish-mash of half-moons and semicircles that pit the ground beneath his feet. He can smell the stagnant water. He can smell the foliage that has fallen from the trees to turn to mulch in the half-dark at the edges of the path. He can smell diesel, and the soft chemical odour of the latex gloves.

'Where do you want us to start? And what are you actually after?'

McAvoy considers the question. In truth, he does not know what he truly suspects. He wishes Pharaoh were beside him; her perfume and stale wine in his nostrils. He wishes Helen Tremberg were still here, following his suggestions and running up to him with new information like an eager terrier.

'Lysol test first. Signs of blood. Signs of struggle. Then fan out. We'll know it when we see it.'

McAvoy turns away before he can see the older man roll his eyes at the vagueness of the brief. Instead, McAvoy squats down. He picks a white stone from the path and holds it in his palm. He wonders what this place saw, what atrocities have happened in this cool, quiet cavern of trees, grasses and dead water.

'Your pocket's going,' says Drew, nodding at McAvoy's coat.

McAvoy takes the call. Andy Daniells is doing his best to keep his voice quiet but McAvoy can tell the bubbly young DC is distinctly enthused.

'Sarge, it's Andy. The boss said you wanted info on a Joel Musgrave? I've been at it. What you want first?'

McAvoy takes a breath. He steps away from the science officers and their mutterings as they start unloading equipment from the back of the van. He talks quietly into the phone, moving towards the treeline. He has a sudden moment of clarity. He has convinced himself of a conspiracy based on a dislike of a man who is cruel to his horses and a child's drawing of the fields around her home. He finds himself making a deal. He is willing to take the flak for being wrong, provided that the girls whose welfare he is concerned about are not actually in any danger. He finds himself desperate to be wrong.

'Andy, I don't even know what I'm hoping for. Tell me what you have.'

The portly DC takes a breath, suggesting there is much to come. 'On HOLMES, there's next to nothing. Same with the usual databases. But it occurred to me that just because we haven't got him in the system, doesn't mean he isn't on other people's radar, so I used the press database.'

McAvoy finds himself standing on damp grass. He raises his face, feeling a line of pure white moonlight kiss his skin. He closes his eyes and bathes in the moment of perfect connection.

'That's not an authorised database,' he says quietly.

'No, but when my bloke was a student he got a log-in and I've been keeping it up. It's a good tool, whatever the brass think about the cost.'

McAvoy cannot disagree with his colleague. There are a score of databases that would make the life of the CID incalculably easier but finding the money to subscribe is an obstacle that Humberside Police has yet to overcome.

'Go on, I'll pretend I haven't heard.'

McAvoy hears Andy shuffle his papers. His voice drops to an excited whisper.

'In 1992 Musgrave was twenty years old. He was studying anthropology at Durham. Spent a summer in Mozambique, right as the civil war was beginning to wind down, but while the blood was still wet. I've found an article in which he talks to the *Sydney Herald* about the work he is doing at a rehabilitation centre in Maputo. That's the capital. It's hard stuff – heart-breaking and horrible. It's in your inbox.'

'Thanks,' says McAvoy, unsure if he means it. 'And?'

'Another piece in 2005. Article in an American glossy about

how this company started by ethical campaigner Joel Musgrave is working to help the natives build a brighter future. It talks about how former child soldiers are being offered a chance at a new life.'

McAvoy swallows and realises his face must look as though he were eating something sour.

'There's more, Andy. Come on.'

'Last May,' says Daniells cautiously, 'Renamo rebels previously thought to have been wiped out began a series of raids on townships in rural Mozambique. Employees of various regeneration and agro companies were run off or taken hostage. I found a piece from Reuters suggesting Popesco paid a large sum to ensure the recovery of several senior members of staff. Telling line in the piece though – no information on the safety of the native workers.'

McAvoy rubs his hand through his hair and looks up at the moon. He begins to walk back and forth, haphazard and erratic, as if following the path of a bee. He stares at the rutted floor then up to the starless heavens. The sky is a mucky grey and the moon casts a sickly yellow light onto the fields.

'The migrant camp,' he says, pressing the heel of his hand into his eye. 'The body. The face . . .'

Daniells drops his voice. 'Sarge, I've also found mention of Musgrave and Popesco in a dossier of case studies used by a company called Blue Lightz.'

McAvoy stops his pacing. He knows the name. 'The security firm?'

Daniells seems to be trying to sound tactful. 'A few ex-cops run it, with former Special Forces and security experts from all over. Big deal. It's flagged on the system. All enquiries to go to NCA but I did a quick sweep online. You know who's in charge of a specialist division?'

McAvoy nods and tries to keep his breathing even as his mind floods with images of his own suffering. For an instant he is back in that hospital bed: all tubes and bandages and the beeping of the heart monitor; feeling Roisin's tears drip onto his ruined features as he tries to say 'I love you' through the pain. It feels as though the path of his life has been dictated by this man. Yes, he knows who runs Blue Lightz. McAvoy has never been a man to indulge in hatred, but he knows what Doug Roper cost him, and he would dearly love to get some of it back.

'Doug Roper,' says Daniells. 'Ex-boss of Humberside Police CID. I'm sure I don't need to give you much more than that. Done well since he left the area. Their firm provides security for Popesco and there's a quote from Musgrave talking about how without their expert help a crisis would have become a catastrophe.'

McAvoy scratches his cheek. He hears the sound of water being disturbed behind him. He smells the unmistakable stench of brackish liquid stirred by unwelcome intruders, then some cursing as Hardeep fails, again, to find the sleeve of his protective suit.

'I'll read the articles and call you back,' says McAvoy, feeling colour rush to his cheeks. He feels sick. Feels himself starting to shake. Hates himself for the effect that his old boss's name still has upon him. Unthinking, he reaches up and touches the scars that cut faint partings into his beard. He suddenly feels horribly far from home. He sees himself as others might: a colossal buffoon blundering about on a muddy path, trying to find a direction in the darkness. He swallows. 'Is the boss still there?'

'In her office, no doubt making life complicated for some poor bugger. I've sent you the briefing notes from tonight as well. Archer and Mallett came along. Was a bit awkward but we're making headway. Your mate Perry came up trumps. Great bit of info in his room. We're getting somewhere. Boss seems pleased, though it's hard to tell.'

'Does she know this? About Musgrave? Roper?'

'No.'

'Tell her,' says McAvoy urgently. 'Tell her what I know.'

'What do you know?' asks Daniells, as tactfully as the question can be couched.

McAvoy considers it and realises he simply cannot put into words the feeling of disquiet that sticks to his skeleton like tar.

'Ask her to call me back,' says McAvoy. 'And thanks, Andy.'

He terminates the call and is about to put the phone away when he glances at the screen. He has three missed phone calls from Verity.

He opens the voicemail and listens to her last message.

Turns on his heel and starts to run.

17

Sunday, 10.55 p.m.

The little digital readout on the dashboard tells the time in
jaunty, angular numbers that look, at least to Angela Verity, like
letters. She reads it, at first, as the word 'LOSS'. A minute ago,
it read 'LOSA', which struck her as unspeakably harsh. Her
mind has always worked this way. She makes words from the
letters in number plates. As a junior constable she nearly wet
herself in the squad car when control informed all cars they
were looking for a vehicle with the number plate 'VA91 NAL'.

She shakes herself back into the moment. She knows her
attention has a tendency to drift. She used to enjoy listening to
radio plays and audiobooks but she kept finding that she was
missing huge chunks of the plot, lost in a daydream or some
meandering remembrance. She knows she will have to work on
this aspect of her character. During surveillance work she has
regularly found herself unable to account for large chunks of
time.

She is in such a place now. Not quite sure of her surroundings. Not quite sure what just happened or where she is
supposed to be. Her mouth tastes peculiar. And there is a pain
running from her neck down to her fingertips. A pain that
grows with each staggered breath . . .

Verity suddenly recalls an impact. Yellow lights and obsidian
waters, metal girders like musical bar-lines. Red brake-lights.

Ghosts of grey-white smoke spiralling upwards from screeching tyres. Erratic mosaics of shattering glass: splintering like ice beneath heavy steps . . .

There is a sound, like a tree-trunk breaking in two, and she jerks her head up. She feels as though she were smashing herself free from pack ice. She is kicking for the surface; coming back to herself.

The tree-trunk breaks again, and Verity is suddenly staring at the scene in front of her through smashed glass and spider webs. She feels as if there were a veil across her vision. She becomes aware of the smell of burned rubber and spilled fuel. She shakes herself again. Feels damp upon her face.

She had been following the car in which Musgrave was passenger. It had wound its way through country roads then up through Great Limber and Melton Ross. They'd passed the petrol station with the sky-high prices and turned onto the dual carriageway. Eight miles. Then they swung right into Barton. She followed them down through the town centre, hanging back, hanging back, until they turned left onto the long road opposite the art gallery with the long roof of red tiles. Their car had looked, for a moment, as if it were approaching a giant mirror. An identical vehicle was heading towards it. They pulled up, window to window. Verity had hung back; her headlights off, nestled into a gap in a row of parked cars. The new 4x4 pulled away and the car in which Musgrave was travelling stayed where it was for perhaps five minutes. Verity took the opportunity to call McAvoy. The call went to voicemail and she ended it. A few moments later the same vehicle had cruised past her. She pressed her face into the passenger seat, smelling the fabric: all wet straw and damp natural fibres. When it had passed, she followed it – a different route this time, back up through the town with its old pubs and rundown townhouses, sporting takeaways in the ground floors and low-rent flats above. She had tailed the vehicle up to the roundabout and right towards the Humber Bridge. There was not much moonlight to see by and the strings and steel of the colossal structure were little more than pencil strokes against the night sky.

10.50 p.m., and she was driving over water; looking left at the blue-black ink that stretched away like an open fan, rippling as if something colossal trembled in its depths.

10.51 p.m., and the 4x4 halted. Just cruised to a stop in the centre of the carriageway. She had checked the time and called McAvoy again. Still nothing.

10.54 p.m. – *you loser, you silly, giddy girl* – and she saw the lights of another vehicle approaching in the other direction. A flat-bed pick-up truck. Old. Red. Y-registered. Big man driving, though she would not be able to say more than that. She had slowed her own car to a near crawl and begun to engage the video function on her mobile phone. Then the pick-up truck stopped, directly opposite the 4x4. She saw something dark. A shape, blacker than the night air. Rectangular. A briefcase. It arced across the metal barrier between the two opposing sides of the road. It missed the back of the pick-up by inches. Bounced off the tailgate and thudded onto the road.

Then she saw the little girl. A flimsy, pale-limbed ragdoll of a thing. She was running, blind, as if her eyes were covered; sprinting down the motorway with her arms in front of her, curving, inexorably, towards the flimsy metal barrier that barred the slope down to the footbridge, and the endless dark water hundreds of feet below.

Verity acted on instinct. She stopped the car and opened her door. Started to climb free from the driver's seat. 'Stop. Police. It's okay—'

The first shot killed her words. It punctured the stillness of the night. It stopped her dead.

Then came the shouts and the crackles and the bang, bang, bang of weapons being discharged. Her windscreen smashed and as she threw herself down behind the steering wheel she glimpsed men in black, holding automatic weapons that blossomed in red roses of fire and filled the sky with a symphony of violence.

10.55 p.m. She bellowed into her mobile phone, begging for help, then dropped it as the windscreen shattered and glass rained upon her like a storm of ice.

Here. Now. Down on the floor. Bleeding from the scalp.

She looks up and the scene before her seems to be moving at half the normal speed. Her head is ringing. There is a sharp, high-pitched wail in her left ear and her cheek feels sticky. She pokes her head out of the car door and sees the pick-up truck, dangling half over the side of the bridge. Two figures, clad in absolute black, are dragging somebody from the passenger seat. The little girl is gone. The 4x4 is screeching backwards towards her, smoke rising from the wheels. And then there is a terrible sound as the pick-up truck falls, in a scream of grinding metal, from the side of the bridge and tumbles, top-first, towards the dark water below.

Verity throws herself from the vehicle just before the 4x4 smashes into its bonnet and pushes it back down the carriageway. She hits the road with an impact that jars her bones and as she rolls over and over on the cold, wet road, she sees a man being dragged across the road by his arms and thrown into the back of the same 4x4 she had glimpsed only minutes before. Had the girl been running towards it? Had she followed the wrong car or had terror simply overwhelmed her?

As the sound in her head reaches a crescendo, Verity feels her knees begin to give way beneath her. As she tries to stand, something seems to pop in her left leg. There is no pain. She just looks at the spreading patch of red on her upper thigh with surprise.

That shouldn't be there. My leg doesn't look like that . . .

She looks up as the other 4x4 careers towards her. She

glimpses a man in a balaclava and sees the gun in his hand erupt in flame.

The burst of gunfire takes her in the sternum, the breast and the clavicle: three holes, neat as stitches, punched through, skin, tissue and bone.

18

Daybreak is still an hour away. There is still no sign of the pale orange sun that will eventually cast a line of flame between the twin darknesses of land and sky. Yet there is so much unnatural light on the bridge that Pharaoh has to turn her back to the harsh glare. She sees herself in silhouette on the rippling water: huge and ungainly; her hair sticking out like snakes. She briefly enjoys the feeling of being colossal.

Far below, the rear wheels of a Toyota Hilux jut, obscenely, from the half-submerged sandbank where it has come to rest. Three police dinghies and a further two rescue vessels bob on the black water: lights turning the divers into silk cut-outs and their shadows into flickering strips of cloth. She looks to the left. There are more police cars on the grass at the water's edge. A news van, quick off the mark, has commandeered a spot within the cordon and the driver is arguing with a uniformed officer about his right to be there. Further inland, half a dozen white-painted cottages gaze out across the waterway. Lights are on in every home. She can see tiny figures milling about on the road, looking up at the chaos overhead. She can hear more vehicles arriving; all raised voices and excited chatter. She can hear the grinding of metal: an ugly twisted screech, like a rope being tightened from both ends, and she realises that the broken guardrail is sagging under its own weight. She smells petrol and gunsmoke; wet sand and disturbed mud. It is a vague, ephemeral cocktail, seamed with the occasional whiff of open ocean, blown, bedraggled, into the Humber Estuary. She smells herself. Cigarettes and coffee and sweet perfume. She's wearing a borrowed coat, a bulky, all-weather affair that carried with it the aroma of spilled beer and damp Alsatian. She reaches out as she senses him. Closes her warm hand upon his big, broken knuckles and feels him flinch at the contact.

'I can see your house from here,' she says, without looking at him. 'Reckon we could persuade Roisin to send up a flask and a slice of banana bread?'

Beneath her hand, McAvoy's grip tightens on the rail. Then his fingers go slack, like an animal releasing a dying breath.

'It's taking all my energy not to jump over the side and swim home,' he says, his voice so devoid of emotion that she has to fight the urge to kick him just to see how he would respond.

'Reckon you'd make it?' asks Pharaoh, peering down into the depths. 'Not many do.'

'I'm a strong swimmer,' he says, then gives a little shake of his head, as though embarrassed at saying something that could be thought of as boastful. 'My dad taught me. Used to swim in the loch. Colder than this.'

'It's the currents though. They drag you under. It's like a bloody washing machine in places. And there are sandbanks everywhere. You might not land in a place deep enough to take you. You might just go straight into the mud and stick there like a cactus. I'd pay good money to see that, to be honest, but with the news crews and the senior officers around it might be frowned upon.'

Pharaoh turns and considers him. He's pale. His face makes her think of moonlight; all translucence and shadows. He's unbuttoned his shirt collar and pulled his tie loose. His coat is unfastened and the tails flap like a cloak. There's mud on the knees of his trousers. She's never seen him so dishevelled.

'If I told you it wasn't your fault, would you give me a kind smile and nod your head and agree with me and then ignore what I've said and carry on brooding and hating yourself?'

McAvoy's mouth twitches and he looks back down at the water. 'Probably.'

'Right then, I won't bother with any of that shit. I'll be your boss and not your friend, if that's what you need. And as your boss, I'm going to have to deliver you a serious bollocking about the fact that you've spent most of the past day and night poking about in a missing persons enquiry from another force, and with only the slimmest shreds of intelligence to go on. I'm going to have to slap your wrist for not keeping me properly informed and for upsetting the great and the good from Lincolnshire Police. But I'm not going to give you a bollocking about what happened to Angela Verity because that's not your fault.'

McAvoy stiffens at the mention of her name. He holds a breath and releases it. Pharaoh wonders whether it will catch the breeze and be snatched away across the water; sailing to Roisin's waiting, parted lips, like a spirit.

'I told her to follow the car,' he says.

'Are you sure?' asks Pharaoh. 'I don't think you would do that, Hector. I've never known you ask somebody to do anything, to be honest. You do it all yourself, which is half your trouble.'

'Well, I agreed with her when she said she would tail them . . .'

'And you insisted she take somebody else, yes?'

He looks down, remembering that dreadful moment of being pulled in too many directions. He should have tried harder. Should have insisted.

'She chose to go it alone. She could never have imagined what would happen. Nor could you. It turned to shit, Hector, but none of that is your fault. If you'd been here you'd probably be dead by now. You're a bigger target.'

McAvoy's reply is lost beneath the sound of the helicopter,

whirring overhead and casting geometric patterns onto the surface of the water. Below, a diver is waving their hand. They've found something.

'What's the latest?' shouts McAvoy, moving closer to Pharaoh. 'Angela? What have they said?'

Their arms come together and she feels the warmth of him. When he leans down to yell in her ear she hopes to Christ he doesn't notice the goose pimples on her skin.

'Touch and go,' shouts Pharaoh, and she starts coughing as the effort of shouting tickles her smoker's lungs. 'She's in surgery. They've got good people working on her. A day or two and she could have some of the coolest scars imaginable and a great story to tell her kids.'

'No kids,' says McAvoy.

'Well, give her time. She's young.'

McAvoy gestures with his head and they move to the rear of one of the police vans that are parked haphazardly on the bridge. White-suited science officers are busy yelling abuse at the police helicopter as the blades play havoc with their orderly collection of samples.

'Bloody chaos,' mutters Pharaoh, tucking in behind the open doors and enjoying being able to hear her own voice. She finds her little black cigarettes and lights one, sucking down a lungful and breathing out a plume of grey that drifts upwards to shroud McAvoy's face.

'What's the official line?' asks McAvoy. He seems embarrassed to ask, in case she might think he is concerned for his own prospects and reputation. She knows him better than that. He just wants to know how to help.

'Downplaying it all, as you can imagine,' says Pharaoh, waving her cigarette and pushing her hair behind her ear at the same time. 'An off-duty female police officer was the victim of a shooting on the Humber Bridge. During the incident, a vehicle left the carriageway and entered the water. Police are looking for the occupants of a further two vehicles thought to have been witnesses to the incident.'

McAvoy considers her. He screws up his face. 'Think anybody will buy that?'

'Well, we don't really know what's happened, so we may as well keep things small.'

Pharaoh sits down on the lip of the van. She drops ash down her cleavage and rubs it away. She feels tired suddenly. She hadn't even made it home when the call came in. She's been fighting fires for six hours. This is her first chance to speak to McAvoy in person, though she has sent him a handful of texts, telling him not to say anything until she's with him and that none of this is his fault. In truth, she doesn't know how the next few hours will pan out. Assistant Chief Constable Mallett is nominally in charge but Pharaoh is conducting things from the scene. Already she knows that this whole debacle is going to cost somebody dear and she is damn sure it isn't going to be herself or any of her team. By the time the first police officers arrived at the scene, Verity was bleeding to death on the damp road and the Toyota was slowly sinking beneath the water. There were no other vehicles in sight. The reports of gunfire had led to the immediate deployment of the armed response unit and its members are now milling about on the bridge, cradling weapons and looking mildly disappointed that they have not got anybody to shoot. The attendants in the toll booths on the Hull side of the bridge reported seeing flashes of fire and the sound of gunshots. The Hilux came through the toll booth at 10.50 p.m. The driver had been a bulky male, wearing a baseball cap and a zipped-up jacket. Pharaoh has no doubt that it contained the hostage-takers. The driver was a white male in a bulky black coat and he had told the attendant to keep the change, having paid the toll with a £2 coin. When Pharaoh asked to see the CCTV footage from the camera in the centre of the bridge, the attendant had informed her that it had not been working all night and that whatever had happened to lead to the shooting of Angela Verity, it had not been captured. But the witnesses had made it pretty clear. The Toyota came to a stop on one side of the bridge and the 4x4 on the other, separated by the central reservation. Another vehicle pulled up. There was a brief hiatus, and then the shooting began.

Pharaoh adjusts her bra strap and pulls a face. 'A 4x4 from the south side. One Hi-Lux, coming from the north, followed a short time later by another 4x4, which smashed the shit out of the Hi-Lux. Not an easy thing to do. Bloody hell, I'd hate to fill in the insurance forms. Then you've got Verity's daft little car in the middle of it all. Sounds like an exchange gone wrong, or a double-cross gone right. If the chopper can't pick up a tail from all this then I think I might chuck myself in.'

'The witnesses?' asks McAvoy. 'Other motorists? People down below?' He waves his hand in the general direction of his house and the huge gaping horseshoe of the estuary mouth with its assorted charcoal streaks and squares. 'There are thousands of people who live within earshot.'

Pharaoh taps her fingers on her teeth, wondering how much she needs to tell him. She can see that his mind is becoming waterlogged, like a sponge at saturation point. Soon, she knows, he will begin to leak.

'Somebody mentioned a girl,' she says with a sigh.

McAvoy goes rigid, and colour floods his cheeks. 'A girl?'

'There was a cyclist. Going towards the south bank. Turned his head at the sound of the shot. Says he could swear he saw a girl.'

'Crystal Heathers,' says McAvoy automatically. 'Early twenties. Stick thin. Probably wearing jodhpurs, boots . . .'

'A little girl,' says Pharaoh. 'Maybe eleven or twelve.'

McAvoy screws up his face. He gives a shake of his head as if there must be a mistake. He looks away, pulling the face he always pulls when he's trying to finish a crossword or answer a bonus question on *University Challenge*. He's thinking, hard.

'Alec's following up on everything you gave him,' says Pharaoh kindly.

McAvoy doesn't seem to hear her. He's staring off towards his house. She can see he's holding his phone as if it's a grenade. He wants to call Roisin so badly she can almost hear the plastic creaking under his grip.

'I heard,' says McAvoy, kicking, non-committally, at something on the breeze. 'Ben and Andy . . .'

'Ben and Andy have moved mountains trying to make sure nobody's asking too many questions about what you've been up to and why you were over the bridge in the first place,' says Pharaoh, sniffing. 'The statement Alec is working on is about as vague as we could word it. As far as the official channels go, you made the most tentative enquiries into the disappearance of Crystal Heathers based on physical evidence recovered from the murder scene at Bronte Hall. As a result of that you came into contact with Trainee DC Angela Verity. When you requested a forensics team, I obliged based on your proven track record of not fucking things up. Angela Verity then followed a vehicle she thought was acting suspiciously. In the course of that unsanctioned pursuit she was shot. DI Harte has therefore questioned the man whom we thought Angela was following when the incident occurred.'

'And?' asks McAvoy, huddling into his coat.

'And Joel Musgrave hasn't left the house all night. There's no 4x4 in his garden. Wife came back this evening. Had a lovely time in London with their daughter. So whoever Angela thought she was following, it wasn't him. Unless he's lying, which is entirely fucking possible'

McAvoy scowls at the darkness, shaking his head. He turns and peers round the back of the van towards the rail. He looks like he's about to jump. Pharaoh puts a hand on his back.

'This Crystal girl has probably just gone off on holiday, like she said. Musgrave's got a cast-iron alibi. There's no physical evidence to suggest anything else. Look, we sometimes get things wrong. We need your help on the case we're actually looking into – a case that involved the attempted murder of a man who meant a lot to you. I understand you've been trying to distract yourself, to be anywhere else but here. But playtime's over. We can get through all this. We can find who shot Angela. She sounds a good soul but you had only just met. You've got no reason to feel like it's all your fault. You've made a hypothesis out of receipts and drawings and conjecture, but if you think Crystal has been held as some sort of hostage at Bronte Hall then you're just going to have to change your thinking because the evidence doesn't add up.'

McAvoy gives her the closest he ever comes to a scowl. He looks at his phone and twitches his face so it looks like he is caught somewhere between smiling and bursting into tears.

McAvoy rubs at the dark patches at his temples. His face is paler than usual and his scars more pronounced. When he speaks, his voice is more heavily accented than Pharaoh is used to. He sounds the way he did when she met him – when he seemed broken by his mistreatment at the hands of Doug Roper.

'His daughter's home, is she?' asks McAvoy. 'His daughter who happens to look around ten or eleven years old and who's supposed to be in London? The daughter who drew a picture of a suspicious vehicle on the very path where she and Crystal hack out? The daughter who loves horses but hasn't been around to look after her own? That daughter? This whole thing seems crooked. I want to ring her school and find out whether she's been here or not but it's the middle of the night, and yes, I know I shouldn't be such a sap. But Trish, you know what I'm thinking here. And I don't think I want to be right . . .'

Pharaoh reaches out and puts a hand on his forearm. She

closes her fingers around the soft grey material of his coat and pulls him closer so she can talk to him properly.

'I read everything Andy sent me,' she says. 'I know where your mind is going.'

'Do you?'

'Alec has questioned Musgrave. He was happy to let them search the house. Daughter's been under the weather, which is why they came home early. Had a nice night in front of a movie and were in bed when Alec rang the bell. This isn't connected to the murder at Bronte Hall. Do you know what we have there? Have you even read the notes on the case we're actually supposed to be investigating? The property developer stuck in the wall with a bicycle spoke?'

McAvoy colours afresh, the way he does when he is being told off. He looks down at his phone and starts scrolling through his inbox.

'The last piece I read on the media database,' says McAvoy, holding the screen up for her to read. 'A hostage-taking in some godforsaken place called Nacololo in the Nacala corridor. Half a dozen Portuguese and Japanese executives and consultants taken by gunmen thought to have been a resurgent Renamo guerrilla group. They were all released unharmed though there was no mention of whether a ransom had been paid.'

'I've read it.'

'Popesco is one of the major agro and bioscience firms operating in that part of the world. Popesco, founded by Joel Musgrave. Popesco, which has been buying up land farmed by the natives for generations.' He stops, as if unsure whether the word 'native' is racist. Then he scowls afresh, annoyed at himself for letting himself be interrupted by his doubts. 'And then we've got the information about the death in Calais. A man called Manu. Another called Aishita. Have you read the piece from when Musgrave was over there as a student?'

Pharaoh looks at him and realises she has never seen him so

wound up. Until now, she had thought he was simply speculating wildly to avoid having to focus directly on the near death of Perry Royle. But she realises that he truly believes what he is saying.

'They buy up land over there,' says McAvoy. 'I read about it in *National Geographic*. They promise work to the locals. They pay them a pittance and make millions and pretend it's an act of philanthropy. I've seen it.'

Pharaoh cocks her head. 'How do you know about this stuff?'

He sags, deflating with each fresh breath. 'The year after I left university I went to Africa,' he says, as if admitting to some terrible past misdeed.

'You?' she asks, considering his pale, freckled skin and red hair. 'Did you not turn to toast?'

'I went out with my mother,' he says, and stares away, back towards the sea.

'Your mother?' asks Pharaoh, surprised. She has met his dad and likes the big, grey-haired crofter who always puts her in mind of some king from Norse mythology. She spent a fortnight at his home near Loch Ewe last summer, repairing the cracks in her relationship with her daughters. McAvoy's mother had not come up in conversation and with the exception of a couple of throwaway comments, Pharaoh had little reason to believe in her as a real person.

'We're not really close,' says McAvoy, then grimaces at the admission. 'Maybe we are. I don't know. She's English.'

'Well, that can't be easy,' says Pharaoh, trying to lighten the mood.

'She came on a walking holiday to Scotland when she was a student,' says McAvoy, looking at the floor. 'Spring 1975. They were staying in a youth hostel.'

'They?'

'Load of students from Cambridge. Dreaming of bagpipes and shortbread and cable-knit sweaters. She met my dad.'

Pharaoh stays silent, waiting for more. Several seconds elapse before she gives a curt nod, indicating he should damn well tell her the rest.

'They had a fling. She fell pregnant.'

'With you?'

'With my brother. Duncan.'

Pharaoh looks into his brown eyes and realises he is looking at something that only he can see. This admission is being dredged up like a bucket from a well.

'She wanted to make a go of things with Dad. They were only young. She was twenty, he was twenty-three. She told her parents and she married Dad. Duncan came along seven months later. I was a year after that. She tried to be a good mammy. Read us books and cooked our meals and bathed us but we were living in a broken-down old croft with my grandfather and the way Dad tells it, she woke up one morning and suddenly the romance of it had all gone. She was just poor and pointless in her own mind and living with strangers in a knackered old croft up a mountain.'

Pharaoh remembers the previous conversations they have had about his childhood. 'She left,' she says, trying to put the point in as kind a way as she can.

'I was four. Dad looked after us. Mam didn't come back into my life for years. Then when I was ten she turned up at the croft in a fancy car with a man who looked like he could buy us and sell us if he wanted to. She needed a divorce from Dad. And she wanted Duncan and me. Her new man had money. He could give us the best. She was sorry things hadn't worked out but she'd never stopped thinking about us.'

Pharaoh thinks of McAvoy's father. Thinks of the proud, handsome man with his broad shoulders and beautiful words; his quiet pride and fierce love.

'Why did you go?' asks Pharaoh, finding it impossible to imagine him being tempted by the offer.

McAvoy scrunches up his features: his face a mouth, biting down on a painful memory.

'The school I was at didn't know what to do with me,' he says, looking at his boots. 'I'd read everything. They let me spend my lessons just reading books or drawing or fiddling with the only knackered old computer in the place. Dad spoke to the head and he said that if I had the chance, I should go to a school that could challenge me. And Mam's new man was promising to pay. Duncan told them where to get off. He wanted nothing to do with her.'

'And you?'

'I thought I could make everybody happy,' he says, and his voice cracks. 'They said if I went to this boarding school I could go back to Dad in the holidays and see them every now and then. But it didn't work out like that. There was always something planned for me. Every break they took me away; spoiling me, treating me to things I hadn't earned. They showed me the world and by the time I was able to choose for myself, the idea of going back to the croft seemed impossible because so much time had elapsed and I felt like I'd betrayed everybody.'

'Oh Hector . . .'

'Don't feel sorry for me,' says McAvoy, flashing fire. 'I let them buy me. And it was the same after university. I dropped out and didn't know what to do with myself. I tried to go back home but I didn't feel I had any right to go there. By then Mam was what she had always wanted to be – an academic, an intellectual, a brain for hire. She was a bioscientist and she and her husband made a fortune selling their expertise to companies like Popesco. And they bought me again, just like they had when I was ten. They offered me a placement with one of their subsidiary firms. This was 1997. Maybe 1998. I spent two months in Congo, working for one of their subsidiaries, teaching natives how to run their farms like Westerners. We were in a compound, safe from the horrors, but I saw enough. I saw what people can do to each other. I saw what Western companies will do. I saw so much greed purporting to be philanthropy. I couldn't take it. I came home. Spent two years teaching rugby and then another year back with Dad before I finally became a policeman. But I saw enough of Africa to know that people will steal and steal and steal again and then expect their victims to say thank you.'

Pharaoh looks at him. There is sweat at his temples and his eyes are damp and angry. 'And you think Musgrave is like that? Why? Based on what? And how does any of it connect to what happened at Bronte Hall?'

McAvoy throws up his hands. 'I don't know,' he says feebly. 'Trish, I think I've killed somebody because I'm angry at my mam for walking out on us when I was a kid! Jesus, Angela could die . . .'

Pharaoh pulls him close and puts her hand to the back of his head. He resists for only a second and then his face is against her shoulder and his whole body is trembling against hers. She strokes his short, damp hair and shushes him like a frightened animal. She tries to ignore her own breath as it trickles out in short, staccato bursts.

'Hector, you haven't killed anybody. You're a good man. You're the best man I've ever known. You were following a lead. That's what you do. It's what you're for. We all have agendas and hang-ups and preconceptions. It's taken me a long time to find yours but the fact that you're very much against capitalist thieves is not exactly a terrible admission.'

She feels him give a half-hearted laugh against her. Hears him sniff. It is with regret bordering upon bereavement that she lets him leave her embrace.

'Can I talk to him?' he asks, and his damp eyes are round and open and utterly desperate.

'Musgrave? Alec's talked to him.'

'There's more to this. Read the article. Read it again. Manu. Aishita . . .'

'Hector, you've been awake for hours. You're not on top of your game.' She swallows hard, hating herself for the advice she is going to give. 'Go home. Hug the kids. Hug Roisin. Start again after a few hours.'

'I just need to ask him something. One thing, Trish. Please.'

Pharaoh sighs and closes her eyes. She cannot decide whether she is acting like a superior officer or an indulgent mum. 'Tell me, in all honesty, what do you think you're investigating?'

McAvoy pinches the bridge of his nose between forefinger and thumb, trying to massage the words into some form of cohesive theory. 'The groom,' he says. 'Crystal. I think somebody has taken her. Perhaps they kept her hostage at Bronte Hall. I don't know. But supposing somebody took Musgrave's daughter. Snatched her, because her father's a big player at a big company. Popesco. They have hostage insurance. They have specialists on hand to deal with these kinds of things. Blue Lightz. That's what they do. Mercenaries and crooked cops and all the worst people you can imagine. They don't want Crystal getting in the way or going to the police. So they keep her somewhere, while the specialists come up with a way to line their own pockets.'

'And Musgrave? He'd have to be one cold bastard if he was going to let people take risks with his daughter's safety,' says Pharaoh, chewing the inside of her mouth. She is trying to stretch her imagination. To see like McAvoy does. He follows the evidence wherever it may lead. But is he following evidence this time? Pharaoh isn't sure. Some braids on a blanket and a child's drawing are not enough to build a case around. And yet she trusts his instincts. What's more, she trusts her own. She will only let him go so far down any path that leads to him getting hurt.

Pharaoh squints at the lights of the helicopter. Her hair flaps across her face like a flag. 'And then we're back to the case that we're supposed to be looking into, yes?'

McAvoy nods, earnest and wet-faced. 'Then you can do what you want with me.'

Pharaoh cannot help but snort with laughter. She recovers, rolling her eyes and tutting. Then she reaches up and cups his face with both hands. Their shadows become one as the angle of the spotlight changes. They fuse together; stretching away over the water until their conjoined shapes flicker and dance at the very doorway of McAvoy's home.

19

The newsreader is a damp watercolour of pinks and browns; static on a screen that reflects the face of the man who watches. The features of both men seem to shimmer and distort, as if a rock has been thrown into a clear pool. For a moment, the watcher has duplicate eyes; the same pert, straight nose; the same curved lips with their subtle daubs of crushed cherry. Then the image on the screen changes and the watcher's face is his own once more. His eyes are black and seamed with tiny silver speckles, like coal that has been polished and buffed to a high sheen. His face is thin and handsome, his jawline sharp as folded paper. There is a smudge of stubble on his upper lip and a tuft of pointed hair beneath the lower. His expression is unreadable; his features absolutely still. It is impossible to tell whether the news report enthuses or disgusts him. He looks utterly impassive. If photographed, anybody trying to ascertain his mood would only be able to transfer their own insecurities and preconceptions onto the image. His truth is a deep, unfathomable thing and there are few who can read his mood with any degree of accuracy.

On the small, sleek tablet, he watches rolling footage of the scene at the Humber Bridge. There is a reporter at the scene. She's overweight with shag-scuffed hair and freckles. She's trying to look solemn. She's wearing a dark blue raincoat, and behind her a group of onlookers is assembled in an assortment of tiny front yards, looking at this interruption in their daily lives with interest. His face does not change as he spots *her*, the pikey bitch and her two fucking brats, looking footloose and perfect in their pyjamas and dressing gowns; shielding their eyes from the glare of the spotlights and staring up at the bridge as if it were a spaceship.

'Humberside Police has been at pains to downplay this incident but there is no doubting that gunshots were heard a little before 11 p.m. last night and this morning police divers are assembled around what looks like a pick-up truck, which, according to witnesses, fell from the Humber Bridge last night during an incident that left an off-duty policewoman fighting for her life.'

Doug Roper breathes in. Exhales, musically, with a soft, throaty hum. He is sitting in the back of a Porsche Cayenne. There is a girl on the back seat with him. She's fifteen. Skinny and knock-kneed. She smells the way he insisted: of damp hair and the day's previous clients. She is bleeding from the wound on her scalp where a clump of hair has been pulled out but she is too far gone on coke and champagne to be aware of it. Nor does she notice the news bulletin that is entertaining her companion. She will sleep for another few hours. She will wake with internal injuries and a speckling of burns about her buttocks and thighs but she will never remember being here, outside the house on Billionaires' Row.

Roper switches off the device and opens the car door. Steps out into the cold, dark night. Feels the kiss of raindrops on his hands and face.

Waiting on the driveway is his driver and closest associate. His name is Nestor. He is capable of inflicting extraordinary pain without ever allowing himself to appear energised by the act. Indeed, he has perfected the art of looking unremarkable. He is clean-shaven, with short brown hair and spectacles. His nose looks as though it may have been broken but anybody giving a physical description would find it difficult to say for certain. He wears a black jumper beneath a dark raincoat and when he speaks, his voice is completely accentless. Only when he strips does he become unforgettable. His body is a gallery of blue-black ink, from the huge tattoo of a church on his stomach to the epaulettes carved on his shoulders. He has stars on his knees and a devil winding its way across his back. He is more ink than skin. He is Roper's most trusted associate and he is very good at what he does.

'Quietly,' says Roper, nodding back towards the car and the dead computer screen. 'That's what I said. That's what I insisted upon. I'm not sure they fully understood.'

Nestor shrugs. He was not involved in the operation that has displeased his boss. Had he been, it would not have gone wrong.

'Clients are happy,' says Nestor. 'There was always going to be fuss.'

Roper rubs his face with a soft, clean hand. He gives a little nod. 'Do you think I was greedy?' he asks, and there is a smile in his eyes that does not reach his lips.

'Greed is not a sin,' says Nestor, after a brief pause. 'Greed is just hunger under a different name.'

Roper stands in the shadow of the huge mansion house and considers the unremarkable man who has been both ally and confidant for years. 'You're a philosopher, Nestor. If it wasn't for your other skills you could write motivational speeches.'

Nestor shrugs, and his sweater slips down to reveal the upper arches of a Kremlin tattoo.

'They've gone,' says Nestor. 'Dropped him off and went their separate ways. They were trying to make it seem like a job well done.'

'And was it?' asks Roper.

Nestor considers this. After a moment he reaches into his jacket and removes a packet of cigarettes. He removes one, with its flat, pinched filter, and lights it with the Ronson lighter that had been a gift upon his last birthday. 'It was always going to be loud,' says Nestor. 'They got her back, so the clients are happy.

And we got one of the bastards, so we get to send a message. There's no footage. It could be worse.'

Roper reaches out and takes the cigarette from Nestor's lips and places it between his own. It is a sweet, pungent Russian tobacco and it makes him think of a childhood spent listening to conversations he was not supposed to; hiding beneath the counter at his father's barbershop while dark-haired, flat-faced men sat with their hands covered and their necks exposed while a man they trusted took a blade to their tattooed throats.

'The press are interested,' says Roper.

'Only for now. There were gunshots. A cop got hurt. It was to be expected.'

'Why was she there?' asks Roper, wrinkling his nose as he gets a whiff of standing water and decaying foliage. 'This dying cop?'

'She spotted the car as it left Musgrove's. Followed. Got hurt by accident. Crossfire.'

Roper grimaces, unimpressed by the way fate has tried to fuck him over. He turns from Nestor. This street is one of the most sought-after addresses in the capital but for every occupied mansion on this palatial row there is another derelict home; set back from the road and protected by black, wrought-iron fences and the services of Blue Lightz Security Ltd. Recently, the *Guardian* reported on the scandal of so many opulent properties standing dishevelled and unoccupied at a time when the notion of affordable housing in London is becoming laughable. The article revealed that seemingly endless luxury homes had been bought by foreign investors and then left to rot; unloved and untended. The article failed to mention that one security firm looked after each of the ramshackle properties. And that company, in turn, had links to venture capitalists who would soon be buying the rundown homes at a fraction of their market value and selling them on at colossal profit. Neither did the piece mention the arms and legs that needed to be twisted in order for the owners to accept the services of Blue Lightz, or the offers of their venture capital associates.

'Crying shame,' says Nestor, turning to look at the huge, buttermilk-coloured mansion with its columns and porticos and high sash windows. 'Could be a beautiful home.'

'It will be again,' says Roper, extinguishing the cigarette against the underside of his leather shoes and depositing the butt in the pocket of his soft grey suit. 'Affordable housing. That's what London needs. Luxury apartments. Two million a pop. Safe from the scum of the earth.'

Nestor follows Roper as he heads towards the rear of the property. It has stood empty for nearly twenty-five years and the only people who have ventured inside since it was last occupied have done so to steal the limited contents, or to deter those with criminal intentions. The house belongs to TK Holdings, which paid just over £1 million for it eight months ago. The old man whose name is on the lease is now so demented he would be fortunate to remember his own name – let alone the volume of documents he signed at the request of his nephew, a solicitor from Shepherd's Bush who expunged his gambling debts by promising to supply a patsy for all Roper's property deals.

Roper gazes wistfully at the front of the mansion house. There are chipboard panels and coils of barbed wire in front of the upper windows; lethal, razor-edged barbs designed by the Russian army and bought in bulk by Blue Lightz for a steal.

'I might take the penthouse,' says Nestor quietly as they pass the double garage and crunch over the gravel to the outbuilding that houses the abandoned pool.

'The penthouse, Nestor?' asks Roper, amused.

'It will be luxurious, yes?'

Roper stops, and feels soft rain on his face and moonlight upon his back as he stands, motionless, in the tender half-dark of the morning. 'You think we'll renovate?'

'Of course.'

Roper scratches his head, amazed, as ever, at the naiveté of people who live their lives around violence and still believe the world to be a safe place.

'It is insured for £35 million. Insured with a company that we have an interest in. Before the year is out, it will burn, my friend.'

Nestor looks up at the house and appears a little saddened.

'You're not happy with your home, Nestor?' asks Roper. His ally lives in a large, three-bedroomed apartment in Chelsea and owns a further two properties in Bermondsey.

'I like the idea of owning a penthouse,' says Nestor, pouting.

'Then you shall, my friend. Pick a building. Tell me which one you want. It's yours.'

Nestor smiles, showing teeth stained yellow. 'Thank you, boss.'

'Has he spoken?' asks Roper, sliding open the double glass doors and stepping into the dark of the abandoned gym and swimming pool.

'He's said sorry a lot. Begged for his life. Told us he'll talk if we spare him.'

Roper shakes his head, disappointed at the weakness of man. Nestor closes the doors behind them and flicks on the bank of spotlights that his team erected months before. This place has been used for violence many times.

'Softer bulbs next time,' says Roper disapprovingly, as his shadow falls into the empty swimming pool. The pool is fifteen metres long and the tiles on its bottom show an Indian elephant surrounded by palm trees. A tall, out-of-shape man cowers in the deep end. He is naked and the blood from his head wounds has trickled all the way to his bare toes.

'He says it was his friend. A man called Sebag. Sebag and an African. He says he had no choice.'

Roper holds up a hand to shush his friend. He does not want to know too much.

'Vasiliy,' says Roper wistfully, as he lowers himself into the shallow end of the pool. His muscles flex as he moves. Everything about him is effortless and strong. 'It's Vasiliy, yes? Did I say that right? I'd hate to get it wrong. Hate to cause offence. You're my guest, after all.'

The wounded man in the deep end tries to make himself understood but his words come out as animal, incomprehensible screeches. He sounds as though he were drowning. A screwdriver has been pushed through his cheeks and blocks the hinge of his jaw.

'That looks nasty,' says Roper compassionately. 'And Christ, I wouldn't want that happening to my ankles. Hope you didn't plan on a career in athletics. Hope you didn't plan on breathing much after today, truth be told.'

Vasiliy gives a damp, pain-fuelled screech. He shuffles back into the corner of the pool. His chest is black with dried blood and the floor of the pool is slippy with his spilled fluids.

'Sebag, yes?' asks Roper, nodding, as if he understands.

Vasiliy nods. His eyes are full of tears and there is no fight in him.

'Let me see if I can answer some questions without having to ask them,' says Roper, and he begins the elaborate process of lighting a cigarette with his Ronson lighter, enjoying the flash as the gold band captures the light. 'Sebag runs a team of casuals. Grunts. Eastern Europeans who can lift and carry and do a little decorating and bacon-slicing if there is a need for it. He's ambitious. Thinks he's tough. The sort of man who says "yes" when he should run a mile. Somebody approaches him with an offer. Do this job with me and you will make money. Sebag says yes. Ropes you in. But it goes wrong, because you and Sebag are fucking morons. Better, stronger, more able men shoot your vehicle to bits. And you get dragged away to be treated horribly by a man who pays as much heed to your screams as he does to the crying of a ladybird. Am I about right?'

Vasiliy wraps his arms about himself. He looks broken. He looks as if he would like to die.

Roper shakes his head. He appears almost forlorn at having to do things like this.

'I don't know whether Sebag survived the fall,' he says. 'It's your friend that interests me. The one who came to you. I'd like to know a lot more about him and what he wants. And after that, all that really remains is the recompense. And Vasiliy, I warn you, I take recompense very seriously.'

On the lip of the pool, Nestor watches, transfixed, as the man he has known for most of his life produces a knife from the pocket of his trousers. He hits Vasiliy in the throat so hard that for a moment, it seems his eyes will pop out of his head.

Vasiliy falls. And Roper kneels above him.

Vasiliy is not a senior member of the criminal organisation to which he is affiliated. The ink upon his chest is little more than a token gesture. He has not been anointed as a full *vory*. Roper takes such associations seriously. He has spent his life believing in the sanctity of the life he has chosen. He believes, with absolute conviction, that the man he is about to kill has forfeited his right to life.

Nestor has seen many executions. In Siberia he witnessed a thief being sawn in half by three *vory*. Nestor had even helped to hold him down; watched him spitting out a spray of blood as the woodsaw bit through flesh, cartilage and bone. Nestor remembers that the victim survived until he was almost entirely sawn in half. He had looked upon his injuries almost with amusement, as if expecting an explanation for his laughable dissection.

'I don't often do this any more, Vasiliy,' says Roper apologetically. 'Be patient with me. It may hurt more than intended.'

It takes twenty minutes for Roper to cut the tattoo of a cat in a top hat from Vasiliy's chest. The tattoo is inexpertly done and it almost saddens Roper to see a picture with such power reduced to such a pitiful assemblage of blurs and blobs. The knife slips, several times, and eventually Nestor has to enter the pool and hold the victim's wrists so he cannot thrash around.

Vasiliy has lost consciousness by the time Roper starts forcing the patch of tattooed flesh into his throat. Nestor has to slap him to bring him around.

Later, both men agree, that Vasiliy went to his death like a coward. He choked upon a flap of his own skin; breathing his last ragged breaths around a twist of inked, bloodied meat. He could have died as a brave soldier, spitting out curses and vowing eternal damnation on his murderers. Instead, his death was a miserable thing. It brought Nestor little pleasure, and Roper even less. Roper holds on to the hope that his next murder will feel more exciting. He has always seen the truth in his father's contention that when a man has tired of killing, he has tired of life.

20

A thatched cottage painted the colour of dying lilies. Pillarbox-red front door. It has an enclosed garden: neat lawns and well-tended trees. In spring swallows will nest in the eaves and wild foxgloves and forget-me-nots will bloom alongside the planted roses and the white and silver dazzle of snow-in-summer.

There are two men inside this picturesque holiday cottage. One lies, naked and starfished, on a single bed in a guest room decorated for a child. He sleeps like a man revelling in the luxury of space. Despite the cold and the blustery morning breeze, his window is open. He sleeps better in the fresh air.

Downstairs is a figure more corpse than man. He wears striped pyjama bottoms and is sprawled on a well-worn sofa. He looks as though he should be surrounded by debris and smashed roof beams. He looks as though he has been dropped from a passing air ambulance.

Colin Ray feels as though he were waking from the heaviest drinking session of his life. His skull is pounding. The pain grips his jaw like the hands of a giant and he fears that if he were to do something hasty, like breathe, his entire head would crumple inwards like over-ripe fruit. And yet he finds his lips twitching into a smile. He has not felt true pain for a long time. When the Headhunters first took him, they beat him whenever they felt the urge. But the cracked ribs and broken bones, black eyes and fractured shins, were all sharp, neat pains that did little but make him even angrier. It was when they started injecting him that he began to lose sight of himself. His perimeters began to distort. He felt himself spreading. Puddling. His memories became hazy. He grew unsure what was real and what was imagination. His teeth dropped out at the back. Some days he would spit up cupfuls of blood without knowing whether it stemmed from his mouth or a deeper wound. Faces swam in the swirl. He remembered wives. Angry rows and bitter recriminations. There had been a son, perhaps. A small, tanned boy with brown eyes who liked to call him 'Dad'. He had tried. Tried so hard to remember the few days before they came for him. Kept telling himself, over and over, to remember *her*, her betrayal: her lies. And the other one. Broad shoulders. Hand stuffed in a packet of crisps. Big doe eyes and scars on her arms, as if she had stood in front of a bomb as it went off . . .

He slithers off the sofa, exhaling gently. He clutches his head, afraid it might explode. He can still smell the iodine and chemicals but there is something more familiar in among the cocktail. He can smell himself. Just the faintest trace of it. The copper. The thief-taker who spent the best part of thirty years spraying bile and spittle in the face of every little bastard who dared to think they were above the law. Colin Ray. The one they were all scared of. Ratty eyes and yellow teeth; hands like claws. He was a legend. He'd caught robbers and gangsters, rapists and murderers. He'd been suspended more times than anybody he knew and he had never apologised in his life.

There is a mirror above the sofa in the living room of the little cottage and Ray makes the decision to face it. He has only glimpsed himself in the weeks since the two men came for him. He has seen himself in the surface of the TV or the polished sheen of the tabletop. Now he realises it is time to see what they have turned him into.

He approaches the mirror with his eyes shut. Positions himself by sense and touch. Then he opens his eyes.

Ray looks upon himself. Five foot ten. Skinny enough for his collarbone and upper ribs to poke through his chest in a way that makes him think of a body long dead. His skin is buttery. Waxy. His eyes are coins on snow. He looks at his palm and spits on it, pushing his hair back from his long, lean face.

'Could be worse, Col,' says Ray, and he sniffs noisily. He swallows down a mouthful of mucus and gives a nod, as if he were checking himself before heading off to a club.

'You're bloody gorgeous,' says Owen, from the doorway.

Ray turns and sees the handsome bastard lounging against the frame. He's bare-chested. Muscular and scarred. He's shaved his greying hair down to the wood and it suits his round, well-proportioned face.

'Prettier than you, nancy-boy,' says Ray, and he pats his pyjama pockets looking for his cigarettes. He lights one and sucks the smoke into his lungs. He coughs as he breathes out and clutches his head, laughing into his own reflection.

'Feeling better?'

'Fucking peachy,' says Ray.

Ray takes another drag of his cigarette. Scratches his balls. Picks something from a tooth and examines his fingernails. The first shafts of morning sun find the gap in the hastily drawn curtains and Ray watches, fascinated, as the dust motes dance and eddy in the tunnel of illumination.

'Colin?' asks Owen. 'You're swaying, mate. Can I get you something? Whiskey? Mahon won't be back for a bit. He got up early. Took a call. Some incident up north. Colin?'

Owen hurries over to where Ray stands and Ray feels him put his arm around him, as if comforting an old man. He shrugs him off and pure fury floods his entire system. He turns on him, eyes filled with loathing.

'Don't fucking touch me. Don't ever fucking touch me, you rapist bastard.'

Owen steps back, hurt in his expression. The shaft of sunlight paints one half of his face a perfect magnolia.

'Rapist? What you talking—'

'You think I'm just some old nobody, don't you? That I'm broken. Dying. I remember, son. I remember who I am. I'm a fucking copper, no matter what anybody says. I know what you are. I remember. You were getting sent down when I arrived in Hull. Raped some slag in the woods. They caught you with a gun. Dropped the rape charges because you pleaded guilty and you went and did your time.'

Owen shakes his head angrily. 'Roper set me up. That's what all this is for! That's why we came for you. You know what he's capable of. We just didn't know you wouldn't remember any of it. Mahon wanted to kill you but I spoke up for you, Col. I know what Roper can do. I'd found out the truth . . .'

Ray slams both hands into the side of his head: a child blocking his ears. 'Roper! Fucking Doug Roper! Standing over me. Shaking his head. Inside her. Touching her . . .'

'Her?' asks Owen, stepping back. His skin is now in the light. The scars beaten onto his skin by endless tormentors gleam in the soft radiance.

Ray stops himself. He remembers it all. What she did to him. *Her.*

Shaz Fucking Archer.

Remembers what he swore to himself as her men plunged the hypodermic full of *krokdil* into his system.

'You're going to pay, Shaz. I'm going to make you watch him burn.'

Manu feels as though he has become part of the earth. His skin is heavy with the mud that clothes him. It took all his energy to drag himself here. He fell asleep without scraping the cloying substance from his clothes and skin. Now it feels as though his body is too cumbersome to lift. He wants to carry on lying here, embryonic, curled up among the leaves and the mire.

'Get up, little brother,' says Aishita, squatting beside him. There is mud on his boots but the rest of him is spotless and sodden. He has found a stream. Has washed himself clean.

Manu shakes his head. Presses his face back into the mire.

'He will wake soon,' says Aishita, pointing at Sebag's slumbering form. 'Now is the time, if we are to kill him.'

Manu raises his head. Sebag is as filthy as he is. He lies on his back, hands out at his sides. The mud on his neck is streaked with red though whether the blood is his own or somebody else's, Manu could not say.

'He's too strong,' says Manu petulantly. 'You do it.'

Aishita spreads his hands. 'I would gladly, little brother. Hand me a rock and I will smash his skull.'

Manu shifts his position. Raises a hand and scrapes mud from his face in clawed handfuls. He looks again at Aishita and the weight of failure floods him.

'They lied,' says Manu quietly. 'They set us up.'

Aishita nods gently. 'It was always a risk.'

'But we asked for so little. And there was so much at stake.'

'Perhaps he was lied to. I did not see his face.'

Manu props himself up. An excruciating pain shoots down his left arm and he falls back into the mud.

'They took Vasiliy.'

'Yes.'

'What will they do to him?'

'What would we have done to him?'

Manu considers this. His mind is engorged with memories of horrors witnessed and committed. He was once instructed to make an example of a soldier who had tried to run back to his village. The boy was no more than twelve. Manu maybe a year older. He had cut off the boy's nose, lips and hands, then buried him in the hard, dry earth. He and Aishita had eaten their evening meal to the sound of his screams. The following morning, little meat remained upon his face. The ants had done their work as effectively as the wriggling creatures that had burrowed into his bloodied limbs below the ground.

'We don't need him,' says Aishita, glancing at Sebag. 'We bought passage with a promise and that promise has become a lie. When he wakes, he will want to kill you, Manu.'

'It was not my fault. We did everything the way we planned. They broke their word.'

'Do you think that matters?'

Manu forces himself to sit up. Slowly, he takes in the view before him. He does not remember arriving here. Has only vague memories of his desperate, stumbling run across endless fields and woods, ducking low with every swoop of the helicopter and hearing Aishita's voice in his ear; his instruction to keep on, keep on. He looks at the peculiar place he has found shelter. The floor is all dirt and damp leaves but the walls are made of interwoven sticks shored up with rocks and the roof is an earth and brick construction. It smells of vegetation. Moss and felled pine.

'What is this place?' asks Manu.

'A rich man's land,' says Aishita, and spits. He scratches at the centre of his chest, as if it pains him. 'You told me of such places. Places where wise men would live, alone, and give wisdom to those who sought them out.'

Manu has a sudden memory of sharing this confidence. They had still been in Calais. They had yet to make friends with the Eritrean. They were cold and alone and they had little to talk about that did not involve their shared history of murder and war. Aishita had asked Manu to tell him of England and Manu had done so. He told him how rich men lived in great castles that their ancestors had won in battle. That today's royal family were the descendants of great warriors who had secured their throne with spilled blood. He told him of the great houses with their cool marble floors and wide staircases; footmen and carriages. He told him of the great mausoleums built on ancestral land to honour the dead. Told him of hermits; paid by great men to live on their land. He had learned this from a book, given to him so many years ago in the place with the soft sheets and the classrooms, the quiet voices and the games of football. It had been given to him by a young man with kind eyes and blond hair.

Manu crawls forward, slithering on his belly towards the opening of the hermitage. He peers out. The sky is a dreary grey-blue and a light rain swirls listlessly on the cool air. He looks out across mile upon mile of greenery. Woodland and grassland; copses of trees and brown earth striped by tractor teeth. He looks down at his feet.

'They will follow our footprints. They will find us.'

Aishita places a hand upon his shoulder. Brushes dirt from his back. 'Manu, did we come here for money or revenge?'

Manu screws up his eyes. He feels weak. Too weak for what must be done. 'For both. I wanted him to know. To feel the pain . . .'

'And he has.'

'But I want a future. I want a life. I have nothing and they have so much. So much, because of me.'

As he speaks, Manu feels himself growing angry and the anger seems to make him strong. He sits up. Starts kicking his boots against one another.

'We are not far from his home,' says Aishita, in the same voice he once used to coax his men into following him when their fear threatened to undo them. 'He will believe himself safe. We could still take what is owed.'

Manu snarls and the dried mud upon his face cracks. 'He will be laughing at us,' he says quietly. 'Laughing as he has done for so long.'

'He needs to learn,' says Aishita, his eyes cold. 'We have come far for our revenge. You bought your freedom with promises of money and blood. You brought me here, to a place of grey skies and rain. You persuaded strong, dangerous men to help you and you vowed there would be reward. You have survived, again, when others have fallen. Be what you truly are, Manu.'

As Aishita speaks, Sebag begins to stir. He growls, like a waking bear. If Manu is to kill him, now is the time. But to kill such an ally would be to accept that this is over. That he has failed. He needs Sebag's strength the way he needs Aishita's. His enemy will believe himself victorious. He will be vulnerable. Perhaps this is the way it was meant to be all along.

Manu takes Aishita's hand and pulls himself upright. He stands over Sebag and ensures he is the first thing he sees when he wakes. He is suddenly staring into a flickering picture: a ragged strip of memory. Glass breaking and the sound of groaning metal. The sudden lurch as the vehicle slipped backwards, teetering on the lip of the great bridge. Then the rush of cold air and the smash and splash as he was thrown into water so cold that he felt he was being crushed by it. And then Aishita. Dragging him towards the moonlight that danced upon the inky surface. His hands and knees, sinking into mud. Sebag, trapped and bellowing for help. And Manu had gone back. He had hauled him free. Clawed their way onto firm land. And together they had run.

'Don't stand over me,' growls Sebag, propping himself up. He pats his jacket, where he keeps his knife. Anger flashes in his face. 'You fucked us. You promised us they'd pay . . .'

Manu blocks out the light. Sebag squints, taking in the silhouette that seems to be a part of the forest floor.

'They will,' says Manu. 'They'll pay everything we're owed.'

21

Monday, 10.32 a.m.

A soft rain is falling from a joyless sky, making the green of the undulating Lincolnshire landscape seem somehow more lush and verdant. It looks to McAvoy as if somebody has started colouring in a pencil sketch and then got bored after completing the land. The only variety in the images flashing by the window is to be found in the occasional purple tree or clump of tangled wildflowers speckled with tiny pink blooms. All else is grey and green, grey and green, as though all the colour has bleached from above and sunk into the earth; descending like sand in an hourglass.

'It's the mustard,' says Pharaoh, indicating her sandwich and nodding approvingly. 'I don't even like mustard. But it just works, y'know. What you got?'

McAvoy looks across from the driver's seat. He has been allowed to drive Pharaoh's little sports car so that she can fully appreciate the packed lunch that Roisin made them before they left the house. 'I think it was cold sausages and goat's cheese with mango chutney.'

Pharaoh pulls a face. 'That doesn't seem worthy of her.'

'It's my favourite. After Nutella, anyway.'

Pharaoh broods on this for a while. 'White bread?'

'Of course.'

'Maybe, then. Did she put in a dessert? Flapjack? That's almost savoury. No cake? Ooh, yes, lemon drizzle . . .'

McAvoy concentrates on the road. The rain is coming down properly now. He has the windows open a crack so the car does not steam up and each time they pass through a village or hamlet he can hear the gentle trickle of overflowing gutters and the slap-slap-slap of water hitting stone. He feels a little brighter. He snatched three hours of sleep, on Pharaoh's orders. Roisin was waiting for him when he staggered home. She held him, wordlessly, and checked him for fresh injuries. Then she led him upstairs to bed and lay down beside him. When he woke, Roisin had not moved. She had not slept either. Just lay there, listening to him breathe and stroking his hands with her soft, perfect fingers.

'Have you any idea what "kk" means?' asks Pharaoh, as they begin the descent into Rothwell. 'Ooh, that pub looks cute. I've been there, I think.'

McAvoy shoots her a glance. 'kk? In a text you mean? It means okay, I think.'

Pharaoh seems pleased with this. 'It's from Sophia,' she explains. 'I thought she'd joined the Klan, or something. Why kk, though? It's no shorter than "ok".' She stops talking as she opens a file on her phone. Preliminary findings from the bridle-way near Musgrave's home. 'Tyre tracks from a 4x4,' she says, and every word is laced with scorn. 'That helps, in rural bloody Lincolnshire. Footprints . . . ooh, good, right, one of the boot-prints at the water's edge matches a print from the death room at Bronte Hall. Testing for fibres as we speak. That's promising. Come on, cheer up, you look like you've put your hand in your pocket and found a turd.'

McAvoy decides not to comment. He feels a little better than he did before he passed out. Roisin has put him back together.

'This the place?' asks Pharaoh, looking up from her sand-wich. 'Christ.'

McAvoy pulls into the driveway of Musgrave's home. It is a perfect white island between the green and the grey and the tumbling rain makes it look somehow more spectacular. McAvoy finds himself feeling like some nineteenth-century tenant farmer going to see his landlord to beg for more time to find the rent. The sensation shocks him. He suddenly wonders whether he has simply taken against Musgrave because of his own associations and preconceptions. McAvoy has despised prejudice his entire life. He blushes at the very thought of making a remark that could be construed as offensive. And yet he knows, deep inside himself, that Musgrave reminds him of the rich Englishman that his mother took up with, and so many others who made their money exploiting people like his father, like the poor bastards in Africa; like Crystal Heathers.

'She's a bonny one,' says Pharaoh, as they come to a halt. She's pointing at a wooden bench-swing, standing on the grass beneath a striped awning. A young girl sits upon it, listlessly rocking back and forth. The doorway of the main house stands open and an attractive middle-aged woman forms a pleasingly colourful shape against the darkness.

McAvoy checks his pockets and feels the reassuring shapes of his folded papers in his inside pocket; his glasses in the left-hand pocket of his long coat and his notebook in the right. He checks for the objects the way another man would check for wallet, keys and gun.

'That's Primrose?'

McAvoy nods, opening the door.

'Go steady,' says Pharaoh, brushing crumbs from her front. She stole a couple of hours' sleep in the caravan that stands in the McAvoys' back yard and has changed into a black dress that she left there one night when she was too drunk to drive home. Roisin has washed, dried and ironed it for her. It smells crisp and floral and warm and Pharaoh would be just as happy to cuddle it like a teddy as wear it.

McAvoy is already out of the car. He does not hunch into his coat or pull up his collar the way most people do when stepping into a downpour. He accepts the rain for what it is. Knows there is no way to avoid getting wet.

'Primrose?' asks McAvoy, walking around the car and approaching the swing.

Primrose stops swinging. Her posture hardens a little. She puts McAvoy in mind of a dog who has heard an unexpected noise.

'I'm Aector,' says McAvoy, and he walks a little smaller so as not to intimidate her with his size. 'It's a hard name to say. You can call me Hector, if you want. Or whatever name you would prefer. I'm a policeman. I'd like to talk to you.'

McAvoy comes to a halt in front of the girl. She's a pretty thing. Hair cut short, like a boy's. Earrings in delicate lobes. Big eyes and a cute, upturned nose. She's wearing leggings, flowery boots and a sloppy grey jumper. She's pale. Gaunt. There are sticking plasters on the nails of her right hand. Beside her on the bench is a yellow tiger; stained the same grey as the sky but smiling despite it all.

'Excuse me . . . hello . . .'

The woman from the doorway is running across the grass towards them. Her hair is piled up on top of her head and she is wearing a loose, one-piece playsuit that flaps as she approaches them. She looks as pale as her daughter. Her eyes are wide and her mouth is set in a grim, grey line. She wears no make-up or jewellery and the rain quickly soaks through her flimsy garment so that it clings to her slim, toned body. She is barefoot, and her feet squelch into the mud of her front lawn as she comes to a halt in front of McAvoy and Pharaoh.

'Mrs Musgrave, please, we're police officers.'

She stops, hands on hips, panting. She doubles over, and it seems the quick sprint has exhausted her. McAvoy examines her physique. Clearly she is a fit, active person. And yet a brief burst of speed has left her breathless?

'I'm sorry, I'm so sorry,' mutters Viola Musgrave, trying to laugh it off. She extends a damp hand and McAvoy takes it in his own. It's trembling, like a dying bird. 'Primrose, have you said hello to the nice man?'

'We were just getting to know each other,' says McAvoy, releasing her hand and looking back to Primrose. She has barely looked up. The angle of the rain has shifted and her leggings are now starting to stain a darker blue but she does not seem concerned by it. She does not even look as though she has registered that they are here.

'Bad sleep last night,' says Viola, flashing white teeth. She pushes a loose strand of damp hair from her face and seems to notice that it is raining. She looks down at herself and the loose clothes that cling to her body and make her appear to be at once naked and multicoloured. She wraps her arms around herself.

'We could pop somewhere dry,' says Pharaoh, as Viola tries to cover herself. 'Here, take Hector's coat.'

McAvoy shrugs out of his long coat and hands it to Viola, who takes it gratefully, and covers herself up. She's not much taller than Pharaoh and she seems to disappear into its folds.

'Primrose? Do you want to come in? A hot chocolate maybe? Marshmallows? Some biscuits?'

The girl levers herself off the chair and stands in the rain. In moments the downpour has plastered her short hair to her scalp and McAvoy notices it has been inexpertly cut; hacked shorter in some places than others. Roisin would say it had been cut with a knife and fork.

'My husband's not at home,' says Viola, leading them back across the grass. There is mud up her legs and the soles of her feet are dirty.

McAvoy offers her his arm as they climb the steps to the house, concerned she may slip. When he turns back to Pharaoh he sees that she is waiting for Primrose. She puts out her hand and the little girl takes it, without a word being spoken.

'I'll take my boots off,' says McAvoy and begins to bend down, but Viola shakes her head.

'It doesn't matter. I'm in and out with muddy boots all the time. We're getting new carpets anyway.'

McAvoy stands in the lobby of the big, high-ceilinged property and looks down at the wooden floor. It is covered with a variety of muddy bootprints.

'Towel?' asks Viola, and leads them through to the kitchen, with its terracotta tiles and big cooking range: artful prints and expensive pots and pans hanging from the wrought-iron grille overhead.

McAvoy glances back and sees that Pharaoh and Primrose are not behind them. 'Your girl's beautiful,' says McAvoy. 'Mine's almost through the terrible twos. She's going to break hearts. We all think our kids are beautiful, I suppose. Your Primrose really is a pretty thing.'

Viola shakes her hair loose and starts towelling it dry with a stripy dishtowel. When she is done she tosses it to McAvoy, who wipes his face, hair and hands. He can smell her. Skin cream. Hair serum. Patchouli and horse-hair.

'I'm McAvoy,' he says cheerily, and nods his thanks as she hands him back his sodden coat. He points in the vague direction of outside. 'That's Trish. She's a detective superintendent. I think Primrose is showing her where the bathroom is. Shall we get the kettle on for when they're back? That hot chocolate sounded good.'

Viola pauses for a moment, then nods, smiling a little too brightly. She disappears into a neighbouring room and comes back with a zip-up fleece top that she pulls on over her one-piece and zips to the throat. 'Don't tell anybody you saw me like this,' says Viola, as she begins fiddling with a complex coffee-maker that is all dials and dashes. 'Some fashion designer, eh? This is quite the look.'

'That looks like most of the high fashion I've seen,' says

McAvoy. 'It always looks like something you wouldn't want your dad to catch a glimpse of you in.'

'You're dressed nicely,' says Viola, expertly looking him up and down. 'That's a Hugo Boss, yes? Not sure about the tie but it has an old-fashioned kind of charm. And the waistcoat works. Very dapper.'

'I take no credit,' says McAvoy, and sweeps his eyes over the room. It's chaotic. There's a smell of bleach. He focuses on the edges: the nooks and crannies and grooves. Focuses on the places that people miss when they are wiping away blood. His eyes linger on a tiny splash of red, smeared around the lip of the table.

'Your wife?'

'Great eye for fashion. Better taste in clothes than she has in men.'

There is a hiss of steam as Viola twists a dial on the fancy coffee machine. She turns, smiling, and looks past him to where Pharaoh has reappeared in the doorway, still holding the little girl's hand. 'Tea, yes? And hot chocolate, Prim? Would you like one?'

McAvoy knows Pharaoh's body language like he knows his own. Her face is stone. There are red spots on her chest and on her cheeks and the frizzy strands of hair that she can never persuade to stay in a ponytail are coiling around her head with static. There is an air of Medusa about her general appearance.

'Primrose has been in the wars,' says Pharaoh, eyes wide. 'Nasty bruises on her knees and shins. Worse ones on her scalp. These little hairs behind her ears? Haircut this morning, was it? Did you do it yourself or bring in a lawnmower? Only all those pictures on the staircase show a smiling, tanned girl with long hair. And this poor lass looks like she's been working as a chimney sweep for a month.'

Viola looks to McAvoy but his smile is gone.

'We have some rough and tumble,' she says, straightening her back. 'And she's an outdoorsy sort of girl—'

'Yes, your husband said,' says McAvoy. 'Showed us the stables, actually. Which one's Primrose's pony? Remind me? Is it the poor sod with the buttercup burn and the colic? Hasn't been groomed properly in days? The one with the spur wedged in his side?'

Beside McAvoy, Primrose raises her head. 'Storm?' she asks, and looks at Pharaoh, questioningly. 'Can I see Storm?'

'Of course you can,' interrupts Viola, shrill and nervous, and she rushes to her daughter and takes her from Pharaoh. She kneels down and cups her face with her hands, smiling at her with bright, wet eyes. 'We'll spoil him, eh? Proper pamper him? Get him something lovely . . .'

'Crystal Heathers,' says McAvoy, leaning back against the table and looking at mother and daughter. 'She's missing.'

'Crystal?' asks Primrose, and she looks at McAvoy as if for the first time. Something seems to kick her in the guts and then she is burying her head in her mother's shoulder. 'I'm tired,' she mumbles, and Viola starts stroking her daughter's hair with short, angry gestures.

'You've been in London, I hear,' says Pharaoh. 'The pair of you? No phones, were there not? Bad signal area?'

McAvoy gives her no time to answer. Stands up straight, blocking the paltry light. 'You told DI Harte that you got home last night. Maybe 9 p.m.? Sat with Mr Musgrave and watched a film then went to bed. Didn't leave?'

'That's right,' says Viola, and as she raises herself from the floor she picks up her daughter like a toddler.

'And Crystal. You've heard nothing more from her? She just left you in the lurch and went off for a holiday, did she?'

Viola nods, pressing Primrose tighter to herself.

'Did you hear about the incident on the Humber Bridge last night?' asks Pharaoh, moving down to the far end of the kitchen.

She looks out of the window at the driving rain, forming puddles and pools in the pitted surface of the courtyard. 'A police officer got shot. She'd been investigating Crystal's disappearance. Hard worker. Young girl. Really took it to heart.'

'Your husband used to work for Popesco, is that right?' asks McAvoy, from the other side of the room. Viola has to whip her head around to keep up with the questions.

'Yes, it was his firm . . .'

'He's spent time in Africa, I understand. Lot of consultancy work, but going back years he was a proper Good Samaritan. Helped at a rehab centre. Got to know a lot of people who had suffered. Helped them find their feet. I admire that. Tried Africa myself but I couldn't stand how useless I was. There was so little I could do to help people. Had to come home to feel like I was making the slightest difference to people's lives. Joel stuck with his beliefs, I see. Helped so many people get a better life.'

'DI Harte didn't ask us any of this,' mutters Viola, pressing herself back into the table and disturbing the vase of dead flowers that stands at its centre. Dead petals fall, like feathers.

McAvoy crosses to her. Lowers his head and tries to put his eyes into her gaze. 'I think I know what's been happening, Mrs Musgrave. I think I know what you've been through.'

'We found a receipt from Thomas Bell's Equestrian in an abandoned mansion house in Hull,' says Pharaoh, approaching Viola from the other side. She reaches out and strokes Primrose's hair. 'Horrible place. Cold and damp and dark. We found a body there. Somebody who made his name helping immigrants into the country for a price. Somebody skewered him to the wall.'

'Enough!'

McAvoy and Pharaoh turn at the sudden interruption. They have not heard a car pull up. They have not heard footsteps.

'Get away from my wife and child,' says Joel Musgrave. He is radiating fury; standing, sodden to the skin, dripping water onto the tiles and staring at McAvoy in a way that makes him feel like he may burst into flames. McAvoy becomes aware of himself, looming over this woman and child, wrong-footing them with questions, slipping into their confidence just so he can trip them up.

'Mr Musgrave,' he says, and he feels shame appear on his cheeks in burning patches. 'We were asking your wife about Crystal—'

'Get out,' says Musgrave, teeth locked. 'Leave us alone.'

'Mr Musgrave,' says Pharaoh, putting herself between him and McAvoy and matching his stare with one of her own. 'You would do well to talk to us. I'm sure you realise by now that this situation is not going to get any easier.'

'Please,' says Musgrave, and some of the fight goes out of him. He flicks a glance at the window and the rain beyond. He blinks, rapidly, shaking his head as if in conversation with himself. 'You have to go. My lawyer will be here in moments.' He looks at his daughter with tired, gentle eyes. 'Did you speak to her? Alone? Without an adult? They could suspend you in an instant.'

McAvoy runs a hand through his hair. 'They sound like somebody else's words, Mr Musgrave.'

'Just go,' says Viola softly, into her daughter's damp hair.

Pharaoh is about to speak when her phone starts to ring. She curses, then apologises to Primrose for using a bad word in front of her. She answers with her name.

McAvoy watches her. She gives nothing away. Talks, quietly and rapidly, absorbing information, places, dates and names. She hangs up with a thank you.

'The pick-up that went into the Humber last night,' says Pharaoh, to the room in general. 'Stolen from an address off the Boulevard. Not far from one of the houses on the list of properties protected by Blue Lightz. Uniform have pulled the plywood off. Gordon Street Police Station, if you'd believe it.

Used to be a lovely nick in its day. Abandoned now, of course. But it's been used for the past twenty-four hours. Definite signs of life.'

'Please,' says Musgrave, raising a hand. He looks a little green, suddenly, as if his mouth were full of bile.

'We've got CCTV footage from the petrol station at Doncaster, too. Black 4x4 with a smashed bumper. False plates, of course, but the guy who filled up did so using a company credit card. Traceable to a security consultancy in London. A security consultancy that has helped Popesco out with all sorts of problems . . .'

Musgrave turns away. 'You have to leave.'

'We're going,' says Pharaoh, giving Viola a pitying shake of her head. 'Hector, have you got some reading materials for our family? Some pictures they might want to look at?'

McAvoy wants to say no. He wants to apologise and leave, taking all the cold and the violence and the bad memories with him. Instead he unfolds the papers from his pocket. Places the newspaper articles on the kitchen table. On the top is an image of a dead man, skewered through the chest into a damp plaster wall. The worst of the wounds have been pixelated, in a forlorn attempt at decency.

McAvoy stops and puts himself in Musgrave's eyeline. 'Have they taken her with them? Crystal? I understand. You tried to control it. Things have escalated. But if you can help . . .'

'Your daughter has been through something traumatic, Mr Musgrave,' says Pharaoh, rummaging in her pocket for her cigarettes. She lights one, slow and deliberate. Breathes out a plume of smoke. 'I thought maybe Hector was getting carried away but now I look at you, I see it. I reckon I could prove it, given time, but if you've been as fucking stupid as I think you have, you won't see jail. You'll be too busy being dead.'

'Go,' says Musgrave, and he manages a half-hearted smirk.

Pharaoh jerks her head and McAvoy follows like a dog. They step through the great front door and into the teeming rain.

'You think Blue Lightz killed Kahrivardan?' asks Pharaoh, stopping sharply. She looks pale. Tense, as if every part of her is insisting she go back in and hit people until they are honest with her.

'Perhaps,' says McAvoy, trying to stop his head spinning. 'More likely he discovered the hostage-takers at his property and they did him in to keep him quiet.'

'So who has Crystal?'

'My guess is that Blue Lightz has the answers. It's all . . . him!'

'You nearly swore there,' says Pharaoh, and she manages a smile. 'Go on. Call him a cunt.'

'Aye,' says McAvoy, and he pushes his hands into his pockets to hide the whiteness of his knuckles. 'Doug Bloody Roper.'

22

Joel Musgrave buries his face in his wife's hair. He presses his lips to her cheek, her neck, her shoulder. He pushes his face against his daughter's as if trying to press them all inside himself for safe keeping. This is his fault. He gambled with a life and it is going to cost him his own.

'We should have told them,' whispers Viola damply against his shirt. 'They seemed nice. I know what you said but, Joel . . . look at her, at Primrose . . . they can help . . .'

'It's too late,' says Musgrave, and his grip tightens on his child. He feels Primrose stiffen. She can smell them. Smell the bad men. Viola seems to sense the change in the texture of the air. She raises her hands to her face but the scream dies in her throat.

Slowly, pitifully, Musgrave turns as the door to the larder opens. The big man with the Russian accent is standing there, streaked with dirt. Beside him is the small, wiry African who looks upon Musgrave with such bright, burning loathing that it makes Musgrave feel as though his sins were being projected onto the wall behind him.

'Well done,' says Sebag. The knife in his hand disappears into the cuff of his jacket, which obscures his fingers, so it seems that the blade is a part of him. There is blood on his face and neck. 'That could have gone very badly.'

'You have to leave us alone,' says Musgrave. 'This wasn't my fault. Please, Manu, I tried . . .'

Manu tips his head back, listening to the words of his companion. His mouth twitches.

'We came for revenge. Came to help you see what betrayal and pain feel like. My friend here did not. He came for money. I will take money too. That's what you said, is it not? That money makes everything easier. Let us see.'

Slowly, Manu reaches down and takes the knife from Sebag's unresisting hand. He looks at the gleaming blade as if it is an old friend; a trusted ally. 'We're going to take what we came for, Joel.'

'Manu, this isn't who you are.' There is a desperate plea in Musgrave's voice. He looks as though he were witnessing a faithful old dog shake a baby in its teeth. 'Remember all I did for you. It wasn't my fault . . .'

Manu ignores him. He looks at Viola. At Primrose. He shakes his head, almost sorry that this is how things have to be. 'I know how to break men, Joel. You thought that the soldier I used to be was a demon – something that could be sent away. You thought that kindness and clean sheets and opportunity would work like medicine on the darkness inside me. But if a good man can be made with kindness, then a devil can be made through betrayal. Through violence. Through heartbreak. You may have been kind to me once. You thought you fixed me. But your betrayal undid everything. You showed me who I was. Aishita helped me become that man again. And now I'm going to do what I was created to do. I'm going to break your soul, and make you beg. And I'm going to smile as I do it.'

23

Halfway up Baker Street in Marylebone, London,
Monday, 6.18 p.m.

A huge, glass-fronted building that reflects the oily black sky and stares down on a jumbled jewellery box of coloured lights: buses, taxis, shops and restaurants; of vehicles grinding along the sodden road in a raucous symphony of hissing brakes and grinding gears, honking horns and rubber turning on tarmac.

Pharaoh parks in a space reserved for taxis. She has already alerted the borough commander to their presence and given the local control room her registration plate. Any traffic warden or uniformed cop who thinks about putting a ticket on her windscreen will find themselves regretting it.

She shoots McAvoy a glance. He's the colour of cold ashes. He's taken his coat off, at her insistence, but he holds it in his lap and looks like a teenager watching a horror movie from behind a cushion.

'It might not be him we see,' says Pharaoh, trying to catch his eye. 'And if it is, you just front it out. He's an old colleague. You go way back. You had your disagreements but you're doing fine. You're pleased to see he's doing so well. You don't need to pick at old scabs, Hector. And if he says anything shitty I'll punch him in the fucking throat.'

McAvoy gives her a nod. He's barely spoken for the past

hour. He's played with his phone a lot. Sent endless messages to Roisin and received words of encouragement in return.

Pharaoh peers up at the looming office block. It's unashamedly modern, with metal support beams propping up a colossal glass awning, which bleeds, in turn, into the fabric of the ten-storey construction. The ground floor houses coffee shops and a gym before giving way to the reception area.

'Shall we?'

McAvoy looks as though he were going to see a consultant for the results of a biopsy. He disentangles himself from the car and climbs out. As he tries to put himself back into his coat his car keys tumble from the pocket and he curses, putting his arm in the wrong sleeve.

'Hector, it's fine, it's fine . . .'

She understands what this is doing to him. Cannot blame him for his pain. Doug Roper almost cost him everything. It was four or five years ago, before Pharaoh had even met McAvoy. She knew Roper by reputation. Knew the slick, soulless fucker to be one hell of an operator with a clean-up record that was the pride of Humberside Police. She'd heard rumours, of course. Everybody had heard the stories about Doug and the Major Incident Team. Word was that guilt was not important. A conviction was what mattered, and Doug was the very best at putting people away. That's what he did with Shane Cadbury, the fat, dim-witted sex-pest who was found with Ella Butterworth's body in his grimy hovel on the Bransholme estate. Roper built a case against him that looked too strong to break. It was McAvoy, only recently transferred across from uniform, who found the holes in the case. It was McAvoy who identified the real killer. It was McAvoy who almost lost his life taking him down. And while McAvoy was in hospital, having his brutal wounds stitched back together, the top brass allowed Roper to slip away without a stain on his character and with his pension intact. For a long time afterwards, McAvoy was a pariah. He was labelled as a grass. He was accused of telling all sorts of lies about their beloved Roper. He had to half kill himself to regain respect and, even now, there are those who believe he is little more than an errand boy for the powers that be and who call him Pharaoh's poodle.

'Trish, I don't know if I can do this.'

The streetlight above his head illuminates the raindrops that form a mist around his big, open face. In this yellow light he looks like a ruined painting; a damp watercolour crumpled in an unforgiving hand.

'Hector, you're a fucking superstar. You catch killers. You can punch people so hard that there's always a risk of decapitation. Your family adore you. The team would have posters of you stuck to their workstations if I let them. And I've never met anybody I'm so proud to call a friend.' She looks up at him, exasperated at how steadfastly he clings to his own perceived uselessness. 'You're also investigating a murder and a hit and run. You suspect a kidnapping, maybe two. And the man in this office knows something about it. So forget the past. Forget what you think you know about him or what you fear he knows about you. Let's question him like anybody else and then let's get the fuck back up north before anybody suggests we get a room for the night and stay in fucking London.'

McAvoy's mouth twitches. He nods. Coughs. Straightens his clothes. Pharaoh slips her arm through his as they approach the desk and the blonde, impossibly beautiful girl who sits behind it; red lips and tasteful make-up, long lashes and teeth like sugar cubes.

'Blue Lightz, please,' says Pharaoh, looking at the girl and feeling very fat, very old and very inclined to punch anybody who dares to look pretty and young in her company.

'Are they expecting you?' asks the girl, with a big, wide-eyed smile.

Pharaoh grins, setting her mouth in a grim line. 'I have no fucking doubt.'

He's waiting as they come out of the elevator on the seventh floor. The double doors slide open and he's already there to meet them. He's smiling, but in a way that suggests he has been taught the art by somebody who has never seen the real thing.

'Hello, hello, hello,' says Roper. 'What's all this then?'

Pharaoh steps out of the lift ahead of McAvoy. 'Doug,' says Pharaoh, extending a hand. 'A long time.'

'Indeed,' says Roper. 'We never really got to know each other back in the good old days. Just a quick meet-and-greet, was it?'

'Something like that,' says Pharaoh. She turns, inviting McAvoy to join them. He hangs back, like a child who has been told to Sing Happy Birthday to his grandmother and then forgotten the words.

'McAvoy,' says Roper, and this time his smile seems real. 'I'd forgotten the size of you. How's it going? I heard through the grapevine you and Trish here were thick as thieves these days. An odd couple but who am I to judge? Doctors did a great job, I see. And the ladies do love a scar.'

McAvoy looks at him. He barely seems a day older than the last time they met. He's still handsome. Still in great shape. Looks like something from a catalogue in his grey suit with its soft blue check. 'How are you, sir?' asks McAvoy, almost too quietly for it to be heard.

'I'm good, thanks,' says Roper. 'Can't complain, though I frequently do. Old coppers, eh? The collective noun should be "a moan".'

'I think we'd get away lightly if that were all we were called,' says Pharaoh. 'Is there somewhere we can have a chat?'

Roper gestures for them to follow him. The corridor is a wide, airy affair and the walls have been stencilled with testimonials from satisfied and delighted clients of Blue Lightz. He takes them through an empty lobby, and pushes open a door set into the glossy white wall. Were McAvoy alone he doubts he would have been able to find it.

'Boardroom,' says Roper, holding the door open for his guests. 'Take a seat where you like. I'm supposed to be at the head but that kind of thing has never worried me.'

As he passes Roper, McAvoy catches that familiar smell. Aramis aftershave and untipped cigarettes. The last time he smelled it, he was lying in a puddle of his own blood, watching the rain fall from a blue-black sky, sinking into the dead leaves and the mud at the Humber Bridge Country Park. It is all he can do to keep his feet.

'Nice,' says Pharaoh begrudgingly. 'Very tasteful. Not sure what the apples are for but I'm sure it's very feng shui.'

The boardroom is smaller than McAvoy had anticipated. It is filled almost to the edge with a modern, black-topped table. A dozen swivel chairs have been pushed neatly around the individual seating stations, which are marked with an upturned glass tumbler and a shiny green apple, a fresh jotter and a fountain pen. A large, blank screen fills one wall. Black curtains have been drawn across the window facing the street. There is no art on the walls. No personality of any kind.

'I've never really asked,' says Roper, appearing to think about it for the first time. 'They're there when we come in. Somebody must have a part-share in an orchard. Or they're worried we're not getting our five-a-day.'

'I get mine,' says McAvoy suddenly. 'Since they've added Jaffa Cakes to the list of approved fruits. Sorry, that's Fin's joke . . .'

There is a pause before Roper and Pharaoh give him an encouraging laugh. His cheeks colour. He wants to run from the room.

'I have a feeling I know what you're after,' says Roper, and sits down gently in one of the chairs. His movements are feline. There is no sound as he alters his position.

'You got a call,' says Pharaoh. 'Still got some friends up north, I presume.' She is sitting on the desk, backside creasing a jotter, but the angle makes it hard for her to look at him so she pulls out one of the seats and sits down.

McAvoy stays where he is, standing by the door. He can't seem to get his feet to move. He finds himself looking at the side of Roper's face. He has always been intimidated by this man. At first, he wanted to impress him. Wanted his approval. But as he learned his investigative methods and saw his callous disregard for people's fragility, McAvoy began to see him differently. By the end, he was half convinced that Roper was a monster. Were it not for the injuries he had endured he would have continued digging into his past. But by the time McAvoy was back on his feet, Roper was gone and McAvoy had fresh battles to fight. Here, now, he finds himself so overcome by a desire to understand him that he is tempted to pull the top of his head off and take a look inside.

'You've no doubt read up on what this company does,' says Roper.

'I have. Not today, of course. We're talking a good way back down the road. We've been fascinated by Blue Lightz for a while.'

Roper smiles. 'We?'

'Oh y'know, interested parties,' says Pharaoh vaguely.

'It's better to be talked about than not talked about,' says Roper. He shoots McAvoy a glance. 'You comfy there, McAvoy? Can I get you something? Tea, coffee? Bowl of water and a packet of ham?'

McAvoy stares at him. Shakes his head. He tries not to break his phone as he squeezes it in his left hand. He has been afraid of this man for so long.

'You're a security consultancy,' says Pharaoh. 'You offer advice. Expert support. Close protection. Logistical assistance. There are a lot of buzzwords on the website to be honest, Doug. A lot of it sounded very much like marketing bollocks to me. So we'll brush right over that. What I want to know is why one of your vehicles was on the Humber Bridge last night at the exact time an officer from Lincolnshire Police was shot.'

Roper nods once, as if digesting this. He exhales, looking as though he were making a difficult decision.

'We're friends to the police,' says Roper, and he leans back in his chair, putting his feet on the desk. He's wearing brogues. Suave, brown and white dinner shoes. There is a green stone lodged in the tread. McAvoy finds himself staring at it. Staring at anything to avoid looking into Roper's eyes.

'Friends? I don't doubt it,' says Pharaoh. 'Half your staff have been coppers.'

'We offer expertise. That's what the company is about. A lot of what we do is in a grey area that the police have traditionally struggled to negotiate. Corporate espionage. Data theft. Things that are criminal but damn hard to get a conviction. That's our bread and butter.'

'Special operations,' says McAvoy, and his voice seems to come from a long way off. 'You head up a special division.'

'I do, I do,' says Roper, smiling encouragingly at McAvoy. 'You're so clever, Detective Sergeant. Yes, you're right. For my sins, as it were. My division is a harder thing to describe. I run a small team of very professional men and women who have a background in various areas of law enforcement, close protection and the military. Their skills are an asset to companies and individuals who have found themselves in, shall we say, awkward situations.'

'Like what?' asks Pharaoh, and picks up an apple. She takes a bite and chews noisily.

'Say, for example, that you have an employee who has been stealing important, confidential material from your firm. In some instances, that can be dealt with by means of disciplinary action and the intervention of the police. But if the information being sold is of a sensitive nature, it can be useful to deal with it without having to trouble the courts.'

Pharaoh puts the apple down on the table and grins, wet-mouthed, at Roper. 'You just have your boys bump them off, do you? Sounds like a fucking hit squad, Doug.'

Roper laughs. It does not suit him. His laugh is a cartoon sound: a trio of snorting breaths, at odds with his well-groomed appearance.

'If only life were so simple,' he says wistfully. 'No, we are very good at recovering said information. We are good at securing promises from the said individual that no such transgression will be repeated. I'm only giving you an example here, of course. Our remit is very wide-ranging. Our cybercrime division alone has a turnover of £63 million a year. We have clients all over the world. Really, if I'd known how much money there was to be made protecting big businesses I doubt I would ever have become a policeman. But if I hadn't become a policeman, who knows what I would be instead. It all gets a bit metaphysical, if you think too deeply.'

McAvoy realises Roper is looking at him. He forces himself to meet his stare. Feels something shift in his belly, as fear gives way to anger. Roper looks better than ever. Rich. Respected. Successful. McAvoy can feel his scars as if they were on fire. Can taste Roisin's tears. Can feel the sting of every insult that was thrown at the copper who cost good old Doug his job.

'Popesco,' says McAvoy drily. 'They have a kidnap and ransom policy for their senior and mid-level staff.'

'I'm afraid I can't discuss individual clients,' says Roper, looking apologetic.

'Joel Musgrave,' says McAvoy. 'He's a non-executive director of Popesco. His name has cropped up in several different strands of our investigations.'

'And what is it you're investigating, McAvoy?'

McAvoy pauses. 'Murder,' he says. 'A hit and run. The shooting of a policewoman.' He looks at Roper and finally lets some venom bleed into his tone. 'Kidnap and ransom.'

'A vehicle belonging to Blue Lightz was spotted very near the scene of a major incident on the Humber Bridge last night,' says Pharaoh. 'That vehicle might well have been used to ram another vehicle over the side of the bridge. Its occupants are, at the very least, witnesses that we need to trace. I'm going to need your personnel records, Doug. Just for the purposes of elimination.'

Roper licks the inside of his lower lip. Scratches his hairline. Looks as though he is pained by the effort of not being able to help them as extensively as he would wish.

'It's going to be tricky,' he says ruefully. 'We're a huge company. We have operatives on various deployments all over the world at any one time. We have a fleet of vehicles but they are from a subsidiary company that also rents them out to other security firms. It will all be in the paperwork, somewhere, but it will take some finding. And then there's the fact that many of our employees are self-employed and work for us on a consultancy basis. Some of these men have a background in counter-terrorism and the security services. Some of the IDs they are using have been given to them by their own governments. It's a hornets' nest. But if it's what you need, for old times' sake, I'll do all I can. It just won't happen quickly, I'm afraid. You should probably have telephoned rather than come all this way. But at least you get a night on the town, eh? Nice meal, maybe a show. The company has a property portfolio and I'm sure I could arrange somewhere comfortable for you tonight.'

McAvoy realises that Roper has been looking at him for the entire time he has been talking. Were he to raise his hand and cover the lower half of Roper's face; were he to simply look at his eyes, he does not know if he would see mockery, loathing or indifference.

'There was a job in Africa,' says McAvoy. 'Mozambique. Last year. Nacololo. Popesco employees taken by armed guerrillas. Blue Lightz was helpful in the recovery of Popesco's employees. Could you talk us through that? Special operations division, was it?'

Roper does not take his eyes off McAvoy. 'Humberside Police has extended its boundary, has it? Missed that.'

'Answer the question, Doug,' says Pharaoh.

Roper pauses, considering it. 'We've helped a lot of agro companies in West Africa. It's bandit country. People get kidnapped. Ransom is paid. They come home. We have expert negotiators and a tactical unit who can help if things don't go according to plan. The incident you're referring to was actually a textbook operation. I wasn't personally involved but I'm proud to have recruited the men who took care of things. The client was delighted and we dealt with it without loss of life.'

'Loss of life?' asks McAvoy. 'Loss of white life, you mean? The hostage-takers. Did they go off on a lovely holiday with their money? Or are they rotting somewhere full of bullet holes?'

Roper shoots Pharaoh a glance. 'He always this melodramatic? Rotting somewhere full of bullet holes? Jesus, McAvoy. You never were any fun but now you're positively maudlin. How on earth does Roisin put up with you?'

McAvoy seems to freeze where he stands. For a second he is a great slab of stone.

'Roisin?' asks Pharaoh, looking from one man to the other as the atmosphere in the room becomes cold. 'You remember all your old officers' partners, do you?'

'Oh yes,' says Roper. 'Anders, isn't it? Your husband? Had a terrible stroke a few years back and left you with four daughters and no money. Of course I remember. I've got a good memory for things like that. I was a cop a long time.'

'Wish I could return the favour,' says Pharaoh, but her smile looks weak and strained. 'Wish I could tell you what I know about you. But you always were a mystery, weren't you? No wife. No kids. A Londoner, originally, but there's not much in the files other than that.'

'I'm an open book,' says Roper, spreading his hands. 'A little digging and you can find out almost anything about anybody. You should know that.'

McAvoy can hear static. The rain against the glass sounds like the noise of a broken TV. The beeping of the cars, far below, is a heart monitor. He remembers the feeling of the hospital bed beneath his aching body. Remembers Roisin's hand, holding his, begging him to come back to her.

'Like I say, we're happy to help the police,' says Roper, looking from one to the other. 'First thing tomorrow I'll do some digging. See if I can get some answers. If members of my unit were up in Yorkshire I want to know about it. After all, there's not a lot of money to be made up there. Took me long enough to get away from the place – I'm in no rush to go back.'

At the table, Pharaoh drums her fingers on the wood. She seems to be making up her mind about something. She looks at McAvoy. Something passes between them. As he looks into her eyes he realises what she is saying. Realises she is giving him permission to do whatever he wants. She'll sort it out. She'll cover for him.

'It's been interesting,' says McAvoy, his throat dry. 'We shouldn't leave it as long.'

Roper slithers out of the chair. He does not extend his hand to the two officers. Does not bother with the charade of a smile.

'I have your contact details,' he says. 'I'll get to you.'

Pharaoh pockets the expensive-looking fountain pen from the table and flicks her apple with her mid-finger so that it rolls onto the floor. It is a pitiful act of disdain but McAvoy enjoys the look on her face as she does it.

He opens the door. Stalks back to the elevator with Pharaoh a pace behind. They do not speak until they are back on the ground floor, exiting the building and into the rain and the breeze and the anonymity of the evening.

'So . . .' begins Pharaoh, and she slips her arm through his, steering him into the throng of pedestrians who mutter into mobile phones and dart between vehicles as if they don't give a damn about their lives.

McAvoy does not look at her. Looks straight ahead, jaw locked as if it's being held in place with a screwdriver.

'He said her name,' he mutters. 'He was laughing at me.'

'You look upset, Hector.'

He turns to face her. Wrinkles his nose. Breathes in her cigarettes and perfume and closes his hand around his telephone and its page after page of loving words from his wife and children.

'I'm angry,' he says, and the words seem to amuse him. His smile looks like a slash wound in a blank face. 'I'm so fucking angry I can barely see.'

Beside him, Pharaoh grins. He feels her squeeze his biceps and hears her words as though they were being spoken by the wind.

'Use it, Hector. Hold onto the fire. Hold onto the temper . . .'

The fire in his eyes turns scarlet and gold.

24

Tuesday morning, still dark

Roisin's hand folds itself into McAvoy's with a practised ease. Her small, tanned fingers find the spaces between his fingers and the soft pads of her fingertips brush his big, broken knuckles softly.

McAvoy has been home for an hour but has not yet gone to bed. Roisin was waiting up for him. She kept the kettle at boiling point and was pouring him a hot chocolate the second he walked through the door. He had picked her up as he hugged her. Hadn't realised he was doing it. They stayed that way for a time, forehead to forehead, breathing one another in. Then he told her what had happened. About the way Primrose had seemed. About his continuing fears for Crystal. About Roper.

They stand, now, on the stretch of grass opposite their front door. Up above, the familiar solid bulk of the bridge seems strangely tainted. They cannot see or hear it, but there is police tape flapping from the twisted metal guardrail, its ragged spikes puncturing the blue-black cotton of the night sky.

Before them, the Humber is a shimmering mass of silver and black and the broken spotlight thrown by the moon makes its surface look somehow alive. The divers are long gone. The Toyota has been retrieved. Sniffer dogs failed to pick up any scent of the vanished occupants but footprints found near the wildlife reserve at Barton gave the search teams a place to start and when last McAvoy checked, at least two of the pick-up's passengers had made it as far as Ulceby, seven miles inland, before the trail petered out.

'I think we should move,' says Roisin, leaning her head on his arm.

McAvoy laughs softly, and presses his face to the crown of her head. 'Was it the hand grenade in the living room, the body on the front lawn or the car falling off the bridge that swung it for you?'

'I can handle all that,' says Roisin, and she withdraws her hand for long enough to light the hand-rolled cigarette she has retrieved from the pocket of her leopard-print silk dressing gown. 'It's the postman. He keeps reading our mail.'

McAvoy looks at her face and enjoys her cheeky smile. He feels warmer just looking at her.

'Where would you like to go?' asks McAvoy. 'I've got £4.70 in my pocket and if I sell everything I own I can just about afford to buy you breakfast.'

'Doesn't matter,' says Roisin, picking a strand of tobacco from the lip-gloss on her lower lip. 'We'd still end up with Trish asleep in the back garden.'

'She brought me home,' protests McAvoy. 'She just kind of assumed . . .'

Roisin smiles at him. 'I don't mind. I feel a bit less intimidated by her now I've heard how loud she snores.'

'She snores?'

'Honestly, I thought somebody was mincing a walrus.'

McAvoy considers her, wondering if she is joking. 'You're not intimidated by anybody, Roisin.'

'Maybe.' Roisin shrugs. 'But when your husband's boss is sexy and tough and clever it can be hard not to let the green-eyed monster come out to play.'

'She's my friend. Our friend. You know where my heart lives.'

Roisin nods, examining the tip of her cigarette. 'I thought you might stay over. In London.'

McAvoy watches the water. Takes half a dozen full breaths before speaking again.

'It would have made sense. We could have got a place. Stayed somewhere comfortable. Got a feed and a good night's sleep then started the day fresh and ready.'

'But you didn't.'

He angles himself so he is looking into her eyes. 'No. We didn't. We didn't even suggest it. We both knew we had to come home. I knew where I needed to be and it was here, with you. She knew that too.'

Roisin puts a hand on his face. He kisses her wrist.

'I'll make her the coffee she likes when she wakes up. And I've got croissants . . .'

McAvoy puts his arm around her. He feels her fragile frame beneath the silk of her gown. She's naked beneath. Barefoot. Her hair is loose and tumbles to her shoulders. She keeps flicking it behind her ears, but it refuses to yield to her admonitions.

'He was still a slick bastard, was he?' asks Roisin, and she wrinkles her nose and crosses herself, spitting to ward off the devil. 'Evil fecker.'

McAvoy scratches his forehead. Nods. Shrugs. Doesn't know if he can handle thinking about it any more.

'You really think he's involved in all this?'

McAvoy sucks his cheek and stares at the slowly moving water. The Humber held back a Roman invasion two millennia ago. It has dragged thousands of men to their deaths. As he watches it he wonders, for a moment, how much of what he does actually matters. This waterway alone has killed more men than he could hope to find justice for in a hundred careers as a policeman. When he catches whoever hurt Perry, will the world be better? Will the streets be safer for his children? Or will he simply have found a narrative he can live with: that a good man got hurt because bad men did bad things.

'I don't really know what I believe,' says McAvoy honestly. 'I know Roper was a crooked cop. He didn't care about the truth or justice or the people left behind. He cared about himself and how he could use tragedy to his advantage. And he left me to die, I've no doubt about that. Wanted me to bleed out because of what I knew about him.' He purses his lips, as if frightened that untested truths will spill forth. Then he plunges on. 'This company. Blue Lightz. The 4x4s on the bridge definitely belonged to them. And Roper was so damn unhelpful. They have the resources to hold the police off as long as they want. Was it a legitimate piece of business? That's what they get paid for. His company offers skills that other people don't provide. If Popesco has been targeted by business rivals or people out to make easy money then of course they will bring in a specialist team to handle that. Did they even mean to push the Toyota off the bridge? I don't know. Should they have to answer for it? Yes, of course.'

Roisin flicks her cigarette butt onto the breeze, digesting all he has told her. 'The girl,' she says. 'The girl with the pony . . .'

'Primrose.'

'Aye. Primrose. Jaysus. You say she had bruises.'

'She looked poorly.'

'And she'd not looked after her pony.'

'Which sounds like the opposite of what would be expected of her.'

'And the groom. Crystal. She's still not been in touch with her mammy?'

McAvoy shakes his head.

'Tell me again about the dad. Sounds a fecking bastard from what you've said but he must have been kind once.'

McAvoy is about to reach into his coat for his notes when he realises he doesn't need them any more. He can recall most of the newspaper articles from memory.

'There's a place in Maputo. Mozambique. It rehabilitates former child soldiers. There was a piece written in an Australian newspaper years ago. It mentioned a kid called Manu. He'd been taken from his village by Renamo bandits and trained to kill. They made him kill his own father. There was mention of rape but the article sort of brushed over that. It said he was with them for four years. He was part of a bandit group run by an older boy. Aishita. He was at the centre in Maputo too. There's a line from it that sticks in my memory. "*The first man that Manu killed was his father. He shot him because he had been told to. The next person he killed was an old woman who would not stop screaming. Manu stuck a knife in her. Then his bandit brothers cut her up. They carried pieces of her in their rucksacks, in case they got hungry on the trail and could find no other villages to raid.*"'

'Jaysus.'

'The article talked about how he was one of just a few. But it was clear he had a special bond with a young student who was over there on a gap year, helping put these people back together. That was Joel Musgrave.'

'He really cared?'

'The article suggests so and we've no reason to doubt it. Then, years later, we've got a piece in a glossy mag talking about how Popesco is helping the natives make the most of their land. Learn new farming practices. Helping them become the bread basket of Africa. One of the foremen on this plantation in Nacololo is called Manu. There's a line in the piece. Musgrave says: "On a personal level it's great to see people I've seen grow up – people I've known since the darkest times of the nation's past – become somebody they can be proud of."'

'And you think that's the same person? What's that got to do with the past couple of days?'

'I don't know. But I do know that last year a load of Popesco employees were taken hostage. The white executives were freed. It was a textbook operation. And the next time the name Manu came up was in reference to a body found in an immigration jungle at Calais. Bicycle spoke through the heart.'

'And you think he might be here . . .'

McAvoy shrugs and hates himself for his uncertainty. 'We've got a dead people-trafficker. We've got a missing girl. We've got a rich family and a daughter who looks like she hasn't seen sunlight in days. We've got hostage negotiation specialists refusing to cooperate in our investigation. I can see a shape, Roisin, but I'm so far from making a case that it's laughable.'

'And what does Her Majesty think?' asks Roisin, jerking her head back at the house.

'She thinks it's far-fetched but that she's heard a lot more ridiculous stories that have turned out to be true.'

'So what do you do next?'

McAvoy pushes his hair back from his face. In truth, he doesn't know. Come morning, Pharaoh will start chopping the case into a workable investigation. Tasks will be allocated and teams will be briefed. McAvoy's suspicions will be just one strand of a streamlined, information-driven major investigation. He feels almost relieved.

'It's Crystal, isn't it?' asks Roisin, smiling. 'The groom. The girl who was sorting her life out and then just packed it all in. You'd rather believe something had happened to her than that she would let herself down and disappear off on holiday like that.'

There is no malice in the way Roisin says it. She just knows her husband. McAvoy does not turn away from her, even as the red spots appear on his cheeks.

'Nobody would have given a damn,' he mutters. 'Only Angela Verity. She knew something wasn't right but I only got wind of it because of a bloody receipt at a crime scene in Hull. And I don't know if I gave it my attention because it was linked to my own case or because I agreed with Angela that Crystal didn't sound the sort of person to abandon her horses or to leave a family in the lurch. It just felt wrong.' He stops. Frowns. Spreads his hands. 'I don't know if I've concocted this whole thing on my own prejudices. Musgrave's a rich man. A lord of the manor. He's got everything. He can give his wife and kids whatever they ask for. Crystal was his serf. His underling. And he didn't seem to give a damn that she had buggered off. Acted like that was just normal for people like that. I used to base everything on evidence and procedure and now I don't even know if I can trust my instincts.'

Roisin listens. Lets him talk. He gives her another ten minutes of his doubts and his fears, and then she tells him to shut up because it's getting cold and that if he says anything else about not being good enough for her, she will put her next cigarette out on his forehead. Then she kisses him.

In the warmth of her embrace and the tenderness of her hands upon his face, he feels something a little like peace. It will not last. But it will sustain him for long enough to work out what the hell he should do next.

25

Primrose is waking up. The pain hasn't hit her yet. She just knows she's cold and damp and she's lying on a chilly stone floor. She feels wrong, somehow. She can't pinpoint it yet – just a general feeling of wrongness, as if she's woken up in the middle of the night with a tummy ache. She hurts. She feels dirty, as if she fell asleep after a ride out on Storm and didn't bother having a bath. She wonders if she should have one now. She's getting older. Can make such decisions for herself. Perhaps Crystal can help her run it . . .

It rushes in like flame. One moment she is lying on the floor, snuffling into the hay and the wet stone. And then her head is full of these past days. The bad men. The men who dragged her from the saddle and stuffed their dirty hands in her mouth. She remembers her thudding heart; that glimpse of Crystal, fighting and clawing and telling her to run. Remembers the dark room with its sad wallpaper and the threadbare rug and the sounds of violence that bled in from nearby. Remembers the cell, with its stink of unwashed men. Remembers darkness. The sting of a needle. Rough hands upon her; movement. A sudden flash of light and the feeling of wind upon her sun-starved face. She was on the bridge. Darkness and rain and the strange sensation of running down the dual carriageway towards the lights of the oncoming car. She had to cross the barrier. Had to climb into her father's arms. Then everything changed. She remembers the shouts and the guns and the smell of the man who bundled her into the back of his car. Then later. The policeman. The nice lady. Her father, staring deep into her and telling her that she must never, ever, tell anybody the truth about what happened. And then they were there. The bad men, caked in mud and fury. One of them searched their home, checking for surveillance equipment. They stumbled upon the cellar. Dragged Crystal from the darkness; horse bit around her face and rage in her eyes. Primrose had screamed when she saw her. During her captivity, she did not know whether Crystal was alive or dead. Seeing her in the flesh brought no answers. The girl who emerged from the cellar looked as though she had clawed her way free from a grave. She was the only one who tried to fight. The one who never stopped screaming threats and promising to do unspeakable violence. Kept it up the whole time that they worked on Joel. Didn't lose her fight as his fingernails fell like blossom and his skin bubbled beneath the unforgiving surface of the super-heated blade. He told them all he knew within moments, but it was a long time before they were satisfied.

'Primrose? Are you awake? Oh my girl, are you all right?'

'Mummy? Mummy, it hurts . . .'

Primrose pulls herself upright. There are ropes around her wrists, biting into the skin. Her arms are aching. She feels around with her bare toes. Her eyes adjust and she sees that her mother is hanging by her arms a little way off. She looks somehow ghostly, like a picture in a spooky book.

'Mummy, point your feet, you might be able to reach the floor.'

'I can't move. I hurt so much . . .'

'Try.'

There is silence for a time. Fear scuttles up Primrose's arms like cold spiders.

'Mummy, are you there? I'm cold. My arms hurt . . .'

They have been here in the wine cellar since yesterday evening. Primrose is bound on the floor with her hands behind her back. Viola's arms were twisted about one another before she was suspended. The pose almost comical, like something from a Latin dance. Then duct tape had been lashed about her wrists and she had been hooked over the jutting nail. 'It's okay, baby. I'm here. Don't worry.'

'Mummy, are they gone? It was them, Mummy. They smelled the same. They smelled the same . . .'

Viola reaches out. Points her feet again. Takes her weight upon her pointed toes. She yanks down with her arms. Pushes up with her toes and puts her whole body weight into it. Slams her toes back into the ground. Feels her tendons creaking. Hears something tear. Feels blood spray upon her face and onto her bare shoulders as she wrenches, over and over . . .

Primrose allows herself a gasp of triumph as she sees her mother tumble forward, slamming onto the ground as if fired from a cannon. Viola gives a cry of triumph and then she is clambering forward, searching for her daughter. Primrose finds herself hauled upwards to be wrapped within an embrace that burns as blood rushes into the dead parts of her.

Fiddling, scratching, Viola finds her daughter's bonds and tries to claw them open. When she fails to do so she hunkers down on her knees and chews through the tape. Primrose's hands come apart with a sudden tearing sound and in the same instant Viola is grabbing her by the hand and pushing her up the stairs towards the door.

Primrose stumbles as she climbs the wooden stairs. Blood is rushing in her head. She pushes at the hatch. Please. Please! She begins to giggle and cry as it opens and she climbs into the cool night air. She collapses into the straw and the mud.

Viola follows her daughter into the open air. She feels as though every bone in her body were aflame. Something felt like it broke as she fought to free herself. One arm seems to be ignoring her commands. And yet it doesn't seem to matter. All that she thought was important has been altered these past few hours. Here, now, she would give anything to have been told the truth from the start. Joel. Fucking Joel. For all the tears she spilled as she watched his desecration, it had been mingled with the desire to grab the knife and help her daughter's kidnappers punish him for his sins.

She bites down on her fingers to stop herself trembling. She had believed her husband. Believed every word that spilled out of his mouth. He could handle it. She would be safe. Everything was going to work out. He was good at this. Every obstacle could be viewed as an opportunity if played right. Crystal needed to be silenced. She was going to go to the police. Viola had struggled with that claim more than any other. Crystal adored Primrose. Saw her as a little sister. She would never have put the child at risk. But Joel had been so insistent. They needed to keep her out of the way for a while. Viola needed to switch her phone off and go to London and come back when all this was over. Only now does she understand. Joel wasn't afraid of Crystal putting his daughter's welfare in further jeopardy. He was afraid she would scupper his plan to make some money from his daughter's kidnapping. Afraid that she would tell Viola about the things that have occurred between her and Joel. Viola recalls the man she married. Charming, funny, handsome . . . but there was a side to him. An ambition. A need to matter. She has read endless textbooks on personality disorders during their marriage. She suspects that Joel is a narcissist. A megalomaniac. She has even underlined certain passages in tomes written about psychopathy. But it was only when she saw Manu drag Crystal from the stables and across to the house; when she saw what Joel had allowed to happen to her, that she really saw the truth of the man she married.

'They said not to call the police,' says Primrose desperately, staring at her mother. 'But how do we get him back? And Crystal. She looked so thin and sore. Did Daddy know she was there? Why didn't he look after her? She fought so hard when the bad men took me. She was like a tiger . . .'

In the bright light of the kitchen, mother and daughter hold one another and come to the same decision without speaking a word. They know what they have been told. They know the consequences of making the wrong decision. They have suffered because people chose to do things their own way rather than the way they had been instructed.

'The nice man,' says Primrose softly. 'With the kind eyes . . .'

Viola runs to the fridge. The detective had left them a card, slipping it under a fridge magnet on his way to the door. The telephone is on the wall; a little-used anachronism in her life of smartphones and tablets.

'Do it, Mummy. We have to.'

Viola punches the numbers with her thumb. She wants to slide to the floor. Wants to pull her daughter close and lie on the ground, wailing at the misery of it all.

'Hello,' she says, when the call is answered. 'Sergeant McAvoy. We need your help . . .'

26

It is not yet lunchtime but already the day seems to be darkening. The rain falls like arrows, arcing down from a sky the colour of putty. The grass is long enough to soak him to the knees and his short jacket does nothing to stop the wind that twists about him like so many lengths of wet rope. He leans with his back to the knotted trunk of a sycamore and watches as the man he has come here to kill fiddles with a bunch of keys and huddles inside his leather jacket: cursing the rain as he tries to open the thick wooden door of the church.

The little building is off to Owen's right; all big grey stones and dark windows and rusty railings beneath a flat, crenelated roof.

Owen watches Pavel fumble again with the keys. He wants to go and help him. It would hurry things up. But the lock is not destined to be opened. Mahon filled it with matchsticks an hour ago.

As Owen watches, a block of the landscape detaches itself from the grey and the green and the driving rain. It becomes a shape. Six-foot-plus of gnarled muscle and scars . . .

Mahon crosses the gap between himself and the Serbian in a dozen swift, easy strides. His steps are light. He leaves little impression on the sodden grass.

Pavel is not a big man. He's skinny, and his dark hair is thinning on top. He's not an impressive specimen, with the pale, gaunt features of a man who spends most of his days indoors. Were he to pass him in the street, Mahon doubts he would see much to admire. But Pavel has skills. He was a communications officer with the Serbian military and was found to have such an innate understanding of computing and algorithms that he was selected for a special programme. A year after it began, that special programme came to the attention of NATO and the corrupt colonel who made millions claiming supplies and wages for a fictional regiment, that marched only in the hazy world of online databases, went on the run. Pavel did too. He wound up in Ukraine, and gravitated towards men like himself. He spent his time in internet cafés, helping set up an online marketplace for a shady network of hackers who promised huge rewards and complete anonymity to their customers from the world of organised crime. Pavel was arrested in 2003. He spent time in a Siberian gulag, but his time was softer than most. By now he had been spotted. He had been identified as a man useful to the *vory*. And when he was released, his passage to the UK was not an uncomfortable one. For the past three years he has lived in a pleasant apartment in Pimlico and helped his paymasters bury their money in accounts the world over. His own contribution to the Headhunters' pot has been significant. He tests firewalls and security systems for their clients. When he finds weakness he exploits it. He shows their clients where they went wrong. And he shows them how to fix it. He never gives them their money back. Were it not for his bad habits, Pavel would be an almost flawless asset to his organisation. But Pavel is just a man. He has weaknesses. He has desires. He can be lured to isolated, private places like this, through his baser instincts alone.

Owen closes his eyes a fraction too late.

Mahon does not give Pavel the chance to turn. He puts his whole hand on the back of the man's head and slams his forehead into the wet, damp wood.

Pavel falls to the ground without a word.

Quickly, Mahon retrieves the matches from the lock and puts

the pieces in his pocket. He takes the keys from the wet flag-stone and soundlessly opens the door. He drags Pavel into the cool quiet of the old church. There is no furniture inside. The pews have long since been ripped out and the stained-glass windows hang ragged and sharp, encased between two panes of tattered mesh.

Mahon does not turn as his companions enter the church. He hears the policeman speak first.

'You hit him too bloody hard. He's no good with his brain smashed.'

'I hit him just right,' says Mahon, and he begins stripping Pavel of his clothes.

'He's bleeding,' says Owen.

'Of course he is. He'll wake up when I want him to.'

'You'd know, of course,' sneers Ray. He's got a thin cigar and is slurping at it with his monkfish lips.

'What are you going to do to him?' asks Owen.

Mahon says nothing. He knows that Owen is solid. The poor bastard has suffered more than any of them. He can watch what comes next without blinking. He does not expect the same of Ray.

'He's going to torture the fucker,' says Ray.

'Problem with that?'

'Me? No, mate. I'm starting to enjoy all this.'

Mahon considers Ray for a second. He's leaning against the wall of the abandoned church. He's started dressing the way he used to. He's picked up a tatty charity shop suit and has tied a 1970s tie into a tight knot at his throat. He wears a damp, mush-room-coloured anorak, with his hands pushed deep in the pockets.

'He knows it all,' says Mahon, nodding at the half-naked man on the floor of the church. 'Every password. Every name. In half an hour, so will we.'

'And then?' asks Ray.

Mahon says nothing. He reaches back and Owen hands him a black case. It contains a laptop computer, half a dozen small towels and two blue plastic bottles.

'Pavel. Hey. Come back to us. We're going to have a little chat.'

Owen watches the whole thing. Ray only looks away a couple of times. Both men have heard of water torture before. They knew when Mahon spread the towel over Pavel's face that the next few moments would be full of choking, drowning, gurgling horror. Yet neither man expected Mahon to use bleach.

Later, Owen experiences a sensation of returning to his own body without being aware of having left. Time has passed, but wherever his mind has been, he has taken no notes. It is as if he has turned over two pages at once. Suddenly, he is aware that the shouts and screams have stopped, and he is staring at a mess of handprints, scribbled threats and phone numbers, all tangled around one another in the dust on the back of an abandoned pew. Somebody has written 'Your guna die'. The years may have altered Owen in ways he never imagined but the part of him that was a journalist feels incapable of leaving the message unedited. He makes quick, deft marks in the dust and adds the missing apostrophe.

'What are you doing?' asks Ray, at his shoulder.

'It was bothering me.'

Ray looks at him as if he were insane. 'That was bothering you? We're in an abandoned church. I'm standing in an inch of solid pigeon shit in the pissing rain and we've got a half-dead Serbian trying to connect to a Wi-Fi signal that only works once every twenty minutes and you're spending your time correcting the grammar in graffiti. I love it. I'm with fucking crazy people.'

Owen finds himself quite pleased to have at least broken the silence. Ray has barely spoken all afternoon and Mahon can go for hours without so much as opening his eyes or parting his lips. Owen has spent the last few hours leaning back against a grey stone column, greasy with damp moss, listening to the flapping of the birds in the bell tower and watching what little light there was slowly bleed into darkness. There is virtually no light at all inside the church now. The soft blue glow of the laptop casts almost no illumination. It shows the sickness in Pavel's face. Eyes that are seamed with burst blood vessels. Broken nose and bleeding lips. Mahon has allowed him to put his clothes back on but his shivers come regardless. He looks like a dying man. He's muttering to himself in his own language. Keeps taking his hands from the keyboard to wrap himself in an embrace. And yet he is still doing as he is told. Still monitoring the frequencies used by his colleagues and waiting for the moment when he finds what Mahon is looking for.

Owen realises he should feel responsible for this. It was he who flirted with Pavel in the coffee shop this morning. He who slipped him his number and told him to call. He who explained that he knew a little place where they could spend time in the dark without interruption. He who told Pavel where to find the key. And yet Owen does not blame himself. He blames Roper. Blames Roper for every damn thing that has gone wrong in his life since he dared question the untouchable bastard on the true identity of a killer. Since then Owen has lost his job, his home and his family. He has suffered almost beyond endurance. He has done what he has done for one reason and one reason alone. He wants to bring down Doug Roper. And if Pavel has to suffer for that to happen, Owen is fine with that. Mahon has taught him that bad things happen to good people and good things happen to bad people and none of it matters a damn. Good, bad, decent, evil, they are all just words invented by man to explain the strange impulses that force people to do things other than those they are told they should. There is no justice. There is no karma. No reward for decency or punishment for transgression. There is only the slow turning of the earth and the rising of the sun and the moon, again and again. They are hamsters on a wheel. And if they want to kill one man to avenge another, there is not a power in the universe to stop them.

'We nearly fucking there?' grumbles Ray. He is smoking a cigar. A pile of old prayer books smoulders at his feet, a soft red glow and a plume of grey mingling in the shadows.

Owen looks at Ray with a disapproving glare.

'Your fucking problem?' spits Ray. 'I'm cold. You think this fire is gonna piss God off? Look at his fucking house.'

Owen looks away. Stares up at the organ pipes. At the peeling ceiling and the decomposing saints that peer down from the high walls. He wonders if it would be wrong to pray, even if just to give voice to his true desires. Sometimes he does not know what he thinks about something until he speaks aloud.

Suddenly, there is a crackle from the laptop. Pavel holds up a hand and the silence of the church seems to grow more oppressive. There is a burst of static and then a garbled rush of speech. The language is unmistakably Eastern European.

'There,' says Pavel. 'That man is Linskey. He is a soldier. Important. Answers to Nestor and Nestor answers to the boss. He runs one of the teams. I have given you names. I have found their channel. They can speak freely here. Is a safe site.'

'I don't fucking speak Russian,' growls Mahon.

'It is not Russian. It is a program I create. It sounds crazy to anybody listening in. But to them, with the right code, it is clear as bell, yes?'

Mahon has been crouching down next to Pavel. Now he stands up, unfolding himself like a sculpture coming to life.

'Make it make sense. Get me what I need.'

Owen looks at both of his companions. They have been through much. They have killed bad men. He does not know if they have done any good work but he feels less of a victim than he has for years. He wonders if all men would be like this, if treated as he has been. Wonders, for a second, what it would take to push somebody like McAvoy into a place from which there would be no return. Owen finds himself thinking about the big cop. For years he hated him. Viewed him as one of his persecutors; a liar who had abandoned him. But in recent months he has learned the truth. McAvoy, like him, was one of Roper's victims. He, too, had been tormented by the hateful bastard. But never once did he suggest asking McAvoy to be complicit in their campaign of revenge. Never once did it occur to him that McAvoy would be able to look the other way as they dispensed a very different form of justice.

'. . . good day's work,' comes the voice, through the computer. 'Two bites of the cherry. Message sent. They'll pay up, we'll handle it and they'll pay us for our time on top of whatever we can make in ransom. There's a girl, too, if you're interested. Bit scabby but could still earn. Sometimes people don't want to fuck the Eastern Europeans, know what I mean? She'd do. Meek as anything. Could do what you like to her and she'd barely make a sound . . .'

Owen and Ray close their eyes as they listen to the conversation. Mahon focuses on every word, filing away every scrap of detail.

'Where?' asks Mahon, and Pavel looks at him with eyes filled with tears and blood.

'I have helped you. I have given you everything. Please. I do not want to die like this. I have not done enough bad things to deserve . . .'

Mahon glances, just once, at the bottle of bleach that rests on an overturned pew by his knees. Pavel gives a broken sob and begins scrolling through screen after screen of files and private correspondence: emails sent and received, chatrooms visited, all in the depths of the dark net. At last he has a list of properties within twenty miles of the spot where Linskey logged in and accessed the private site. The properties all have a connection with Blue Lightz or one of its subsidiaries.

Owen crosses to where Mahon stands. Catches the trace of his constant aroma: damp leaves and wet fur, thick mud and splintered trees. Owen and Mahon consider the list. Six properties. Two on the same street. An abandoned pool hall, two office blocks and an apartment building by St Katharine Docks. Owen sucks his teeth and tries to think like the man he despises most. Imagines the comfort of shadows.

'Two on the same street,' says Owen, pointing at a virtual pin on a map of London. 'They're all abandoned down there. Billionaires' Row but not a tenant in sight. He'd like that. It would make sense.'

Mahon nods. He reads the address off the screen then slowly turns to Colin Ray. The former policeman has his hands in his pockets.

'You let me go, yes?' asks Pavel. 'I do good?'

Mahon registers his presence. He blinks, once, like the shutter of a camera opening and closing. Owen never sees the blade. One moment Pavel is looking up, head back, pleading for his life. The next he has fallen forward in a spreading puddle of his own blood, his throat an open envelope.

Mahon does not take his eyes off Colin Ray, or the soft light emanating from his pocket.

'Did she hear all that?' asks Mahon, above the sound of Pavel's blood seeping into the gaps beneath the floorboards.

Ray smiles. It's an ugly, leering, joyless sight. He tosses his cigar and it lands in the puddle of thick red tar. 'I'm a copper,' he says, straightening his tie. 'What do you expect?'

'This,' says Mahon, nodding. 'I expected this.'

Ray rubs his jaw. 'So why did you let me tell her?'

'Because you deserve your own revenge,' says Mahon. 'You need to see somebody in prison. You need information. You would not be happy with cutting his head off.'

Ray laughs at that. 'So what will happen now?' he asks.

'We will hurt them,' he says, nodding at Owen.

'And me? Are you going to open my throat too?'

'No,' says Mahon. 'I would not do that. Your friend in Operation Trident knows almost as much as we do. Whatever happens now, the people who killed Mr Nock will fall. But before that happens, there must be blood.'

'It doesn't have to be like that,' says Ray.

'It does. For me, it does.'

'What if I try to stop you?' asks Ray, and he alters his position slightly. 'I'm not as strong as I was but I'd go down fighting.'

'I know,' says Mahon. 'That is why I must cause you some disadvantage. For this, for many things, I am sorry. I hope you find what it is you are looking for, DCI Ray. I know what it is I seek. And you will not stop me taking it.'

Ray opens his mouth to speak at the moment that Mahon throws the knife. The sound is of an arrow splitting wood. Slowly, Ray turns to look at his left arm. A short dagger has pierced the flesh at his wrist. It has parted tendons and bone. It has pinned him to the rotting wood of the cross.

'I'm sorry,' says Mahon, crossing the space between them. He hits Ray, once, in the side of the head. Wordlessly, Ray slides to the floor; one hand points upwards, skewered and bloody.

Mahon and Owen are gone within moments. They leave the laptop, still logged in to the private site. They leave Pavel and the list of names he gave them between mouthfuls of bleach. They leave Ray, out cold and turning grey as the blood trickles down his arm.

They leave the tiny, echoing voice of Helen Tremberg, yelling into the chilly air of the church like the ghost of a prayer.

'Colin. Colin, can you hear me? Colin? Please. DCI Ray . . .'

27

There is a madness in the man's eyes. A yearning that verges on hysteria. He strains at his bonds as if aflame. His muscles seem to be upon the verge of tearing themselves apart. His shoulder joint is a skull, pushing against flimsy skin. There are only a few planks of wood between his feet and the rolling, blue-black ocean. The sirens who call to him move provocatively, all feline grace and baleful eyes; their bodies childlike but their gestures sensual. McAvoy pities the man. Pities both his pain and his foolishness. The men in the rowing boat, their ears muffled by strips of cloth, look upon their leader with something between admiration and disdain. McAvoy recognises the look.

'Hello,' he says again, and his voice sounds loud in the quiet of the gallery. 'I couldn't hear you . . .'

'It's Viola Musgrave,' comes a small, timid voice. 'Please. Something terrible has happened.'

There are only a couple of other visitors to the Ferens Art Gallery in the centre of Hull. It's a cool, quiet space with high ceilings and polished wooden floors. The assembled artworks are tastefully, graciously spaced. Dusky, lamplit images of humble homes vie for wall space with grand depictions of battle. Portraits stare out upon idyllic landscapes and the soft, red and orange glow of sunrises and sunsets makes the space seem timeless, as though it is both day and night, as well as somewhere in between. McAvoy stands before an image of Ulysses, haunted by the sirens who call to him and his men. He had not meant to linger in front of it. He should be in the staff canteen, talking to one of the gallery guards who has come forward to reveal the fact that on Sunday evening, at his home on the Boulevard, he saw a tall, skinny man breaking into the red Toyota Hilux that the kidnappers were using during the carnage at the bridge. The witness only caught a glimpse of what was occurring as he was driving by at the time. But he thought it might have been important and had worked up the courage to call the police. DS Mackintosh has marked the follow-up urgent and McAvoy, paired with DC Daniells, is here to take a statement. A sketch artist is on the way to the gallery. McAvoy is trying not to linger over the irony. Daniells has mentioned it eight times.

He turns his back on Ulysses' staring eyes. Jams a finger in his ear and asks her to repeat herself. He feels his senses shrinking, as if all the extraneous parts of himself are disappearing to leave just a tiny focal point of concentration. All that matters is what is happening now. All that matters is the words he knows he is about to hear.

'It's Joel,' she says, appearing to take great care over her words. 'They hurt him. They took him.'

'A man called Aishita,' says McAvoy.

She's not listening. She's focusing on saying what she must.

'We didn't want to do any of the things they made us do. We loved Crystal. But they had Primrose.'

McAvoy closes his eyes. He walks without seeing; his footsteps loud on the wooden floor. When he opens them he is standing at the far end of the gallery. He is staring into a picture of a skull containing a long, plumed quill.

'They told us not to talk to the police. I don't know what to do. But you looked like you might understand. Like maybe you could do something that would make it all better, somehow. They've had Primrose all this time. They took her. Crystal saw everything. Came running back to tell us to call the police. And then they called. Manu. He knew Joel from Africa. Told us we couldn't speak to anybody except the directors at Popesco. They sent this man and Joel sent me away. I've been sitting in a hotel for days. He promised me it would all be okay if we did things right. But Joel saw a chance to make money. My company hasn't been doing so well and Popesco is making a fortune but he's only seeing scraps of it. If he was still in charge he'd be in control of a fortune. The men. They . . . hurt him. He told me what he'd done. The gamble he took. The leader – he made Joel look at me, at Prim, and tell us what kind of man he was. He thought he could win. That was his word. Win! Get Primrose back and keep the money. Grab the kidnappers too. But one of the kidnappers had a gun and it all went wrong . . .'

McAvoy concentrates on his breathing. Feels himself shudder at the thought of what the little girl must have seen.

'They came back. The men who took Prim. And they hurt Joel. Beat him until he handed over the money. The Russian was pleased but the other man didn't look satisfied. Said there was more to be had. He wanted everything. Everything! Hurt Joel again and again, demanding to know who at Popesco controlled the money. Who had made the decision back in Africa. Who had betrayed him. And they took him. Tied us up and took him and Crystal.'

McAvoy looks up at the sound of his name. Daniells is standing in the doorway, looking at him questioningly. He is perfectly to scale with the image he stands in front of. He looks almost comical, blending in with the fishwives who haggle over the price of herring in seventeenth-century Amsterdam.

'Was it a man called Aishita?' asks McAvoy again.

Viola pauses, as if hearing him for the first time. 'It was the man Joel had spoken about. Manu. He said he had come thousands of miles for revenge. Said Joel had betrayed him. Said he had become the man his brothers made him. I don't understand, Sergeant McAvoy. Why is any of this happening?'

McAvoy stands still, bathed in the yellow light of the bulb

above him. His gaze takes in brush strokes and gilded frames, gleaming floors and deep blue walls. He wants to stay here. Wants to climb up on the wall and hang, for ever, like an exhibit to be studied and criticised, admired and ignored.

'I need you to tell me everything,' he says, pushing his hair back from his face. 'Is Primrose safe? Where are you now? I'm on my way . . .'

28

It's hard to get lost in the little village of Kirmington, which sits nine miles from the River Humber and a stone's throw from the local airport. There are only half a dozen streets around the pretty sandstone church, but there's no village shop and it's been years since there was a post office on Post Office Lane. Despite this, the sign outside the big white pub on the main road welcomes diners and drinkers to 'the centre of the universe'. Nobody could accuse the owners of the Marrowbone and Cleaver of lacking ambition.

McAvoy pulls up next to a battered agricultural vehicle. A skinny man in a bobble hat is sitting at the wheel, rolling himself a cigarette. His pint is balanced on the dashboard, which is festooned with empty tobacco pouches, cans of fizzy drink and gymkhana rosettes. McAvoy decides not to let himself breathe in. If he can't smell the drugs he doesn't need to get sidetracked. And besides, right now, he's not even sure if he is here as a police officer. He climbs out into the rain-spattered darkness and ignores the thumbs-up from the happy looking fellow in the adjacent vehicle. He concentrates on his breathing. On steadying his heart. His scars are hurting him. Each ridge of pink and puckered flesh feels like a newly carved wound.

He turns towards the pub. It's been pebble-dashed, then painted over in a buttery gloss. The curtains in the conservatory are wide open and McAvoy glimpses a few diners sitting down at wooden tables in a pleasant dining area. He gets a whiff of frying steak and apple crumble, real ale and damp clothes, and then he is pushing open the door and a small brown terrier is jumping up at his legs and a handful of men and women are nodding hellos and telling him he's a big chap as he pushes his way through the packed bar. It's nice inside. Bright and airy, with motorbike memorabilia behind the bar and a large poster warning customers that there is no Wi-Fi and that anybody seeking entertainment should try having a conversation. The barmaids seem to be leading by example.

Viola is waiting in the back bar. She's got a glass of dry white wine in front of her but doesn't look as though she has touched it. A superbike, with instructions not to touch, is mounted in a raised area to her right and behind her there are old photographs of the RAF men who lived and drank here during the war. She starts to stand as she glimpses McAvoy. She's dressed differently to how she looked earlier. Leggings and a running top. Flip-flops. She has chewed her nails down and taken off her rings. Her hair is pulled back in a tight ponytail and her skin looks like split wood. McAvoy picked this place because he knows it is always busy and that the people who drink here, though friendly and well-mannered, would rather die than let anybody walk in and make off with a young woman and her daughter. This is farming country, and there is no shortage of guns.

'Please, don't get up,' says McAvoy, lowering himself into the wooden chair opposite. There are two other drinkers in this side of the bar, chatting about the local landowner between slurps of lager, and as the lights bounce off the horse brasses above the fireplace McAvoy catches the word 'wanker' three times before he stops listening.

'Primrose has gone to the toilet,' says Viola, and her voice seems to catch in her throat. Were Pharaoh here, she would doubt the sincerity of the action and instruct a junior officer to find out whether she studied drama during her university days.

'How is she?'

'Frightened,' says Viola, then shakes her head. 'No, that's not right. Numb, maybe. Only half there . . .'

'What did she see?'

'Everything. Too much.'

'And yet you're alive.'

Viola tries to hold his gaze and fails. She raises her glass but her hand is shaking and she spills wine on her chin and chest as she tries to take a drink.

'You didn't call 999,' says McAvoy. 'You rang me. Why? Am I some sort of alternative to the real police?'

Viola glances towards the door. She seems ready to bolt. McAvoy forces himself to look more sympathetic. She has been through a lot. But a lot of people have been through a lot more.

'I need you to tell me everything,' says McAvoy, his voice low. 'Everything I need.'

Viola is about to reply when the pale, washed-out figure of Primrose emerges from the toilets. She looks like a cartoon; somehow sepia-toned despite the flamboyant colours around her. It was expensive, but her pinafore dress looks like sacking cloth. She seems to be deliberately keeping herself small. Moving like a mouse that has glimpsed the shadow of an eagle overhead. She slinks to the table and, in an action that looks almost boneless, she insinuates herself into her mother's arms. Viola holds her tight, and the embrace fills McAvoy with both sadness and temper. Viola has her daughter, but Crystal is still missing. Joel Musgrave is in danger. A group of corporate gangsters are playing games with people's lives.

'Tell me about Crystal,' he says, not blinking.

'She tried to fight them,' says Primrose, and her voice sounds far away. 'They were hurting Daddy and she got free. They had to hurt her.'

'Bronte Hall,' says McAvoy. 'Is that where they kept her?'

'I haven't pushed,' says Viola, nodding at her daughter.

'I can't interview her,' says McAvoy, shaking his head. 'There are procedures. Processes. We need to do things properly.'

'But what about Joel?' asks Viola, and she smears her hand across her cheek and nose, leaving a trail of mucus like a slash across her perfect features.

McAvoy sits back in his chair and looks at the sad, scared face of the little girl. He understands most of it. Somebody with a grudge against Joel Musgrave kidnapped his daughter. His employers hired a kidnap and ransom team in the employ of Blue Lightz. They urged Musgrave to keep his mouth shut and they tied up the one person who wouldn't keep their mouth shut. Musgrave kept Crystal's whereabouts a secret. Whether he intended to set her free or kill her after the double-cross was complete, McAvoy could not say. But after the catastrophe at the bridge, the hostage-takers had made their way to his home. They had hurt him. Then they had taken him away.

'They took Crystal?' he asks. 'Why?'

'Insurance, I think,' says Viola softly. 'One of the men said they should kill us all. The leader didn't want that. Said they should tie us up until it was all over. But there was no tying up Crystal. Fought like an animal.' She hangs her head. 'Fought harder than me.'

'Where are they going?'

'Gert Van Vuuren,' says Viola, as if somebody were listening. 'Boss of Popesco. The man who okayed the payment. The same man who gave the go-ahead for the operation in Africa.'

'And they're going to take him?'

'Joel told them where he stays when he is in this country. The policy that Popesco has in place for him runs into millions.'

'Was that the plan all along? To get Van Vuuren here so they could hook the big fish?'

'I don't know,' says Viola, shaking her head.

McAvoy is about to push her when Primrose raises her head. 'They made me watch. Such a long time, and Daddy crying and screaming like he was in a film. Crystal tried to hug me but couldn't get close. She was wearing a horse bit, like Storm. Daddy said he had done it to her. That isn't right, is it? Why would he do that?'

A sob escapes Viola's lips as she hugs her daughter. A barmaid with red hair and wonky glasses stops midway towards their table and tucks her pad back into her apron.

McAvoy closes his eyes as he pulls out his phone. He's already strayed too far. However he justifies it, he knows that he has deliberately severed the connection between himself and the rest of the team. He has never made up his mind about what he really believes about the great philosophical questions, but if he were to truly think about it, he would confess to a vague certainty that every step he takes brings him closer to Doug Roper. And that is a journey he wants to make alone. It is not heroism. He just knows what happens to innocent bystanders during a crossfire.

Pharaoh has called him six times. Her text messages have evolved into capital letters and exclamation marks. Roisin has sent him a picture of herself with her lower lip sticking out. Andy Daniells has sent him a file marked 'Urgent'. He opens it first and digests the contents. Joel Musgrave's car has been found outside a hotel 140 miles south. Police and paramedics are at the scene due to the amount of blood found in the boot. The staff are unable to offer much on the details of current guests due to some technical problems that have also fried the CCTV.

'Crystal fought so hard,' says Primrose, and she sits up. Doodles with her finger in a drop of spilled wine. 'Do they have her? That's not fair. She's nice. She did nothing wrong. Can you bring her home?'

McAvoy pictures countless scenarios. Thinks about all the possibilities and outcomes. Considers every option. He can think of no other course of action. He has to try. Has to act like a good man first and a policeman second.

'I'll try.'

29

Manu has stayed in a place like this before. Years ago. Back when he was becoming the lie. Back when Joel Musgrave was his friend and his benefactor. Back when Popesco was a company that was going to make his country fat and wealthy and his people masters of their own fates.

A gathering of senior executives had been arranged in a hunting lodge twenty miles from Johannesburg. It had been built in the style of a Tudor mansion: thick, buttery walls and deep brown timbers, open fireplaces and wood-panelled walls. Manu had worn the suit that Joel had sent him from England. He had shaken hands and drunk good brandy and talked to white men and women about the good earth of the Nacala corridor and the excitement among his people for the opportunities that lay ahead. They would work hard, he promised. They wanted to learn. And the white men had smiled and squeezed his shoulder and shown him their maps and projections and graphs and productivity flows and his head had swum with numbers and the scale of their ambition.

We see Mozambique as the future bread basket of the world, they had said. Its people will have good jobs. Good lives. We will teach them how to increase the yield from their crops ten times over. And we will invest, Manu. We will build hospitals and schools . . .

He had not asked the question that he wanted to. He did not want to sour things. Did not ask these kind, selfless philanthropists what would happen to the farmers who did not want to turn their land over to Popesco. Land that they had farmed for generations. Land they had fought to earn and to protect. Land into which they had bled and buried their dead. Land that the government would sell to Popesco from under their very spades and ploughs.

Here, now, in the soft grey light of the evening, he wishes he had asked. Wishes he had turned to Joel and queried him about whether Popesco's words were prayers or promises. They never built the schools. They didn't build the hospitals. The jobs they offered the tenant farmers paid less than they had earned as masters of their own land. And Manu, as the local man who had facilitated it all and brought Popesco into their midst, was a traitor. Manu, who tried so hard and for so long to speak up for his friend Joel. Manu, who promised his people things would get better. Manu, who had been away to university and learned so much and could speak English and Afrikaans. Manu, who had survived his time with the bandits to become an important man in his community. Manu, who tried to save them when the bandits came again . . .

'We can do this,' says Aishita in his ear. 'You can do this.'

Manu says nothing. Just nods and admires the front of the hotel: its glass frontage serving as a shield for the old, two-tiered mansion house. Its façade is seamed with crooked black timbers and the white paint gleams. There are even flowers in the hanging baskets; little explosions of pink and purple, red and white, hanging from chains in the thatched eaves. It is a pleasant place. They are only eight miles from London. Six miles from the private airfield where the private plane landed three hours ago. Sebag had suggested they take him then. Said they should grab him before he had been in the country for five minutes. But the two men who carried the rich man's bag had looked strong and professional and Manu knows he has not yet got the strength to fight such men. Nor does Sebag. The big man is bleeding. Only

Aishita seems to be as strong as he was. Only Aishita seems to want the fight that will come.

'Do it,' says Aishita. 'Before your courage fails you.'

Manu sits in the back of Joel Musgrave's big white car. He holds Joel's phone. He looks again at the hotel. It has stood here for more than 500 years. The frame was built with the timbers of sunken ships that were dragged miles overland from the River Thames. He had read that on Joel's phone. It had made him smile. He liked to think of Englishmen hauling timber across broken, dirty ground. Liked knowing that the country was built on sweat and labour as well as broken promises and camouflaged lies.

'There's no other way,' says Sebag, in the driver's seat. 'We do this or we don't.'

Manu considers the bigger man. He looks pale. Weak. Had not even had the strength to enjoy the girl in the way he had promised.

'Could Musgrave not do it?' asks Sebag. 'We could make him say it to us first. Check how he sounds . . .'

'His teeth are broken,' says Manu. 'He does not sound like himself.'

'You don't sound like him either.'

'I sound more like him than he does.'

Manu closes his eyes. Images bubble up like chunks of meat in a cooking pot. Joel begging him to stop. The girl, lashing out at him with her riding crop and turning to scream at her frightened friend. Deeper memories. Darkness. Flame. The muzzle flashes and the screams and the words 'Renamo, Renamo,' as the bandits emerged from the trees. And the man leading the charge. His old leader. His old comrade. Aishita. He had recognised him at once. Took one look at his former brother-in-arms and let revulsion show in his eyes. Manu, in his Western clothes. Soft beige chinos and a pristine cotton shirt. Aishita had stripped him. Beaten him. Used him as a plaything while the negotiations were conducted on a satellite phone and the company bartered over price. Manu remembers. *Sees*. Sees again as the executives, the white men and women, are loaded into the back of a grit wagon and driven away to their freedom. He again sinks into the dirt, eyes filled with the stinging tears of betrayal. Aishita was almost gentle as he told him the truth of what he meant to his Western paymaster. 'They do not value you, brother. You are replaceable.' Manu had tried to cling to hope. There were still white people here. Still skilled native workers. Popesco had bought the freedom of their most valuable assets but they would not abandon them entirely. They would be back, and back in force. Could they have left him behind because he was a good and reliable man who would look after the remaining workforce? Why was he not with the executives? Slowly, like the first rocks before an avalanche, realisation cascades over and through him. He knew what he was. What he was worth. How little he mattered. He felt himself collapse inside as the enormity of the revelation slammed into him. Popesco would not pay for his release. They had no policy for their native workers. He might dress like a white man and talk like a white man but to Popesco he was just another native and not worth the price of a policy. He should have stayed with his brothers in the jungle. Should have been true to his nature . . .

Manu screws up his eyes for a moment and waits for the pictures to disappear. Then he raises the phone and calls the reception desk of the hotel.

'Hello. I wish to speak to Gert Van Vuuren. Tell him Joel Musgrave is outside.'

Van Vuuren is sitting in a red leather armchair in front of a picture of King Charles. A cafetière is brewing in front of him. He has yet to push the plunger. Likes his coffee to be thick and treacly, like the brooding mid-afternoon darkness that gathers at the old, leaded windows set deep into the wood-panelled walls.

He is feeling better after a shower, shave and a half-decent sandwich. The flight took the best part of thirteen hours and he had slept little either before or during. Although he looks fit and tanned, he knows there is a darkness beneath his eyes. Despite the shower and the change of clothes he can still smell Johannesburg on his skin: traffic and dust and the soft calfskin of the limo. His mistress had sulked when he said he was leaving. Complained that he treated her as a whore and not as his lover. What did the silly bitch expect? He has a wife. Kids. Responsibilities. She'd done well out of him, hadn't she? Got herself a nice house out of the arrangement and was never short of pocket money. All he asked was that she realised what she was. She was sanctuary. She was release. She could be nothing more. She was a black, for God's sake . . .

Van Vuuren looks up at the sound of footsteps. It's a young girl. Blonde hair tied in a ponytail that hangs down the left side of her body over her white blouse. She wears a tight black skirt. Black tights. Flat shoes, like a ballet dancer. She's probably no more than eighteen.

'Mr Van Vuuren. A message from reception. There is a Joel Musgrave here. He wonders if you could meet him outside.'

Van Vuuren's smile does not leave his face. He thanks her with a nod. Asks her name.

'Kelly,' she says, and he can see her giving him a quick inspection. Trim. Well-dressed. Well-preserved. Rich. Very, very rich.

'I'm Gert,' he says, and extends a hand. Hers, in his, feels small and warm. As he lets it go he raises his palm to his face and surreptitiously sniffs his fingers. Hand sanitiser and furniture polish masking the slightest tang of sweet perfume.

'I don't know any other Gerts,' says Kelly. 'Is that foreign?'

'South African.'

'Like Nelson Mandela?' asks Kelly brightly. She seems pleased to be able to offer some association.

'Perhaps,' says Van Vuuren. 'But I'm better looking.'

Kelly smiles at that. Looks around at the other drinkers in this comfortable lounge with its old oil paintings and chandeliers, tasteful sofas and round wooden tables. 'You're enjoying your stay?'

Van Vuuren shrugs. 'I've been before.'

'To England?'

'To this hotel.'

'In that case, it's nice to have you back.'

Van Vuuren is about to make a joke about how nice it would be to have her front, but a buzzing from his pocket interrupts him. He apologises to Kelly and watches as she turns and walks back out the double doors. The seam of her skirt is crooked, like the map of a river.

'Van Vuuren,' he says quietly.

'They're outside,' says Linskey.

'I know. I was just summoned,' snaps Van Vuuren. He has no time for any of this. Pays good money to avoid being involved in such things. 'You promised me I would be safe. This is what you are for.'

'You are safe. My men are watching.'

'Why have they come?' asks Van Vuuren.

'Musgrave must have given you up.'

'Weak bastard,' spits Van Vuuren. He sighs, tired of this. 'What is it you actually want me to do?'

'Wait there,' says Linskey. 'My men will be with you soon.'

Van Vuuren leans forward and presses the plunger on his coffee. Looking up, he realises he is alone in the lounge. He makes himself comfortable.

'What do you think they want?' asks Van Vuuren, and he gives a start as the doors swing open and two of Linskey's men enter the lounge. They are dressed in black. One has the company logo for Blue Lightz on his baseball cap.

'They want what we all want,' says Linskey in his ear. 'Money and respect.'

Van Vuuren snorts. 'They want putting down. Like dogs.'

Linskey's response is lost over the sudden sound of shouting from beyond the glass. Van Vuuren hears the screech of tyres on the wet road and then a sudden crunch of metal on metal. He turns in the direction of the noise. When he looks back, the man in the baseball cap is pointing an object at him that looks a little like a TV remote control.

'What's going on?' asks Van Vuuren, of both the man before him and Linskey, at the end of the line.

'Life is about opportunities,' says Linskey.

'You're my bodyguards,' says Van Vuuren, turning pale. 'You can't! We paid you!'

'And we've done our job very well. We got Musgrave his daughter back. Did you really not know that Musgrave was going to fuck you over? He's a gambling man, that one. Daughter gets kidnapped by a man who hates him and all he sees is a chance to make some money from Popesco. I can't believe you paid up, to be honest. We agreed a 50/50 split. Just a damn shame they were better armed than we thought. And we couldn't have expected them to survive the fall. The boss was a bit pissed off about it but he's a bit like Joel when it comes to pragmatism. Sees an opportunity. And I guarantee you, Popesco will pay a shitload more to get you back than it would pay us to protect you. Don't worry though, we'll handle the negotiations. It will be expensive, but your wife will get your body back.'

Van Vuuren starts to stand, looking around wildly for assistance. It is too public, surely. Too blatant. It occurs to him just how professional these men are. The things they have done for his company and the rules that they have so efficiently disregarded. He knows, with absolute certainty, that all the cameras will have been remotely neutralised.

The man before him points the sleek, black object at Van Vuuren's torso, and shrugs, almost apologetically. Van Vuuren jerks as the small dart sticks in his sternum and the nerve relaxant floods his system.

He falls forward and is caught, deftly, in the arms of the man in the baseball cap. He lowers him back into his seat and talks, softly, into the headset curled behind his ear.

'Do you have them?'

'We do. And a very bloody Musgrave in the boot. There's a girl here too. No clothes on.'

'Bonus. Get going. I'll make the call.'

Deftly, the man in the baseball cap reaches down and retrieves Van Vuuren's phone. He calls Blue Lightz. Asks to be put through to special operations. Tells the receptionist the codeword and is immediately forwarded on to the mobile of the kidnap and ransom specialist.

The phone in Doug Roper's pocket begins to ring. He takes off the baseball cap and answers the call. Puts both phones to his ears and smiles at the unconscious man before him.

'Mr Van Vuuren. I do believe you've been kidnapped.'

Roper pauses. Takes a sip of Van Vuuren's coffee. Scowls. Not strong enough.

'Don't worry,' he says, into both phones. 'I'll take care of everything.'

30

Tuesday night, 8.11 p.m.

The service station near Doncaster.

A squat, inelegant vehicle parked up in a near-empty sprawl of tarmac. Lights off, windows closed, mist on the inside of the windows and a small tail of damp overcoat sticking out of the closed door.

A fat black fly is crawling on the steering wheel. McAvoy doesn't know where it came from. It wasn't here a moment ago. It's a sizeable specimen. Red head and grey wings. It looks almost like a toy. Looks the sort of thing that pranksters would leave on top of a friend's sandwich if they popped away from their desk for a minute. McAvoy watches it for a moment. Glances out of the window for confirmation. It's dark. It's February. A gentle rain is falling from clouds that look like smoke. He wonders where it has come from. Has a sudden, horrible fear that it is an augury of something sinister. Cannot help but run through the possibilities. The people-carrier has been parked at Courtland Road nick for most of the day. He checked the back seat when he climbed inside. When did he last open the boot? Could somebody have targeted him? Could there be something sinister inside his vehicle? He feels the colour leaching from his face. A few years ago he would have thought any such fear to be irrational and paranoid. But McAvoy knows, to his cost, that bad people are capable of almost anything. He has been targeted before. His family has been targeted before . . .

'You get all that, Sarge?'

McAvoy's spiral of worries comes to an abrupt halt as Andy Daniells's voice jumps out of the mobile phone that sits in its holder on the windscreen. The fly seems as startled as McAvoy. It takes off, buzzing angrily, and hits the glass to McAvoy's right. It stays there, making a noise that reminds McAvoy of the sound he could make as a child when he held a piece of fat grass to his lips between his thumbs and blew.

'Sarge?'

'Sorry, Andy,' says McAvoy, and gives his laptop his attention. 'It's coming through now.'

'I can hear buzzing,' says Daniells. 'Is it a bad line or are you going undercover dressed as a hive?'

'It's a fly,' says McAvoy. 'Bloody great big thing. Just turned up.'

'Must have set its alarm for the wrong time. Bet it's going to be pissed off when it sees the weather.'

McAvoy manages a smile. Starts scrolling through the information on the screen before him. Flicks the fly away as it lands on the back of his hand.

Daniells clears his throat; a nervous, awkward sound. 'You're going to do something a bit, erm, McAvoy, aren't you, Sarge?'

'That's a thing, is it?' asks McAvoy distractedly.

'Sort of. There are people who say you only work two weeks of the year. You spend the rest of it recuperating.'

McAvoy pauses and considers this. 'I've never called in sick in my life.'

'No, the nurses usually do it for you. Or you're in a coma and using a mobile would interfere with the equipment . . .'

'It's fine, Andy. If this becomes a major police operation the prime responsibilities alter. It becomes about catching who is responsible. That isn't what the Musgraves need. That isn't what Crystal needs. Getting them back unharmed is their prime wish. And if I do things quietly there's more chance of that happening.'

He hears Daniells make a noise of begrudging acceptance. 'Where are you now?'

'Service station at Doncaster. I can be on the M1 in thirty seconds.'

'That would be great if you knew where to go.'

'I have to hope something presents itself,' says McAvoy.

He carries on reading through the property portfolio he has opened from Daniells's email. Every building is registered in the name of TK Holdings or uses one of Blue Lightz's subsidiaries for its security. In most cases there is an overlap. McAvoy flicks through page after page of abandoned houses, boarded-up schools, repossessed terraces and office blocks. Many have been marked for redevelopment. Others just squat on the landscape, slowly collapsing inwards and sinking into the earth.

'Helen's down there,' says Daniells pointedly. 'She'd help.'

'I know she would.'

'So are you going to call her?'

'Probably not. Please, don't fuss. It will probably be a wasted trip anyway. I just want to know I tried.'

'And you, Sarge? What about you?'

McAvoy shakes his head. He finds the question impossible to answer. He wonders, for a moment, if Andy thinks he is trying to be a hero. Wonders if he is taking the danger and the burden and carrying it himself for whatever glory it may bring. He finds the very idea grotesque. There is no part of him that wants to start the car and drive, alone, to a place that could contain fresh miseries for his weighed-down soul. He wants to go home. Wants to hug Roisin and play with his kids and never have to suffer pain again. But that cannot be. There is a chance he can save a life. Perhaps more than one. He has to take it. That is the job. That is what he's for.

'Anything?'

McAvoy stops scrolling on a picture of a dilapidated mansion house. It looks caged behind red-brick walls and black railings. It is an off-white colour and there are coils of barbed wire around the high windows and chipboard across the door. McAvoy opens the accompanying image. Looks at the property from above. Widens the image until the screen is filled with a hazy green. The pathway is made of shiny stones. Jagged pebbles, like tiny axe-heads. The kind of stones he has seen upon tombs. The kind of stones he has seen pressed into the tread of an expensive brogue. He thinks about the man he knows. About the merciless bastard who would enjoy taking slow revenge on anybody who caused him a moment's disquiet. He knows Roper. Knows how he thinks. If he has Manu, the Russian; if he has Crystal, has Musgrave – he will enjoy taking his time working out his frustrations.

'I know where I'm going,' says McAvoy. 'I'll call you. Thanks, Andy.'

Daniells is about to ask for more when McAvoy terminates the call. He turns on the engine and opens the window a crack. Cool air blows in. With a soft buzz, the fly disappears into the dark and the rain.

He reverses out of the parking space. Takes a breath. Calls Pharaoh and breathes a sigh of relief as he gets her voicemail.

'Trish. It's me. I've got to go and do something. It's just . . . one of those things. You know? Sometimes it just needs to be done. This needs to be done. It will be fine, I know it will. But, look, if there are problems, speak to Andy. And, look . . . Roisin. The kids . . .' He pauses, not wanting to speak further in case the wall of gristle in his throat comes up like a sluice gate. 'They know why I do these things. You do, too, I think. I'm sorry. I'm rambling. Don't worry. I'll call you later.'

He ends the call before he speaks again, quietly.

'Tell them I love them,' he whispers, swinging the vehicle around the roundabout and putting his foot down.

'Tell yourself too.'

31

At first the voice is smoke. Manu catches only the faintest trace of it, touching his senses like steam touching skin. He shakes his head; a dog with a tick, a baby refusing the spoon. Inside his head there is a low, dull buzzing – an electric toothbrush pushed inside his skull. He screws up his eyes. Tries to raise his hands to rub his face. He realises he cannot move. His arms are behind him, stickily pinned at the wrist. He feels pain, now. Pain in his shoulders, where the joints bulge against his flesh. Pain in his ribs, as if he has been dropped from a height. A low, grinding throb in his teeth and jaw. He lifts his head a little. His face is touching skin. He breathes in. Smells soap and sweat. Raises his head further and dares to open his eyes.

A white man is looking down at him as if from a podium. His feet are higher than Manu's head. He wears black clothes, but the light in this place is a dull indigo-grey and he struggles to make out the man's features. His shoes look expensive. So does the gun he holds, loosely, in his right hand.

Manu turns to his left. He keeps his actions groggy and uncertain so he can absorb as much of his surroundings as possible before he can be told to stop looking. There is a young woman to his left. She smells worse than his own rancid skin and clothes. Her breath is shallow and the air that leaves her cracked lips carries the scent of the grave. She is laid out, crossways, on the lap of Joel Musgrave. Joel is kneeling up, arms tied behind him at the wrist. There is blood on his face and dripping from his ear but he has hunched himself forward in a pitiful attempt to shield the girl lying across him.

There is another man next to Musgrave. He has white hair. He is spitting and cursing in a language that Manu cannot immediately place. Then realisation hits him like water. The man is Popesco. The boss. The money. He is barking in Afrikaans. His words are full of rage but there is a tremor in his voice that betrays his fear. This is who he came for. The man he was about to take when the vehicle smashed into their own. This is the one who decided that the price of his freedom was too great for Popesco to pay. Joel had failed to persuade him otherwise. Manu does not believe he even tried.

Manu rolls his head to his right. He is pressed against Sebag, who is leaning against a smooth tiled wall, hands tied. Sebag is not looking at the man above them. He is staring at the piece of meat that hangs, slack, a few feet ahead of them. The meat was a man, once. Its name was Vasiliy. The thing that hangs beneath the diving board is barely recognisable as human and the blood that has pooled on the tiles beneath his feet seems more like tar.

'Aishita?' whispers Manu, in his own language. 'Aishita, my brother?'

Gert continues to shout. There is no response from Aishita. Manu wonders how he got away. The men in black came from nowhere. He and Sebag had barely exited the vehicle when he felt the sting of the dart in the back of his neck and he had hit the damp ground. There was little shouting. Sebag had barely managed three steps before he, too, was sedated in an operation that was crisp and ruthless in its efficiency. How had Aishita evaded the men?

Manu's thoughts begin to coalesce, like droplets of liquid metal dribbling and pooling at the base of a container. He begins to remember who he is. What he wants. Who he hates. He and Aishita have travelled thousands of miles for revenge and reward. For a time, Manu was Popesco's mascot. Their emblem. They held him up to his people as proof of their decency.

Look at Manu, they had said. He was taken by bandits. He was stolen away and made to do terrible, terrible things. But he has been returned to you. He has been healed. And Popesco has helped him become an important man. We have paid for his education. We have sent him to South Africa to study. He will tell you how good the future can be if you take Popesco into your hearts. He is one of you. He will help you become wealthy. He will tell you of the schools and the hospitals we have built and the crops we can teach you to grow. All we ask is that you vacate your homes. We will give you jobs. Build you houses. We respect you. We need you to be a part of what we want to build. This is a great step forward for Mozambique . . .

Manu had spoken like a preacher. Told village after village of the good people at Popesco and the great future they could enjoy thanks to their benevolence. He had kept quiet when those promises turned to nothing. He persuaded himself to be loyal and unquestioning when months went by without schools or hospitals opening their doors. He stayed silent even as the great bulldozers churned down homes and smashed through fields and villagers wept at the destruction of all they knew. He did what Joel asked him. Joel, who had been so kind to him. Joel, who had talked to him as an equal and who had not judged him for the things he had been forced to do. Joel, who had promised he would not forget him. Joel, who was going to found a company when he finished his studies and who made him a promise he would return some day and help him become the great man he was destined to be. Joel, who sold Popesco to people whose dream for Africa was so very different to his own. Who sold Popesco to men who cared only for profit and who saw their black workers as little more than honey bees. Sold to Gert and his consortium.

When the bandits came to the farm in Nacololo, it was the

white workers they targeted. Renamo had not been a true force for more than twenty years but there were plenty of former child soldiers who did not want to lay down their guns when peace was declared. They had become guerrillas for hire. They took hostages and lived handsomely on the ransoms that Western companies were glad to pay. When Manu heard their guns he was a child once more. Back in his village. Back among the flames and the tears and the sound of blade and bullet striking flesh. He stood immobile as the white men and women tried to flee from the swarthy young men in camouflage clothes and scarves. He had stood, frozen, as the big man with the scarred arms had stalked towards him as though approaching a fallen gladiator. Then the man had pulled down his face mask and he had said Manu's name. He had called him 'little brother'. He had embraced him. Folded him in his greasy, dirt-streaked arms and held him fast. He had only released him so he could look into his eyes; both hands upon his face and his machine gun jutting against Manu's belly. It has been so long, Aishita had said. Look what they have made you. You, who were so merciless. You, who fought by my side.

And then his face had changed. He looked at Manu's Western clothes. Looked at the name badge that clipped to the pocket of his pristine shirt. And Aishita had twisted his face into a scowl. He had spat at Manu's feet. And then he had clubbed him to the ground.

Manu spent more than a month as a captive of the bandits. Aishita beat him each day. The white hostages were fed. They were given water. The threats made for their futures were delivered half-heartedly. A ransom was due to be paid. They would be free soon, if they behaved. Nobody spoke up for Manu; staked out beneath the sun, watching steam rise from his belly and thighs as the sun slowly cooked him from within.

'I will send them this,' said Aishita, and there was no happiness in his smile as he sliced off Manu's ear and slipped it into his pocket. 'I will show you how much you matter to your new friends.'

The men in black came in the night. They moved like jungle cats and their weapons were polished and silent. They had been sent by Popesco. The bandits died with barely a sound. The white men and women were set free. Manu heard them talking as they were loaded into wagons. Popesco had paid for their release but a message needed to be sent. Nobody ever came looking for Manu. Perhaps the whites already thought him dead. He had been kept apart from them, along with the handful of other natives who had not managed to flee their assault. But it was clear that Popesco had not valued him. They had not sent men to free him. They had betrayed him. Joel had betrayed him. They had made him think himself important. They had convinced him he was not the bad man who had done such terrible things in the jungle in the name of a cause that was not his own. They had lied. Joel had lied. Only Aishita had ever told him the truth about himself. Only Aishita, who had called him 'little brother' and who had marvelled at his ability to inflict pain without feeling and whose capacity for horror matched his own. Aishita, who is at once beside him, and within.

As he remembers that day, so long ago, Manu allows the pain in his ribs and wrists to cut through the fog of his wits. He remembers everything. Those endless miles. The grey road beneath his frozen face. The begging and the stealing and the murder as he gathered the money to buy passage; each step taking him closer to the man who had refused to help him. Remembers the fat man in Calais who would not help him unless he could promise him something better than the handful of grubby notes he had pushed into his hand. Manu had told him why he was going to England. His enemy had a daughter. Under the terms of Popesco's policies, ransom would automatically be paid when any of the board of directors were taken. The same applied to their children. Manu knew of the girl called Primrose. Joel had shown him pictures many times. She meant everything to him. And that knowledge had helped Manu decide how to hurt him. The fat truck driver had made a phone call. They had shaken hands. He just needed a little more money and he knew that his new friend Golgol had a secret stash to help him reach England. Manu saw an opportunity and Aishita, whispering as if into the deepest recesses of his skull, had told him that in the act of killing, he would be slaying a lie. He would be stabbing the man he had pretended to be. He would be stepping back into his old skin as warrior, killer and soldier.

Manu had done what had to be done. He had taken his money. Bought passage to England. Had climbed from the back of the wagon on a quiet road that smelled of sea-spray and diesel oil, fishmeal and chocolate. Two men had been waiting for him. Sebag and Vasiliy. They had driven him and Aishita through a city unlike any he had seen: grand buildings and gaudy lights, a strange jumble of sound and silence beneath a grey-black sky. They had taken him to a house with a mattress in the front garden and wood across the windows and doors. They had led him inside and given him food and a place to lie. They had let him sleep and talked over him as he passed in and out of consciousness. The big man had scared him. He had scars and tattoos and looked as though he could rip Manu's arms off if he chose. But Aishita had promised him they could be trusted. They would help him. They needed money to make themselves important. The big man, Sebag, had once been a soldier. They listened to Manu's plan. They whistled when he told them how much Popesco would pay for the safe return of such an important man.

Manu learned he was in Hull, only twenty miles from where Joel Musgrave lay down to sleep each night in his comfortable bed in his beautiful house with his perfect wife and child. Together, they worked out how to take the girl. She rode horses.

Sometimes, she rode out alone. Sometimes there was an older girl with her. They figured out the pattern. Worked out when to make their move. The older girl was not supposed to be there. Their reconnaissance had implied that this was one of the days when she did not accompany the young girl. She had surprised them all. Sebag had been forced to smash her in the head with a steering wheel lock from their stolen van. They had taken Primrose to a place they knew to be empty. Sebag and Vasiliy sometimes provided workmen for the man they called Mahesh. The tumbledown mansion house was to be refurbished and remodelled. Sebag told Manu that provided Mahesh did not find out, it would be a safe place to keep the girl. But it took longer than they had hoped for Musgrave to come up with the money. Tearfully, he told them that the company's kidnap and ransom policy did not cover him for such incidents. Popesco was not going to pay and he did not have that kind of money himself. He begged for time so he could persuade his old partner to help him. Sebag grew angry. Vasiliy grew frightened. Manu had felt his revenge slipping away from him.

Then a man called Linskey answered the phone at the Musgrave house and told them they would get all that they sought if they gave him a little more time. First he needed proof of life. Manu had little time to spare. They were already being hunted by the authorities for what had happened to the landlord at Bronte Hall and for running down the old white man as he stood between themselves and escape. They were holed up in an old police station, bickering, trying to hold it together, trying to stay a step ahead. But Manu had done what Musgrave asked for, even if he had chosen his own way to comply. He needed them to understand how serious he was. The skills he had at his disposal. The exploding plasma pack had been a statement. There would still be enough blood to establish proof of life, even if it had to be scraped from Musgrave's face. After that it should have been simple. The exchange was organised and Manu had every intention of being true to his word. Musgrave had suffered the way he himself had suffered. Manu had shown him who he truly was. But the exchange was a disaster. Men with guns and the same logos on their uniforms as the team in Mozambique double-crossed them and sent their vehicle plunging into the icy water. Sebag had pulled a gun that Manu did not know he possessed. There were bullets and explosions and the sound of metal on metal. Manu had survived through will alone. And he had woken close enough to Musgrave's house to know what he had to do.

'You lot look like the worst fucking pop group I have ever seen,' says the man above him.

Manu looks up. The man is crouching down and his face swims into focus. He is handsome, though his eyes are black, like those of a shark.

'I'm sure you've all been introduced,' says the man. 'If you haven't, I'm awfully sorry.'

Manu swivels his eyes left and right. He is in an empty swimming pool. The ceiling is far above his head. There are timbers missing and the walls to his left and right have been spray-painted with crude and unreadable symbols. There is a smell of damp and rotting meat.

'You must feel a right prick,' says the man, pointing at Manu. 'All this way and now you're tied up next to the man you were here to crush. Bloody shame. I almost admire you. Thing is, life's not always nice to people. If you ask me, karma is just something losers tell themselves when they've been beaten. Life doesn't give a damn. I admired the idea though. Hostage-taking in Africa is a messy affair. A lot of variables. We make good money out of it but there's always the risk somebody important will die. And it's a painful thing to hand over a million or two when you know your payment for arranging the whole thing is about 10 per cent. Thankfully, when you play both sides, you can get both.'

The man smiles down at Manu, cocking his head. His teeth are very white. Manu senses movement. One of the men is climbing, deftly, into the empty pool.

'If it helps, you can tell yourself this is all part of your own plan. In a way, it is. You targeting Musgrave means there's no chance anybody will question the identity of the kidnappers who came after Gert. And Gert is a bugger to get hold of. Thankfully, Blue Lightz provides his security. So now I can handle the negotiations from both sides and avoid all the messiness. Popesco can pay up, and they can pay me for sorting it out, and when Gert dies, I'll at least be able to serve up the man who did it and an incredible sob story to warm their cockles. A shame Musgrave will have to go too, because he's really rather irrelevant in the grand scheme, but you're the one who had him in the boot of your car. Not my fault, really.'

The man spreads his hands, looking apologetic. He turns his gaze to where Van Vuuren has released another stream of Afrikaans curses.

'Please, Nestor. Make him be quiet.'

Manu turns his head and watches the man behind Van Vuuren draw a blade across his throat. A spray of blood shoots from his severed neck to gush across the side of the swimming pool as if somebody has stamped on a tube full of red paint.

'Jesus,' hisses Musgrave, next to Manu. He tucks himself more securely over the girl who he kept prisoner in his wine cellar. He seems more protective of her now the risk to her life comes from actions other than his own.

'I make good money anyway,' says the man, without commenting on the vile gurgling sounds that spill from Van Vuuren's throat. 'But this will be a nice clean payday. Psychologically, you're an interesting study. I'd like to spend more time getting to know you and trying to truly understand what it feels like to be you. I killed for the first time when I was a kid but nobody ever called me a child soldier or tried to put me in a lovely rehab centre where I could draw and play foot-ball and learn to be human again. You fucking Africans, you get all the luck.' He turns to Nestor. 'Scrape up a bagful – we need proof of life. I liked the way these pricks did the trick with the exploding plasma bag. Very effective. Might use that next time.'

Manu looks up into the man's eyes and knows he is going to die. He knows that his blood will mingle with Musgrave's. He does not find the idea so terrible. So much has changed, and he is so very tired.

There is the sound of footsteps to Manu's right. A smaller man with receding hair has walked briskly to the man's side to show him a readout on a laptop.

'Doug, there's a vehicle on the road doesn't check out. Stolen from a car park in Richmond day before yesterday. Surveillance van en route. Some bloody people-carrier out there too . . .'

'Who does that belong to?'

The man plays with the computer he holds open in his hands. There is an automatic weapon hanging from a strap around his neck and a Blue Lightz logo on his body armour.

A name is whispered in the leader's ear. An expression of delight flickers across his face.

There is a tiny glint of a smile playing on the man's face as he moves, slowly, away from the lip of the pool and into the shad-ows. Manu hears him say one word before he disappears and it is almost lost beneath Manu's own whispered prayer.

'McAvoy.'

32

McAvoy's thoughts are all static and cloud. His chest is tight and his blood seems to have turned upon him and begun flowing in the opposite direction, as if in mutiny. The only part of him that wants to continue edging towards the big white house is his conscience. Every other aspect of his being wants to run back to the vehicle and drive home.

He moves across the wet, tangled grass that is framed by the circular drive of splintered green glass. Ahead, the white house is an ugly, eerie presence. There should be security lights, he thinks. I should have disturbed something when I climbed over the wall and into the garden. They must have disconnected the alarms. And if they've done that . . .

He does not want to finish the thought. He keeps low, hunched forward, and scurries, soundlessly, along the inside of the front wall. The windows are boarded up and he uses the light of his phone to inspect the edges of the wood. The nail-heads are rusty. The board has not been moved in some time.

Keeping his back to the wall, McAvoy edges his way to the side of the mansion. Facing out onto the road, he feels a soft mist of rain upon his brow. He pushes his hair back from his face. He's sodden with sweat; soaked to the knees from the knotted grass; dirty and torn from his climb over the surrounding wall.

He reaches the edge of the property and cautiously peers around. The grounds are carpeted with a mulch of dead leaves. A skeleton of a dead bush sprouts from an overgrown pile of stones. The tiny sword of moonlight that slices through the clouds illuminates a dirty conservatory; all moss-streaked pillars and broken glass. There is a man hiding behind one of the supporting walls. He is just a blob of spilled ink. But he seems to sense McAvoy's presence. He turns, and McAvoy looks at a man he has not seen in a very long time. He looks at the huge, scarred killer who saved his life and took many more. He looks at Mahon.

McAvoy opens his mouth to speak but the words die as he sees the two men in black come running from the rear of the house. They run past Mahon as if he were shadow.

The light makes it almost impossible to say for sure, but McAvoy is certain that he glimpses a cracked, toothless smile as Mahon alters his position and raises the shotgun that he clutches like a walking stick.

'Stop . . . no!'

McAvoy's jaw snaps closed around the word as the man behind him puts a handgun to his head, and pulls the trigger.

McAvoy hits the ground as if dropped by angels.

'Stay down,' says Owen, and raises the gun. It's black, with a taped handle, and it fits in his grip like the palm of a lover.

The two men turn at the sound of the shot. The taller of the pair is only a few feet away from where Mahon stands, silent and still. Mahon raises the shotgun and blows away half the man's face and shoulder. The shot peppers the other figure, who yells and throws up his arms. Owen shoots him in the kneecap and he falls forward. Mahon takes three steps towards him and turns the shotgun. He clubs the man twice across the back of the head. His skull caves in upon the second strike.

Owen looks down at McAvoy. He has one bloodied hand to the side of his head. Red is oozing from his ear. He is turning his head groggily; a wounded animal looking for the creature that has hurt it.

'Here,' says Owen, and tucks a small recording device into the big man's coat pocket. 'Don't make him kill you. Just stay the fuck on the ground. It has to be this way, Aector. Please.'

As he looks at the figure sprawled on the floor before him, Owen has a memory. Five years ago. The dirty, sodden floor of the Humber Bridge Country Park. McAvoy, bleeding out onto a carpet of mud and leaves. Another of Roper's victims; set up and butchered because he had untangled his tapestry of lies. Owen had saved his life, then. Had kept his heart pumping and talked to him of his wife and his infant. McAvoy had survived and for his troubles Owen went to prison to be brutalised by Roper's thugs. It makes sense to Owen. Makes sense that McAvoy be here, now, when he and Mahon take their revenge.

'There's a church near Richmond. Abandoned, spooky place. You'll find Colin Ray in it. A Serbian hacker too. Colin's alive, if you can call it that. The Serbian's in pieces. Use what you find. Take down what's left. And don't come after us, Aector. You really, really don't want to do that.'

Owen has positioned himself in McAvoy's eyeline so he can read his lips. He knows that McAvoy's eardrums have perforated and that his head is now one ball of throbbing agony. He feels McAvoy clutch at his clothes, looking up, helpless, from the floor. Owen looks at him and shakes his head sadly. Then he kicks his hand away and brings his boot down hard on McAvoy's face. He thuds back against the ground and lies still.

'Bad penny, that one,' growls Mahon, behind Owen. 'Good man though. You did him a decent turn.'

Owen smells Mahon; that tang of corruption and old blood. He breathes in. Fills himself with it. Makes himself brave and capable with the scent of this huge, decades-old killer.

'He's inside,' says Mahon.

'How many?'

'Linskey and two others. Nestor and another.'

'The people in the pool?'

'Not our problem,' says Mahon, snapping the shotgun open and inserting another cartridge. 'We can wait here, if you like. There'll be sirens soon. They'll have to come past us to get away. We can pick them off.'

Owen turns and looks up at Mahon's scarred face. His eyes are a perfect blue but Owen knows that the corrective surgery he had on his mangled face left him with nerve damage in his retinas and he sees the world in a haze of amber, as if staring at the world through whiskey and piss. There is an emptiness in his eyes. A sadness. Mahon lived to serve Mr Nock and Mr Nock has been dead for two years. In that time, Mahon has carved a bloody trench through the men he holds accountable for his master's downfall. He is now within spitting distance of the architect of all that pain. He is close enough to Roper to be able to smell him. Owen knows that once he takes Roper's head, Mahon will have nowhere left to go. He will have nothing left to do.

'Afterwards,' says Owen quietly. 'When he's gone . . .'

'There's money in my old cottage,' says Mahon, looking away. He reaches into his coat and pulls out his cigarettes. He smokes harsh, unfiltered fags and they are one of the few things Owen has ever seen him actually enjoy. He sucks smoke into his lungs and holds it. 'Go now. Take it. Have a life. Live a little. Do what you like. Leave the rest to me.'

Owen scowls. Shakes his head. 'No way. This is what it's all been for.'

'And if it goes wrong? If he kills you? Imagine that, for a second. All this way and you lose. He wins.'

'Let's not let that happen.'

'Time's running out, Owen. You can go. You've had your revenge. After tonight, whatever happens, he's done.'

'You're not going in alone.'

'I've always gone in alone,' says Mahon.

They stand over the fallen body of McAvoy and weigh up their options. Mahon cocks his head. He can hear the faint sound of sirens. He turns, just as a bullet slams into the wall by his shoulder and spits up a chip of brick dust.

'Run,' yells Owen and pushes Mahon towards the conservatory, dragging him by the arm that hangs by his side. Bullets pepper the wall and then there is a crash as the windows begin to smash as the automatic weapons rake their surface.

Owen feels a sudden burning agony in his hip and yells in pain. Mahon stops in front of the shattered glass and raises his shotgun. He looks at Owen, down to one knee at his side, and gives him a curt nod.

'For Mr Nock,' he says.

And walks into the line of fire; back straight, and cigarette glowing red at his lips.

33

Manu feels around behind him for something he can use to unfasten his bonds. Musgrave is whimpering. Sebag is scurrying on his knees into the shelter of the swimming pool wall. Above, Nestor and the man who has done this to him are crouching behind a low marble wall. The leader's face is expressionless. Nestor is talking into a mobile phone.

Manu pushes backwards. Finds a piece of shattered marble with his groping fingers. Turns it in his hands and begins to saw at the tape around his wrists. He feels calm. Gunfire. Tears. Screams. This has been the symphony of his life. He curses as he fumbles with the shard of tile, then finds himself grinning as big, strong hands appear behind him and take the shard. The bonds split in two with one easy slice. Manu turns and looks into the big, broad face of Aishita. He is unsullied. Unscathed. There is no mud or blood upon him. He looks as he has always done: a perfect emblem of brutality.

'Do it,' says Aishita, nodding at Musgrave and putting the tile in his hand. 'Open his throat.'

Manu crouches in the darkness and closes his hand around the tile. Musgrave is two steps in front of him, cowering over the girl, trying to protect her with his body as the gunshots rake the room. It would take no effort at all. One slice of the makeshift dagger and Musgrave would spill his blood across her face and onto the floor of the pool. Manu would have his revenge.

'This is how it must be. This is what we have come for. You have killed so many people, little brother. You have salted the earth with blood. He betrayed you. Your life was worth nothing to him. He fed you a lie. You are not one of them, Manu. You are a soldier. A warrior. A man. You are Renamo!'

Manu closes his eyes. For an instant he is back in that accursed place. Staked out. Bleeding. Flies feeding on the crusted blood where his ear used to sit. Aishita had crouched beside him, then. Had looked at him with eyes that seemed to be experiencing pain for the very first time. Manu had braced himself for the end. He heard the shot. And then he felt the weight of the man who had made him a killer flood across his chest. He felt Aishita mingle with his own self. Aishita, so strong and determined. Aishita, who knew how to turn pain into an art. Aishita, who killed himself to show his protégé how to die like a warrior. Manu felt himself changing. Felt the other man's strength and cruelty, brutality and rage. Felt the sheer raw power of hatred. He turned his gaze upon the image of Joel Musgrave that he held in his mind and he swore bloody vengeance on the man who convinced him he was more than a child soldier who had been forced to kill his father. He vowed vengeance. And then Aishita had spoken to him in his own voice. Told him he would be forever by his side. Would give him the strength he needed. And he had spoken the truth. Aishita had given him the strength to ram the skewer through Golgol's chest. Aishita had taken control when the man who owned Bronte Hall had turned up unexpectedly and found Primrose Musgrave bound in a dank, dark room. Aishita had placed the bicycle spoke in Manu's hand and together they had driven it through the man's chest as he stood before Sebag and told him they would all go to prison for this. That the house was only his in name. It belonged to bad men. Dangerous men. Men who would kill him as soon as draw breath. Aishita and Manu, together, had pushed him into the wall and left him to die, feet kicking against the damp plaster. When he drove the nails into his wrists, he thought of Christ. Wondered about repentance and rebirth.

'Kill him, Manu. That is who you are. That is what I trained you to do. You, who shot your father. You, who cut men and stabbed men and raped women. Forced fathers to rape daughters, sons to rape mothers. You: a perfect beast. You—'

'You don't have to hurt anybody else.' Manu turns at the girl's words. She looks broken. Hollow. Her skin is pale and her lips grey but there is a quiet ferocity in her eyes. Musgrave kept her captive so she would not reveal the truth about Primrose's abduction. She bit and fought and scratched and forced Musgrave to hurt her – all for the young girl whose welfare she had promised to safeguard. Here, now, she could take the tile from Manu and plunge it into the man responsible for her suffering. Yet she resists. Her eyes offer forgiveness, as she battles and defies her basest urgings.

'She is weak, Manu. Weak like all of them. Do it. Take what you are owed!'

The girl, the one called Crystal, is looking deep inside him, somehow communicating directly with the dying embers of the man he once was. 'You don't seem evil. Don't do evil things.'

'Ignore her, little brother. Listen to me. Listen to your leader. Listen to the calling of your blood!'

Aishita's words are heard only by Manu, deep inside his head. Aishita has spoken to him every day since he killed himself. He has been Manu's constant companion on the long road from Mozambique. He has been his conscience and strength and the fuel for all his rage. But in this moment, this now, Manu finds that all he wants is silence. Wants to feel, if only for the length of a dying heartbeat, that he is in control of his own actions.

'Kill Musgrave. Now. Do it. Do it!'

The words stop as Manu pushes upwards with the jagged edge. Aishita's eyes widen as he looks down at the blood spilling from his belly and pulsing over Manu's hand. He sounds as though he were drowning.

Manu looks down. There is a piece of jagged tile deep in his guts. His blood is flooding over his thighs. He feels himself fall. Sees Aishita flickering. Blurring, as though viewed through flapping curtains.

His head strikes the tiles. He feels weak. Feels himself fading. Emptying. Turns his head and looks through the disappearing shape of Aishita into the wide, staring eyes of Joel Musgrave.

'Manu,' he says, voice breaking. 'Why . . . ?'

He feels soft hands upon him. The girl. Her rough, cold hands stroking the sweat from his brow even as tears fall like rain upon his face.

'Manu?'

Manu would like to smile at the man who saved him. Would like to put his whole strength into one act of contrition. Of apology. He would like to tell Joel that it was not his idea that Primrose be taken. Not his idea that they demand money for her return. Not he who had sustained himself across countless miles with visions of brutality and vile deeds. But he would be lying. Aishita was merely the voice of his own thoughts. He did what he chose to. Did what he wanted to.

Manu's eyes roll back as he breathes his last. His final vision, glimpsed through dying eyes, is of an old man with a shotgun walking into machine-gun fire as if walking into rain.

Mahon's second shot takes a chunk out of the marble wall behind which Nestor is crouching. Nestor shouts and throws himself clear. He stumbles, feet slipping on the ferns that sprout through the bare brick floor. Mahon reloads as he walks. He slams the shotgun shut and fires, blowing Nestor backwards in a gory cloud of blood and bone.

'Mahon, look out . . .'

The shout distracts Roper, who turns and shoots at the doorway. Owen is thrown backwards as the bullets strafe him across his entire left side. He falls backwards onto the grass.

Mahon is trying to reload. He cracks the shotgun and slips in a new cartridge but before he can snap it closed, Roper flips his own weapon back towards Mahon.

'You're the one, eh? The one who can't be killed? The spirit of vengeance, angel of death. I'm disappointed. You look like a frail old fucker to me.'

Mahon snaps the barrel closed and pulls the trigger in one movement. A trio of bullets from Roper's weapon thud into his chest but the shot from Mahon's great shotgun blasts the weapon from Roper's hands.

Mahon falls backwards into the empty pool, landing on the bodies, some living, some dead, that cower below.

Roper is bleeding. Cursing. He walks forward and looks down at where Mahon lies. He looks towards Nestor, his fallen friend and comrade. Looks like he wants to spit. He reaches down and takes Nestor's phone.

'We need an evac. There's a unit on the way. It will take some cleaning up. Best if I'm not here—'

'Roper!'

He turns at the sound of his name.

Framed by jagged shards of glass, blood dripping from his ear, face white as bone, McAvoy is looking at him the way he has never been looked at before. Roper understands people. Knows their fears and desires. Knows how to hurt. Where to squeeze. He has never been looked at like this before. Never seen such absolute, cold fury in somebody's eyes.

Roper sucks his teeth, weighing things up. He looks at his bleeding hands and broken gun. Nods to himself, making up his mind. Then he turns and runs for the stairs.

34

There is a crack in McAvoy's vision, like a photograph ripped in two and stuck back together. He can hear nothing but his own breath. There is blood dripping under his collar. He stumbles as he charges forward. Feels half-drunk, as if he can't get his feet to go in the direction he wants.

He staggers around the lip of the swimming pool, only half aware of the shapes moving within. He glimpses a corpse, almost headless and oozing blood. He lurches for the exit and throws himself into the corridor that leads to the main house. He sees a spot of blood and runs on, smearing his hand across the ugly miasma of blood and sweat and darkness that blinds him.

Onward, banging off the walls, tumbling through an open door. He looks up. Roper is running up a curved staircase. Plants grow from the broken tiles and the walls are black with damp. The high ceilings with their smashed chandeliers seem as far away as the heavens.

McAvoy catches the bottom step with his boot and falls. The pain in his head explodes afresh but he drags himself to his feet and runs up the stairs. Roper is waiting at the top, peering down from a balcony-style landing like a monarch waving to the poor.

McAvoy is sure he is saying something but he cannot hear his own voice. All he can see is Roper, his mouth parted in a mocking smile, waiting there to hurt him, to end him, swinging towards his exposed head with a half-brick in his bleeding hand.

The brick strikes McAvoy hard in the temple and he feels his feet go out from under him. Roper curses as he drops the brick and knees McAvoy twice in the jaw. McAvoy slithers back down the curved steps. Roper turns away but McAvoy reaches up and grabs the back of his trousers. He holds on. Jerks him backwards. Roper kicks back. Catches McAvoy in the face. For an instant, his head clears. He can hear. Can hear Roper, hissing and spitting in a language he does not understand. Can hear his own voice, saying 'no', over and over.

Roper kicks him again. Boots him like a dog who will not let go. The pressure eases and he jerks forward, triumphant. He looks back. Sees the bloodied, broken beast he has left lying on the stairs. He cannot resist. Needs to enjoy the moment.

'You tried, McAvoy,' says Roper, standing over him. 'Gave it your absolute all. It's been a costly night. I'm bleeding. I've lost good men. Some bad ones too. When I go to bed tonight there'll be a part of me that feels I may have played this whole thing wrong. But all in all, it's been a good day. I've solved problems, made money and I've put you down. I like that thought best. There's something about you. You're too bloody wholesome. Too fucking nice. I never knew how to motivate you or frighten you or get you on side. So it's best that I just kill you. And I do hope you know that before you're even cold in the ground, I'll have had a dozen fresh-off-the-wagon lads have themselves quite the party with the people you hold dear. I'll burn your fucking house down, Aector, and you won't be there to stop it. I'll bend Trish over the desk myself and make her look in a mirror as I hurt her. And Roisin . . . oh Roisin . . .'

McAvoy does not feel himself come back to life. Does not make a conscious decision to move. One moment he is lying, sprawled and broken, on the steps. The next he is lunging forward, hands around Roper's throat, roaring something inhuman and barrelling him backwards along the landing.

McAvoy becomes aware of himself an instant before he slams Roper into the chipboard that covers the window. He has a tiny heartbeat of clarity, of realisation, that the chipboard will not hold. And then he has powered Roper through the flimsy wood and the glass behind and they are falling, together, through the second-floor window.

Something sharp makes him catch his breath. He feels tiny, sharp knives in his legs. There is cold air on his face. A shaft of silver light.

McAvoy twists, his hands still around Roper's throat, and looks up at the coils of barbed wire that have snagged around his shins and uncoiled into a lethal twist of jagged metal. He looks down.

Roper is screaming. A length of barbed wire has looped around his face. The barbs have caught in his jawline and cheek, his eyelid and scalp. The two men dangle from the window like flies in a web.

'Stop,' says McAvoy desperately, as Roper twists in his grasp. 'Roper, I can't hold you, stop . . .'

Roper wriggles and flails, twisting against the barbs that puncture his flesh. Then there is a sound like tearing silk and Roper slithers free from McAvoy's grasp and plunges towards the ground.

McAvoy sees him fall. Sees the vile, skinless mess plummet earthwards. Sees the bloodied jawbone open in a scream, rudely interrupted as he slams into the ground.

For a moment there is no sound at all. McAvoy just stares down at the figure who lies on a pathway made of jagged glass.

McAvoy forces himself to look away. His breath catches as he looks at the strips of meat that hang from the barbs below him. Roper's face: ripped off and shredded on the points of steel.

'McAvoy. Christ, McAvoy . . .'

Groggily, he focuses. Squints through blood and agony at the reassuring bulk of Helen Tremberg.

Hangs, upside down, and feels the tears and blood run into his hair, before the tiny crimson droplets plunge down onto the thing that used to be Doug Roper, and which stares, bloodily, at a sky of perfect blackness.

35

'This is the last time,' says Pharaoh, looking at him furiously. 'I can't afford the grapes and the flowers. And it's not bloody cheap getting to London. They refund the tickets, yeah, but I have to shell it out in the first place and that means the credit card again. You're an expensive friend. And in case you didn't know it, you look bloody awful. I would have to be dropped from an aeroplane into a cheese grater to look as bad as you.'

She stops and shakes her head, then crosses to the bed. She leans down and kisses him on the forehead the way she would like to kiss him on the lips. She presses herself against him. Has one warm hand upon his cheek. His face is in her cleavage; all perfume and sweat and coffee and smoke. He catches his breath and she snatches away a tear. Both cough, refusing to look at one another properly. Then she throws herself down into the plastic chair at his bedside.

'She's gone for a coffee, before you ask,' says Pharaoh, and she takes a black cigarette from her case and puts it to her lips. She seems set on lighting it but decides, at the last, that it would be one act of social disobedience too far. 'The kids didn't come down. The novelty of you being in hospital has clearly worn off.'

McAvoy smiles and the act pains him. Pharaoh watches the memories flood into his consciousness and sees his face change. He seems to get smaller, his shape changing beneath the crisp white bedcovers.

'It's okay,' she says soothingly, and puts a hand on his. 'You lost some blood and your legs aren't looking too pretty but you're going to be fine. You suffered a perforated eardrum and the teensiest of fractured skulls but nothing worth making a fuss about.'

'Crystal,' croaks McAvoy. 'Is she . . . ?'

Pharaoh plays with her phone and then holds it in front of his face. He is groggy and his thoughts are sluggish but he makes sense of the image. Crystal Heathers, dressed in borrowed clothes, muddy and weak and bloodied, sitting in the back of an ambulance with a telephone pressed to her face and tears in her eyes.

'Wouldn't go to hospital until they let her speak to Primrose,' says Pharaoh. 'Tough lass. Fought like a tiger. She doesn't know who she has to thank yet but I reckon if you ever want a free horsey ride, you're not going to have to look very hard.'

McAvoy nods, and everything hurts. He remembers the room at Bronte Hall. Braided tassels and a bucket of urine and Perry's blood drying on his skin. So much pain. So many bodies. All because he had blundered into something as a favour to an old man. 'Helen Tremberg,' says McAvoy, remembering. He clutches Pharaoh's hand like a child.

'Tremberg found a scene from a bloody horror movie. Joel Musgrave and Crystal Heathers cowering in a swimming pool. A great bloody Russian whimpering next to the body of his mate. An African and a South African vying for the title of "most dead".'

'Roper. Mahon. Owen . . .'

'We found what looks very much like it used to be Doug Roper's face hanging from a coil of barbed wire. Mahon isn't going to be coming back to life this time. Owen's on life support. Doesn't look good. Still, we told him that Roper was dead and the readout on his monitor did a little dance so wherever he is, he's probably quite pleased.'

'Blue Lightz,' splutters McAvoy, trying to sit up.

'Shush yourself,' says Pharaoh, patting the air. 'We know. There was a recording device in your pocket. Showed footage of a man in a Blue Lightz uniform cutting the throat of the chief exec of Popesco – a company they were hired to protect. It shows Doug Roper giving the order. Well done.'

'I didn't film it . . .'

'No. But for the sake of argument, yes you did. Blue Lightz is in meltdown. Word has got out that we have the footage. And with Roper missing a face, they don't really have the friends in authority to clean all this up.'

'Who was with Helen? How did she even know?' He pinches his nose. 'Colin Ray . . .'

Pharaoh shakes her head but grins, as if she can't quite believe it. 'He's in a different hospital, just in case you and he should go to the toilet at the same time and start arguing over who has had the shittiest couple of years. He's hurt and he's going to need a lot of care and attention but he's alive. Spitting venom and bile and asking for red wine and cigars so he can't be feeling all that bad. He's already had his clothes on twice and isn't taking to hospitalisation at all well. I think he wants to go lie down in a sewer like a wounded rat. He says he can't remember much of where he's been but he's held together with lies and sticky-tape so who knows what game he's playing. I just know that of all the things Shaz Archer asked about when she phoned Operation Trident, it was whether or not Colin remembered anything that seemed to trouble her the most.'

McAvoy's features twitch. He looks old, suddenly. The grey in his beard and the dark thumbprints beneath his eye conspire with the grey walls and the white linen to make him look like a thing leached of colour; a black and white image of somebody who has endured too much.

'Verity?' he asks.

'Sore. Bit of a mess. Not up to a full ship's complement in the spleen department. But she hasn't shut up since she woke up. Keeps asking whether you're cross at her. Said something about a Valentine's night at her local. What is it you do to these people?'

McAvoy concentrates on breathing. The familiar hospital smell; the tang of his own blood.

'I never went there to do any of this,' he says at last. 'I just thought they might have been involved. That maybe Crystal might be there. It just seemed as though I had to be there. As though it were for me to do. I judged Joel Musgrave because of my own prejudices . . .'

'You?' snorts Pharaoh. 'Prejudiced? Fuck off.'

'I feel like I've done everything wrong.'

Pharaoh rolls her eyes at him, shaking her head. 'Operation Trident is bringing down one of the most lethal criminal gangs they've ever dealt with and it's all thanks to intelligence you've helped provide. We now know that the linchpin of the whole organisation was a man called Nestor Vachnadze, who just happens to be dead and in no position to claim otherwise. We know that the Headhunters used Blue Lightz as a legitimate cover for their criminal operation and that they hired mercenaries and talent-spotted criminals to create a small but perfectly formed protection outfit that took a chunk of earnings from criminal groups across the country in exchange for access to their resources and skills and the tempting offer of not being brutally killed.'

'Roper,' says McAvoy. 'What do they think?'

'They know. Everybody knows. Knows what you knew years before the rest of them. Roper was the devil.'

McAvoy looks down at himself and wipes his eyes with the heels of his hands. 'I don't feel any different.'

'You never will,' says Pharaoh with a laugh. 'This is how you're meant to feel. It's what makes you, you.'

They sit in silence for a spell, until Pharaoh feels her hand start to sweat and she hears footsteps coming down the corridor. Hears the kind of high heels she would never dare to wear. Hears Roisin. She withdraws her hand and smiles at him.

'You did good,' she says. 'Procedurally, you are going to get whipped with a bamboo pole when we get back to the office but I'm sure you can take that. You might even like it.'

The door opens and Roisin stands in the entrance, smiling at them both. She's holding a cardboard tray with three expensive drinks wedged into the gaps. She's wearing red shoes with a huge pair of lips stitched onto the upper and has matched them with a polka-dot rockabilly dress and tights with a seam up the back. She hands her husband a hot chocolate and passes a black coffee to Pharaoh. She puts a hand on McAvoy's cheek.

'Perry sends his love. He's not exactly peachy but he's refusing to die until he at least gets a chance to call you some names. Apparently, none of this would have happened if he had just gone and checked out Bronte Hall for himself. Blames you entirely. But in a nice way.'

McAvoy manages a tight smile. Wonders whether, right now, Perry could make good on his threats to kick his arse.

'I'm very proud of you,' says Roisin quietly. 'But if you do this again, I'm going to do unspeakable things to you, okay?'

McAvoy nods, and Roisin leans forward to press her forehead to his. Tears spill onto his white T-shirt but he makes no sound at all. After a time, Roisin retreats to the chair on the far side of the bed from Pharaoh. They eye one another, then nod.

'Would you call him a high-maintenance friend?' asks Roisin, smiling.

'I'd call him a pain in the arse,' says Pharaoh.

McAvoy sits in the bed and looks from one to the other. Closes his eyes and lets the calm of the moment wash over him.

Epilogue

There's a statue of Philip Larkin at the rear of the Royal Hotel. It's cast in bronze and captures the poet striding towards the bustle of Hull's Paragon Station with briefcase in hand and coat-tails flapping on the Whitsun breeze. A student is taking a selfie with his arm around the great man; backpack held on by both straps and elbow patches on his corduroy jacket. Larkin would have hated him.

As Shaz Archer glides across the ornate floor of the Victorian rail interchange, her footsteps startle a dirty white pigeon, which flutters up at the student and causes him to take a picture of himself mid-yelp: mouth open and twisted, captured for ever in the act of squealing feebly. Archer gives him a look of pure contempt as she pushes past him and up the stairs into the comfortable old hotel with its high ceilings and plush carpets, its comfortable art deco sofas, huge rugs and potted plants. Were she able, she would stamp on the student's throat until his head came off. She detests such specimens. Abhors these weak reflections of the few men she has ever found to be worthy of her time.

She used to meet *him* here. Used to sweat and swear, moan and writhe, raising herself up for his caresses almost as eagerly as she sought the pain he inflicted so exquisitely.

The sense of nostalgia that Archer feels would turn to tears if she was one for crying. She loved him, in her way. Needed him. Adores what he helped her to become. And now he is gone and she has been left to deal with the circling jackals and wolves.

She knows she is up to the challenge. Relishes it, in a way. She spends a fortune on manicures but she fancies that her stiletto-sharp nails look prettiest when mottled with blood.

Professional Standards has requested she meet them within the week. Her Police Federation rep has told her to get her story straight. Operation Trident has been calling, asking for a meeting to compare notes on their recent investigation into the organised crime outfit dubbed the Headhunters. She is having to work hard to stay on top of things. They'd known this day would come, of course. She knows how to turn it all to her advantage. If necessary, she can hand over the memory cards and SIM cards showing how hard she worked on her private undercover operation to gain access to the outfit. She can give them enough information on Nestor to walk out of the whole thing like a hero. She has an answer for whatever questions they ask. The money is hidden and clean. Roper taught her well.

Archer sees her reflection in the dull metal of the lift doors as she waits for the elevator that will take her to the room she is staying in on the third floor. She does not want to be at home right now. Archer admires her reflection. She hasn't let the stresses of the past three days affect her appearance. She's wearing her soft leather riding boots and a blue dress that stops halfway between her knees and her backside. She's removed the most expensive jewellery for fear of drawing extra attention but she has not neglected her other affectations. She is perfectly made up: all elongated lashes, blushed cheeks and red lips. She can feel the admiring glances of the assorted drinkers and staff. Knows what they want. Knows what she does to people and how much they are willing to sacrifice of themselves for the right to inhale her perfection. She has plans. She knows what the future holds and she intends to enjoy every single second. There may be one or two wrinkles to smooth over, but she's very good at that.

Archer hears the lift arrive and dabs at the corner of her mouth with a perfectly manicured finger, allowing the young man on reception to see her perfect pink tongue. She can see him taking a mental picture to enjoy later. The doors open and she steps inside: glass mirrors on the other three walls so she can enjoy herself from every angle.

The doors are sliding closed when she gets the whiff of him. Cigars and sweat; clothes dried in a damp room; red wine and tobacco; stiff socks and dead flowers. She wrinkles her nose and a shotgun blast of memories hits her in the gut.

She looks up as Colin Ray slides into the lift; a hunched figure in raincoat and dark trousers, hair slicked back from a wolfish, pallid face: all yellow teeth and bleeding gums.

'Hello, Shaz,' says Colin.

Acknowledgements

Hello again. Take a moment for yourself. You've done jolly well and it's appreciated.

As ever, I'd like to take a self-indulgent moment and say thanks to the people who have helped turn a peculiar idea into a (hopefully) readable novel. Ruth, I couldn't (and wouldn't) do this without you. Cicely, you're doing the North proud in that London. Kerry, you're more than just a great publicist, you're my friend and confidante and you mean the world to me. To all in the art department, thanks for taking the pictures from my head and turning them into something real.

Librarians, not enough people realise that you are the fourth emergency service. Thanks for your support. Never forget, any politician who suggests closing a library deserves to be thinly grated from the feet up.

Oli, if you don't know by now, I'm very grateful for your patience and good humour. Munson, Mark and McAvoy, forever onward.

On the research front, I'd like to express my thanks to the many cops, scientists and serial killers who helped with the creation of this novel. Albert, if I'm ever murdered, you're the chap I want looking into it. Rebecca Bradley, Lisa Cutts, thanks for filling in the colossal gaps in my knowledge. Jan, your knowledge of poisonous plants is both fascinating and slightly worrying.

On the personal front, I'd like to say cheers to Cheese. You've been a good friend through a hard time and if it weren't for our decompression sessions in the barn, I'm not sure I'd have come through. I'm also aware that I have just created a euphemism.

Babs, you continue to be the best friend I could ask for. Susi, you're a bloody good writer and an equally fab person. Nick Q, you're a truly decent soul and definitely among Hull's top two crime writers. And Professor Lavery. I'm raising a mug of coffee in your honour. You're one of the most admirable people I have ever met. Thanks for being my mate and mentor.

Finally, my family. Sarah, as ex-wives go, you're the best I could wish for. Thanks for being my friend. Elora, you are the story I'm most proud of, now and always. Artemisia, welcome to the world. You've instantly made it a better place. Connor, Amber, Honey, you're expensive, but worth it. And Nicola, my sunflower. The shadows pass, the light remains. Until I met you, I presumed poets were skilful liars. You put different colours in my inkwell. You've shown me the beauty of truth and the truth of beauty. And yes, I just stole a line from Keats